I0831140

THE IDIOT

VOLUME ONE OF TWO

The Idiot

Dostoevsky, Fyodor 1821 – 1881
First Published by The Russian Messenger
in 1868–69
Thanslated by Eva Martin
Martin, Eva 1883 – 1940

Text set in 18 point Helvetica.
Chapter headings set in Helvetica Neue.

ISBN: 978-1-83412-397-4 Volume One
ISBN: 978-1-83412-398-1 Volume Two

THE IDIOT

VOLUME ONE OF TWO

FYODOR DOSTOEVSKY

Translated by Eva Martin

GRAND TYPE CLASSICS

CONTENTS

VOLUME ONE

Part One

CHAPTER ONE

TOWARDS THE END of November, during a thaw, at nine o'clock one morning, a train on the Warsaw and Petersburg railway was approaching the latter city at full speed. The morning was so damp and misty that it was only with great difficulty that the day succeeded in breaking; and it was impossible to distinguish anything more than a few yards away from the carriage windows.

Some of the passengers by this particular

train were returning from abroad; but the third-class carriages were the best filled, chiefly with insignificant persons of various occupations and degrees, picked up at the different stations nearer town. All of them seemed weary, and most of them had sleepy eyes and a shivering expression, while their complexions generally appeared to have taken on the colour of the fog outside.

When day dawned, two passengers in one of the third-class carriages found themselves opposite each other. Both were young fellows, both were rather poorly dressed, both had remarkable faces, and both were evidently anxious to start a conversation. If they had but known why, at this particular moment, they were both remarkable persons, they would undoubtedly have wondered at the strange chance which had set them down opposite to one another in a third-class carriage of the Warsaw Railway Company.

One of them was a young fellow of about twenty-seven, not tall, with black curling hair, and small, grey, fiery eyes. His nose was broad and flat, and he had high cheek bones; his thin lips were constantly compressed into an impudent, ironical–it might almost be called a malicious–smile; but his forehead was high and well formed, and atoned for a good deal of the ugliness of the lower part of his face. A special feature of this physiognomy was its death-like pallor, which gave to the whole man an indescribably emaciated appearance in spite of his hard look, and at the same time a sort of passionate and suffering expression which did not harmonize with his impudent, sarcastic smile and keen, self-satisfied bearing. He wore a large fur–or rather astrachan–overcoat, which had kept him warm all night, while his neighbour had been obliged to bear the full severity of a Russian November night entirely unprepared. His wide sleeveless mantle with a large cape to it–the sort of cloak one sees upon travellers during the winter months in Switzerland or North Italy–was by no means adapted to the long cold journey through Russia, from Eydkuhnen to St. Petersburg.

The wearer of this cloak was a young fellow, also of about twenty-six or twenty-seven years of age, slightly above the middle height, very fair, with a thin, pointed and very light coloured beard; his eyes were large and blue, and had an intent look about them, yet that heavy expression which some people affirm to be a peculiarity as well as evidence, of an epileptic subject. His face was decidedly a pleasant one for all that; refined, but quite colourless, except for the circumstance that at this moment it was blue with cold. He held a bundle made up of an old faded silk handkerchief that apparently contained all his travelling wardrobe, and wore thick shoes and gaiters, his whole appearance being very un-Russian.

His black-haired neighbour inspected these peculiarities, having nothing better to do, and at length remarked, with that rude enjoyment of the discomforts of others which the common classes so often show:

"Cold?"

"Very," said his neighbour, readily, "and this is a thaw, too. Fancy if it had been a hard frost! I never thought it would be so cold in the old country. I've grown quite out of the way of it."

"What, been abroad, I suppose?"

"Yes, straight from Switzerland."

"Wheugh! my goodness!" The black-haired young fellow whistled, and then laughed.

The conversation proceeded. The readiness of the fair-haired young man in the cloak to answer all his opposite neighbour's questions was surprising. He seemed to have no suspicion of any impertinence or inappropriateness in the fact of such questions being put to him. Replying to them, he made known to the inquirer that he certainly had been long absent from Russia, more than four years; that he had been sent abroad for his health; that he had suffered from some strange nervous malady–a kind of epilepsy, with convulsive spasms. His interlocutor burst out laughing several times at his answers; and more than ever, when to the question, "whether he had been cured?" the patient replied:

"No, they did not cure me."

"Hey! that's it! You stumped up your money for nothing, and we believe in those fellows, here!" remarked the black-haired individual, sarcastically.

"Gospel truth, sir, Gospel truth!" exclaimed another passenger, a shabbily dressed man of about forty, who looked like a clerk, and possessed a red nose and a very blotchy face. "Gospel truth! All they do is to get hold of our good Russian money free, gratis, and for nothing."

"Oh, but you're quite wrong in my particular instance," said the Swiss patient, quietly.

"Of course I can't argue the matter, because I know only my own case; but my doctor gave me money–and he had very little–to pay my journey back, besides having kept me at his own expense, while there, for nearly two years."

"Why? Was there no one else to pay for you?" asked the black-haired one.

"No–Mr. Pavlicheff, who had been supporting me there, died a couple of years ago. I wrote to Mrs. General Epanchin at the time (she is a distant relative of mine), but she did not answer my letter. And so eventually I came back."

"And where have you come to?"

"That is–where am I going to stay? I–I really don't quite know yet, I–"

Both the listeners laughed again.

"I suppose your whole set-up is in that bundle, then?" asked the first.

"I bet anything it is!" exclaimed the red-nosed passenger, with extreme satisfaction, "and that he has precious little in the luggage van!–though of course poverty is no crime–we must remember that!"

It appeared that it was indeed as they had surmised. The young fellow hastened to admit the fact with wonderful readiness.

"Your bundle has some importance, however," continued the clerk, when they had laughed their fill (it was observable that the subject of their mirth joined in the laughter when he saw them laughing); "for though I dare say it is not stuffed full of friedrichs d'or and louis d'or–judge from your costume and gaiters–still–if you can add to your possessions such a valuable property as a relation like Mrs. General Epanchin, then your bundle becomes a significant object at once. That is, of course, if you really are a relative of Mrs. Epanchin's, and have not made a little error through–well, absence of mind, which is very common to human beings; or, say–through a too luxuriant fancy?"

"Oh, you are right again," said the fair-haired traveller, "for I really am **almost** wrong when I say she and I are related. She is hardly a relation at all; so little, in fact, that I was not in the least surprised to have no answer to my letter. I expected as much."

"H'm! you spent your postage for nothing, then. H'm! you are candid, however–and that is commendable. H'm! Mrs. Epanchin–oh yes! a most eminent person. I know her. As for Mr. Pavlicheff, who supported you in Switzerland, I know him too–at least, if it was Nicolai Andreevitch of that name? A fine fellow he was–and had a property of four thousand souls in his day."

"Yes, Nicolai Andreevitch–that was his name," and the young fellow looked earnestly and with curiosity at the all-knowing gentleman with the red nose.

This sort of character is met with pretty frequently in a certain class. They are people who know everyone–that is, they know where a man is employed, what his salary is, whom he knows, whom he married, what money his wife had, who are his cousins, and second cousins, etc., etc. These men generally have about a hundred pounds a year to live on, and they spend their whole time and talents in the amassing of this style of knowledge, which they reduce–or raise–to the standard of a science.

During the latter part of the conversation the black-haired young man had become very impatient. He stared out of the window, and fidgeted, and evidently longed for the end of the journey. He was very absent; he would appear to listen–and heard nothing; and he would laugh of a sudden, evidently with no idea of what he was laughing about.

"Excuse me," said the red-nosed man to the young fellow with the bundle, rather suddenly; "whom have I the honour to be talking to?"

"Prince Lef Nicolaievitch Muishkin," replied the latter, with perfect readiness.

"Prince Muishkin? Lef Nicolaievitch? H'm!

I don't know, I'm sure! I may say I have never heard of such a person," said the clerk, thoughtfully. "At least, the name, I admit, is historical. Karamsin must mention the family name, of course, in his history–but as an individual–one never hears of any Prince Muishkin nowadays."

"Of course not," replied the prince; "there are none, except myself. I believe I am the last and only one. As to my forefathers, they have always been a poor lot; my own father was a sublieutenant in the army. I don't know how Mrs. Epanchin comes into the Muishkin family, but she is descended from the Princess Muishkin, and she, too, is the last of her line."

"And did you learn science and all that, with your professor over there?" asked the black-haired passenger.

"Oh yes–I did learn a little, but–"

"I've never learned anything whatever," said the other.

"Oh, but I learned very little, you know!"

added the prince, as though excusing himself. "They could not teach me very much on account of my illness."

"Do you know the Rogojins?" asked his questioner, abruptly.

"No, I don't–not at all! I hardly know anyone in Russia. Why, is that your name?"

"Yes, I am Rogojin, Parfen Rogojin."

"Parfen Rogojin? dear me–then don't you belong to those very Rogojins, perhaps–" began the clerk, with a very perceptible increase of civility in his tone.

"Yes–those very ones," interrupted Rogojin, impatiently, and with scant courtesy. I may remark that he had not once taken any notice of the blotchy-faced passenger, and had hitherto addressed all his remarks direct to the prince.

"Dear me–is it possible?" observed the clerk, while his face assumed an expression of great deference and servility–if not of absolute alarm: "what, a son of that very Semen Rogojin–hereditary honourable citizen–who died a month or so ago and left two million and a half of roubles?"

"And how do **you** know that he left two million and a half of roubles?" asked Rogojin, disdainfully, and not deigning so much as to look at the other. "However, it's true enough that my father died a month ago, and that here am I returning from Pskoff, a month after, with hardly a boot to my foot. They've treated me like a dog! I've been ill of fever at Pskoff the whole time, and not a line, nor farthing of money, have I received from my mother or my confounded brother!"

"And now you'll have a million roubles, at least–goodness gracious me!" exclaimed the clerk, rubbing his hands.

"Five weeks since, I was just like yourself," continued Rogojin, addressing the prince, "with nothing but a bundle and the clothes I wore. I ran away from my father and came to Pskoff to my aunt's house, where I caved in at once with fever, and he went and died while I was away. All honour to my respected father's memory–but he uncommonly nearly killed me, all the same. Give you my word, prince, if I hadn't cut and run then, when I did, he'd have murdered me like a dog."

"I suppose you angered him somehow?" asked the prince, looking at the millionaire with considerable curiosity. But though there may have been something remarkable in the fact that this man was heir to millions of roubles there was something about him which surprised and interested the prince more than that. Rogojin, too, seemed to have taken up the conversation with unusual alacrity it appeared that he was still in a considerable state of excitement, if not absolutely feverish, and was in real need of someone to talk to for the mere sake of talking, as safety-valve to his agitation.

As for his red-nosed neighbour, the latter–since the information as to the identity of Rogojin–hung over him, seemed to be living on the honey of his words and in the breath of his nostrils, catching at every syllable as though it were a pearl of great price.

"Oh, yes; I angered him–I certainly did anger him," replied Rogojin. "But what puts me out so is my brother. Of course my mother couldn't do anything–she's too old–and whatever brother Senka says is law for her! But why couldn't he let me know? He sent a telegram, they say. What's the good of a telegram? It frightened my aunt so that she sent it back to the office unopened, and there it's been ever since! It's only thanks to Konief that I heard at all; he wrote me all about it. He says my brother cut off the gold tassels from my father's coffin, at night 'because they're worth a lot of money!' says he. Why, I can get him sent off to Siberia for that alone, if I like; it's sacrilege. Here, you–scarecrow!" he added, addressing the clerk at his side, "is it sacrilege or not, by law?"

"Sacrilege, certainly–certainly sacrilege," said the latter.

"And it's Siberia for sacrilege, isn't it?"

"Undoubtedly so; Siberia, of course!"

"They will think that I'm still ill," continued Rogojin to the prince, "but I sloped off quietly, seedy as I was, took the train and came away. Aha, brother Senka, you'll have to open your gates and let me in, my boy! I know he told tales about me to my father–I know that well enough but I certainly did rile my father about Nastasia Philipovna that's very sure, and that was my own doing."

"Nastasia Philipovna?" said the clerk, as though trying to think out something.

"Come, you know nothing about **her**," said Rogojin, impatiently.

"And supposing I do know something?" observed the other, triumphantly.

"Bosh! there are plenty of Nastasia Philipovnas. And what an impertinent beast you are!" he added angrily. "I thought some creature like you would hang on to me as soon as I got hold of my money."

"Oh, but I do know, as it happens," said the clerk in an aggravating manner. "Lebedeff knows all about her. You are pleased to reproach me, your excellency, but what if I prove that I am right after all? Nastasia Phillpovna's family name is Barashkoff–I know, you see–and she is a very well known lady, indeed, and comes of a good family, too. She is connected with one Totski, Afanasy Ivanovitch, a man of considerable property, a director of companies, and so on, and a great friend of General Epanchin, who is interested in the same matters as he is."

"My eyes!" said Rogojin, really surprised at last. "The devil take the fellow, how does he know that?"

"Why, he knows everything–Lebedeff knows everything! I was a month or two with Lihachof after his father died, your excellency, and while he was knocking about–he's in the debtor's prison now–I was with him, and he couldn't do a thing without Lebedeff; and I got to know Nastasia Philipovna and several people at that time."

"Nastasia Philipovna? Why, you don't mean to say that she and Lihachof–" cried

Rogojin, turning quite pale.

"No, no, no, no, no! Nothing of the sort, I assure you!" said Lebedeff, hastily. "Oh dear no, not for the world! Totski's the only man with any chance there. Oh, no! He takes her to his box at the opera at the French theatre of an evening, and the officers and people all look at her and say, 'By Jove, there's the famous Nastasia Philipovna!' but no one ever gets any further than that, for there is nothing more to say."

"Yes, it's quite true," said Rogojin, frowning gloomily; "so Zaleshoff told me. I was walking about the Nefsky one fine day, prince, in my father's old coat, when she suddenly came out of a shop and stepped into her carriage. I swear I was all of a blaze at once. Then I met Zaleshoff–looking like a hair-dresser's assistant, got up as fine as I don't know who, while I looked like a tinker. 'Don't flatter yourself, my boy,' said he; 'she's not for such as you; she's a princess, she is, and her name is Nastasia Philipovna Barashkoff, and she lives with Totski, who wishes to get rid of her because he's growing rather old–fifty-five or so–and wants to marry a certain beauty, the loveliest woman in all Petersburg.' And then he told me that I could see Nastasia Philipovna at the opera-house that evening, if I liked, and described which was her box. Well, I'd like to see my father allowing any of us to go to the theatre; he'd sooner have killed us, any day. However, I went for an hour or so and saw Nastasia Philipovna, and I never slept a wink all night after. Next morning my father happened to give me two government loan bonds to sell, worth nearly five thousand roubles each. 'Sell them,' said he, 'and then take seven thousand five hundred roubles to the office, give them to the cashier, and bring me back the rest of the ten thousand, without looking in anywhere on the way; look sharp, I shall be waiting for you.' Well, I sold the bonds, but I didn't take the seven thousand roubles to the office; I went straight to the English shop and chose a pair of earrings, with a diamond the size of a nut in each. They cost four hundred roubles more than I had, so I gave my name, and they trusted me. With the earrings I went at once to Zaleshoff's. 'Come on!' I said, 'come on to Nastasia Philipovna's,' and off we went without more ado. I tell you I hadn't a notion of what was about me or before me or below my feet all the way; I saw nothing whatever. We went straight into her drawing-room, and then she came out to us.

"I didn't say right out who I was, but Zaleshoff said: 'From Parfen Rogojin, in memory of his first meeting with you yesterday; be so kind as to accept these!'

"She opened the parcel, looked at the earrings, and laughed.

"'Thank your friend Mr. Rogojin for his kind attention,' says she, and bowed and went off. Why didn't I die there on the spot? The worst of it all was, though, that the beast Zaleshoff got all the credit of it! I was short and abominably dressed, and stood and stared in her face and never said a word, because I was shy, like an ass! And there was he all in the fashion, pomaded and dressed out, with a smart tie on, bowing and scraping; and I bet anything she took him for me all the while!

"'Look here now,' I said, when we came out, 'none of your interference here after this–do you understand?' He laughed: 'And how are you going to settle up with your father?' says he. I thought I might as well jump into the Neva at once without going home first; but it struck me that I wouldn't, after all, and I went home feeling like one of the damned."

"My goodness!" shivered the clerk. "And his father," he added, for the prince's instruction, "and his father would have given a man a ticket to the other world for ten roubles any day–not to speak of ten thousand!"

The prince observed Rogojin with great

curiosity; he seemed paler than ever at this moment.

“What do you know about it?” cried the latter. “Well, my father learned the whole story at once, and Zaleshoff blabbed it all over the town besides. So he took me upstairs and locked me up, and swore at me for an hour. ‘This is only a foretaste,’ says he; ‘wait a bit till night comes, and I’ll come back and talk to you again.’

“Well, what do you think? The old fellow went straight off to Nastasia Philipovna, touched the floor with his forehead, and began blubbering and beseeching her on his knees to give him back the diamonds. So after awhile she brought the box and flew out at him. ‘There,’ she says, ‘take your earrings, you wretched old miser; although they are ten times dearer than their value to me now that I know what it must have cost Parfen to get them! Give Parfen my compliments,’ she says, ‘and thank him very much!’ Well, I meanwhile had borrowed twenty-five roubles from a friend, and off I went to Pskoff to my aunt's. The old woman there lectured me so that I left the house and went on a drinking tour round the public-houses of the place. I was in a high fever when I got to Pskoff, and by nightfall I was lying delirious in the streets somewhere or other!"

"Oho! we'll make Nastasia Philipovna sing another song now!" giggled Lebedeff, rubbing his hands with glee. "Hey, my boy, we'll get her some proper earrings now! We'll get her such earrings that–"

"Look here," cried Rogojin, seizing him fiercely by the arm, "look here, if you so much as name Nastasia Philipovna again, I'll tan your hide as sure as you sit there!"

"Aha! do–by all means! if you tan my hide you won't turn me away from your society. You'll bind me to you, with your lash, for ever. Ha, ha! here we are at the station, though."

Sure enough, the train was just steaming

in as he spoke.

Though Rogojin had declared that he left Pskoff secretly, a large collection of friends had assembled to greet him, and did so with profuse waving of hats and shouting.

"Why, there's Zaleshoff here, too!" he muttered, gazing at the scene with a sort of triumphant but unpleasant smile. Then he suddenly turned to the prince: "Prince, I don't know why I have taken a fancy to you; perhaps because I met you just when I did. But no, it can't be that, for I met this fellow" (nodding at Lebedeff) "too, and I have not taken a fancy to him by any means. Come to see me, prince; we'll take off those gaiters of yours and dress you up in a smart fur coat, the best we can buy. You shall have a dress coat, best quality, white waistcoat, anything you like, and your pocket shall be full of money. Come, and you shall go with me to Nastasia Philipovna's. Now then will you come or no?"

"Accept, accept, Prince Lef Nicolaievitch"

said Lebedef solemnly; "don't let it slip! Accept, quick!"

Prince Muishkin rose and stretched out his hand courteously, while he replied with some cordiality:

"I will come with the greatest pleasure, and thank you very much for taking a fancy to me. I dare say I may even come today if I have time, for I tell you frankly that I like you very much too. I liked you especially when you told us about the diamond earrings; but I liked you before that as well, though you have such a dark-clouded sort of face. Thanks very much for the offer of clothes and a fur coat; I certainly shall require both clothes and coat very soon. As for money, I have hardly a copeck about me at this moment."

"You shall have lots of money; by the evening I shall have plenty; so come along!"

"That's true enough, he'll have lots before evening!" put in Lebedeff.

"But, look here, are you a great hand with

the ladies? Let's know that first?" asked Rogojin.

"Oh no, oh no!" said the prince; "I couldn't, you know–my illness–I hardly ever saw a soul."

"H'm! well–here, you fellow–you can come along with me now if you like!" cried Rogojin to Lebedeff, and so they all left the carriage.

Lebedeff had his desire. He went off with the noisy group of Rogojin's friends towards the Voznesensky, while the prince's route lay towards the Litaynaya. It was damp and wet. The prince asked his way of passers-by, and finding that he was a couple of miles or so from his destination, he determined to take a droshky.

CHAPTER TWO

GENERAL EPANCHIN LIVED IN his own house near the Litaynaya. Besides this large residence–five-sixths of which was let in flats and lodgings–the general was owner of another enormous house in the Sadovaya bringing in even more rent than the first. Besides these houses he had a delightful little estate just out of town, and some sort of factory in another part of the city. General Epanchin, as everyone knew, had a good deal to do with certain government monopolies; he was also a voice, and an important one, in many rich public companies of various descriptions; in fact, he enjoyed the reputation of being a well-to-do man of busy habits, many ties, and affluent means. He had made himself indispensable in several quarters, amongst others in his department of the government; and yet it was a known fact that Fedor Ivanovitch Epanchin was a man of no education whatever, and had absolutely risen from the ranks.

This last fact could, of course, reflect nothing but credit upon the general; and yet, though unquestionably a sagacious man, he had his own little weaknesses–very excusable ones,–one of which was a dislike to any allusion to the above circumstance. He was undoubtedly clever. For instance, he made a point of never asserting himself when he would gain more by keeping in the background; and in consequence many exalted personages valued him principally for his humility and simplicity, and because "he knew his place." And yet if these good people could only have had a peep into the mind of this excellent fellow who "knew his place" so well! The fact is that, in spite of his knowledge of the world and his really remarkable abilities, he always liked to appear to be carrying out other people's ideas rather than his own. And also, his luck seldom failed him, even at cards, for which he had a passion that he did not attempt to conceal. He played for high stakes, and moved, altogether, in very varied society.

As to age, General Epanchin was in the very prime of life; that is, about fifty-five years of age,–the flowering time of existence, when real enjoyment of life begins. His healthy appearance, good colour, sound, though discoloured teeth, sturdy figure, preoccupied air during business hours, and jolly good humour during his game at cards in the evening, all bore witness to his success in life, and combined to make existence a bed of roses to his excellency. The general was lord of a flourishing family, consisting of his wife and three grown-up daughters. He had married young, while still a lieutenant, his wife being a girl of about his own age, who possessed neither beauty nor education, and who brought him no more than fifty souls of landed property, which little estate served, however, as a nest-egg for far more important accumulations. The general never regretted his early marriage, or regarded it as a foolish youthful escapade; and he so respected and feared his wife that he was very near loving her. Mrs. Epanchin came of the princely stock of Muishkin, which if not a brilliant, was, at all events, a decidedly ancient family; and she was extremely proud of her descent.

With a few exceptions, the worthy couple had lived through their long union very happily. While still young the wife had been able to make important friends among the aristocracy, partly by virtue of her family descent, and partly by her own exertions; while, in after life, thanks to their wealth and to the position of her husband in the service, she took her place among the higher circles as by right.

During these last few years all three of the general's daughters–Alexandra, Adelaida, and Aglaya–had grown up and matured. Of course they were only Epanchins, but their mother's family was noble; they might expect considerable fortunes; their father had hopes of attaining to very high rank indeed in his country's service–all of which was satisfactory. All three of the girls were decidedly pretty, even the eldest, Alexandra, who was just twenty-five years old. The middle daughter was now twenty-three, while the youngest, Aglaya, was twenty. This youngest girl was absolutely a beauty, and had begun of late to attract considerable attention in society. But this was not all, for every one of the three was clever, well educated, and accomplished.

It was a matter of general knowledge that the three girls were very fond of one another, and supported each other in every way; it was even said that the two elder ones had made certain sacrifices for the sake of the idol of the household, Aglaya. In society they not only disliked asserting themselves, but were actually retiring. Certainly no one could blame them for being too arrogant or haughty, and yet everybody was well aware that they were proud and quite understood their own value. The eldest was musical, while the second was a clever artist, which fact she had concealed until lately. In a word, the world spoke well of the girls; but they were not without their enemies, and occasionally people talked with horror of the number of books they had read.

They were in no hurry to marry. They liked good society, but were not too keen about it. All this was the more remarkable, because everyone was well aware of the hopes and aims of their parents.

It was about eleven o'clock in the forenoon when the prince rang the bell at General Epanchin's door. The general lived on the first floor or flat of the house, as modest a lodging as his position permitted. A liveried servant opened the door, and the prince was obliged to enter into long explanations with this gentleman, who, from the first glance, looked at him and his bundle with grave suspicion. At last, however, on the repeated positive assurance that he really was Prince Muishkin, and must absolutely see the general on business, the bewildered domestic showed him into a little ante-chamber leading to a waiting-room that adjoined the general's study, there handing him over to another servant, whose duty it was to be in this ante-chamber all the morning, and announce visitors to the general. This second individual wore a dress coat, and was some forty years of age; he was the general's special study servant, and well aware of his own importance.

"Wait in the next room, please; and leave your bundle here," said the door-keeper, as he sat down comfortably in his own easy-chair in the ante-chamber. He looked at the prince in severe surprise as the latter settled himself in another chair alongside, with his bundle on his knees.

"If you don't mind, I would rather sit here with you," said the prince; "I should prefer it to sitting in there."

"Oh, but you can't stay here. You are a visitor–a guest, so to speak. Is it the general himself you wish to see?"

The man evidently could not take in the idea of such a shabby-looking visitor, and had decided to ask once more.

"Yes–I have business–" began the prince.

"I do not ask you what your business may be, all I have to do is to announce you; and unless the secretary comes in here I cannot do that."

The man's suspicions seemed to increase

more and more. The prince was too unlike the usual run of daily visitors; and although the general certainly did receive, on business, all sorts and conditions of men, yet in spite of this fact the servant felt great doubts on the subject of this particular visitor. The presence of the secretary as an intermediary was, he judged, essential in this case.

"Surely you–are from abroad?" he inquired at last, in a confused sort of way. He had begun his sentence intending to say, "Surely you are not Prince Muishkin, are you?"

"Yes, straight from the train! Did not you intend to say, 'Surely you are not Prince Muishkin?' just now, but refrained out of politeness?"

"H'm!" grunted the astonished servant.

"I assure you I am not deceiving you; you shall not have to answer for me. As to my being dressed like this, and carrying a bundle, there's nothing surprising in that–the fact is, my circumstances are not particularly rosy at this moment."

"H'm!–no, I'm not afraid of that, you see; I have to announce you, that's all. The secretary will be out directly–that is, unless you–yes, that's the rub–unless you–come, you must allow me to ask you–you've not come to beg, have you?"

"Oh dear no, you can be perfectly easy on that score. I have quite another matter on hand."

"You must excuse my asking, you know. Your appearance led me to think–but just wait for the secretary; the general is busy now, but the secretary is sure to come out."

"Oh–well, look here, if I have some time to wait, would you mind telling me, is there any place about where I could have a smoke? I have my pipe and tobacco with me."

"**Smoke?**" said the man, in shocked but disdainful surprise, blinking his eyes at the prince as though he could not believe his senses. "No, sir, you cannot smoke here, and I wonder you are not ashamed of the very suggestion. Ha, ha! a cool idea that, I declare!"

"Oh, I didn't mean in this room! I know I can't smoke here, of course. I'd adjourn to some other room, wherever you like to show me to. You see, I'm used to smoking a good deal, and now I haven't had a puff for three hours; however, just as you like."

"Now how on earth am I to announce a man like that?" muttered the servant. "In the first place, you've no right in here at all; you ought to be in the waiting-room, because you're a sort of visitor–a guest, in fact–and I shall catch it for this. Look here, do you intend to take up you abode with us?" he added, glancing once more at the prince's bundle, which evidently gave him no peace.

"No, I don't think so. I don't think I should stay even if they were to invite me. I've simply come to make their acquaintance, and nothing more."

"Make their acquaintance?" asked the man, in amazement, and with redoubled suspicion. “Then why did you say you had business with the general?”

“Oh well, very little business. There is one little matter–some advice I am going to ask him for; but my principal object is simply to introduce myself, because I am Prince Muishkin, and Madame Epanchin is the last of her branch of the house, and besides herself and me there are no other Muishkins left.”

“What–you’re a relation then, are you?” asked the servant, so bewildered that he began to feel quite alarmed.

“Well, hardly so. If you stretch a point, we are relations, of course, but so distant that one cannot really take cognizance of it. I once wrote to your mistress from abroad, but she did not reply. However, I have thought it right to make acquaintance with her on my arrival. I am telling you all this in order to ease your mind, for I see you are still far from comfortable on my account. All you have to do is to announce me as Prince

Muishkin, and the object of my visit will be plain enough. If I am received–very good; if not, well, very good again. But they are sure to receive me, I should think; Madame Epanchin will naturally be curious to see the only remaining representative of her family. She values her Muishkin descent very highly, if I am rightly informed."

The prince's conversation was artless and confiding to a degree, and the servant could not help feeling that as from visitor to common serving-man this state of things was highly improper. His conclusion was that one of two things must be the explanation–either that this was a begging impostor, or that the prince, if prince he were, was simply a fool, without the slightest ambition; for a sensible prince with any ambition would certainly not wait about in ante-rooms with servants, and talk of his own private affairs like this. In either case, how was he to announce this singular visitor?

"I really think I must request you to step

into the next room!" he said, with all the insistence he could muster.

"Why? If I had been sitting there now, I should not have had the opportunity of making these personal explanations. I see you are still uneasy about me and keep eyeing my cloak and bundle. Don't you think you might go in yourself now, without waiting for the secretary to come out?"

"No, no! I can't announce a visitor like yourself without the secretary. Besides the general said he was not to be disturbed–he is with the Colonel C–. Gavrila Ardalionovitch goes in without announcing."

"Who may that be? a clerk?"

"What? Gavrila Ardalionovitch? Oh no; he belongs to one of the companies. Look here, at all events put your bundle down, here."

"Yes, I will if I may; and–can I take off my cloak"

"Of course; you can't go in **there** with it on, anyhow."

The prince rose and took off his mantle,

revealing a neat enough morning costume–a little worn, but well made. He wore a steel watch chain and from this chain there hung a silver Geneva watch. Fool the prince might be, still, the general's servant felt that it was not correct for him to continue to converse thus with a visitor, in spite of the fact that the prince pleased him somehow.

"And what time of day does the lady receive?" the latter asked, reseating himself in his old place.

"Oh, that's not in **my** province! I believe she receives at any time; it depends upon the visitors. The dressmaker goes in at eleven. Gavrila Ardalionovitch is allowed much earlier than other people, too; he is even admitted to early lunch now and then."

"It is much warmer in the rooms here than it is abroad at this season," observed the prince; "but it is much warmer there out of doors. As for the houses–a Russian can't live in them in the winter until he gets accustomed to them."

"Don't they heat them at all?"

"Well, they do heat them a little; but the houses and stoves are so different to ours."

"H'm! were you long away?"

"Four years! and I was in the same place nearly all the time,–in one village."

"You must have forgotten Russia, hadn't you?"

"Yes, indeed I had–a good deal; and, would you believe it, I often wonder at myself for not having forgotten how to speak Russian? Even now, as I talk to you, I keep saying to myself 'how well I am speaking it.' Perhaps that is partly why I am so talkative this morning. I assure you, ever since yesterday evening I have had the strongest desire to go on and on talking Russian."

"H'm! yes; did you live in Petersburg in former years?"

This good flunkey, in spite of his conscientious scruples, really could not resist continuing such a very genteel and agreeable conversation.

"In Petersburg? Oh no! hardly at all, and now they say so much is changed in the place that even those who did know it well are obliged to relearn what they knew. They talk a good deal about the new law courts, and changes there, don't they?"

"H'm! yes, that's true enough. Well now, how is the law over there, do they administer it more justly than here?"

"Oh, I don't know about that! I've heard much that is good about our legal administration, too. There is no capital punishment here for one thing."

"Is there over there?"

"Yes–I saw an execution in France–at Lyons. Schneider took me over with him to see it."

"What, did they hang the fellow?"

"No, they cut off people's heads in France."

"What did the fellow do?–yell?"

"Oh no–it's the work of an instant. They put a man inside a frame and a sort of broad knife falls by machinery–they call the thing a guillotine–it falls with fearful force and weight–the head springs off so quickly that you can't wink your eye in between. But all the preparations are so dreadful. When they announce the sentence, you know, and prepare the criminal and tie his hands, and cart him off to the scaffold–that's the fearful part of the business. The people all crowd round–even women–though they don't at all approve of women looking on."

"No, it's not a thing for women."

"Of course not–of course not!–bah! The criminal was a fine intelligent fearless man; Le Gros was his name; and I may tell you–believe it or not, as you like–that when that man stepped upon the scaffold he **cried**, he did indeed,–he was as white as a bit of paper. Isn't it a dreadful idea that he should have cried–cried! Whoever heard of a grown man crying from fear–not a child, but a man who never had cried before–a grown man of forty-five years. Imagine what must have been going on in that man's mind at such a moment; what dreadful convulsions his whole spirit must have endured; it is an outrage on the soul that's what it is. Because it is said 'thou shalt not kill,' is he to be killed because he murdered some one else? No, it is not right, it's an impossible theory. I assure you, I saw the sight a month ago and it's dancing before my eyes to this moment. I dream of it, often."

The prince had grown animated as he spoke, and a tinge of colour suffused his pale face, though his way of talking was as quiet as ever. The servant followed his words with sympathetic interest. Clearly he was not at all anxious to bring the conversation to an end. Who knows? Perhaps he too was a man of imagination and with some capacity for thought.

"Well, at all events it is a good thing that there's no pain when the poor fellow's head flies off," he remarked.

"Do you know, though," cried the prince warmly, "you made that remark now, and everyone says the same thing, and the machine is designed with the purpose of avoiding pain, this guillotine I mean; but a thought came into my head then: what if it be a bad plan after all? You may laugh at my idea, perhaps–but I could not help its occurring to me all the same. Now with the rack and tortures and so on–you suffer terrible pain of course; but then your torture is bodily pain only (although no doubt you have plenty of that) until you die. But **here** I should imagine the most terrible part of the whole punishment is, not the bodily pain at all–but the certain knowledge that in an hour,–then in ten minutes, then in half a minute, then now–this very **instant**–your soul must quit your body and that you will no longer be a man–and that this is certain, **certain!** That's the point–the certainty of it. Just that instant when you place your head on the block and hear the iron grate over your head–then–that quarter of a second is the most awful of all.

"This is not my own fantastical opinion–many people have thought the same; but I feel it so deeply that I'll tell you what I think. I believe that to execute a man for murder is to punish him immeasurably more dreadfully than is equivalent to his crime. A murder by sentence is far more dreadful than a murder committed by a criminal. The man who is attacked by robbers at night, in a dark wood, or anywhere, undoubtedly hopes and hopes that he may yet escape until the very moment of his death. There are plenty of instances of a man running away, or imploring for mercy–at all events hoping on in some degree–even after his throat was cut. But in the case of an execution, that last hope–having which it is so immeasurably less dreadful to die,–is taken away from the wretch and **certainty** substituted in its place! There is his sentence, and with it that terrible certainty that he cannot possibly escape death–which, I consider, must be the most dreadful anguish in the world.

You may place a soldier before a cannon's mouth in battle, and fire upon him–and he will still hope. But read to that same soldier his death-sentence, and he will either go mad or burst into tears. Who dares to say that any man can suffer this without going mad? No, no! it is an abuse, a shame, it is unnecessary–why should such a thing exist? Doubtless there may be men who have been sentenced, who have suffered this mental anguish for a while and then have been reprieved; perhaps such men may have been able to relate their feelings afterwards. Our Lord Christ spoke of this anguish and dread. No! no! no! No man should be treated so, no man, no man!"

The servant, though of course he could not have expressed all this as the prince did, still clearly entered into it and was greatly conciliated, as was evident from the increased amiability of his expression. "If you are really very anxious for a smoke," he remarked, "I think it might possibly be managed, if you are very quick about it. You see they might come out and inquire for you, and you wouldn't be on the spot. You see that door there? Go in there and you'll find a little room on the right; you can smoke there, only open the window, because I ought not to allow it really, and–." But there was no time, after all.

A young fellow entered the ante-room at this moment, with a bundle of papers in his hand. The footman hastened to help him take off his overcoat. The new arrival glanced at the prince out of the corners of his eyes.

"This gentleman declares, Gavrila Ardalionovitch," began the man, confidentially and almost familiarly, "that he is Prince Muishkin and a relative of Madame Epanchin's. He has just arrived from abroad, with nothing but a bundle by way of luggage–."

The prince did not hear the rest, because at this point the servant continued his communication in a whisper.

Gavrila Ardalionovitch listened attentively, and gazed at the prince with great curiosity. At last he motioned the man aside and stepped hurriedly towards the prince.

"Are you Prince Muishkin?" he asked, with the greatest courtesy and amiability.

He was a remarkably handsome young fellow of some twenty-eight summers, fair and of middle height; he wore a small beard, and his face was most intelligent. Yet his smile, in spite of its sweetness, was a little thin, if I may so call it, and showed his teeth too evenly; his gaze though decidedly good-humoured and ingenuous, was a trifle too inquisitive and intent to be altogether agreeable.

"Probably when he is alone he looks quite different, and hardly smiles at all!" thought the prince.

He explained about himself in a few words, very much the same as he had told the footman and Rogojin beforehand.

Gavrila Ardalionovitch meanwhile seemed to be trying to recall something.

"Was it not you, then, who sent a letter a year or less ago–from Switzerland, I think it was–to Elizabetha Prokofievna (Mrs. Epanchin)?"

"It was."

"Oh, then, of course they will remember who you are. You wish to see the general? I'll tell him at once–he will be free in a minute; but you–you had better wait in the antechamber,–hadn't you? Why is he here?" he added, severely, to the man.

"I tell you, sir, he wished it himself!"

At this moment the study door opened, and a military man, with a portfolio under his arm, came out talking loudly, and after bidding good-bye to someone inside, took his departure.

"You there, Gania?" cried a voice from the study, "come in here, will you?"

Gavrila Ardalionovitch nodded to the prince and entered the room hastily.

A couple of minutes later the door opened again and the affable voice of Gania cried:

"Come in please, prince!"

CHAPTER THREE

GENERAL IVAN FEDOROVITCH EPANCHIN was standing in the middle of the room, and gazed with great curiosity at the prince as he entered. He even advanced a couple of steps to meet him.

The prince came forward and introduced himself.

“Quite so,” replied the general, “and what can I do for you?”

“Oh, I have no special business; my principal object was to make your acquaintance. I should not like to disturb you. I do not know your times and arrangements here, you see, but I have only just arrived. I came straight from the station. I am come direct from Switzerland."

The general very nearly smiled, but thought better of it and kept his smile back. Then he reflected, blinked his eyes, stared at his guest once more from head to foot; then abruptly motioned him to a chair, sat down himself, and waited with some impatience for the prince to speak.

Gania stood at his table in the far corner of the room, turning over papers.

"I have not much time for making acquaintances, as a rule," said the general, "but as, of course, you have your object in coming, I–"

"I felt sure you would think I had some object in view when I resolved to pay you this visit," the prince interrupted; "but I give you my word, beyond the pleasure of making your acquaintance I had no personal object whatever."

"The pleasure is, of course, mutual; but life is not all pleasure, as you are aware. There is such a thing as business, and I really do not see what possible reason there can be, or what we have in common to–"

"Oh, there is no reason, of course, and I suppose there is nothing in common between us, or very little; for if I am Prince Muishkin, and your wife happens to be a member of my house, that can hardly be called a 'reason.' I quite understand that. And yet that was my whole motive for coming. You see I have not been in Russia for four years, and knew very little about anything when I left. I had been very ill for a long time, and I feel now the need of a few good friends. In fact, I have a certain question upon which I much need advice, and do not know whom to go to for it. I thought of your family when I was passing through Berlin. 'They are almost relations,' I said to myself, 'so I'll begin with them; perhaps we may get on with each other, I with them and they with me, if they are kind people;' and I have heard that you are very kind people!"

"Oh, thank you, thank you, I'm sure," replied the general, considerably taken aback. "May I ask where you have taken up your quarters?"

"Nowhere, as yet."

"What, straight from the station to my house? And how about your luggage?"

"I only had a small bundle, containing linen, with me, nothing more. I can carry it in my hand, easily. There will be plenty of time to take a room in some hotel by the evening."

"Oh, then you **do** intend to take a room?"

"Of course."

"To judge from your words, you came straight to my house with the intention of staying there."

"That could only have been on your invitation. I confess, however, that I should not have stayed here even if you had invited me, not for any particular reason, but because it is–well, contrary to my practice and nature, somehow."

"Oh, indeed! Then it is perhaps as well that I neither **did** invite you, nor **do** invite you now. Excuse me, prince, but we had better make this matter clear, once for all. We have just agreed that with regard to our relationship there is not much to be said, though, of course, it would have been very delightful to us to feel that such relationship did actually exist; therefore, perhaps–"

"Therefore, perhaps I had better get up and go away?" said the prince, laughing merrily as he rose from his place; just as merrily as though the circumstances were by no means strained or difficult. "And I give you my word, general, that though I know nothing whatever of manners and customs of society, and how people live and all that, yet I felt quite sure that this visit of mine would end exactly as it has ended now. Oh, well, I suppose it's all right; especially as my letter was not answered. Well, good-bye, and forgive me for having disturbed you!"

The prince's expression was so good-natured at this moment, and so entirely free from even a suspicion of unpleasant feeling was the smile with which he looked at the general as he spoke, that the latter suddenly paused, and appeared to gaze at his guest from quite a new point of view, all in an instant.

"Do you know, prince," he said, in quite a different tone, "I do not know you at all, yet, and after all, Elizabetha Prokofievna would very likely be pleased to have a peep at a man of her own name. Wait a little, if you don't mind, and if you have time to spare?"

"Oh, I assure you I've lots of time, my time is entirely my own!" And the prince immediately replaced his soft, round hat on the table. "I confess, I thought Elizabetha Prokofievna would very likely remember that I had written her a letter. Just now your servant–outside there–was dreadfully suspicious that I had come to beg of you. I noticed that! Probably he has very strict instructions on that score; but I assure you I did not come to beg. I came to make some friends. But I am rather bothered at having disturbed you; that's all I care about.–"

"Look here, prince," said the general, with a cordial smile, "if you really are the sort of man you appear to be, it may be a source of great pleasure to us to make your better acquaintance; but, you see, I am a very busy man, and have to be perpetually sitting here and signing papers, or off to see his excellency, or to my department, or somewhere; so that though I should be glad to see more of people, nice people–you see, I–however, I am sure you are so well brought up that you will see at once, and–but how old are you, prince?"

"Twenty-six."

"No? I thought you very much younger."

"Yes, they say I have a 'young' face. As to disturbing you I shall soon learn to avoid doing that, for I hate disturbing people.

Besides, you and I are so differently constituted, I should think, that there must be very little in common between us. Not that I will ever believe there is **nothing** in common between any two people, as some declare is the case. I am sure people make a great mistake in sorting each other into groups, by appearances; but I am boring you, I see, you–"

"Just two words: have you any means at all? Or perhaps you may be intending to undertake some sort of employment? Excuse my questioning you, but–"

"Oh, my dear sir, I esteem and understand your kindness in putting the question. No; at present I have no means whatever, and no employment either, but I hope to find some. I was living on other people abroad. Schneider, the professor who treated me and taught me, too, in Switzerland, gave me just enough money for my journey, so that now I have but a few copecks left. There certainly is one question upon which I am anxious to have advice, but–"

"Tell me, how do you intend to live now, and what are your plans?" interrupted the general.

"I wish to work, somehow or other."

"Oh yes, but then, you see, you are a philosopher. Have you any talents, or ability in any direction–that is, any that would bring in money and bread? Excuse me again–"

"Oh, don't apologize. No, I don't think I have either talents or special abilities of any kind; on the contrary. I have always been an invalid and unable to learn much. As for bread, I should think–"

The general interrupted once more with questions; while the prince again replied with the narrative we have heard before. It appeared that the general had known Pavlicheff; but why the latter had taken an interest in the prince, that young gentleman could not explain; probably by virtue of the old friendship with his father, he thought.

The prince had been left an orphan when

quite a little child, and Pavlicheff had entrusted him to an old lady, a relative of his own, living in the country, the child needing the fresh air and exercise of country life. He was educated, first by a governess, and afterwards by a tutor, but could not remember much about this time of his life. His fits were so frequent then, that they made almost an idiot of him (the prince used the expression "idiot" himself). Pavlicheff had met Professor Schneider in Berlin, and the latter had persuaded him to send the boy to Switzerland, to Schneider's establishment there, for the cure of his epilepsy, and, five years before this time, the prince was sent off. But Pavlicheff had died two or three years since, and Schneider had himself supported the young fellow, from that day to this, at his own expense. Although he had not quite cured him, he had greatly improved his condition; and now, at last, at the prince's own desire, and because of a certain matter which came to the ears of the latter, Schneider had despatched the young man to Russia.

The general was much astonished.

"Then you have no one, absolutely **no** one in Russia?" he asked.

"No one, at present; but I hope to make friends; and then I have a letter from–"

"At all events," put in the general, not listening to the news about the letter, "at all events, you must have learned **something**, and your malady would not prevent your undertaking some easy work, in one of the departments, for instance?"

"Oh dear no, oh no! As for a situation, I should much like to find one for I am anxious to discover what I really am fit for. I have learned a good deal in the last four years, and, besides, I read a great many Russian books."

"Russian books, indeed? Then, of course, you can read and write quite correctly?"

"Oh dear, yes!"

"Capital! And your handwriting?"

"Ah, there I am **really** talented! I may

say I am a real caligraphist. Let me write you something, just to show you," said the prince, with some excitement.

"With pleasure! In fact, it is very necessary. I like your readiness, prince; in fact, I must say–I–I–like you very well, altogether," said the general.

"What delightful writing materials you have here, such a lot of pencils and things, and what beautiful paper! It's a charming room altogether. I know that picture, it's a Swiss view. I'm sure the artist painted it from nature, and that I have seen the very place–"

"Quite likely, though I bought it here. Gania, give the prince some paper. Here are pens and paper; now then, take this table. What's this?" the general continued to Gania, who had that moment taken a large photograph out of his portfolio, and shown it to his senior. "Halloa! Nastasia Philipovna! Did she send it you herself? Herself?" he inquired, with much curiosity and great animation.

"She gave it me just now, when I called in to congratulate her. I asked her for it long ago. I don't know whether she meant it for a hint that I had come empty-handed, without a present for her birthday, or what," added Gania, with an unpleasant smile.

"Oh, nonsense, nonsense," said the general, with decision. "What extraordinary ideas you have, Gania! As if she would hint; that's not her way at all. Besides, what could **you** give her, without having thousands at your disposal? You might have given her your portrait, however. Has she ever asked you for it?"

"No, not yet. Very likely she never will. I suppose you haven't forgotten about tonight, have you, Ivan Fedorovitch? You were one of those specially invited, you know."

"Oh no, I remember all right, and I shall go, of course. I should think so! She's twenty-five years old today! And, you know, Gania, you must be ready for great things; she has promised both myself and

Afanasy Ivanovitch that she will give a decided answer tonight, yes or no. So be prepared!"

Gania suddenly became so ill at ease that his face grew paler than ever.

"Are you sure she said that?" he asked, and his voice seemed to quiver as he spoke.

"Yes, she promised. We both worried her so that she gave in; but she wished us to tell you nothing about it until the day."

The general watched Gania's confusion intently, and clearly did not like it.

"Remember, Ivan Fedorovitch," said Gania, in great agitation, "that I was to be free too, until her decision; and that even then I was to have my 'yes or no' free."

"Why, don't you, aren't you–" began the general, in alarm.

"Oh, don't misunderstand–"

"But, my dear fellow, what are you doing, what do you mean?"

"Oh, I'm not rejecting her. I may have expressed myself badly, but I didn't mean that."

"Reject her! I should think not!" said the general with annoyance, and apparently not in the least anxious to conceal it. "Why, my dear fellow, it's not a question of your rejecting her, it is whether you are prepared to receive her consent joyfully, and with proper satisfaction. How are things going on at home?"

"At home? Oh, I can do as I like there, of course; only my father will make a fool of himself, as usual. He is rapidly becoming a general nuisance. I don't ever talk to him now, but I hold him in check, safe enough. I swear if it had not been for my mother, I should have shown him the way out, long ago. My mother is always crying, of course, and my sister sulks. I had to tell them at last that I intended to be master of my own destiny, and that I expect to be obeyed at home. At least, I gave my sister to understand as much, and my mother was present."

"Well, I must say, I cannot understand it!" said the general, shrugging his shoulders and dropping his hands. "You remember your mother, Nina Alexandrovna, that day she came and sat here and groaned–and when I asked her what was the matter, she says, 'Oh, it's such a **dishonour** to us!' dishonour! Stuff and nonsense! I should like to know who can reproach Nastasia Philipovna, or who can say a word of any kind against her. Did she mean because Nastasia had been living with Totski? What nonsense it is! You would not let her come near your daughters, says Nina Alexandrovna. What next, I wonder? I don't see how she can fail to–to understand–"

"Her own position?" prompted Gania. "She does understand. Don't be annoyed with her. I have warned her not to meddle in other people's affairs. However, although there's comparative peace at home at present, the storm will break if anything is finally settled tonight."

The prince heard the whole of the foregoing conversation, as he sat at the table, writing. He finished at last, and brought the result of his labour to the general's desk.

"So this is Nastasia Philipovna," he said, looking attentively and curiously at the portrait. "How wonderfully beautiful!" he immediately added, with warmth. The picture was certainly that of an unusually lovely woman. She was photographed in a black silk dress of simple design, her hair was evidently dark and plainly arranged, her eyes were deep and thoughtful, the expression of her face passionate, but proud. She was rather thin, perhaps, and a little pale. Both Gania and the general gazed at the prince in amazement.

"How do you know it's Nastasia Philipovna?" asked the general; "you surely don't know her already, do you?"

"Yes, I do! I have only been one day in Russia, but I have heard of the great beauty!" And the prince proceeded to narrate his meeting with Rogojin in the train and the whole of the latter's story.

"There's news!" said the general in some excitement, after listening to the story with engrossed attention.

"Oh, of course it's nothing but humbug!" cried Gania, a little disturbed, however. "It's all humbug; the young merchant was pleased to indulge in a little innocent recreation! I have heard something of Rogojin!"

"Yes, so have I!" replied the general. "Nastasia Philipovna told us all about the earrings that very day. But now it is quite a different matter. You see the fellow really has a million of roubles, and he is passionately in love. The whole story smells of passion, and we all know what this class of gentry is capable of when infatuated. I am much afraid of some disagreeable scandal, I am indeed!"

"You are afraid of the million, I suppose," said Gania, grinning and showing his teeth.

"And you are **not**, I presume, eh?"

"How did he strike you, prince?" asked Gania, suddenly. "Did he seem to be a serious sort of a man, or just a common rowdy fellow? What was your own opinion about the matter?"

While Gania put this question, a new idea suddenly flashed into his brain, and blazed out, impatiently, in his eyes. The general, who was really agitated and disturbed, looked at the prince too, but did not seem to expect much from his reply.

"I really don't quite know how to tell you," replied the prince, "but it certainly did seem to me that the man was full of passion, and not, perhaps, quite healthy passion. He seemed to be still far from well. Very likely he will be in bed again in a day or two, especially if he lives fast."

"No! do you think so?" said the general, catching at the idea.

"Yes, I do think so!"

"Yes, but the sort of scandal I referred

to may happen at any moment. It may be this very evening," remarked Gania to the general, with a smile.

"Of course; quite so. In that case it all depends upon what is going on in her brain at this moment."

"You know the kind of person she is at times."

"How? What kind of person is she?" cried the general, arrived at the limits of his patience. "Look here, Gania, don't you go annoying her tonight. What you are to do is to be as agreeable towards her as ever you can. Well, what are you smiling at? You must understand, Gania, that I have no interest whatever in speaking like this. Whichever way the question is settled, it will be to my advantage. Nothing will move Totski from his resolution, so I run no risk. If there is anything I desire, you must know that it is your benefit only. Can't you trust me? You are a sensible fellow, and I have been counting on you; for, in this matter, that, that–"

"Yes, that's the chief thing," said Gania, helping the general out of his difficulties again, and curling his lips in an envenomed smile, which he did not attempt to conceal. He gazed with his fevered eyes straight into those of the general, as though he were anxious that the latter might read his thoughts.

The general grew purple with anger.

"Yes, of course it is the chief thing!" he cried, looking sharply at Gania. "What a very curious man you are, Gania! You actually seem to be **glad** to hear of this millionaire fellow's arrival–just as though you wished for an excuse to get out of the whole thing. This is an affair in which you ought to act honestly with both sides, and give due warning, to avoid compromising others. But, even now, there is still time. Do you understand me? I wish to know whether you desire this arrangement or whether you do not? If not, say so,–and–and welcome!

No one is trying to force you into the snare, Gavrila Ardalionovitch, if you see a snare in the matter, at least."

"I do desire it," murmured Gania, softly but firmly, lowering his eyes; and he relapsed into gloomy silence.

The general was satisfied. He had excited himself, and was evidently now regretting that he had gone so far. He turned to the prince, and suddenly the disagreeable thought of the latter's presence struck him, and the certainty that he must have heard every word of the conversation. But he felt at ease in another moment; it only needed one glance at the prince to see that in that quarter there was nothing to fear.

"Oh!" cried the general, catching sight of the prince's specimen of caligraphy, which the latter had now handed him for inspection. "Why, this is simply beautiful; look at that, Gania, there's real talent there!"

On a sheet of thick writing-paper the prince had written in medieval characters the legend:

"The gentle Abbot Pafnute signed this."

"There," explained the prince, with great delight and animation, "there, that's the abbot's real signature–from a manuscript of the fourteenth century. All these old abbots and bishops used to write most beautifully, with such taste and so much care and diligence. Have you no copy of Pogodin, general? If you had one I could show you another type. Stop a bit–here you have the large round writing common in France during the eighteenth century. Some of the letters are shaped quite differently from those now in use. It was the writing current then, and employed by public writers generally. I copied this from one of them, and you can see how good it is. Look at the well-rounded a and d. I have tried to translate the French character into the Russian letters–a difficult thing to do, but I think I have succeeded fairly. Here is a fine sentence, written in a good, original hand–'Zeal triumphs over all.' That is the script of the Russian War Office. That is how official documents addressed to important personages should be written. The letters are round, the type black, and the style somewhat remarkable. A stylist would not allow these ornaments, or attempts at flourishes–just look at these unfinished tails!–but it has distinction and really depicts the soul of the writer. He would like to give play to his imagination, and follow the inspiration of his genius, but a soldier is only at ease in the guard-room, and the pen stops half-way, a slave to discipline. How delightful! The first time I met an example of this handwriting, I was positively astonished, and where do you think I chanced to find it? In Switzerland, of all places! Now that is an ordinary English hand. It can hardly be improved, it is so refined and exquisite–almost perfection. This is an example of another kind, a mixture of styles. The copy was given me by a French commercial traveller. It is founded on the English, but the downstrokes are a little blacker, and more marked. Notice that the oval has some slight modification–it is more rounded. This writing allows for flourishes; now a flourish is a dangerous thing! Its use requires such taste, but, if successful, what a distinction it gives to the whole! It results in an incomparable type–one to fall in love with!"

"Dear me! How you have gone into all the refinements and details of the question! Why, my dear fellow, you are not a caligraphist, you are an artist! Eh, Gania?"

"Wonderful!" said Gania. "And he knows it too," he added, with a sarcastic smile.

"You may smile,–but there's a career in this," said the general. "You don't know what a great personage I shall show this to, prince. Why, you can command a situation at thirty-five roubles per month to start with. However, it's half-past twelve," he concluded, looking at his watch; "so to business, prince, for I must be setting to work and shall not see you again today. Sit down a minute. I have told you that I cannot receive you myself very often, but I should like to be of some assistance to you, some small assistance, of a kind that would give you satisfaction. I shall find you a place in one of the State departments, an easy place–but you will require to be accurate. Now, as to your plans–in the house, or rather in the family of Gania here–my young friend, whom I hope you will know better–his mother and sister have prepared two or three rooms for lodgers, and let them to highly recommended young fellows, with board and attendance. I am sure Nina Alexandrovna will take you in on my recommendation. There you will be comfortable and well taken care of; for I do not think, prince, that you are the sort of man to be left to the mercy of Fate in a town like Petersburg. Nina Alexandrovna, Gania's mother, and Varvara Alexandrovna, are ladies for whom I have the highest possible esteem and respect. Nina Alexandrovna is the wife of General Ardalion Alexandrovitch, my old brother in arms, with whom, I regret to say, on account of certain circumstances, I am no longer acquainted. I give you all this information, prince, in order to make it clear to you that I am personally recommending you to this family, and that in so doing, I am more or less taking upon myself to answer for you. The terms are most reasonable, and I trust that your salary will very shortly prove amply sufficient for your expenditure. Of course pocket-money is a necessity, if only a little; do not be angry, prince, if I strongly recommend you to avoid carrying money in your pocket. But as your purse is quite empty at the present moment, you must allow me to press these twenty-five roubles upon your acceptance, as something to begin with. Of course we will settle this little matter another time, and if you are the upright, honest man you look, I anticipate very little trouble between us on that score. Taking so much interest in you as you may perceive I do, I am not without my object, and you shall know it in good time. You see, I am perfectly candid with you. I hope, Gania, you have nothing to say against the prince's taking up his abode in your house?"

"Oh, on the contrary! my mother will be very glad," said Gania, courteously and kindly.

"I think only one of your rooms is engaged as yet, is it not? That fellow Ferd-Ferd–"

"Ferdishenko."

"Yes–I don't like that Ferdishenko. I can't understand why Nastasia Philipovna encourages him so. Is he really her cousin, as he says?"

"Oh dear no, it's all a joke. No more cousin than I am."

"Well, what do you think of the arrangement, prince?"

"Thank you, general; you have behaved very kindly to me; all the more so since I did not ask you to help me. I don't say that out of pride. I certainly did not know where to lay my head tonight. Rogojin asked me to come to his house, of course, but–"

"Rogojin? No, no, my good fellow. I should strongly recommend you, paternally,–or, if you prefer it, as a friend,–to forget all about Rogojin, and, in fact, to stick to the family into which you are about to enter."

"Thank you," began the prince; "and since you are so very kind there is just one matter which I–"

"You must really excuse me," interrupted the general, "but I positively haven't another moment now. I shall just tell Elizabetha Prokofievna about you, and if she wishes to receive you at once–as I shall advise her–I strongly recommend you to ingratiate yourself with her at the first opportunity, for my wife may be of the greatest service to you in many ways. If she cannot receive you now, you must be content to wait till another time. Meanwhile you, Gania, just look over these accounts, will you? We mustn't forget to finish off that matter–"

The general left the room, and the prince never succeeded in broaching the business which he had on hand, though he had endeavoured to do so four times.

Gania lit a cigarette and offered one to the prince. The latter accepted the offer, but did not talk, being unwilling to disturb Gania's work. He commenced to examine the study and its contents. But Gania hardly so much as glanced at the papers lying before him; he was absent and thoughtful, and his smile and general appearance struck the prince still more disagreeably now that the two were left alone together.

Suddenly Gania approached our hero who was at the moment standing over Nastasia Philipovna's portrait, gazing at it.

"Do you admire that sort of woman, prince?" he asked, looking intently at him. He seemed to have some special object in the question.

"It's a wonderful face," said the prince, "and I feel sure that her destiny is not by any means an ordinary, uneventful one.

Her face is smiling enough, but she must have suffered terribly–hasn't she? Her eyes show it–those two bones there, the little points under her eyes, just where the cheek begins. It's a proud face too, terribly proud! And I–I can't say whether she is good and kind, or not. Oh, if she be but good! That would make all well!"

"And would you marry a woman like that, now?" continued Gania, never taking his excited eyes off the prince's face.

"I cannot marry at all," said the latter. "I am an invalid."

"Would Rogojin marry her, do you think?"

"Why not? Certainly he would, I should think. He would marry her tomorrow!–marry her tomorrow and murder her in a week!"

Hardly had the prince uttered the last word when Gania gave such a fearful shudder that the prince almost cried out.

"What's the matter?" said he, seizing Gania's hand.

"Your highness! His excellency begs your

presence in her excellency's apartments!" announced the footman, appearing at the door.

The prince immediately followed the man out of the room.

CHAPTER FOUR

ALL THREE OF THE Miss Epanchins were fine, healthy girls, well-grown, with good shoulders and busts, and strong–almost masculine–hands; and, of course, with all the above attributes, they enjoyed capital appetites, of which they were not in the least ashamed.

Elizabetha Prokofievna sometimes informed the girls that they were a little too candid in this matter, but in spite of their outward deference to their mother these three young women, in solemn conclave, had long agreed to modify the unquestioning obedience which they had been in the habit of according to her; and Mrs. General Epanchin had judged it better to say nothing about it, though, of course, she was well aware of the fact.

It is true that her nature sometimes rebelled against these dictates of reason, and that she grew yearly more capricious and impatient; but having a respectful and well-disciplined husband under her thumb at all times, she found it possible, as a rule, to empty any little accumulations of spleen upon his head, and therefore the harmony of the family was kept duly balanced, and things went as smoothly as family matters can.

Mrs. Epanchin had a fair appetite herself, and generally took her share of the capital mid-day lunch which was always served for the girls, and which was nearly as good as a dinner. The young ladies used to have a cup of coffee each before this meal, at ten o'clock, while still in bed. This was a favourite and unalterable arrangement with them. At half-past twelve, the table was laid in the small dining-room, and occasionally the general himself appeared at the family gathering, if he had time.

Besides tea and coffee, cheese, honey, butter, pan-cakes of various kinds (the lady of the house loved these best), cutlets, and so on, there was generally strong beef soup, and other substantial delicacies.

On the particular morning on which our story has opened, the family had assembled in the dining-room, and were waiting the general's appearance, the latter having promised to come this day. If he had been one moment late, he would have been sent for at once; but he turned up punctually.

As he came forward to wish his wife good-morning and kiss her hands, as his custom was, he observed something in her look which boded ill. He thought he knew the reason, and had expected it, but still, he was not altogether comfortable. His daughters advanced to kiss him, too, and though they did not look exactly angry, there was something strange in their expression as well.

The general was, owing to certain circumstances, a little inclined to be too suspicious at home, and needlessly nervous; but, as an experienced father and husband, he judged it better to take measures at once to protect himself from any dangers there might be in the air.

However, I hope I shall not interfere with the proper sequence of my narrative too much, if I diverge for a moment at this point, in order to explain the mutual relations between General Epanchin's family and others acting a part in this history, at the time when we take up the thread of their destiny. I have already stated that the general, though he was a man of lowly origin, and of poor education, was, for all that, an experienced and talented husband and father. Among other things, he considered it undesirable to hurry his daughters to the matrimonial altar and to worry them too much with assurances of his paternal wishes for their happiness, as is the custom among parents of many grown-up daughters. He even succeeded in ranging his wife on his side on this question, though he found the feat very difficult to accomplish, because unnatural; but the general's arguments were conclusive, and founded upon obvious facts. The general considered that the girls' taste and good sense should be allowed to develop and mature deliberately, and that the parents' duty should merely be to keep watch, in order that no strange or undesirable choice be made; but that the selection once effected, both father and mother were bound from that moment to enter heart and soul into the cause, and to see that the matter progressed without hindrance until the altar should be happily reached.

Besides this, it was clear that the Epanchins' position gained each year, with geometrical accuracy, both as to financial solidity and social weight; and, therefore, the longer the girls waited, the better was their chance of making a brilliant match.

But again, amidst the incontrovertible facts just recorded, one more, equally significant, rose up to confront the family; and this was, that the eldest daughter, Alexandra, had imperceptibly arrived at her twenty-fifth birthday. Almost at the same moment, Afanasy Ivanovitch Totski, a man of immense wealth, high connections, and good standing, announced his intention of marrying. Afanasy Ivanovitch was a gentleman of fifty-five years of age, artistically gifted, and of most refined tastes. He wished to marry well, and, moreover, he was a keen admirer and judge of beauty.

Now, since Totski had, of late, been upon terms of great cordiality with Epanchin, which excellent relations were intensified by the fact that they were, so to speak, partners in several financial enterprises, it so happened that the former now put in a friendly request to the general for counsel with regard to the important step he meditated. Might he suggest, for instance, such a thing as a marriage between himself and one of the general's daughters?

Evidently the quiet, pleasant current of the family life of the Epanchins was about to undergo a change.

The undoubted beauty of the family, **par excellence**, was the youngest, Aglaya, as aforesaid. But Totski himself, though an egotist of the extremest type, realized that he had no chance there; Aglaya was clearly not for such as he.

Perhaps the sisterly love and friendship of the three girls had more or less exaggerated Aglaya's chances of happiness. In their opinion, the latter's destiny was not merely to be very happy; she was to live in a heaven on earth. Aglaya's husband was to be a compendium of all the virtues, and of all success, not to speak of fabulous wealth. The two elder sisters had agreed that all was to be sacrificed by them, if need be, for Aglaya's sake; her dowry was to be colossal and unprecedented.

The general and his wife were aware of this agreement, and, therefore, when Totski suggested himself for one of the sisters, the parents made no doubt that one of the two elder girls would probably accept the offer, since Totski would certainly make no difficulty as to dowry. The general valued the proposal very highly. He knew life, and realized what such an offer was worth.

The answer of the sisters to the communication was, if not conclusive, at least consoling and hopeful. It made known that the eldest, Alexandra, would very likely be disposed to listen to a proposal.

Alexandra was a good-natured girl, though she had a will of her own. She was intelligent and kind-hearted, and, if she were to marry Totski, she would make him a good wife. She did not care for a brilliant marriage; she was eminently a woman calculated to soothe and sweeten the life of any man; decidedly pretty, if not absolutely handsome. What better could Totski wish?

So the matter crept slowly forward. The general and Totski had agreed to avoid any hasty and irrevocable step. Alexandra's parents had not even begun to talk to their daughters freely upon the subject, when suddenly, as it were, a dissonant chord was struck amid the harmony of the proceedings. Mrs. Epanchin began to show signs of discontent, and that was a serious matter. A certain circumstance had crept in, a disagreeable and troublesome factor, which threatened to overturn the whole business.

This circumstance had come into existence eighteen years before. Close to an estate of Totski's, in one of the central provinces of Russia, there lived, at that time, a poor gentleman whose estate was of the wretchedest description. This gentleman was noted in the district for his persistent ill-fortune; his name was Barashkoff, and, as regards family and descent, he was vastly superior to Totski, but his estate was mortgaged to the last acre. One day, when he had ridden over to the town to see a creditor, the chief peasant of his village followed him shortly after, with the news that his house had been burnt down, and that his wife had perished with it, but his children were safe.

Even Barashkoff, inured to the storms of evil fortune as he was, could not stand this last stroke. He went mad and died shortly after in the town hospital. His estate was sold for the creditors; and the little girls–two of them, of seven and eight years of age respectively,–were adopted by Totski, who undertook their maintenance and education in the kindness of his heart. They were brought up together with the children of his German bailiff. Very soon, however, there was only one of them left–Nastasia Philipovna–for the other little one died of whooping-cough. Totski, who was living abroad at this time, very soon forgot all about the child; but five years after, returning to Russia, it struck him that he would like to look over his estate and see how matters were going there, and, arrived at his bailiff's house, he was not long in discovering that among the children of the latter there now dwelt a most lovely little girl of twelve, sweet and intelligent, and bright, and promising to develop beauty of most unusual quality–as to which last Totski was an undoubted authority.

He only stayed at his country seat a few days on this occasion, but he had time to make his arrangements. Great changes took place in the child's education; a good governess was engaged, a Swiss lady of experience and culture. For four years this lady resided in the house with little Nastia, and then the education was considered complete. The governess took her departure, and another lady came down to fetch Nastia, by Totski's instructions. The child was now transported to another of Totski's estates in a distant part of the country. Here she found a delightful little house, just built, and prepared for her reception with great care and taste; and here she took up her abode together with the lady who had accompanied her from her old home. In the house there were two experienced maids, musical instruments of all sorts, a charming "young lady's library," pictures, paint-boxes, a lap-dog, and everything to make life agreeable. Within a fortnight Totski himself arrived, and from that time he appeared to have taken a great fancy to this part of the world and came down each summer, staying two and three months at a time. So passed four years peacefully and happily, in charming surroundings.

At the end of that time, and about four

months after Totski's last visit (he had stayed but a fortnight on this occasion), a report reached Nastasia Philipovna that he was about to be married in St. Petersburg, to a rich, eminent, and lovely woman. The report was only partially true, the marriage project being only in an embryo condition; but a great change now came over Nastasia Philipovna. She suddenly displayed unusual decision of character; and without wasting time in thought, she left her country home and came up to St. Petersburg, straight to Totski's house, all alone.

The latter, amazed at her conduct, began to express his displeasure; but he very soon became aware that he must change his voice, style, and everything else, with this young lady; the good old times were gone. An entirely new and different woman sat before him, between whom and the girl he had left in the country last July there seemed nothing in common.

In the first place, this new woman understood

a good deal more than was usual for young people of her age; so much indeed, that Totski could not help wondering where she had picked up her knowledge. Surely not from her "young lady's library"? It even embraced legal matters, and the "world" in general, to a considerable extent.

Her character was absolutely changed. No more of the girlish alternations of timidity and petulance, the adorable naivete, the reveries, the tears, the playfulness... It was an entirely new and hitherto unknown being who now sat and laughed at him, and informed him to his face that she had never had the faintest feeling for him of any kind, except loathing and contempt–contempt which had followed closely upon her sensations of surprise and bewilderment after her first acquaintance with him.

This new woman gave him further to understand that though it was absolutely the same to her whom he married, yet she had decided to prevent this marriage–for no particular reason, but that she **chose** to do so, and because she wished to amuse herself at his expense for that it was "quite her turn to laugh a little now!"

Such were her words–very likely she did not give her real reason for this eccentric conduct; but, at all events, that was all the explanation she deigned to offer.

Meanwhile, Totski thought the matter over as well as his scattered ideas would permit. His meditations lasted a fortnight, however, and at the end of that time his resolution was taken. The fact was, Totski was at that time a man of fifty years of age; his position was solid and respectable; his place in society had long been firmly fixed upon safe foundations; he loved himself, his personal comforts, and his position better than all the world, as every respectable gentleman should!

At the same time his grasp of things in general soon showed Totski that he now had to deal with a being who was outside the pale of the ordinary rules of traditional behaviour, and who would not only threaten mischief but would undoubtedly carry it out, and stop for no one.

There was evidently, he concluded, something at work here; some storm of the mind, some paroxysm of romantic anger, goodness knows against whom or what, some insatiable contempt–in a word, something altogether absurd and impossible, but at the same time most dangerous to be met with by any respectable person with a position in society to keep up.

For a man of Totski's wealth and standing, it would, of course, have been the simplest possible matter to take steps which would rid him at once from all annoyance; while it was obviously impossible for Nastasia Philipovna to harm him in any way, either legally or by stirring up a scandal, for, in case of the latter danger, he could so easily remove her to a sphere of safety. However, these arguments would only hold good in case of Nastasia acting as others might in such an emergency. She was much more likely to overstep the bounds of reasonable conduct by some extraordinary eccentricity.

Here the sound judgment of Totski stood him in good stead. He realized that Nastasia Philipovna must be well aware that she could do nothing by legal means to injure him, and that her flashing eyes betrayed some entirely different intention.

Nastasia Philipovna was quite capable of ruining herself, and even of perpetrating something which would send her to Siberia, for the mere pleasure of injuring a man for whom she had developed so inhuman a sense of loathing and contempt. He had sufficient insight to understand that she valued nothing in the world–herself least of all–and he made no attempt to conceal the fact that he was a coward in some respects. For instance, if he had been told that he would be stabbed at the altar, or publicly insulted, he would undoubtedly have been frightened; but not so much at the idea of being murdered, or wounded, or insulted, as at the thought that if such things were to happen he would be made to look ridiculous in the eyes of society.

He knew well that Nastasia thoroughly understood him and where to wound him and how, and therefore, as the marriage was still only in embryo, Totski decided to conciliate her by giving it up. His decision was strengthened by the fact that Nastasia Philipovna had curiously altered of late. It would be difficult to conceive how different she was physically, at the present time, to the girl of a few years ago. She was pretty then... but now!... Totski laughed angrily when he thought how short-sighted he had been. In days gone by he remembered how he had looked at her beautiful eyes, how even then he had marvelled at their dark mysterious depths, and at their wondering gaze which seemed to seek an answer to some unknown riddle. Her complexion also had altered. She was now exceedingly pale, but, curiously, this change only made her more beautiful. Like most men of the world, Totski had rather despised such a cheaply-bought conquest, but of late years he had begun to think differently about it. It had struck him as long ago as last spring that he ought to be finding a good match for Nastasia; for instance, some respectable and reasonable young fellow serving in a government office in another part of the country. How maliciously Nastasia laughed at the idea of such a thing, now!

However, it appeared to Totski that he might make use of her in another way; and he determined to establish her in St. Petersburg, surrounding her with all the comforts and luxuries that his wealth could command. In this way he might gain glory in certain circles.

Five years of this Petersburg life went by, and, of course, during that time a great deal happened. Totski's position was very uncomfortable; having "funked" once, he could not totally regain his ease. He was afraid, he did not know why, but he was simply **afraid** of Nastasia Philipovna. For the first two years or so he had suspected that she wished to marry him herself, and that only her vanity prevented her telling him so. He thought that she wanted him to approach her with a humble proposal from his own side. But to his great, and not entirely pleasurable amazement, he discovered that this was by no means the case, and that were he to offer himself he would be refused. He could not understand such a state of things, and was obliged to conclude that it was pride, the pride of an injured and imaginative woman, which had gone to such lengths that it preferred to sit and nurse its contempt and hatred in solitude rather than mount to heights of hitherto unattainable splendour. To make matters worse, she was quite impervious to mercenary considerations, and could not be bribed in any way.

Finally, Totski took cunning means to try to break his chains and be free. He tried to tempt her in various ways to lose her heart; he invited princes, hussars, secretaries of embassies, poets, novelists, even Socialists, to see her; but not one of them all made the faintest impression upon Nastasia. It was as though she had a pebble in place of a heart, as though her feelings and affections were dried up and withered for ever.

She lived almost entirely alone; she read, she studied, she loved music. Her principal acquaintances were poor women of various grades, a couple of actresses, and the family of a poor schoolteacher. Among these people she was much beloved.

She received four or five friends sometimes, of an evening. Totski often came. Lately, too, General Epanchin had been enabled with great difficulty to introduce himself into her circle. Gania made her acquaintance also, and others were Ferdishenko, an ill-bred, and would-be witty, young clerk, and Ptitsin, a money-lender of modest and polished manners, who had risen from poverty. In fact, Nastasia Philipovna's beauty became a thing known to all the town; but not a single man could boast of anything more than his own admiration for her; and this reputation of hers, and her wit and culture and grace, all confirmed Totski in the plan he had now prepared.

And it was at this moment that General Epanchin began to play so large and important a part in the story.

When Totski had approached the general with his request for friendly counsel as to a marriage with one of his daughters, he had made a full and candid confession. He had said that he intended to stop at no means to obtain his freedom; even if Nastasia were to promise to leave him entirely alone in future, he would not (he said) believe and trust her; words were not enough for him; he must have solid guarantees of some sort. So he and the general determined to try what an attempt to appeal to her heart would effect. Having arrived at Nastasia's house one day, with Epanchin, Totski immediately began to speak of the intolerable torment of his position. He admitted that he was to blame for all, but candidly confessed that he could not bring himself to feel any remorse for his original guilt towards herself, because he was a man of sensual passions which were inborn and ineradicable, and that he had no power over himself in this respect; but that he wished, seriously, to marry at last, and that the whole fate of the most desirable social union which he contemplated, was in her hands; in a word, he confided his all to her generosity of heart.

General Epanchin took up his part and spoke in the character of father of a family; he spoke sensibly, and without wasting words over any attempt at sentimentality, he merely recorded his full admission of her right to be the arbiter of Totski's destiny at this moment. He then pointed out that the fate of his daughter, and very likely of both his other daughters, now hung upon her reply.

To Nastasia's question as to what they wished her to do, Totski confessed that he had been so frightened by her, five years ago, that he could never now be entirely comfortable until she herself married. He immediately added that such a suggestion from him would, of course, be absurd, unless accompanied by remarks of a more pointed nature. He very well knew, he said, that a certain young gentleman of good family, namely, Gavrila Ardalionovitch Ivolgin, with whom she was acquainted, and whom she received at her house, had long loved her passionately, and would give his life for some response from her. The young fellow had confessed this love of his to him (Totski) and had also admitted it in the hearing of his benefactor, General Epanchin. Lastly, he could not help being of opinion that Nastasia must be aware of Gania's love for her, and if he (Totski) mistook not, she had looked with some favour upon it, being often lonely, and rather tired of her present life. Having remarked how difficult it was for him, of all people, to speak to her of these matters, Totski concluded by saying that he trusted Nastasia Philipovna would not look with contempt upon him if he now expressed his sincere desire to guarantee her future by a gift of seventy-five thousand roubles. He added that the sum would have been left her all the same in his will, and that therefore she must not consider the gift as in any way an indemnification to her for anything, but that there was no reason, after all, why a man should not be allowed to entertain a natural desire to lighten his conscience, etc., etc.; in fact, all that would naturally be said under the circumstances. Totski was very eloquent all through, and, in conclusion, just touched on the fact that not a soul in the world, not even General Epanchin, had ever heard a word about the above seventy-five thousand roubles, and that this was the first time he had ever given expression to his intentions in respect to them.

Nastasia Philipovna's reply to this long rigmarole astonished both the friends considerably.

Not only was there no trace of her former irony, of her old hatred and enmity, and of that dreadful laughter, the very recollection of which sent a cold chill down Totski's back to this very day; but she seemed charmed and really glad to have the opportunity of talking seriously with him for once in a way. She confessed that she had long wished to have a frank and free conversation and to ask for friendly advice, but that pride had hitherto prevented her; now, however, that the ice was broken, nothing could be more welcome to her than this opportunity.

First, with a sad smile, and then with a twinkle of merriment in her eyes, she admitted that such a storm as that of five years ago was now quite out of the question. She said that she had long since changed her views of things, and recognized that facts must be taken into consideration in spite of the feelings of the heart. What was done was done and ended, and she could not understand why Totski should still feel alarmed.

She next turned to General Epanchin and observed, most courteously, that she had long since known of his daughters, and that she had heard none but good report; that she had learned to think of them with deep and sincere respect. The idea alone that she could in any way serve them, would be to her both a pride and a source of real happiness.

It was true that she was lonely in her present life; Totski had judged her thoughts aright. She longed to rise, if not to love, at least to family life and new hopes and objects, but as to Gavrila Ardalionovitch, she could not as yet say much. She thought it must be the case that he loved her; she felt that she too might learn to love him, if she could be sure of the firmness of his attachment to herself; but he was very young, and it was a difficult question to decide. What she specially liked about him was that he worked, and supported his family by his toil.

She had heard that he was proud and ambitious; she had heard much that was interesting of his mother and sister, she had heard of them from Mr. Ptitsin, and would much like to make their acquaintance, but–another question!–would they like to receive her into their house? At all events, though she did not reject the idea of this marriage, she desired not to be hurried. As for the seventy-five thousand roubles, Mr. Totski need not have found any difficulty or awkwardness about the matter; she quite understood the value of money, and would, of course, accept the gift. She thanked him for his delicacy, however, but saw no reason why Gavrila Ardalionovitch should not know about it.

She would not marry the latter, she said, until she felt persuaded that neither on his part nor on the part of his family did there exist any sort of concealed suspicions as to herself. She did not intend to ask forgiveness for anything in the past, which fact she desired to be known. She did not consider herself to blame for anything that had happened in former years, and she thought that Gavrila Ardalionovitch should be informed as to the relations which had existed between herself and Totski during the last five years. If she accepted this money it was not to be considered as indemnification for her misfortune as a young girl, which had not been in any degree her own fault, but merely as compensation for her ruined life.

She became so excited and agitated during all these explanations and confessions that General Epanchin was highly gratified, and considered the matter satisfactorily arranged once for all. But the once bitten

Totski was twice shy, and looked for hidden snakes among the flowers. However, the special point to which the two friends particularly trusted to bring about their object (namely, Gania's attractiveness for Nastasia Philipovna), stood out more and more prominently; the pourparlers had commenced, and gradually even Totski began to believe in the possibility of success.

Before long Nastasia and Gania had talked the matter over. Very little was said–her modesty seemed to suffer under the infliction of discussing such a question. But she recognized his love, on the understanding that she bound herself to nothing whatever, and that she reserved the right to say "no" up to the very hour of the marriage ceremony. Gania was to have the same right of refusal at the last moment.

It soon became clear to Gania, after scenes of wrath and quarrellings at the domestic hearth, that his family were seriously opposed to the match, and that Nastasia was aware of this fact was equally evident. She said nothing about it, though he daily expected her to do so.

There were several rumours afloat, before long, which upset Totski's equanimity a good deal, but we will not now stop to describe them; merely mentioning an instance or two. One was that Nastasia had entered into close and secret relations with the Epanchin girls–a most unlikely rumour; another was that Nastasia had long satisfied herself of the fact that Gania was merely marrying her for money, and that his nature was gloomy and greedy, impatient and selfish, to an extraordinary degree; and that although he had been keen enough in his desire to achieve a conquest before, yet since the two friends had agreed to exploit his passion for their own purposes, it was clear enough that he had begun to consider the whole thing a nuisance and a nightmare.

In his heart passion and hate seemed to

hold divided sway, and although he had at last given his consent to marry the woman (as he said), under the stress of circumstances, yet he promised himself that he would "take it out of her," after marriage.

Nastasia seemed to Totski to have divined all this, and to be preparing something on her own account, which frightened him to such an extent that he did not dare communicate his views even to the general. But at times he would pluck up his courage and be full of hope and good spirits again, acting, in fact, as weak men do act in such circumstances.

However, both the friends felt that the thing looked rosy indeed when one day Nastasia informed them that she would give her final answer on the evening of her birthday, which anniversary was due in a very short time.

A strange rumour began to circulate, meanwhile; no less than that the respectable and highly respected General Epanchin was himself so fascinated by Nastasia

Philipovna that his feeling for her amounted almost to passion. What he thought to gain by Gania's marriage to the girl it was difficult to imagine. Possibly he counted on Gania's complaisance; for Totski had long suspected that there existed some secret understanding between the general and his secretary. At all events the fact was known that he had prepared a magnificent present of pearls for Nastasia's birthday, and that he was looking forward to the occasion when he should present his gift with the greatest excitement and impatience. The day before her birthday he was in a fever of agitation.

Mrs. Epanchin, long accustomed to her husband's infidelities, had heard of the pearls, and the rumour excited her liveliest curiosity and interest. The general remarked her suspicions, and felt that a grand explanation must shortly take place–which fact alarmed him much.

This is the reason why he was so unwilling to take lunch (on the morning upon which we took up this narrative) with the rest of his family. Before the prince's arrival he had made up his mind to plead business, and "cut" the meal; which simply meant running away.

He was particularly anxious that this one day should be passed–especially the evening–without unpleasantness between himself and his family; and just at the right moment the prince turned up–"as though Heaven had sent him on purpose," said the general to himself, as he left the study to seek out the wife of his bosom.

CHAPTER FIVE

MRS. GENERAL EPANCHIN WAS a proud woman by nature. What must her feelings have been when she heard that Prince Muishkin, the last of his and her line, had arrived in beggar's guise, a wretched idiot, a recipient of charity–all of which details the general gave out for greater effect! He was anxious to steal her interest at the first swoop, so as to distract her thoughts from other matters nearer home.

Mrs. Epanchin was in the habit of holding

herself very straight, and staring before her, without speaking, in moments of excitement.

She was a fine woman of the same age as her husband, with a slightly hooked nose, a high, narrow forehead, thick hair turning a little grey, and a sallow complexion. Her eyes were grey and wore a very curious expression at times. She believed them to be most effective–a belief that nothing could alter.

"What, receive him! Now, at once?" asked Mrs. Epanchin, gazing vaguely at her husband as he stood fidgeting before her.

"Oh, dear me, I assure you there is no need to stand on ceremony with him," the general explained hastily. "He is quite a child, not to say a pathetic-looking creature. He has fits of some sort, and has just arrived from Switzerland, straight from the station, dressed like a German and without a farthing in his pocket. I gave him twenty-five roubles to go on with, and am going to find him some easy place in one of the government offices. I should like you to ply him well with the victuals, my dears, for I should think he must be very hungry."

"You astonish me," said the lady, gazing as before. "Fits, and hungry too! What sort of fits?"

"Oh, they don't come on frequently, besides, he's a regular child, though he seems to be fairly educated. I should like you, if possible, my dears," the general added, making slowly for the door, "to put him through his paces a bit, and see what he is good for. I think you should be kind to him; it is a good deed, you know–however, just as you like, of course–but he is a sort of relation, remember, and I thought it might interest you to see the young fellow, seeing that this is so."

"Oh, of course, mamma, if we needn't stand on ceremony with him, we must give the poor fellow something to eat after his journey; especially as he has not the least idea where to go to," said Alexandra, the eldest of the girls.

"Besides, he's quite a child; we can entertain him with a little hide-and-seek, in case of need," said Adelaida.

"Hide-and-seek? What do you mean?" inquired Mrs. Epanchin.

"Oh, do stop pretending, mamma," cried Aglaya, in vexation. "Send him up, father; mother allows."

The general rang the bell and gave orders that the prince should be shown in.

"Only on condition that he has a napkin under his chin at lunch, then," said Mrs. Epanchin, "and let Fedor, or Mavra, stand behind him while he eats. Is he quiet when he has these fits? He doesn't show violence, does he?"

"On the contrary, he seems to be very well brought up. His manners are excellent–but here he is himself. Here you are, prince–let me introduce you, the last of the Muishkins, a relative of your own, my dear, or at least of the same name. Receive him kindly, please. They'll bring in lunch directly, prince; you must stop and have some, but you must excuse me. I'm in a hurry, I must be off–"

"We all know where **you** must be off to!" said Mrs. Epanchin, in a meaning voice.

"Yes, yes–I must hurry away, I'm late! Look here, dears, let him write you something in your albums; you've no idea what a wonderful caligraphist he is, wonderful talent! He has just written out 'Abbot Pafnute signed this' for me. Well, **au revoir!**"

"Stop a minute; where are you off to? Who is this abbot?" cried Mrs. Epanchin to her retreating husband in a tone of excited annoyance.

"Yes, my dear, it was an old abbot of that name–I must be off to see the count, he's waiting for me, I'm late–Good-bye! **Au revoir**, prince!"–and the general bolted at full speed.

"Oh, yes–I know what count you're going to see!" remarked his wife in a cutting manner, as she turned her angry eyes on the prince. "Now then, what's all this about?–What abbot–Who's Pafnute?" she added, brusquely.

"Mamma!" said Alexandra, shocked at her rudeness.

Aglaya stamped her foot.

"Nonsense! Let me alone!" said the angry mother. "Now then, prince, sit down here, no, nearer, come nearer the light! I want to have a good look at you. So, now then, who is this abbot?"

"Abbot Pafnute," said our friend, seriously and with deference.

"Pafnute, yes. And who was he?"

Mrs. Epanchin put these questions hastily and brusquely, and when the prince answered she nodded her head sagely at each word he said.

"The Abbot Pafnute lived in the fourteenth century," began the prince; "he was in charge of one of the monasteries on the Volga, about where our present Kostroma government lies. He went to Oreol and helped in the great matters then going on in the religious world; he signed an edict there, and I have seen a print of his signature; it struck me, so I copied it. When the general asked me, in his study, to write something for him, to show my handwriting, I wrote 'The Abbot Pafnute signed this,' in the exact handwriting of the abbot. The general liked it very much, and that's why he recalled it just now."

"Aglaya, make a note of 'Pafnute,' or we shall forget him. H'm! and where is this signature?"

"I think it was left on the general's table."

"Let it be sent for at once!"

"Oh, I'll write you a new one in half a minute," said the prince, "if you like!"

"Of course, mamma!" said Alexandra. "But let's have lunch now, we are all hungry!"

"Yes; come along, prince," said the mother, "are you very hungry?"

"Yes; I must say that I am pretty hungry, thanks very much."

"H'm! I like to see that you know your manners; and you are by no means such a person as the general thought fit to describe you. Come along; you sit here, opposite to me," she continued, "I wish to be able to see your face. Alexandra, Adelaida, look after the prince! He doesn't seem so very ill, does he? I don't think he requires a napkin under his chin, after all; are you accustomed to having one on, prince?"

"Formerly, when I was seven years old or so. I believe I wore one; but now I usually hold my napkin on my knee when I eat."

"Of course, of course! And about your fits?"

"Fits?" asked the prince, slightly surprised. "I very seldom have fits nowadays. I don't know how it may be here, though; they say the climate may be bad for me."

"He talks very well, you know!" said Mrs. Epanchin, who still continued to nod at each word the prince spoke. "I really did not expect it at all; in fact, I suppose it was all stuff and nonsense on the general's part, as usual. Eat away, prince, and tell me where you were born, and where you were brought up. I wish to know all about you, you interest me very much!"

The prince expressed his thanks once more, and eating heartily the while, recommenced the narrative of his life in Switzerland, all of which we have heard before. Mrs. Epanchin became more and more pleased with her guest; the girls, too, listened with considerable attention. In talking over the question of relationship it turned out that the prince was very well up in the matter and knew his pedigree off by heart. It was found that scarcely any connection existed between himself and Mrs. Epanchin, but the talk, and the opportunity of conversing about her family tree, gratified the latter exceedingly, and she rose from the table in great good humour.

"Let's all go to my boudoir," she said, "and they shall bring some coffee in there. That's the room where we all assemble and busy ourselves as we like best," she explained. "Alexandra, my eldest, here, plays the piano, or reads or sews; Adelaida paints landscapes and portraits (but never finishes any); and Aglaya sits and does nothing. I don't work too much, either. Here we are, now; sit down, prince, near the fire and talk to us. I want to hear you relate something. I wish to make sure of you first and then tell my old friend, Princess Bielokonski, about you. I wish you to know all the good people and to interest them. Now then, begin!"

"Mamma, it's rather a strange order, that!" said Adelaida, who was fussing among her paints and paint-brushes at the easel. Aglaya and Alexandra had settled themselves with folded hands on a sofa, evidently meaning to be listeners. The prince felt that the general attention was concentrated upon himself.

"I should refuse to say a word if I were ordered to tell a story like that!" observed Aglaya.

"Why? what's there strange about it? He has a tongue. Why shouldn't he tell us something? I want to judge whether he is a good story-teller; anything you like, prince–how you liked Switzerland, what was your first impression, anything. You'll see, he'll begin directly and tell us all about it beautifully."

"The impression was forcible–" the prince began.

"There, you see, girls," said the impatient lady, "he **has** begun, you see."

"Well, then, **let** him talk, mamma," said Alexandra. "This prince is a great humbug and by no means an idiot," she whispered to Aglaya.

"Oh, I saw that at once," replied the latter. "I don't think it at all nice of him to play a part. What does he wish to gain by it, I wonder?"

"My first impression was a very strong one," repeated the prince. "When they took me away from Russia, I remember I passed through many German towns and looked out of the windows, but did not trouble so much as to ask questions about them. This was after a long series of fits. I always used to fall into a sort of torpid condition after such a series, and lost my memory almost entirely; and though I was not altogether without reason at such times, yet I had no logical power of thought. This would continue for three or four days, and then I would recover myself again. I remember my melancholy was intolerable; I felt inclined to cry; I sat and wondered and wondered uncomfortably; the consciousness that everything was strange weighed terribly upon me; I could understand that it was all foreign and strange. I recollect I awoke from this state for the first time at Basle, one evening; the bray of a donkey aroused me, a donkey in the town market. I saw the donkey and was extremely pleased with it, and from that moment my head seemed to clear."

"A donkey? How strange! Yet it is not strange. Anyone of us might fall in love with a donkey! It happened in mythological times," said Madame Epanchin, looking wrathfully at her daughters, who had begun to laugh.

"Go on, prince."

"Since that evening I have been specially fond of donkeys. I began to ask questions about them, for I had never seen one before; and I at once came to the conclusion that this must be one of the most useful of animals–strong, willing, patient, cheap; and, thanks to this donkey, I began to like the whole country I was travelling through; and my melancholy passed away."

"All this is very strange and interesting," said Mrs. Epanchin. "Now let's leave the donkey and go on to other matters. What are you laughing at, Aglaya? and you too, Adelaida? The prince told us his experiences very cleverly; he saw the donkey himself, and what have you ever seen? **You** have never been abroad."

"I have seen a donkey though, mamma!" said Aglaya.

"And I've heard one!" said Adelaida. All three of the girls laughed out loud, and the prince laughed with them.

"Well, it's too bad of you," said mamma. "You must forgive them, prince; they are good girls. I am very fond of them, though I often have to be scolding them; they are all as silly and mad as march hares."

"Oh, why shouldn't they laugh?" said the prince. "I shouldn't have let the chance go by in their place, I know. But I stick up for the donkey, all the same; he's a patient, good-natured fellow."

"Are you a patient man, prince? I ask out of curiosity," said Mrs. Epanchin.

All laughed again.

"Oh, that wretched donkey again, I see!" cried the lady. "I assure you, prince, I was not guilty of the least–"

"Insinuation? Oh! I assure you, I take your word for it." And the prince continued laughing merrily.

"I must say it's very nice of you to laugh. I see you really are a kind-hearted fellow," said Mrs. Epanchin.

"I'm not always kind, though."

"I am kind myself, and **always** kind too, if you please!" she retorted, unexpectedly; "and that is my chief fault, for one ought not to be always kind. I am often angry with these girls and their father; but the worst of it is, I am always kindest when I am cross. I was very angry just before you came, and Aglaya there read me a lesson–thanks, Aglaya, dear–come and kiss me–there–that's enough" she added, as Aglaya came forward and kissed her lips and then her hand. "Now then, go on, prince. Perhaps you can think of something more exciting than about the donkey, eh?"

"I must say, again, I can't understand how you can expect anyone to tell you stories straight away, so," said Adelaida. "I know I never could!"

"Yes, but the prince can, because he is clever–cleverer than you are by ten or twenty times, if you like. There, that's so, prince; and seriously, let's drop the donkey now–what else did you see abroad, besides the donkey?"

"Yes, but the prince told us about the donkey very cleverly, all the same," said Alexandra. "I have always been most interested to hear how people go mad and get well again, and that sort of thing. Especially when it happens suddenly."

"Quite so, quite so!" cried Mrs. Epanchin, delighted. "I see you **can** be sensible now and then, Alexandra. You were speaking of Switzerland, prince?"

"Yes. We came to Lucerne, and I was taken out in a boat. I felt how lovely it was, but the loveliness weighed upon me somehow or other, and made me feel melancholy."

"Why?" asked Alexandra.

"I don't know; I always feel like that when I look at the beauties of nature for the first time; but then, I was ill at that time, of course!"

"Oh, but I should like to see it!" said Adelaida; "and I don't know **when** we shall ever go abroad. I've been two years looking out for a good subject for a picture. I've done all I know. 'The North and South I know by heart,' as our poet observes. Do help me to a subject, prince."

"Oh, but I know nothing about painting. It seems to me one only has to look, and paint what one sees."

"But I don't know **how** to see!"

"Nonsense, what rubbish you talk!" the mother struck in. "Not know how to see! Open your eyes and look! If you can't see here, you won't see abroad either. Tell us what you saw yourself, prince!"

"Yes, that's better," said Adelaida; "the prince **learned to see** abroad."

"Oh, I hardly know! You see, I only went to restore my health. I don't know whether I learned to see, exactly. I was very happy, however, nearly all the time."

"Happy! you can be happy?" cried Aglaya. "Then how can you say you did not learn to see? I should think you could teach **us** to see!"

"Oh! **do** teach us," laughed Adelaida.

"Oh! I can't do that," said the prince, laughing too. "I lived almost all the while in one little Swiss village; what can I teach you? At first I was only just not absolutely dull; then my health began to improve–then every day became dearer and more precious to me, and the longer I stayed, the dearer became the time to me; so much so that I could not help observing it; but why this was so, it would be difficult to say."

"So that you didn't care to go away anywhere else?"

"Well, at first I did; I was restless; I didn't know however I should manage to support life–you know there are such moments, especially in solitude. There was a waterfall near us, such a lovely thin streak of water, like a thread but white and moving. It fell from a great height, but it looked quite low, and it was half a mile away, though it did not seem fifty paces. I loved to listen to it at night, but it was then that I became so restless. Sometimes I went and climbed the mountain and stood there in the midst of the tall pines, all alone in the terrible silence, with our little village in the distance, and the sky so blue, and the sun so bright, and an old ruined castle on the mountain-side, far away. I used to watch the line where earth and sky met, and longed to go and seek there the key of all mysteries, thinking that I might find there a new life, perhaps some great city where life should be grander and richer–and then it struck me that life may be grand enough even in a prison."

"I read that last most praiseworthy thought in my manual, when I was twelve years old," said Aglaya.

"All this is pure philosophy," said Adelaida. "You are a philosopher, prince, and have come here to instruct us in your views."

"Perhaps you are right," said the prince, smiling. "I think I am a philosopher, perhaps, and who knows, perhaps I do wish to teach my views of things to those I meet with?"

"Your philosophy is rather like that of an

old woman we know, who is rich and yet does nothing but try how little she can spend. She talks of nothing but money all day. Your great philosophical idea of a grand life in a prison and your four happy years in that Swiss village are like this, rather," said Aglaya.

"As to life in a prison, of course there may be two opinions," said the prince. "I once heard the story of a man who lived twelve years in a prison–I heard it from the man himself. He was one of the persons under treatment with my professor; he had fits, and attacks of melancholy, then he would weep, and once he tried to commit suicide. **His** life in prison was sad enough; his only acquaintances were spiders and a tree that grew outside his grating–but I think I had better tell you of another man I met last year. There was a very strange feature in this case, strange because of its extremely rare occurrence. This man had once been brought to the scaffold in company with several others, and had had the sentence of death by shooting passed upon him for some political crime. Twenty minutes later he had been reprieved and some other punishment substituted; but the interval between the two sentences, twenty minutes, or at least a quarter of an hour, had been passed in the certainty that within a few minutes he must die. I was very anxious to hear him speak of his impressions during that dreadful time, and I several times inquired of him as to what he thought and felt. He remembered everything with the most accurate and extraordinary distinctness, and declared that he would never forget a single iota of the experience.

"About twenty paces from the scaffold, where he had stood to hear the sentence, were three posts, fixed in the ground, to which to fasten the criminals (of whom there were several). The first three criminals were taken to the posts, dressed in long white tunics, with white caps drawn over their faces, so that they could not see the rifles pointed at them. Then a group of soldiers took their stand opposite to each post. My friend was the eighth on the list, and therefore he would have been among the third lot to go up. A priest went about among them with a cross: and there was about five minutes of time left for him to live.

"He said that those five minutes seemed to him to be a most interminable period, an enormous wealth of time; he seemed to be living, in these minutes, so many lives that there was no need as yet to think of that last moment, so that he made several arrangements, dividing up the time into portions–one for saying farewell to his companions, two minutes for that; then a couple more for thinking over his own life and career and all about himself; and another minute for a last look around. He remembered having divided his time like this quite well. While saying good-bye to his friends he recollected asking one of them some very usual everyday question, and being much interested in the answer. Then having bade farewell, he embarked upon those two minutes which he had allotted to looking into himself; he knew beforehand what he was going to think about. He wished to put it to himself as quickly and clearly as possible, that here was he, a living, thinking man, and that in three minutes he would be nobody; or if somebody or something, then what and where? He thought he would decide this question once for all in these last three minutes. A little way off there stood a church, and its gilded spire glittered in the sun. He remembered staring stubbornly at this spire, and at the rays of light sparkling from it. He could not tear his eyes from these rays of light; he got the idea that these rays were his new nature, and that in three minutes he would become one of them, amalgamated somehow with them.

"The repugnance to what must ensue almost immediately, and the uncertainty, were dreadful, he said; but worst of all was the idea, 'What should I do if I were not to die now? What if I were to return to life again? What an eternity of days, and all mine! How I should grudge and count up every minute of it, so as to waste not a single instant!' He said that this thought weighed so upon him and became such a terrible burden upon his brain that he could not bear it, and wished they would shoot him quickly and have done with it."

The prince paused and all waited, expecting him to go on again and finish the story.

"Is that all?" asked Aglaya.

"All? Yes," said the prince, emerging from a momentary reverie.

"And why did you tell us this?"

"Oh, I happened to recall it, that's all! It fitted into the conversation–"

"You probably wish to deduce, prince," said Alexandra, "that moments of time cannot be reckoned by money value, and that sometimes five minutes are worth priceless treasures. All this is very praiseworthy; but may I ask about this friend of yours, who told you the terrible experience of his life? He was reprieved, you say; in other words, they did restore to him that 'eternity of days.' What did he do with these riches of time? Did he keep careful account of his minutes?"

"Oh no, he didn't! I asked him myself. He said that he had not lived a bit as he had intended, and had wasted many, and many a minute."

"Very well, then there's an experiment, and the thing is proved; one cannot live and count each moment; say what you like, but one **cannot**."

"That is true," said the prince, "I have thought so myself. And yet, why shouldn't one do it?"

"You think, then, that you could live more wisely than other people?" said Aglaya.

"I have had that idea."

"And you have it still?"

"Yes–I have it still," the prince replied.

He had contemplated Aglaya until now, with a pleasant though rather timid smile, but as the last words fell from his lips he began to laugh, and looked at her merrily.

"You are not very modest!" said she.

"But how brave you are!" said he. "You are laughing, and I–that man's tale impressed me so much, that I dreamt of it afterwards; yes, I dreamt of those five minutes..."

He looked at his listeners again with that same serious, searching expression.

"You are not angry with me?" he asked suddenly, and with a kind of nervous hurry, although he looked them straight in the face.

"Why should we be angry?" they cried.

"Only because I seem to be giving you a lecture, all the time!"

At this they laughed heartily.

"Please don't be angry with me," continued the prince. "I know very well that I have seen less of life than other people, and have less knowledge of it. I must appear to speak strangely sometimes..."

He said the last words nervously.

"You say you have been happy, and that proves you have lived, not less, but more than other people. Why make all these excuses?" interrupted Aglaya in a mocking tone of voice. "Besides, you need not mind about lecturing us; you have nothing to boast of. With your quietism, one could live happily for a hundred years at least. One might show you the execution of a felon, or show you one's little finger. You could draw a moral from either, and be quite satisfied. That sort of existence is easy enough."

"I can't understand why you always fly into a temper," said Mrs. Epanchin, who had been listening to the conversation and examining the faces of the speakers in turn. "I do not understand what you mean. What has your little finger to do with it? The prince talks well, though he is not amusing. He began all right, but now he seems sad."

"Never mind, mamma! Prince, I wish you

had seen an execution," said Aglaya. "I should like to ask you a question about that, if you had."

"I have seen an execution," said the prince.

"You have!" cried Aglaya. "I might have guessed it. That's a fitting crown to the rest of the story. If you have seen an execution, how can you say you lived happily all the while?"

"But is there capital punishment where you were?" asked Adelaida.

"I saw it at Lyons. Schneider took us there, and as soon as we arrived we came in for that."

"Well, and did you like it very much? Was it very edifying and instructive?" asked Aglaya.

"No, I didn't like it at all, and was ill after seeing it; but I confess I stared as though my eyes were fixed to the sight. I could not tear them away."

"I, too, should have been unable to tear my eyes away," said Aglaya.

"They do not at all approve of women going to see an execution there. The women who do go are condemned for it afterwards in the newspapers."

"That is, by contending that it is not a sight for women they admit that it is a sight for men. I congratulate them on the deduction. I suppose you quite agree with them, prince?"

"Tell us about the execution," put in Adelaida.

"I would much rather not, just now," said the prince, a little disturbed and frowning slightly.

"You don't seem to want to tell us," said Aglaya, with a mocking air.

"No,–the thing is, I was telling all about the execution a little while ago, and–"

"Whom did you tell about it?"

"The man-servant, while I was waiting to see the general."

"Our man-servant?" exclaimed several voices at once.

"Yes, the one who waits in the entrance hall, a greyish, red-faced man–"

"The prince is clearly a democrat," remarked Aglaya.

"Well, if you could tell Aleksey about it, surely you can tell us too."

"I do so want to hear about it," repeated Adelaida.

"Just now, I confess," began the prince, with more animation, "when you asked me for a subject for a picture, I confess I had serious thoughts of giving you one. I thought of asking you to draw the face of a criminal, one minute before the fall of the guillotine, while the wretched man is still standing on the scaffold, preparatory to placing his neck on the block."

"What, his face? only his face?" asked Adelaida. "That would be a strange subject indeed. And what sort of a picture would that make?"

"Oh, why not?" the prince insisted, with some warmth. "When I was in Basle I saw a picture very much in that style–I should like to tell you about it; I will some time or other; it struck me very forcibly."

"Oh, you shall tell us about the Basle picture another time; now we must have all about the execution," said Adelaida. "Tell us about that face as it appeared to your imagination–how should it be drawn?–just the face alone, do you mean?"

"It was just a minute before the execution," began the prince, readily, carried away by the recollection and evidently forgetting everything else in a moment; "just at the instant when he stepped off the ladder on to the scaffold. He happened to look in my direction: I saw his eyes and understood all, at once–but how am I to describe it? I do so wish you or somebody else could draw it, you, if possible. I thought at the time what a picture it would make. You must imagine all that went before, of course, all–all. He had lived in the prison for some time and had not expected that the execution would take place for at least a week yet–he had counted on all the formalities and so on taking time; but it so happened that his papers had been got ready quickly. At five o'clock in the morning he was asleep–it was October, and at five in the morning it was cold and dark. The governor of the prison comes in on tip-toe and touches the sleeping man's shoulder gently. He starts up. 'What is it?' he says. 'The execution is fixed for ten o'clock.' He was only just awake, and would not believe at first, but began to argue that his papers would not be out for a week, and so on. When he was wide awake and realized the truth, he became very silent and argued no more–so they say; but after a bit he said: 'It comes very hard on one so suddenly' and then he was silent again and said nothing.

"The three or four hours went by, of course, in necessary preparations–the priest, breakfast, (coffee, meat, and some wine they gave him; doesn't it seem ridiculous?) And yet I believe these people give them a good breakfast out of pure kindness of heart, and believe that they are doing a good action. Then he is dressed, and then begins the procession through the town to the scaffold. I think he, too, must feel that he has an age to live still while they cart him along. Probably he thought, on the way, 'Oh, I have a long, long time yet. Three streets of life yet! When we've passed this street there'll be that other one; and then that one where the baker's shop is on the right; and when shall we get there? It's ages, ages!' Around him are crowds shouting, yelling–ten thousand faces, twenty thousand eyes. All this has to be endured, and especially the thought: 'Here are ten thousand men, and not one of them is going to be executed, and yet I am to die.' Well, all that is preparatory.

"At the scaffold there is a ladder, and just there he burst into tears–and this was a strong man, and a terribly wicked one, they say! There was a priest with him the whole time, talking; even in the cart as they drove along, he talked and talked. Probably the other heard nothing; he would begin to listen now and then, and at the third word or so he had forgotten all about it.

"At last he began to mount the steps; his legs were tied, so that he had to take very small steps. The priest, who seemed to be a wise man, had stopped talking now, and only held the cross for the wretched fellow to kiss. At the foot of the ladder he had been pale enough; but when he set foot on the scaffold at the top, his face suddenly became the colour of paper, positively like white notepaper. His legs must have become suddenly feeble and helpless, and he felt a choking in his throat–you know the sudden feeling one has in moments of terrible fear, when one does not lose one's wits, but is absolutely powerless to move? If some dreadful thing were suddenly to happen; if a house were just about to fall on one;–don't you know how one would long to sit down and shut one's eyes and wait, and wait? Well, when this terrible feeling came over him, the priest quickly pressed the cross to his lips, without a word–a little silver cross it was–and he kept on pressing it to the man's lips every second. And whenever the cross touched his lips, the eyes would open for a moment, and the legs moved once, and he kissed the cross greedily, hurriedly–just as though he were anxious to catch hold of something in case of its being useful to him afterwards, though he could hardly have had any connected religious thoughts at the time. And so up to the very block.

"How strange that criminals seldom swoon at such a moment! On the contrary, the brain is especially active, and works incessantly–probably hard, hard, hard–like an engine at full pressure. I imagine that various thoughts must beat loud and fast through his head–all unfinished ones, and strange, funny thoughts, very likely!–like this, for instance: 'That man is looking at me, and he has a wart on his forehead! and the executioner has burst one of his buttons, and the lowest one is all rusty!' And meanwhile he notices and remembers everything. There is one point that cannot be forgotten, round which everything else dances and turns about; and because of this point he cannot faint, and this lasts until the very final quarter of a second, when the wretched neck is on the block and the victim listens and waits and **knows**–that's the point, he **knows** that he is just **now** about to die, and listens for the rasp of the iron over his head. If I lay there, I should certainly listen for that grating sound, and hear it, too! There would probably be but the tenth part of an instant left to hear it in, but one would certainly hear it. And imagine, some people declare that when the head flies off it is **conscious** of having flown off! Just imagine what a thing to realize! Fancy if consciousness were to last for even five seconds!

"Draw the scaffold so that only the top

step of the ladder comes in clearly. The criminal must be just stepping on to it, his face as white as note-paper. The priest is holding the cross to his blue lips, and the criminal kisses it, and knows and sees and understands everything. The cross and the head–there's your picture; the priest and the executioner, with his two assistants, and a few heads and eyes below. Those might come in as subordinate accessories–a sort of mist. There's a picture for you." The prince paused, and looked around.

"Certainly that isn't much like quietism," murmured Alexandra, half to herself.

"Now tell us about your love affairs," said Adelaida, after a moment's pause.

The prince gazed at her in amazement.

"You know," Adelaida continued, "you owe us a description of the Basle picture; but first I wish to hear how you fell in love. Don't deny the fact, for you did, of course. Besides, you stop philosophizing when you are telling about anything."

"Why are you ashamed of your stories the moment after you have told them?" asked Aglaya, suddenly.

"How silly you are!" said Mrs. Epanchin, looking indignantly towards the last speaker.

"Yes, that wasn't a clever remark," said Alexandra.

"Don't listen to her, prince," said Mrs. Epanchin; "she says that sort of thing out of mischief. Don't think anything of their nonsense, it means nothing. They love to chaff, but they like you. I can see it in their faces–I know their faces."

"I know their faces, too," said the prince, with a peculiar stress on the words.

"How so?" asked Adelaida, with curiosity.

"What do **you** know about our faces?" exclaimed the other two, in chorus.

But the prince was silent and serious. All awaited his reply.

"I'll tell you afterwards," he said quietly.

"Ah, you want to arouse our curiosity!" said Aglaya. "And how terribly solemn you are about it!"

"Very well," interrupted Adelaida, "then if you can read faces so well, you **must** have been in love. Come now; I've guessed–let's have the secret!"

"I have not been in love," said the prince, as quietly and seriously as before. "I have been happy in another way."

"How, how?"

"Well, I'll tell you," said the prince, apparently in a deep reverie.

CHAPTER SIX

"HERE YOU ALL ARE," began the prince, "settling yourselves down to listen to me with so much curiosity, that if I do not satisfy you you will probably be angry with me. No, no! I'm only joking!" he added, hastily, with a smile.

"Well, then–they were all children there, and I was always among children and only with children. They were the children of the village in which I lived, and they went to the school there–all of them. I did not teach them, oh no; there was a master for that, one Jules Thibaut. I may have taught them some things, but I was among them just as an outsider, and I passed all four years of my life there among them. I wished for nothing better; I used to tell them everything and hid nothing from them. Their fathers and relations were very angry with me, because the children could do nothing without me at last, and used to throng after me at all times. The schoolmaster was my greatest enemy in the end! I had many enemies, and all because of the children. Even Schneider reproached me. What were they afraid of? One can tell a child everything, anything. I have often been struck by the fact that parents know their children so little. They should not conceal so much from them. How well even little children understand that their parents conceal things from them, because they consider them too young to understand! Children are capable of giving advice in the most important matters. How can one deceive these dear little birds, when they look at one so sweetly and confidingly? I call them birds because there is nothing in the world better than birds!

"However, most of the people were angry with me about one and the same thing; but Thibaut simply was jealous of me. At first he had wagged his head and wondered how it was that the children understood what I told them so well, and could not learn from him; and he laughed like anything when I replied that neither he nor I could teach them very much, but that **they** might teach us a good deal.

"How he could hate me and tell scandalous stories about me, living among children as he did, is what I cannot understand. Children soothe and heal the wounded heart. I remember there was one poor fellow at our professor's who was being treated for madness, and you have no idea what those children did for him, eventually. I don't think he was mad, but only terribly unhappy. But I'll tell you all about him another day. Now I must get on with this story.

"The children did not love me at first; I was such a sickly, awkward kind of a fellow then–and I know I am ugly. Besides, I was a foreigner. The children used to laugh at me, at first; and they even went so far as to throw stones at me, when they saw me kiss Marie. I only kissed her once in my life–no, no, don't laugh!" The prince hastened to suppress the smiles of his audience at this point. "It was not a matter of **love** at all! If only you knew what a miserable creature she was, you would have pitied her, just as I did. She belonged to our village. Her mother was an old, old woman, and they used to sell string and thread, and soap and tobacco, out of the window of their little house, and lived on the pittance they gained by this trade. The old woman was ill and very old, and could hardly move. Marie was her daughter, a girl of twenty, weak and thin and consumptive; but still she did heavy work at the houses around, day by day.

Well, one fine day a commercial traveller betrayed her and carried her off; and a week later he deserted her. She came home dirty, draggled, and shoeless; she had walked for a whole week without shoes; she had slept in the fields, and caught a terrible cold; her feet were swollen and sore, and her hands torn and scratched all over. She never had been pretty even before; but her eyes were quiet, innocent, kind eyes.

"She was very quiet always–and I remember once, when she had suddenly begun singing at her work, everyone said, 'Marie tried to sing today!' and she got so chaffed that she was silent for ever after. She had been treated kindly in the place before; but when she came back now–ill and shunned and miserable–not one of them all had the slightest sympathy for her. Cruel people! Oh, what hazy understandings they have on such matters! Her mother was the first to show the way. She received her wrathfully, unkindly, and with contempt. 'You have disgraced me,' she said. She was the first to cast her into ignominy; but when they all heard that Marie had returned to the village, they ran out to see her and crowded into the little cottage–old men, children, women, girls–such a hurrying, stamping, greedy crowd. Marie was lying on the floor at the old woman's feet, hungry, torn, draggled, crying, miserable.

"When everyone crowded into the room she hid her face in her dishevelled hair and lay cowering on the floor. Everyone looked at her as though she were a piece of dirt off the road. The old men scolded and condemned, and the young ones laughed at her. The women condemned her too, and looked at her contemptuously, just as though she were some loathsome insect.

"Her mother allowed all this to go on, and nodded her head and encouraged them. The old woman was very ill at that time, and knew she was dying (she really did die a couple of months later), and though she felt the end approaching she never thought of forgiving her daughter, to the very day of her death. She would not even speak to her. She made her sleep on straw in a shed, and hardly gave her food enough to support life.

"Marie was very gentle to her mother, and nursed her, and did everything for her; but the old woman accepted all her services without a word and never showed her the slightest kindness. Marie bore all this; and I could see when I got to know her that she thought it quite right and fitting, considering herself the lowest and meanest of creatures.

"When the old woman took to her bed finally, the other old women in the village sat with her by turns, as the custom is there; and then Marie was quite driven out of the house. They gave her no food at all, and she could not get any work in the village; none would employ her. The men seemed to consider her no longer a woman, they said such dreadful things to her. Sometimes on Sundays, if they were drunk enough, they used to throw her a penny or two, into the mud, and Marie would silently pick up the money. She had began to spit blood at that time.

"At last her rags became so tattered and torn that she was ashamed of appearing in the village any longer. The children used to pelt her with mud; so she begged to be taken on as assistant cowherd, but the cowherd would not have her. Then she took to helping him without leave; and he saw how valuable her assistance was to him, and did not drive her away again; on the contrary, he occasionally gave her the remnants of his dinner, bread and cheese. He considered that he was being very kind. When the mother died, the village parson was not ashamed to hold Marie up to public derision and shame. Marie was standing at the coffin's head, in all her rags, crying.

"A crowd of people had collected to see how she would cry. The parson, a young fellow ambitious of becoming a great preacher, began his sermon and pointed to Marie. 'There,' he said, 'there is the cause of the death of this venerable woman'–(which was a lie, because she had been ill for at least two years)–'there she stands before you, and dares not lift her eyes from the ground, because she knows that the finger of God is upon her. Look at her tatters and rags–the badge of those who lose their virtue. Who is she? her daughter!' and so on to the end.

"And just fancy, this infamy pleased them, all of them, nearly. Only the children had altered–for then they were all on my side and had learned to love Marie.

"This is how it was: I had wished to do something for Marie; I longed to give her some money, but I never had a farthing while I was there. But I had a little diamond pin, and this I sold to a travelling pedlar; he gave me eight francs for it–it was worth at least forty.

"I long sought to meet Marie alone; and at

last I did meet her, on the hillside beyond the village. I gave her the eight francs and asked her to take care of the money because I could get no more; and then I kissed her and said that she was not to suppose I kissed her with any evil motives or because I was in love with her, for that I did so solely out of pity for her, and because from the first I had not accounted her as guilty so much as unfortunate. I longed to console and encourage her somehow, and to assure her that she was not the low, base thing which she and others strove to make out; but I don't think she understood me. She stood before me, dreadfully ashamed of herself, and with downcast eyes; and when I had finished she kissed my hand. I would have kissed hers, but she drew it away. Just at this moment the whole troop of children saw us. (I found out afterwards that they had long kept a watch upon me.) They all began whistling and clapping their hands, and laughing at us. Marie ran away at once; and when I tried to talk to them, they threw stones at me. All the village heard of it the same day, and Marie's position became worse than ever. The children would not let her pass now in the streets, but annoyed her and threw dirt at her more than before. They used to run after her–she racing away with her poor feeble lungs panting and gasping, and they pelting her and shouting abuse at her.

"Once I had to interfere by force; and after that I took to speaking to them every day and whenever I could. Occasionally they stopped and listened; but they teased Marie all the same.

"I told them how unhappy Marie was, and after a while they stopped their abuse of her, and let her go by silently. Little by little we got into the way of conversing together, the children and I. I concealed nothing from them, I told them all. They listened very attentively and soon began to be sorry for Marie. At last some of them took to saying 'Good-morning' to her, kindly, when they met her. It is the custom there to salute anyone you meet with 'Good-morning' whether acquainted or not. I can imagine how astonished Marie was at these first greetings from the children.

"Once two little girls got hold of some food and took it to her, and came back and told me. They said she had burst into tears, and that they loved her very much now. Very soon after that they all became fond of Marie, and at the same time they began to develop the greatest affection for myself. They often came to me and begged me to tell them stories. I think I must have told stories well, for they did so love to hear them. At last I took to reading up interesting things on purpose to pass them on to the little ones, and this went on for all the rest of my time there, three years. Later, when everyone–even Schneider–was angry with me for hiding nothing from the children, I pointed out how foolish it was, for they always knew things, only they learnt them in a way that soiled their minds but not so from me. One has only to remember one's own childhood to admit the truth of this. But nobody was convinced... It was two weeks before her mother died that I had kissed Marie; and when the clergyman preached that sermon the children were all on my side.

"When I told them what a shame it was of the parson to talk as he had done, and explained my reason, they were so angry that some of them went and broke his windows with stones. Of course I stopped them, for that was not right, but all the village heard of it, and how I caught it for spoiling the children! Everyone discovered now that the little ones had taken to being fond of Marie, and their parents were terribly alarmed; but Marie was so happy. The children were forbidden to meet her; but they used to run out of the village to the herd and take her food and things; and sometimes just ran off there and kissed her, and said, '**Je vous aime, Marie!**' and then trotted back again. They imagined that I was in love with Marie, and this was the only point on which I did not undeceive them, for they got such enjoyment out of it. And what delicacy and tenderness they showed!

"In the evening I used to walk to the waterfall. There was a spot there which was quite closed in and hidden from view by large trees; and to this spot the children used to come to me. They could not bear that their dear Leon should love a poor girl without shoes to her feet and dressed all in rags and tatters. So, would you believe it, they actually clubbed together, somehow, and bought her shoes and stockings, and some linen, and even a dress! I can't understand how they managed it, but they did it, all together. When I asked them about it they only laughed and shouted, and the little girls clapped their hands and kissed me. I sometimes went to see Marie secretly, too. She had become very ill, and could hardly walk. She still went with the herd, but could not help the herdsman any longer. She used to sit on a stone near, and wait there almost motionless all day, till the herd went home. Her consumption was so advanced, and she was so weak, that she used to sit with closed eyes, breathing heavily. Her face was as thin as a skeleton's, and sweat used to stand on her white brow in large drops. I always found her sitting just like that. I used to come up quietly to look at her; but Marie would hear me, open her eyes, and tremble violently as she kissed my hands. I did not take my hand away because it made her happy to have it, and so she would sit and cry quietly. Sometimes she tried to speak; but it was very difficult to understand her. She was almost like a madwoman, with excitement and ecstasy, whenever I came. Occasionally the children came with me; when they did so, they would stand some way off and keep guard over us, so as to tell me if anybody came near. This was a great pleasure to them.

"When we left her, Marie used to relapse at once into her old condition, and sit with closed eyes and motionless limbs. One day she could not go out at all, and remained at home all alone in the empty hut; but the children very soon became aware of the fact, and nearly all of them visited her that day as she lay alone and helpless in her miserable bed.

"For two days the children looked after her, and then, when the village people got to know that Marie was really dying, some of the old women came and took it in turns to sit by her and look after her a bit. I think they began to be a little sorry for her in the village at last; at all events they did not interfere with the children any more, on her account.

"Marie lay in a state of uncomfortable delirium the whole while; she coughed dreadfully. The old women would not let the children stay in the room; but they all collected outside the window each morning, if only for a moment, and shouted '**Bon jour, notre bonne Marie!**' and Marie no sooner caught sight of, or heard them, and she became quite animated at once, and, in spite of the old women, would try to sit up and nod her head and smile at them, and thank them. The little ones used to bring her nice things and sweets to eat, but she could hardly touch anything. Thanks to them, I assure you, the girl died almost perfectly happy. She almost forgot her misery, and seemed to accept their love as a sort of symbol of pardon for her offence, though she never ceased to consider herself a dreadful sinner. They used to flutter at her window just like little birds, calling out: '**Nous t'aimons, Marie!**'

"She died very soon; I had thought she would live much longer. The day before her death I went to see her for the last time, just before sunset. I think she recognized me, for she pressed my hand.

"Next morning they came and told me that

Marie was dead. The children could not be restrained now; they went and covered her coffin with flowers, and put a wreath of lovely blossoms on her head. The pastor did not throw any more shameful words at the poor dead woman; but there were very few people at the funeral. However, when it came to carrying the coffin, all the children rushed up, to carry it themselves. Of course they could not do it alone, but they insisted on helping, and walked alongside and behind, crying.

"They have planted roses all round her grave, and every year they look after the flowers and make Marie's resting-place as beautiful as they can. I was in ill odour after all this with the parents of the children, and especially with the parson and schoolmaster. Schneider was obliged to promise that I should not meet them and talk to them; but we conversed from a distance by signs, and they used to write me sweet little notes. Afterwards I came closer than ever to those little souls, but even then it was very dear to me, to have them so fond of me.

"Schneider said that I did the children great harm by my pernicious 'system'; what nonsense that was! And what did he mean by my system? He said afterwards that he believed I was a child myself–just before I came away. 'You have the form and face of an adult' he said, 'but as regards soul, and character, and perhaps even intelligence, you are a child in the completest sense of the word, and always will be, if you live to be sixty.' I laughed very much, for of course that is nonsense. But it is a fact that I do not care to be among grown-up people and much prefer the society of children. However kind people may be to me, I never feel quite at home with them, and am always glad to get back to my little companions. Now my companions have always been children, not because I was a child myself once, but because young things attract me. On one of the first days of my stay in Switzerland,

I was strolling about alone and miserable, when I came upon the children rushing noisily out of school, with their slates and bags, and books, their games, their laughter and shouts–and my soul went out to them. I stopped and laughed happily as I watched their little feet moving so quickly. Girls and boys, laughing and crying; for as they went home many of them found time to fight and make peace, to weep and play. I forgot my troubles in looking at them. And then, all those three years, I tried to understand why men should be for ever tormenting themselves. I lived the life of a child there, and thought I should never leave the little village; indeed, I was far from thinking that I should ever return to Russia. But at last I recognized the fact that Schneider could not keep me any longer. And then something so important happened, that Schneider himself urged me to depart. I am going to see now if can get good advice about it. Perhaps my lot in life will be changed; but that is not the principal thing. The principal thing is the entire change that has already come over me. I left many things behind me–too many. They have gone. On the journey I said to myself, 'I am going into the world of men. I don't know much, perhaps, but a new life has begun for me.' I made up my mind to be honest, and steadfast in accomplishing my task. Perhaps I shall meet with troubles and many disappointments, but I have made up my mind to be polite and sincere to everyone; more cannot be asked of me. People may consider me a child if they like. I am often called an idiot, and at one time I certainly was so ill that I was nearly as bad as an idiot; but I am not an idiot now. How can I possibly be so when I know myself that I am considered one?

"When I received a letter from those dear little souls, while passing through Berlin, I only then realized how much I loved them. It was very, very painful, getting that first little letter. How melancholy they had been when they saw me off! For a month before, they had been talking of my departure and sorrowing over it; and at the waterfall, of an evening, when we parted for the night, they would hug me so tight and kiss me so warmly, far more so than before. And every now and then they would turn up one by one when I was alone, just to give me a kiss and a hug, to show their love for me. The whole flock went with me to the station, which was about a mile from the village, and every now and then one of them would stop to throw his arms round me, and all the little girls had tears in their voices, though they tried hard not to cry. As the train steamed out of the station, I saw them all standing on the platform waving to me and crying 'Hurrah!' till they were lost in the distance.

"I assure you, when I came in here just now and saw your kind faces (I can read faces well) my heart felt light for the first time since that moment of parting. I think

I must be one of those who are born to be in luck, for one does not often meet with people whom one feels he can love from the first sight of their faces; and yet, no sooner do I step out of the railway carriage than I happen upon you!

"I know it is more or less a shamefaced thing to speak of one's feelings before others; and yet here am I talking like this to you, and am not a bit ashamed or shy. I am an unsociable sort of fellow and shall very likely not come to see you again for some time; but don't think the worse of me for that. It is not that I do not value your society; and you must never suppose that I have taken offence at anything.

"You asked me about your faces, and what I could read in them; I will tell you with the greatest pleasure. You, Adelaida Ivanovna, have a very happy face; it is the most sympathetic of the three. Not to speak of your natural beauty, one can look at your face and say to one's self, 'She has the face of a kind sister.' You are simple and merry, but you can see into another's heart very quickly. That's what I read in your face.

"You too, Alexandra Ivanovna, have a very lovely face; but I think you may have some secret sorrow. Your heart is undoubtedly a kind, good one, but you are not merry. There is a certain suspicion of 'shadow' in your face, like in that of Holbein's Madonna in Dresden. So much for your face. Have I guessed right?

"As for your face, Lizabetha Prokofievna, I not only think, but am perfectly **sure**, that you are an absolute child–in all, in all, mind, both good and bad–and in spite of your years. Don't be angry with me for saying so; you know what my feelings for children are. And do not suppose that I am so candid out of pure simplicity of soul. Oh dear no, it is by no means the case! Perhaps I have my own very profound object in view."

CHAPTER SEVEN

WHEN THE PRINCE CEASED speaking all were gazing merrily at him–even Aglaya; but Lizabetha Prokofievna looked the jolliest of all.

"Well!" she cried, "we **have** 'put him through his paces,' with a vengeance! My dears, you imagined, I believe, that you were about to patronize this young gentleman, like some poor **protégé**picked up somewhere, and taken under your magnificent protection. What fools we were, and what a specially big fool is your father! Well done, prince! I assure you the general actually asked me to put you through your paces, and examine you. As to what you said about my face, you are absolutely correct in your judgment. I am a child, and know it. I knew it long before you said so; you have expressed my own thoughts. I think your nature and mine must be extremely alike, and I am very glad of it. We are like two drops of water, only you are a man and I a woman, and I've not been to Switzerland, and that is all the difference between us."

"Don't be in a hurry, mother; the prince says that he has some motive behind his simplicity," cried Aglaya.

"Yes, yes, so he does," laughed the others.

"Oh, don't you begin bantering him," said mamma. "He is probably a good deal cleverer than all three of you girls put together. We shall see. Only you haven't told us anything about Aglaya yet, prince; and Aglaya and I are both waiting to hear."

"I cannot say anything at present. I'll tell you afterwards."

"Why? Her face is clear enough, isn't it?"

"Oh yes, of course. You are very beautiful, Aglaya Ivanovna, so beautiful that one is afraid to look at you."

"Is that all? What about her character?" persisted Mrs. Epanchin.

"It is difficult to judge when such beauty is concerned. I have not prepared my judgment. Beauty is a riddle."

"That means that you have set Aglaya a riddle!" said Adelaida. "Guess it, Aglaya! But she's pretty, prince, isn't she?"

"Most wonderfully so," said the latter, warmly, gazing at Aglaya with admiration. "Almost as lovely as Nastasia Philipovna, but quite a different type."

All present exchanged looks of surprise.

"As lovely as **who?**" said Mrs. Epanchin. "As **Nastasia Philipovna?** Where have you seen Nastasia Philipovna? What Nastasia Philipovna?"

"Gavrila Ardalionovitch showed the general her portrait just now."

"How so? Did he bring the portrait for my husband?"

"Only to show it. Nastasia Philipovna gave it to Gavrila Ardalionovitch today, and the latter brought it here to show to the general."

"I must see it!" cried Mrs. Epanchin. "Where is the portrait? If she gave it to him, he must have it; and he is still in the study. He never leaves before four o'clock on Wednesdays. Send for Gavrila Ardalionovitch at once. No, I don't long to see **him** so much. Look here, dear prince, **be** so kind, will you? Just step to the study and fetch this portrait! Say we want to look at it. Please do this for me, will you?"

"He is a nice fellow, but a little too simple," said Adelaida, as the prince left the room.

"He is, indeed," said Alexandra; "almost laughably so at times."

Neither one nor the other seemed to give expression to her full thoughts.

"He got out of it very neatly about our faces, though," said Aglaya. "He flattered us all round, even mamma."

"Nonsense!" cried the latter. "He did not flatter me. It was I who found his appreciation flattering. I think you are a great deal more foolish than he is. He is simple, of course, but also very knowing. Just like myself."

"How stupid of me to speak of the portrait," thought the prince as he entered the study, with a feeling of guilt at his heart, "and yet, perhaps I was right after all." He had an idea, unformed as yet, but a strange idea.

Gavrila Ardalionovitch was still sitting in the study, buried in a mass of papers. He looked as though he did not take his salary from the public company, whose servant he was, for a sinecure.

He grew very wroth and confused when the prince asked for the portrait, and explained how it came about that he had spoken of it.

"Oh, curse it all," he said; "what on earth

must you go blabbing for? You know nothing about the thing, and yet–idiot!" he added, muttering the last word to himself in irrepressible rage.

"I am very sorry; I was not thinking at the time. I merely said that Aglaya was almost as beautiful as Nastasia Philipovna."

Gania asked for further details; and the prince once more repeated the conversation. Gania looked at him with ironical contempt the while.

"Nastasia Philipovna," he began, and there paused; he was clearly much agitated and annoyed. The prince reminded him of the portrait.

"Listen, prince," said Gania, as though an idea had just struck him, "I wish to ask you a great favour, and yet I really don't know–"

He paused again, he was trying to make up his mind to something, and was turning the matter over. The prince waited quietly. Once more Gania fixed him with intent and questioning eyes.

"Prince," he began again, "they are rather angry with me, in there, owing to a circumstance which I need not explain, so that I do not care to go in at present without an invitation. I particularly wish to speak to Aglaya, but I have written a few words in case I shall not have the chance of seeing her" (here the prince observed a small note in his hand), "and I do not know how to get my communication to her. Don't you think you could undertake to give it to her at once, but only to her, mind, and so that no one else should see you give it? It isn't much of a secret, but still–Well, will you do it?"

"I don't quite like it," replied the prince.

"Oh, but it is absolutely necessary for me," Gania entreated. "Believe me, if it were not so, I would not ask you; how else am I to get it to her? It is most important, dreadfully important!"

Gania was evidently much alarmed at the idea that the prince would not consent to take his note, and he looked at him now with an expression of absolute entreaty.

"Well, I will take it then."

"But mind, nobody is to see!" cried the delighted Gania "And of course I may rely on your word of honour, eh?"

"I won't show it to anyone," said the prince.

"The letter is not sealed–" continued Gania, and paused in confusion.

"Oh, I won't read it," said the prince, quite simply.

He took up the portrait, and went out of the room.

Gania, left alone, clutched his head with his hands.

"One word from her," he said, "one word from her, and I may yet be free."

He could not settle himself to his papers again, for agitation and excitement, but began walking up and down the room from corner to corner.

The prince walked along, musing. He did not like his commission, and disliked the idea of Gania sending a note to Aglaya at all; but when he was two rooms distant from the drawing-room, where they all were, he stopped as though recalling something; went to the window, nearer the light, and began to examine the portrait in his hand.

He longed to solve the mystery of something in the face of Nastasia Philipovna, something which had struck him as he looked at the portrait for the first time; the impression had not left him. It was partly the fact of her marvellous beauty that struck him, and partly something else. There was a suggestion of immense pride and disdain in the face almost of hatred, and at the same time something confiding and very full of simplicity. The contrast aroused a deep sympathy in his heart as he looked at the lovely face. The blinding loveliness of it was almost intolerable, this pale thin face with its flaming eyes; it was a strange beauty.

The prince gazed at it for a minute or two, then glanced around him, and hurriedly raised the portrait to his lips. When, a minute after, he reached the drawing-room door, his face was quite composed. But just as he reached the door he met Aglaya coming out alone.

"Gavrila Ardalionovitch begged me to give you this," he said, handing her the note.

Aglaya stopped, took the letter, and gazed strangely into the prince's eyes. There was no confusion in her face; a little surprise, perhaps, but that was all. By her look she seemed merely to challenge the prince to an explanation as to how he and Gania happened to be connected in this matter. But her expression was perfectly cool and quiet, and even condescending.

So they stood for a moment or two, confronting one another. At length a faint smile passed over her face, and she passed by him without a word.

Mrs. Epanchin examined the portrait of Nastasia Philipovna for some little while, holding it critically at arm's length.

"Yes, she is pretty," she said at last, "even very pretty. I have seen her twice, but only at a distance. So you admire this kind of beauty, do you?" she asked the prince, suddenly.

"Yes, I do–this kind."

"Do you mean especially this kind?"

"Yes, especially this kind."

"Why?"

"There is much suffering in this face," murmured the prince, more as though talking to himself than answering the question.

"I think you are wandering a little, prince," Mrs. Epanchin decided, after a lengthened survey of his face; and she tossed the portrait on to the table, haughtily.

Alexandra took it, and Adelaida came up, and both the girls examined the photograph. Just then Aglaya entered the room.

"What a power!" cried Adelaida suddenly, as she earnestly examined the portrait over her sister's shoulder.

"Whom? What power?" asked her mother,

crossly.

"Such beauty is real power," said Adelaida. "With such beauty as that one might overthrow the world." She returned to her easel thoughtfully.

Aglaya merely glanced at the portrait–frowned, and put out her underlip; then went and sat down on the sofa with folded hands. Mrs. Epanchin rang the bell.

"Ask Gavrila Ardalionovitch to step this way," said she to the man who answered.

"Mamma!" cried Alexandra, significantly.

"I shall just say two words to him, that's all," said her mother, silencing all objection by her manner; she was evidently seriously put out. "You see, prince, it is all secrets with us, just now–all secrets. It seems to be the etiquette of the house, for some reason or other. Stupid nonsense, and in a matter which ought to be approached with all candour and open-heartedness. There is a marriage being talked of, and I don't like this marriage–"

"Mamma, what are you saying?" said Alexandra again, hurriedly.

"Well, what, my dear girl? As if you can possibly like it yourself? The heart is the great thing, and the rest is all rubbish–though one must have sense as well. Perhaps sense is really the great thing. Don't smile like that, Aglaya. I don't contradict myself. A fool with a heart and no brains is just as unhappy as a fool with brains and no heart. I am one and you are the other, and therefore both of us suffer, both of us are unhappy."

"Why are you so unhappy, mother?" asked Adelaida, who alone of all the company seemed to have preserved her good temper and spirits up to now.

"In the first place, because of my carefully brought-up daughters," said Mrs. Epanchin, cuttingly; "and as that is the best reason I can give you we need not bother about any other at present. Enough of words, now! We shall see how both of you (I don't count Aglaya) will manage your business, and whether you, most revered Alexandra Ivanovna, will be happy with your fine mate."

"Ah!" she added, as Gania suddenly entered the room, "here's another marrying subject. How do you do?" she continued, in response to Gania's bow; but she did not invite him to sit down. "You are going to be married?"

"Married? how–what marriage?" murmured Gania, overwhelmed with confusion.

"Are you about to take a wife? I ask,–if you prefer that expression."

"No, no I–I–no!" said Gania, bringing out his lie with a tell-tale blush of shame. He glanced keenly at Aglaya, who was sitting some way off, and dropped his eyes immediately.

Aglaya gazed coldly, intently, and composedly at him, without taking her eyes off his face, and watched his confusion.

"No? You say no, do you?" continued the pitiless Mrs. General. "Very well, I shall remember that you told me this Wednesday morning, in answer to my question, that you are not going to be married. What day is it, Wednesday, isn't it?"

"Yes, I think so!" said Adelaida.

"You never know the day of the week; what's the day of the month?"

"Twenty-seventh!" said Gania.

"Twenty-seventh; very well. Good-bye now; you have a good deal to do, I'm sure, and I must dress and go out. Take your portrait. Give my respects to your unfortunate mother, Nina Alexandrovna. **Au revoir**, dear prince, come in and see us often, do; and I shall tell old Princess Bielokonski about you. I shall go and see her on purpose. And listen, my dear boy, I feel sure that God has sent you to Petersburg from Switzerland on purpose for me. Maybe you will have other things to do, besides, but you are sent chiefly for my sake, I feel sure of it. God sent you to me! **Au revoir!** Alexandra, come with me, my dear."

Mrs. Epanchin left the room.

Gania–confused, annoyed, furious–took up his portrait, and turned to the prince with a nasty smile on his face.

"Prince," he said, "I am just going home. If you have not changed your mind as to living with us, perhaps you would like to come with me. You don't know the address, I believe?"

"Wait a minute, prince," said Aglaya, suddenly rising from her seat, "do write something in my album first, will you? Father says you are a most talented caligraphist; I'll bring you my book in a minute." She left the room.

"Well, **au revoir**, prince," said Adelaida, "I must be going too." She pressed the prince's hand warmly, and gave him a friendly smile as she left the room. She did not so much as look at Gania.

"This is your doing, prince," said Gania, turning on the latter so soon as the others were all out of the room. "This is your doing, sir! **You** have been telling them that I am going to be married!" He said this in a hurried whisper, his eyes flashing with rage and his face ablaze. "You shameless tattler!"

"I assure you, you are under a delusion," said the prince, calmly and politely. "I did not even know that you were to be married."

"You heard me talking about it, the general and me. You heard me say that everything was to be settled today at Nastasia Philipovna's, and you went and blurted it out here. You lie if you deny it. Who else could have told them? Devil take it, sir, who could have told them except yourself? Didn't the old woman as good as hint as much to me?"

"If she hinted to you who told her you must know best, of course; but I never said a word about it."

"Did you give my note? Is there an answer?" interrupted Gania, impatiently.

But at this moment Aglaya came back, and the prince had no time to reply.

"There, prince," said she, "there's my

album. Now choose a page and write me something, will you? There's a pen, a new one; do you mind a steel one? I have heard that you caligraphists don't like steel pens."

Conversing with the prince, Aglaya did not even seem to notice that Gania was in the room. But while the prince was getting his pen ready, finding a page, and making his preparations to write, Gania came up to the fireplace where Aglaya was standing, to the right of the prince, and in trembling, broken accents said, almost in her ear:

"One word, just one word from you, and I'm saved."

The prince turned sharply round and looked at both of them. Gania's face was full of real despair; he seemed to have said the words almost unconsciously and on the impulse of the moment.

Aglaya gazed at him for some seconds with precisely the same composure and calm astonishment as she had shown a little while before, when the prince handed her the note, and it appeared that this calm surprise and seemingly absolute incomprehension of what was said to her, were more terribly overwhelming to Gania than even the most plainly expressed disdain would have been.

"What shall I write?" asked the prince.

"I'll dictate to you," said Aglaya, coming up to the table. "Now then, are you ready? Write, 'I never condescend to bargain!' Now put your name and the date. Let me see it."

The prince handed her the album.

"Capital! How beautifully you have written it! Thanks so much. **Au revoir**, prince. Wait a minute," she added, "I want to give you something for a keepsake. Come with me this way, will you?"

The prince followed her. Arrived at the dining-room, she stopped.

"Read this," she said, handing him Gania's note.

The prince took it from her hand, but gazed at her in bewilderment.

"Oh! I **know** you haven't read it, and that

you could never be that man's accomplice. Read it, I wish you to read it."

The letter had evidently been written in a hurry:

"My fate is to be decided today" (it ran), **"you know how. This day I must give my word irrevocably. I have no right to ask your help, and I dare not allow myself to indulge in any hopes; but once you said just one word, and that word lighted up the night of my life, and became the beacon of my days. Say one more such word, and save me from utter ruin. Only tell me, 'break off the whole thing!' and I will do so this very day. Oh! what can it cost you to say just this one word? In doing so you will but be giving me a sign of your sympathy for me, and of your pity; only this, only this; nothing more, nothing. I dare not indulge in any hope, because I am unworthy of it. But if you say but this word, I will take up my cross again with joy, and return once more to**

my battle with poverty. I shall meet the storm and be glad of it; I shall rise up with renewed strength.

"Send me back then this one word of sympathy, only sympathy, I swear to you; and oh! do not be angry with the audacity of despair, with the drowning man who has dared to make this last effort to save himself from perishing beneath the waters.

"G.L."

"This man assures me," said Aglaya, scornfully, when the prince had finished reading the letter, "that the words 'break off everything' do not commit me to anything whatever; and himself gives me a written guarantee to that effect, in this letter. Observe how ingenuously he underlines certain words, and how crudely he glosses over his hidden thoughts. He must know that if he 'broke off everything,' **first**, by himself, and without telling me a word about it or having the slightest hope on my account, that in that case I should perhaps be able to change my opinion of him, and even accept his–friendship. He must know that, but his soul is such a wretched thing. He knows it and cannot make up his mind; he knows it and yet asks for guarantees. He cannot bring himself to **trust**, he wants me to give him hopes of myself before he lets go of his hundred thousand roubles. As to the 'former word' which he declares 'lighted up the night of his life,' he is simply an impudent liar; I merely pitied him once. But he is audacious and shameless. He immediately began to hope, at that very moment. I saw it. He has tried to catch me ever since; he is still fishing for me. Well, enough of this. Take the letter and give it back to him, as soon as you have left our house; not before, of course."

"And what shall I tell him by way of answer?"

"Nothing–of course! That's the best answer. Is it the case that you are going to live in his house?"

"Yes, your father kindly recommended me to him."

"Then look out for him, I warn you! He won't forgive you easily, for taking back the letter."

Aglaya pressed the prince's hand and left the room. Her face was serious and frowning; she did not even smile as she nodded good-bye to him at the door.

"I'll just get my parcel and we'll go," said the prince to Gania, as he re-entered the drawing-room. Gania stamped his foot with impatience. His face looked dark and gloomy with rage.

At last they left the house behind them, the prince carrying his bundle.

"The answer–quick–the answer!" said Gania, the instant they were outside. "What did she say? Did you give the letter?" The prince silently held out the note. Gania was struck motionless with amazement.

"How, what? my letter?" he cried. "He never delivered it! I might have guessed it, oh! curse him! Of course she did not understand what I meant, naturally! Why–why–**why** didn't you give her the note, you–"

"Excuse me; I was able to deliver it almost immediately after receiving your commission, and I gave it, too, just as you asked me to. It has come into my hands now because Aglaya Ivanovna has just returned it to me."

"How? When?"

"As soon as I finished writing in her album for her, and when she asked me to come out of the room with her (you heard?), we went into the dining-room, and she gave me your letter to read, and then told me to return it."

"To **read?**" cried Gania, almost at the top of his voice; "to **read**, and you read it?"

And again he stood like a log in the middle of the pavement; so amazed that his mouth remained open after the last word had left it.

"Yes, I have just read it."

"And she gave it you to read herself–

herself?"

"Yes, herself; and you may believe me when I tell you that I would not have read it for anything without her permission."

Gania was silent for a minute or two, as though thinking out some problem. Suddenly he cried:

"It's impossible, she cannot have given it to you to read! You are lying. You read it yourself!"

"I am telling you the truth," said the prince in his former composed tone of voice; "and believe me, I am extremely sorry that the circumstance should have made such an unpleasant impression upon you!"

"But, you wretched man, at least she must have said something? There must be **some** answer from her!"

"Yes, of course, she did say something!"

"Out with it then, damn it! Out with it at once!" and Gania stamped his foot twice on the pavement.

"As soon as I had finished reading it, she

told me that you were fishing for her; that you wished to compromise her so far as to receive some hopes from her, trusting to which hopes you might break with the prospect of receiving a hundred thousand roubles. She said that if you had done this without bargaining with her, if you had broken with the money prospects without trying to force a guarantee out of her first, she might have been your friend. That's all, I think. Oh no, when I asked her what I was to say, as I took the letter, she replied that 'no answer is the best answer.' I think that was it. Forgive me if I do not use her exact expressions. I tell you the sense as I understood it myself."

Ungovernable rage and madness took entire possession of Gania, and his fury burst out without the least attempt at restraint.

"Oh! that's it, is it!" he yelled. "She throws my letters out of the window, does she! Oh! and she does not condescend to bargain, while I **do**, eh? We shall see, we shall see! I shall pay her out for this."

He twisted himself about with rage, and grew paler and paler; he shook his fist. So the pair walked along a few steps. Gania did not stand on ceremony with the prince; he behaved just as though he were alone in his room. He clearly counted the latter as a nonentity. But suddenly he seemed to have an idea, and recollected himself.

"But how was it?" he asked, "how was it that you (idiot that you are)," he added to himself, "were so very confidential a couple of hours after your first meeting with these people? How was that, eh?"

Up to this moment jealousy had not been one of his torments; now it suddenly gnawed at his heart.

"That is a thing I cannot undertake to explain," replied the prince. Gania looked at him with angry contempt.

"Oh! I suppose the present she wished to make to you, when she took you into the dining-room, was her confidence, eh?"

"I suppose that was it; I cannot explain it

otherwise."

"But why, **why?** Devil take it, what did you do in there? Why did they fancy you? Look here, can't you remember exactly what you said to them, from the very beginning? Can't you remember?"

"Oh, we talked of a great many things. When first I went in we began to speak of Switzerland."

"Oh, the devil take Switzerland!"

"Then about executions."

"Executions?"

"Yes–at least about one. Then I told the whole three years' story of my life, and the history of a poor peasant girl–"

"Oh, damn the peasant girl! go on, go on!" said Gania, impatiently.

"Then how Schneider told me about my childish nature, and–"

"Oh, **curse** Schneider and his dirty opinions! Go on."

"Then I began to talk about faces, at least about the **expressions** of faces, and said that Aglaya Ivanovna was nearly as lovely as Nastasia Philipovna. It was then I blurted out about the portrait–"

"But you didn't repeat what you heard in the study? You didn't repeat that–eh?"

"No, I tell you I did **not**."

"Then how did they–look here! Did Aglaya show my letter to the old lady?"

"Oh, there I can give you my fullest assurance that she did **not**. I was there all the while–she had no time to do it!"

"But perhaps you may not have observed it, oh, you damned idiot, you!" he shouted, quite beside himself with fury. "You can't even describe what went on."

Gania having once descended to abuse, and receiving no check, very soon knew no bounds or limit to his licence, as is often the way in such cases. His rage so blinded him that he had not even been able to detect that this "idiot," whom he was abusing to such an extent, was very far from being slow of comprehension, and had a way of taking in an impression, and afterwards giving it out again, which was very un-idiotic indeed. But something a little unforeseen now occurred.

"I think I ought to tell you, Gavrila Ardalionovitch," said the prince, suddenly, "that though I once was so ill that I really was little better than an idiot, yet now I am almost recovered, and that, therefore, it is not altogether pleasant to be called an idiot to my face. Of course your anger is excusable, considering the treatment you have just experienced; but I must remind you that you have twice abused me rather rudely. I do not like this sort of thing, and especially so at the first time of meeting a man, and, therefore, as we happen to be at this moment standing at a crossroad, don't you think we had better part, you to the left, homewards, and I to the right, here? I have twenty-five roubles, and I shall easily find a lodging."

Gania was much confused, and blushed for shame "Do forgive me, prince!" he cried, suddenly changing his abusive tone for one of great courtesy. "For Heaven's sake, forgive me! You see what a miserable plight I am in, but you hardly know anything of the facts of the case as yet. If you did, I am sure you would forgive me, at least partially. Of course it was inexcusable of me, I know, but–"

"Oh, dear me, I really do not require such profuse apologies," replied the prince, hastily. "I quite understand how unpleasant your position is, and that is what made you abuse me. So come along to your house, after all. I shall be delighted–"

"I am not going to let him go like this," thought Gania, glancing angrily at the prince as they walked along. "The fellow has sucked everything out of me, and now he takes off his mask–there's something more than appears, here we shall see. It shall all be as clear as water by tonight, everything!"

But by this time they had reached Gania's house.

CHAPTER EIGHT

THE FLAT OCCUPIED by Gania and his family was on the third floor of the house. It was reached by a clean light staircase, and consisted of seven rooms, a nice enough lodging, and one would have thought a little too good for a clerk on two thousand roubles a year. But it was designed to accommodate a few lodgers on board terms, and had been taken a few months since, much to the disgust of Gania, at the urgent request of his mother and his sister,

Varvara Ardalionovna, who longed to do something to increase the family income a little, and fixed their hopes upon letting lodgings. Gania frowned upon the idea. He thought it **infra dig**, and did not quite like appearing in society afterwards–that society in which he had been accustomed to pose up to now as a young man of rather brilliant prospects. All these concessions and rebuffs of fortune, of late, had wounded his spirit severely, and his temper had become extremely irritable, his wrath being generally quite out of proportion to the cause. But if he had made up his mind to put up with this sort of life for a while, it was only on the plain understanding with his inner self that he would very soon change it all, and have things as he chose again. Yet the very means by which he hoped to make this change threatened to involve him in even greater difficulties than he had had before.

The flat was divided by a passage which

led straight out of the entrance-hall. Along one side of this corridor lay the three rooms which were designed for the accommodation of the "highly recommended" lodgers. Besides these three rooms there was another small one at the end of the passage, close to the kitchen, which was allotted to General Ivolgin, the nominal master of the house, who slept on a wide sofa, and was obliged to pass into and out of his room through the kitchen, and up or down the back stairs. Colia, Gania's young brother, a school-boy of thirteen, shared this room with his father. He, too, had to sleep on an old sofa, a narrow, uncomfortable thing with a torn rug over it; his chief duty being to look after his father, who needed to be watched more and more every day.

The prince was given the middle room of the three, the first being occupied by one Ferdishenko, while the third was empty.

But Gania first conducted the prince to the family apartments. These consisted of a “salon,” which became the dining-room when required; a drawing-room, which was only a drawing-room in the morning, and became Gania’s study in the evening, and his bedroom at night; and lastly Nina Alexandrovna’s and Varvara’s bedroom, a small, close chamber which they shared together.

In a word, the whole place was confined, and a “tight fit” for the party. Gania used to grind his teeth with rage over the state of affairs; though he was anxious to be dutiful and polite to his mother. However, it was very soon apparent to anyone coming into the house, that Gania was the tyrant of the family.

Nina Alexandrovna and her daughter were both seated in the drawing-room, engaged in knitting, and talking to a visitor, Ivan Petrovitch Ptitsin.

The lady of the house appeared to be a woman of about fifty years of age, thin-faced, and with black lines under the eyes.

She looked ill and rather sad; but her face was a pleasant one for all that; and from the first word that fell from her lips, any stranger would at once conclude that she was of a serious and particularly sincere nature. In spite of her sorrowful expression, she gave the idea of possessing considerable firmness and decision.

Her dress was modest and simple to a degree, dark and elderly in style; but both her face and appearance gave evidence that she had seen better days.

Varvara was a girl of some twenty-three summers, of middle height, thin, but possessing a face which, without being actually beautiful, had the rare quality of charm, and might fascinate even to the extent of passionate regard.

She was very like her mother: she even dressed like her, which proved that she had no taste for smart clothes. The expression of her grey eyes was merry and gentle, when it was not, as lately, too full of thought and anxiety. The same decision and firmness was to be observed in her face as in her mother's, but her strength seemed to be more vigorous than that of Nina Alexandrovna. She was subject to outbursts of temper, of which even her brother was a little afraid.

The present visitor, Ptitsin, was also afraid of her. This was a young fellow of something under thirty, dressed plainly, but neatly. His manners were good, but rather ponderously so. His dark beard bore evidence to the fact that he was not in any government employ. He could speak well, but preferred silence. On the whole he made a decidedly agreeable impression. He was clearly attracted by Varvara, and made no secret of his feelings. She trusted him in a friendly way, but had not shown him any decided encouragement as yet, which fact did not quell his ardour in the least.

Nina Alexandrovna was very fond of him, and had grown quite confidential with him of late. Ptitsin, as was well known, was engaged in the business of lending out money on good security, and at a good rate of interest. He was a great friend of Gania's.

After a formal introduction by Gania (who greeted his mother very shortly, took no notice of his sister, and immediately marched Ptitsin out of the room), Nina Alexandrovna addressed a few kind words to the prince and forthwith requested Colia, who had just appeared at the door, to show him to the "middle room."

Colia was a nice-looking boy. His expression was simple and confiding, and his manners were very polite and engaging.

"Where's your luggage?" he asked, as he led the prince away to his room.

"I had a bundle; it's in the entrance hall."

"I'll bring it you directly. We only have a cook and one maid, so I have to help as much as I can. Varia looks after things, generally, and loses her temper over it. Gania says you have only just arrived from Switzerland?"

"Yes."

"Is it jolly there?"

"Very."

"Mountains?"

"Yes."

"I'll go and get your bundle."

Here Varvara joined them.

"The maid shall bring your bed-linen directly. Have you a portmanteau?"

"No; a bundle–your brother has just gone to the hall for it."

"There's nothing there except this," said Colia, returning at this moment. "Where did you put it?"

"Oh! but that's all I have," said the prince, taking it.

"Ah! I thought perhaps Ferdishenko had taken it."

"Don't talk nonsense," said Varia, severely. She seemed put out, and was only just polite with the prince.

"Oho!" laughed the boy, "you can be nicer than that to **me**, you know–I'm not Ptitsin!"

"You ought to be whipped, Colia, you silly boy. If you want anything" (to the prince) "please apply to the servant. We dine at half-past four. You can take your dinner with us, or have it in your room, just as you please. Come along, Colia, don't disturb the prince."

At the door they met Gania coming in.

"Is father in?" he asked. Colia whispered something in his ear and went out.

"Just a couple of words, prince, if you'll excuse me. Don't blab over **there** about what you may see here, or in this house as to all that about Aglaya and me, you know. Things are not altogether pleasant in this establishment–devil take it all! You'll see. At all events keep your tongue to yourself for **today**."

"I assure you I 'blabbed' a great deal less than you seem to suppose," said the prince, with some annoyance. Clearly the relations between Gania and himself were by no means improving.

"Oh well; I caught it quite hot enough today, thanks to you. However, I forgive you."

"I think you might fairly remember that I was not in any way bound, I had no reason to be silent about that portrait. You never asked me not to mention it."

"Pfu! what a wretched room this is–dark, and the window looking into the yard. Your coming to our house is, in no respect, opportune. However, it's not **my** affair. I don't keep the lodgings."

Ptitsin here looked in and beckoned to Gania, who hastily left the room, in spite of the fact that he had evidently wished to say something more and had only made the remark about the room to gain time. The prince had hardly had time to wash and tidy himself a little when the door opened once more, and another figure appeared.

This was a gentleman of about thirty, tall, broad-shouldered, and red-haired; his face was red, too, and he possessed a pair of thick lips, a wide nose, small eyes, rather bloodshot, and with an ironical expression in them; as though he were perpetually winking at someone. His whole appearance gave one the idea of impudence; his dress was shabby.

He opened the door just enough to let his head in. His head remained so placed for a few seconds while he quietly scrutinized the room; the door then opened enough to admit his body; but still he did not enter. He stood on the threshold and examined the prince carefully. At last he gave the door a final shove, entered, approached the prince, took his hand and seated himself and the owner of the room on two chairs side by side.

"Ferdishenko," he said, gazing intently and inquiringly into the prince's eyes.

"Very well, what next?" said the latter, almost laughing in his face.

"A lodger here," continued the other, staring as before.

"Do you wish to make acquaintance?"

asked the prince.

"Ah!" said the visitor, passing his fingers through his hair and sighing. He then looked over to the other side of the room and around it. "Got any money?" he asked, suddenly.

"Not much."

"How much?"

"Twenty-five roubles."

"Let's see it."

The prince took his banknote out and showed it to Ferdishenko. The latter unfolded it and looked at it; then he turned it round and examined the other side; then he held it up to the light.

"How strange that it should have browned so," he said, reflectively. "These twenty-five rouble notes brown in a most extraordinary way, while other notes often grow paler. Take it."

The prince took his note. Ferdishenko rose.

"I came here to warn you," he said. "In the

first place, don't lend me any money, for I shall certainly ask you to."

"Very well."

"Shall you pay here?"

"Yes, I intend to."

"Oh! I **don't** intend to. Thanks. I live here, next door to you; you noticed a room, did you? Don't come to me very often; I shall see you here quite often enough. Have you seen the general?"

"No."

"Nor heard him?"

"No; of course not."

"Well, you'll both hear and see him soon; he even tries to borrow money from me. **Avis au lecteur.** Good-bye; do you think a man can possibly live with a name like Ferdishenko?"

"Why not?"

"Good-bye."

And so he departed. The prince found out afterwards that this gentleman made it his business to amaze people with his originality and wit, but that it did not as a rule "come off." He even produced a bad impression on some people, which grieved him sorely; but he did not change his ways for all that.

As he went out of the prince's room, he collided with yet another visitor coming in. Ferdishenko took the opportunity of making several warning gestures to the prince from behind the new arrival's back, and left the room in conscious pride.

This next arrival was a tall red-faced man of about fifty-five, with greyish hair and whiskers, and large eyes which stood out of their sockets. His appearance would have been distinguished had it not been that he gave the idea of being rather dirty. He was dressed in an old coat, and he smelled of vodka when he came near. His walk was effective, and he clearly did his best to appear dignified, and to impress people by his manner.

This gentleman now approached the prince slowly, and with a most courteous smile; silently took his hand and held it in his own, as he examined the prince's features as though searching for familiar traits therein.

"'Tis he, 'tis he!" he said at last, quietly, but with much solemnity. "As though he were alive once more. I heard the familiar name–the dear familiar name–and, oh! how it reminded me of the irrevocable past–Prince Muishkin, I believe?"

"Exactly so."

"General Ivolgin–retired and unfortunate. May I ask your Christian and generic names?"

"Lef Nicolaievitch."

"So, so–the son of my old, I may say my childhood's friend, Nicolai Petrovitch."

"My father's name was Nicolai Lvovitch."

"Lvovitch," repeated the general without the slightest haste, and with perfect confidence, just as though he had not committed himself the least in the world, but merely made a little slip of the tongue. He sat down, and taking the prince's hand, drew him to a seat next to himself.

"I carried you in my arms as a baby," he observed.

"Really?" asked the prince. "Why, it's twenty years since my father died."

"Yes, yes–twenty years and three months. We were educated together; I went straight into the army, and he–"

"My father went into the army, too. He was a sub-lieutenant in the Vasiliefsky regiment."

"No, sir–in the Bielomirsky; he changed into the latter shortly before his death. I was at his bedside when he died, and gave him my blessing for eternity. Your mother–" The general paused, as though overcome with emotion.

"She died a few months later, from a cold," said the prince.

"Oh, not cold–believe an old man–not from a cold, but from grief for her prince. Oh–your mother, your mother! heigh-ho! Youth–youth! Your father and I–old friends as we were–nearly murdered each other for her sake."

The prince began to be a little incredulous.

"I was passionately in love with her when she was engaged–engaged to my friend. The prince noticed the fact and was furious. He came and woke me at seven o'clock one morning. I rise and dress in amazement; silence on both sides. I understand it all. He takes a couple of pistols out of his pocket–across a handkerchief–without witnesses. Why invite witnesses when both of us would be walking in eternity in a couple of minutes? The pistols are loaded; we stretch the handkerchief and stand opposite one another. We aim the pistols at each other's hearts. Suddenly tears start to our eyes, our hands shake; we weep, we embrace–the battle is one of self-sacrifice now! The prince shouts, 'She is yours;' I cry, 'She is yours–' in a word, in a word–You've come to live with us, hey?"

"Yes–yes–for a while, I think," stammered

the prince.

"Prince, mother begs you to come to her," said Colia, appearing at the door.

The prince rose to go, but the general once more laid his hand in a friendly manner on his shoulder, and dragged him down on to the sofa.

"As the true friend of your father, I wish to say a few words to you," he began. "I have suffered–there was a catastrophe. I suffered without a trial; I had no trial. Nina Alexandrovna my wife, is an excellent woman, so is my daughter Varvara. We have to let lodgings because we are poor–a dreadful, unheard-of come-down for us–for me, who should have been a governor-general; but we are very glad to have **you**, at all events. Meanwhile there is a tragedy in the house."

The prince looked inquiringly at the other.

"Yes, a marriage is being arranged–a marriage between a questionable woman and a young fellow who might be a flunkey.

They wish to bring this woman into the house where my wife and daughter reside, but while I live and breathe she shall never enter my doors. I shall lie at the threshold, and she shall trample me underfoot if she does. I hardly talk to Gania now, and avoid him as much as I can. I warn you of this beforehand, but you cannot fail to observe it. But you are the son of my old friend, and I hope–"

"Prince, be so kind as to come to me for a moment in the drawing-room," said Nina Alexandrovna herself, appearing at the door.

"Imagine, my dear," cried the general, "it turns out that I have nursed the prince on my knee in the old days." His wife looked searchingly at him, and glanced at the prince, but said nothing. The prince rose and followed her; but hardly had they reached the drawing-room, and Nina Alexandrovna had begun to talk hurriedly, when in came the general. She immediately relapsed into silence. The master of the house may have observed this, but at all events he did not take any notice of it; he was in high good humour.

"A son of my old friend, dear," he cried; "surely you must remember Prince Nicolai Lvovitch? You saw him at–at Tver."

"I don't remember any Nicolai Lvovitch. Was that your father?" she inquired of the prince.

"Yes, but he died at Elizabethgrad, not at Tver," said the prince, rather timidly. "So Pavlicheff told me."

"No, Tver," insisted the general; "he removed just before his death. You were very small and cannot remember; and Pavlicheff, though an excellent fellow, may have made a mistake."

"You knew Pavlicheff then?"

"Oh, yes–a wonderful fellow; but I was present myself. I gave him my blessing."

"My father was just about to be tried when he died," said the prince, "although I never knew of what he was accused. He died in hospital."

"Oh! it was the Kolpakoff business, and of course he would have been acquitted."

"Yes? Do you know that for a fact?" asked the prince, whose curiosity was aroused by the general's words.

"I should think so indeed!" cried the latter. "The court-martial came to no decision. It was a mysterious, an impossible business, one might say! Captain Larionoff, commander of the company, had died; his command was handed over to the prince for the moment. Very well. This soldier, Kolpakoff, stole some leather from one of his comrades, intending to sell it, and spent the money on drink. Well! The prince–you understand that what follows took place in the presence of the sergeant-major, and a corporal–the prince rated Kolpakoff soundly, and threatened to have him flogged. Well, Kolpakoff went back to the barracks, lay down on a camp bedstead, and in a quarter of an hour was dead: you quite understand? It was, as I said, a strange, almost impossible, affair. In due course Kolpakoff was buried; the prince wrote his report, the deceased's name was removed from the roll. All as it should be, is it not? But exactly three months later at the inspection of the brigade, the man Kolpakoff was found in the third company of the second battalion of infantry, Novozemlianski division, just as if nothing had happened!"

"What?" said the prince, much astonished.

"It did not occur–it's a mistake!" said Nina Alexandrovna quickly, looking, at the prince rather anxiously. "**Mon mari se trompe**," she added, speaking in French.

"My dear, '**se trompe**' is easily said. Do you remember any case at all like it? Everybody was at their wits' end. I should be the first to say '**qu'on se trompe**,' but unfortunately I was an eye-witness, and was also on the commission of inquiry. Everything proved that it was really he, the very same soldier Kolpakoff who had been given the usual military funeral to the sound of the drum. It is of course a most curious case–nearly an impossible one. I recognize that... but–"

"Father, your dinner is ready," said Varvara at this point, putting her head in at the door.

"Very glad, I'm particularly hungry. Yes, yes, a strange coincidence–almost a psychological–"

"Your soup'll be cold; do come."

"Coming, coming," said the general. "Son of my old friend–" he was heard muttering as he went down the passage.

"You will have to excuse very much in my husband, if you stay with us," said Nina Alexandrovna; "but he will not disturb you often. He dines alone. Everyone has his little peculiarities, you know, and some people perhaps have more than those who are most pointed at and laughed at. One thing I must beg of you–if my husband applies to you for payment for board and lodging, tell him that you have already paid me. Of course anything paid by you to the general would be as fully settled as if paid to me, so far as you are concerned; but I wish it to be so, if you please, for convenience' sake. What is it, Varia?"

Varia had quietly entered the room, and was holding out the portrait of Nastasia Philipovna to her mother.

Nina Alexandrovna started, and examined the photograph intently, gazing at it long and sadly. At last she looked up inquiringly at Varia.

"It's a present from herself to him," said Varia; "the question is to be finally decided this evening."

"This evening!" repeated her mother in a tone of despair, but softly, as though to herself. "Then it's all settled, of course, and there's no hope left to us. She has anticipated her answer by the present of her portrait. Did he show it you himself?" she added, in some surprise.

"You know we have hardly spoken to each other for a whole month. Ptitsin told me all about it; and the photo was lying under the table, and I picked it up."

"Prince," asked Nina Alexandrovna, "I wanted to inquire whether you have known my son long? I think he said that you had only arrived today from somewhere."

The prince gave a short narrative of what we have heard before, leaving out the greater part. The two ladies listened intently.

"I did not ask about Gania out of curiosity," said the elder, at last. "I wish to know how much you know about him, because he said just now that we need not stand on ceremony with you. What, exactly, does that mean?"

At this moment Gania and Ptitsin entered the room together, and Nina Alexandrovna immediately became silent again. The prince remained seated next to her, but Varia moved to the other end of the room; the portrait of Nastasia Philipovna remained lying as before on the work-table. Gania observed it there, and with a frown of annoyance snatched it up and threw it across to his writing-table, which stood at the other end of the room.

"Is it today, Gania?" asked Nina Alexandrovna, at last.

"Is what today?" cried the former. Then suddenly recollecting himself, he turned sharply on the prince. "Oh," he growled, "I see, you are here, that explains it! Is it a disease, or what, that you can't hold your tongue? Look here, understand once for all, prince–"

"I am to blame in this, Gania–no one else," said Ptitsin.

Gania glanced inquiringly at the speaker.

"It's better so, you know, Gania–especially as, from one point of view, the matter may be considered as settled," said Ptitsin; and sitting down a little way from the table he began to study a paper covered with pencil writing.

Gania stood and frowned, he expected a family scene. He never thought of apologizing to the prince, however.

"If it's all settled, Gania, then of course Mr. Ptitsin is right," said Nina Alexandrovna. "Don't frown. You need not worry yourself, Gania; I shall ask you no questions. You need not tell me anything you don't like. I assure you I have quite submitted to your will." She said all this, knitting away the while as though perfectly calm and composed.

Gania was surprised, but cautiously kept silence and looked at his mother, hoping that she would express herself more clearly. Nina Alexandrovna observed his cautiousness and added, with a bitter smile:

"You are still suspicious, I see, and do not believe me; but you may be quite at your ease. There shall be no more tears, nor questions–not from my side, at all events. All I wish is that you may be happy, you know that. I have submitted to my fate; but my heart will always be with you, whether we remain united, or whether we part. Of course I only answer for myself–you can hardly expect your sister–"

"My sister again," cried Gania, looking at her with contempt and almost hate. "Look here, mother, I have already given you my word that I shall always respect you fully and absolutely, and so shall everyone else in this house, be it who it may, who shall cross this threshold."

Gania was so much relieved that he gazed at his mother almost affectionately.

"I was not at all afraid for myself, Gania, as you know well. It was not for my own sake that I have been so anxious and worried all this time! They say it is all to be settled today. What is to be settled?"

"She has promised to tell me tonight at her own house whether she consents or not," replied Gania.

"We have been silent on this subject for three weeks," said his mother, "and it was better so; and now I will only ask you one question. How can she give her consent and make you a present of her portrait when you do not love her? How can such a–such a–"

"Practised hand–eh?"

"I was not going to express myself so. But how could you so blind her?"

Nina Alexandrovna's question betrayed intense annoyance. Gania waited a moment and then said, without taking the trouble to conceal the irony of his tone:

"There you are, mother, you are always like that. You begin by promising that there are to be no reproaches or insinuations or questions, and here you are beginning them at once. We had better drop the subject–we had, really. I shall never leave you, mother; any other man would cut and run from such a sister as this. See how she is looking at me at this moment! Besides, how do you know that I am blinding Nastasia Philipovna? As for Varia, I don't care–she can do just as she pleases. There, that's quite enough!"

Gania's irritation increased with every word he uttered, as he walked up and down the room. These conversations always touched the family sores before long.

"I have said already that the moment she comes in I go out, and I shall keep my word," remarked Varia.

"Out of obstinacy" shouted Gania. "You haven't married, either, thanks to your obstinacy. Oh, you needn't frown at me, Varvara! You can go at once for all I care; I am sick enough of your company. What, you are going to leave us are you, too?" he cried, turning to the prince, who was rising from his chair.

Gania's voice was full of the most uncontrolled and uncontrollable irritation.

The prince turned at the door to say something, but perceiving in Gania's expression that there was but that one drop wanting to make the cup overflow, he changed his mind and left the room without a word. A few minutes later he was aware from the noisy voices in the drawing room, that the conversation had become more quarrelsome than ever after his departure.

He crossed the salon and the entrance-hall, so as to pass down the corridor into his own room. As he came near the front door he heard someone outside vainly endeavouring to ring the bell, which was evidently broken, and only shook a little, without emitting any sound.

The prince took down the chain and opened the door. He started back in amazement–for there stood Nastasia Philipovna. He knew her at once from her photograph. Her eyes blazed with anger as she looked at him. She quickly pushed by him into the hall, shouldering him out of her way, and said, furiously, as she threw off her fur cloak:

"If you are too lazy to mend your bell, you should at least wait in the hall to let people in when they rattle the bell handle. There, now, you've dropped my fur cloak–dummy!"

Sure enough the cloak was lying on the ground. Nastasia had thrown it off her towards the prince, expecting him to catch it, but the prince had missed it.

"Now then–announce me, quick!"

The prince wanted to say something, but was so confused and astonished that he could not. However, he moved off towards the drawing-room with the cloak over his arm.

"Now then, where are you taking my cloak to? Ha, ha, ha! Are you mad?"

The prince turned and came back, more confused than ever. When she burst out laughing, he smiled, but his tongue could not form a word as yet. At first, when he had opened the door and saw her standing before him, he had become as pale as death; but now the red blood had rushed back to his cheeks in a torrent.

"Why, what an idiot it is!" cried Nastasia, stamping her foot with irritation. "Go on, do! Whom are you going to announce?"

"Nastasia Philipovna," murmured the prince.

"And how do you know that?" she asked him, sharply.

"I have never seen you before!"

"Go on, announce me–what's that noise?"

"They are quarrelling," said the prince, and entered the drawing-room, just as matters in there had almost reached a crisis. Nina Alexandrovna had forgotten that she had "submitted to everything!" She was defending Varia. Ptitsin was taking her part, too. Not that Varia was afraid of standing up for herself. She was by no means that sort of a girl; but her brother was becoming ruder and more intolerable every moment. Her usual practice in such cases as the present was to say nothing, but stare at him, without taking her eyes off his face for an instant. This manoeuvre, as she well knew, could drive Gania distracted.

Just at this moment the door opened and the prince entered, announcing:

"Nastasia Philipovna!"

Part One

CHAPTER NINE

SILENCE IMMEDIATELY FELL ON the room; all looked at the prince as though they neither understood, nor hoped to understand. Gania was motionless with horror.

Nastasia's arrival was a most unexpected and overwhelming event to all parties. In the first place, she had never been before. Up to now she had been so haughty that she had never even asked Gania to introduce her to his parents. Of late she had not so much as mentioned them. Gania was partly glad of this; but still he had put it to her debit in the account to be settled after marriage.

He would have borne anything from her rather than this visit. But one thing seemed to him quite clear–her visit now, and the present of her portrait on this particular day, pointed out plainly enough which way she intended to make her decision!

The incredulous amazement with which all regarded the prince did not last long, for Nastasia herself appeared at the door and passed in, pushing by the prince again.

"At last I've stormed the citadel! Why do you tie up your bell?" she said, merrily, as she pressed Gania's hand, the latter having rushed up to her as soon as she made her appearance. "What are you looking so upset about? Introduce me, please!"

The bewildered Gania introduced her first to Varia, and both women, before shaking hands, exchanged looks of strange import. Nastasia, however, smiled amiably; but

Varia did not try to look amiable, and kept her gloomy expression. She did not even vouchsafe the usual courteous smile of etiquette. Gania darted a terrible glance of wrath at her for this, but Nina Alexandrovna mended matters a little when Gania introduced her at last. Hardly, however, had the old lady begun about her "highly gratified feelings," and so on, when Nastasia left her, and flounced into a chair by Gania's side in the corner by the window, and cried: "Where's your study? and where are the–the lodgers? You do take in lodgers, don't you?"

Gania looked dreadfully put out, and tried to say something in reply, but Nastasia interrupted him:

"Why, where are you going to squeeze lodgers in here? Don't you use a study? Does this sort of thing pay?" she added, turning to Nina Alexandrovna.

"Well, it is troublesome, rather," said the latter; "but I suppose it will 'pay' pretty well.

We have only just begun, however–"

Again Nastasia Philipovna did not hear the sentence out. She glanced at Gania, and cried, laughing, "What a face! My goodness, what a face you have on at this moment!"

Indeed, Gania did not look in the least like himself. His bewilderment and his alarmed perplexity passed off, however, and his lips now twitched with rage as he continued to stare evilly at his laughing guest, while his countenance became absolutely livid.

There was another witness, who, though standing at the door motionless and bewildered himself, still managed to remark Gania's death-like pallor, and the dreadful change that had come over his face. This witness was the prince, who now advanced in alarm and muttered to Gania:

"Drink some water, and don't look like that!"

It was clear that he came out with these words quite spontaneously, on the spur of the moment. But his speech was productive of much–for it appeared that all Gania's rage now overflowed upon the prince. He seized him by the shoulder and gazed with an intensity of loathing and revenge at him, but said nothing–as though his feelings were too strong to permit of words.

General agitation prevailed. Nina Alexandrovna gave a little cry of anxiety; Ptitsin took a step forward in alarm; Colia and Ferdishenko stood stock still at the door in amazement;–only Varia remained coolly watching the scene from under her eyelashes. She did not sit down, but stood by her mother with folded hands. However, Gania recollected himself almost immediately. He let go of the prince and burst out laughing.

"Why, are you a doctor, prince, or what?" he asked, as naturally as possible. "I declare you quite frightened me! Nastasia Philipovna, let me introduce this interesting character to you–though I have only known him myself since the morning."

Nastasia gazed at the prince in

bewilderment. “Prince? He a Prince? Why, I took him for the footman, just now, and sent him in to announce me! Ha, ha, ha, isn’t that good!”

“Not bad that, not bad at all!” put in Ferdishenko, “**se non è vero**–”

“I rather think I pitched into you, too, didn’t I? Forgive me–do! Who is he, did you say? What prince? Muishkin?” she added, addressing Gania.

“He is a lodger of ours,” explained the latter.

“An idiot!”–the prince distinctly heard the word half whispered from behind him. This was Ferdishenko’s voluntary information for Nastasia’s benefit.

“Tell me, why didn’t you put me right when I made such a dreadful mistake just now?” continued the latter, examining the prince from head to foot without the slightest ceremony. She awaited the answer as though convinced that it would be so foolish that she must inevitably fail to restrain her laughter over it.

"I was astonished, seeing you so suddenly–" murmured the prince.

"How did you know who I was? Where had you seen me before? And why were you so struck dumb at the sight of me? What was there so overwhelming about me?"

"Oho! ho, ho, ho!" cried Ferdishenko. "**Now** then, prince! My word, what things I would say if I had such a chance as that! My goodness, prince–go on!"

"So should I, in your place, I've no doubt!" laughed the prince to Ferdishenko; then continued, addressing Nastasia: "Your portrait struck me very forcibly this morning; then I was talking about you to the Epanchins; and then, in the train, before I reached Petersburg, Parfen Rogojin told me a good deal about you; and at the very moment that I opened the door to you I happened to be thinking of you, when–there you stood before me!"

"And how did you recognize me?"

"From the portrait!"

"What else?"

"I seemed to imagine you exactly as you are–I seemed to have seen you somewhere."

"Where–where?"

"I seem to have seen your eyes somewhere; but it cannot be! I have not seen you–I never was here before. I may have dreamed of you, I don't know."

The prince said all this with manifest effort–in broken sentences, and with many drawings of breath. He was evidently much agitated. Nastasia Philipovna looked at him inquisitively, but did not laugh.

"Bravo, prince!" cried Ferdishenko, delighted.

At this moment a loud voice from behind the group which hedged in the prince and Nastasia Philipovna, divided the crowd, as it were, and before them stood the head of the family, General Ivolgin. He was dressed in evening clothes; his moustache was dyed.

This apparition was too much for Gania. Vain and ambitious almost to morbidness, he had had much to put up with in the last two months, and was seeking feverishly for some means of enabling himself to lead a more presentable kind of existence. At home, he now adopted an attitude of absolute cynicism, but he could not keep this up before Nastasia Philipovna, although he had sworn to make her pay after marriage for all he suffered now. He was experiencing a last humiliation, the bitterest of all, at this moment–the humiliation of blushing for his own kindred in his own house. A question flashed through his mind as to whether the game was really worth the candle.

For that had happened at this moment, which for two months had been his nightmare; which had filled his soul with dread and shame–the meeting between his father and Nastasia Philipovna. He had often tried to imagine such an event, but had found the picture too mortifying and exasperating, and had quietly dropped it. Very likely he anticipated far worse things than was at all necessary; it is often so with vain persons. He had long since determined, therefore, to get his father out of the way, anywhere, before his marriage, in order to avoid such a meeting; but when Nastasia entered the room just now, he had been so overwhelmed with astonishment, that he had not thought of his father, and had made no arrangements to keep him out of the way. And now it was too late–there he was, and got up, too, in a dress coat and white tie, and Nastasia in the very humour to heap ridicule on him and his family circle; of this last fact, he felt quite persuaded. What else had she come for? There were his mother and his sister sitting before her, and she seemed to have forgotten their very existence already; and if she behaved like that, he thought, she must have some object in view.

Ferdishenko led the general up to Nastasia Philipovna.

"Ardalion Alexandrovitch Ivolgin," said the smiling general, with a low bow of great dignity, "an old soldier, unfortunate, and the father of this family; but happy in the hope of including in that family so exquisite–"

He did not finish his sentence, for at this moment Ferdishenko pushed a chair up from behind, and the general, not very firm on his legs, at this post-prandial hour, flopped into it backwards. It was always a difficult thing to put this warrior to confusion, and his sudden descent left him as composed as before. He had sat down just opposite to Nastasia, whose fingers he now took, and raised to his lips with great elegance, and much courtesy. The general had once belonged to a very select circle of society, but he had been turned out of it two or three years since on account of certain weaknesses, in which he now indulged with all the less restraint; but his good manners remained with him to this day, in spite of all.

Nastasia Philipovna seemed delighted

at the appearance of this latest arrival, of whom she had of course heard a good deal by report.

"I have heard that my son–" began Ardalion Alexandrovitch.

"Your son, indeed! A nice papa you are! **You** might have come to see me anyhow, without compromising anyone. Do you hide yourself, or does your son hide you?"

"The children of the nineteenth century, and their parents–" began the general, again.

"Nastasia Philipovna, will you excuse the general for a moment? Someone is inquiring for him," said Nina Alexandrovna in a loud voice, interrupting the conversation.

"Excuse him? Oh no, I have wished to see him too long for that. Why, what business can he have? He has retired, hasn't he? You won't leave me, general, will you?"

"I give you my word that he shall come and see you–but he–he needs rest just now."

"General, they say you require rest," said

Nastasia Philipovna, with the melancholy face of a child whose toy is taken away.

Ardalion Alexandrovitch immediately did his best to make his foolish position a great deal worse.

"My dear, my dear!" he said, solemnly and reproachfully, looking at his wife, with one hand on his heart.

"Won't you leave the room, mamma?" asked Varia, aloud.

"No, Varia, I shall sit it out to the end."

Nastasia must have overheard both question and reply, but her vivacity was not in the least damped. On the contrary, it seemed to increase. She immediately overwhelmed the general once more with questions, and within five minutes that gentleman was as happy as a king, and holding forth at the top of his voice, amid the laughter of almost all who heard him.

Colia jogged the prince's arm.

"Can't **you** get him out of the room, somehow? **Do**, please," and tears of annoyance stood in the boy's eyes. "Curse that Gania!" he muttered, between his teeth.

"Oh yes, I knew General Epanchin well," General Ivolgin was saying at this moment; "he and Prince Nicolai Ivanovitch Muishkin–whose son I have this day embraced after an absence of twenty years–and I, were three inseparables. Alas one is in the grave, torn to pieces by calumnies and bullets; another is now before you, still battling with calumnies and bullets–"

"Bullets?" cried Nastasia.

"Yes, here in my chest. I received them at the siege of Kars, and I feel them in bad weather now. And as to the third of our trio, Epanchin, of course after that little affair with the poodle in the railway carriage, it was all **up** between us."

"Poodle? What was that? And in a railway carriage? Dear me," said Nastasia, thoughtfully, as though trying to recall something to mind.

"Oh, just a silly, little occurrence, really not

worth telling, about Princess Bielokonski's governess, Miss Smith, and–oh, it is really not worth telling!"

"No, no, we must have it!" cried Nastasia merrily.

"Yes, of course," said Ferdishenko. "C'est du nouveau."

"Ardalion," said Nina Alexandrovitch, entreatingly.

"Papa, you are wanted!" cried Colia.

"Well, it is a silly little story, in a few words," began the delighted general. "A couple of years ago, soon after the new railway was opened, I had to go somewhere or other on business. Well, I took a first-class ticket, sat down, and began to smoke, or rather **continued** to smoke, for I had lighted up before. I was alone in the carriage. Smoking is not allowed, but is not prohibited either; it is half allowed–so to speak, winked at. I had the window open."

"Suddenly, just before the whistle, in came two ladies with a little poodle, and sat down opposite to me; not bad-looking women; one was in light blue, the other in black silk. The poodle, a beauty with a silver collar, lay on light blue's knee. They looked haughtily about, and talked English together. I took no notice, just went on smoking. I observed that the ladies were getting angry–over my cigar, doubtless. One looked at me through her tortoise-shell eyeglass.

"I took no notice, because they never said a word. If they didn't like the cigar, why couldn't they say so? Not a word, not a hint! Suddenly, and without the very slightest suspicion of warning, 'light blue' seizes my cigar from between my fingers, and, wheugh! out of the window with it! Well, on flew the train, and I sat bewildered, and the young woman, tall and fair, and rather red in the face, too red, glared at me with flashing eyes.

"I didn't say a word, but with extreme courtesy, I may say with most refined courtesy, I reached my finger and thumb over towards the poodle, took it up delicately by the nape of the neck, and chucked it out of the window, after the cigar. The train went flying on, and the poodle's yells were lost in the distance."

"Oh, you naughty man!" cried Nastasia, laughing and clapping her hands like a child.

"Bravo!" said Ferdishenko. Ptitsin laughed too, though he had been very sorry to see the general appear. Even Colia laughed and said, "Bravo!"

"And I was right, truly right," cried the general, with warmth and solemnity, "for if cigars are forbidden in railway carriages, poodles are much more so."

"Well, and what did the lady do?" asked Nastasia, impatiently.

"She–ah, that's where all the mischief of it lies!" replied Ivolgin, frowning. "Without a word, as it were, of warning, she slapped me on the cheek! An extraordinary woman!"

"And you?"

The general dropped his eyes, and

elevated his brows; shrugged his shoulders, tightened his lips, spread his hands, and remained silent. At last he blurted out:

"I lost my head!"

"Did you hit her?"

"No, oh no!–there was a great flare-up, but I didn't hit her! I had to struggle a little, purely to defend myself; but the very devil was in the business. It turned out that 'light blue' was an Englishwoman, governess or something, at Princess Bielokonski's, and the other woman was one of the old-maid princesses Bielokonski. Well, everybody knows what great friends the princess and Mrs. Epanchin are, so there was a pretty kettle of fish. All the Bielokonskis went into mourning for the poodle. Six princesses in tears, and the Englishwoman shrieking!

"Of course I wrote an apology, and called, but they would not receive either me or my apology, and the Epanchins cut me, too!"

"But wait," said Nastasia. "How is it that, five or six days since, I read exactly the same story in the paper, as happening between a Frenchman and an English girl? The cigar was snatched away exactly as you describe, and the poodle was chucked out of the window after it. The slapping came off, too, as in your case; and the girl's dress was light blue!"

The general blushed dreadfully; Colia blushed too; and Ptitsin turned hastily away. Ferdishenko was the only one who laughed as gaily as before. As to Gania, I need not say that he was miserable; he stood dumb and wretched and took no notice of anybody.

"I assure you," said the general, "that exactly the same thing happened to myself!"

"I remembered there was some quarrel between father and Miss Smith, the Bielokonski's governess," said Colia.

"How very curious, point for point the same anecdote, and happening at different ends of Europe! Even the light blue dress the same," continued the pitiless Nastasia. "I must really send you the paper."

"You must observe," insisted the general, "that my experience was two years earlier."

"Ah! that's it, no doubt!"

Nastasia Philipovna laughed hysterically.

"Father, will you hear a word from me outside!" said Gania, his voice shaking with agitation, as he seized his father by the shoulder. His eyes shone with a blaze of hatred.

At this moment there was a terrific bang at the front door, almost enough to break it down. Some most unusual visitor must have arrived. Colia ran to open.

CHAPTER TEN

THE ENTRANCE-HALL SUDDENLY became full of noise and people. To judge from the sounds which penetrated to the drawing-room, a number of people had already come in, and the stampede continued. Several voices were talking and shouting at once; others were talking and shouting on the stairs outside; it was evidently a most extraordinary visit that was about to take place.

Everyone exchanged startled glances.

Gania rushed out towards the dining-room, but a number of men had already made their way in, and met him.

"Ah! here he is, the Judas!" cried a voice which the prince recognized at once. "How d'ye do, Gania, you old blackguard?"

"Yes, that's the man!" said another voice.

There was no room for doubt in the prince's mind: one of the voices was Rogojin's, and the other Lebedeff's.

Gania stood at the door like a block and looked on in silence, putting no obstacle in the way of their entrance, and ten or a dozen men marched in behind Parfen Rogojin. They were a decidedly mixed-looking collection, and some of them came in in their furs and caps. None of them were quite drunk, but all appeared to be considerably excited.

They seemed to need each other's support, morally, before they dared come in; not one of them would have entered alone but with the rest each one was brave enough.

Even Rogojin entered rather cautiously at the head of his troop; but he was evidently preoccupied. He appeared to be gloomy and morose, and had clearly come with some end in view. All the rest were merely chorus, brought in to support the chief character. Besides Lebedeff there was the dandy Zalesheff, who came in without his coat and hat, two or three others followed his example; the rest were more uncouth. They included a couple of young merchants, a man in a great-coat, a medical student, a little Pole, a small fat man who laughed continuously, and an enormously tall stout one who apparently put great faith in the strength of his fists. A couple of "ladies" of some sort put their heads in at the front door, but did not dare come any farther. Colia promptly banged the door in their faces and locked it.

"Hallo, Gania, you blackguard! You didn't expect Rogojin, eh?" said the latter, entering the drawing-room, and stopping before

Gania.

But at this moment he saw, seated before him, Nastasia Philipovna. He had not dreamed of meeting her here, evidently, for her appearance produced a marvellous effect upon him. He grew pale, and his lips became actually blue.

"I suppose it is true, then!" he muttered to himself, and his face took on an expression of despair. "So that's the end of it! Now you, sir, will you answer me or not?" he went on suddenly, gazing at Gania with ineffable malice. "Now then, you–"

He panted, and could hardly speak for agitation. He advanced into the room mechanically; but perceiving Nina Alexandrovna and Varia he became more or less embarrassed, in spite of his excitement. His followers entered after him, and all paused a moment at sight of the ladies. Of course their modesty was not fated to be long-lived, but for a moment they were abashed. Once let them begin to shout, however, and nothing on earth should disconcert them.

"What, you here too, prince?" said Rogojin, absently, but a little surprised all the same "Still in your gaiters, eh?" He sighed, and forgot the prince next moment, and his wild eyes wandered over to Nastasia again, as though attracted in that direction by some magnetic force.

Nastasia looked at the new arrivals with great curiosity. Gania recollected himself at last.

"Excuse me, sirs," he said, loudly, "but what does all this mean?" He glared at the advancing crowd generally, but addressed his remarks especially to their captain, Rogojin. "You are not in a stable, gentlemen, though you may think it–my mother and sister are present."

"Yes, I see your mother and sister," muttered Rogojin, through his teeth; and Lebedeff seemed to feel himself called upon to second the statement.

"At all events, I must request you to step into the salon," said Gania, his rage rising quite out of proportion to his words, "and then I shall inquire–"

"What, he doesn't know me!" said Rogojin, showing his teeth disagreeably. "He doesn't recognize Rogojin!" He did not move an inch, however.

"I have met you somewhere, I believe, but–"

"Met me somewhere, pfu! Why, it's only three months since I lost two hundred roubles of my father's money to you, at cards. The old fellow died before he found out. Ptitsin knows all about it. Why, I've only to pull out a three-rouble note and show it to you, and you'd crawl on your hands and knees to the other end of the town for it; that's the sort of man you are. Why, I've come now, at this moment, to buy you up! Oh, you needn't think that because I wear these boots I have no money. I have lots of money, my beauty,–enough to buy up you and all yours together. So I shall, if I like to! I'll buy you up! I will!" he yelled, apparently growing more and more intoxicated and excited. "Oh, Nastasia Philipovna! don't turn me out! Say one word, do! Are you going to marry this man, or not?"

Rogojin asked his question like a lost soul appealing to some divinity, with the reckless daring of one appointed to die, who has nothing to lose.

He awaited the reply in deadly anxiety.

Nastasia Philipovna gazed at him with a haughty, ironical expression of face; but when she glanced at Nina Alexandrovna and Varia, and from them to Gania, she changed her tone, all of a sudden.

"Certainly not; what are you thinking of? What could have induced you to ask such a question?" she replied, quietly and seriously, and even, apparently, with some astonishment.

"No? No?" shouted Rogojin, almost out of his mind with joy. "You are not going to, after all? And they told me–oh, Nastasia Philipovna–they said you had promised to marry him, **him!** As if you **could** do it!–him–pooh! I don't mind saying it to everyone–I'd buy him off for a hundred roubles, any day pfu! Give him a thousand, or three if he likes, poor devil, and he'd cut and run the day before his wedding, and leave his bride to me! Wouldn't you, Gania, you blackguard? You'd take three thousand, wouldn't you? Here's the money! Look, I've come on purpose to pay you off and get your receipt, formally. I said I'd buy you up, and so I will."

"Get out of this, you drunken beast!" cried Gania, who was red and white by turns.

Rogojin's troop, who were only waiting for an excuse, set up a howl at this. Lebedeff stepped forward and whispered something in Parfen's ear.

"You're right, clerk," said the latter, "you're right, tipsy spirit–you're right!–Nastasia Philipovna," he added, looking at her like some lunatic, harmless generally, but suddenly wound up to a pitch of audacity, "here are eighteen thousand roubles, and–and you shall have more–." Here he threw a packet of bank-notes tied up in white paper, on the table before her, not daring to say all he wished to say.

"No–no–no!" muttered Lebedeff, clutching at his arm. He was clearly aghast at the largeness of the sum, and thought a far smaller amount should have been tried first.

"No, you fool–you don't know whom you are dealing with–and it appears I am a fool, too!" said Parfen, trembling beneath the flashing glance of Nastasia. "Oh, curse it all! What a fool I was to listen to you!" he added, with profound melancholy.

Nastasia Philipovna, observing his woe-begone expression, suddenly burst out laughing.

"Eighteen thousand roubles, for me? Why, you declare yourself a fool at once," she said, with impudent familiarity, as she rose from the sofa and prepared to go. Gania watched the whole scene with a sinking of the heart.

"Forty thousand, then–forty thousand roubles instead of eighteen! Ptitsin and another have promised to find me forty thousand roubles by seven o'clock tonight. Forty thousand roubles–paid down on the nail!"

The scene was growing more and more disgraceful; but Nastasia Philipovna continued to laugh and did not go away. Nina Alexandrovna and Varia had both risen from their places and were waiting, in silent horror, to see what would happen. Varia's eyes were all ablaze with anger; but the scene had a different effect on Nina Alexandrovna. She paled and trembled, and looked more and more like fainting every moment.

"Very well then, a **hundred** thousand! a hundred thousand! paid this very day. Ptitsin! find it for me. A good share shall stick to your fingers–come!"

"You are mad!" said Ptitsin, coming up

quickly and seizing him by the hand. "You're drunk–the police will be sent for if you don't look out. Think where you are."

"Yes, he's boasting like a drunkard," added Nastasia, as though with the sole intention of goading him.

"I do **not** boast! You shall have a hundred thousand, this very day. Ptitsin, get the money, you gay usurer! Take what you like for it, but get it by the evening! I'll show that I'm in earnest!" cried Rogojin, working himself up into a frenzy of excitement.

"Come, come; what's all this?" cried General Ivolgin, suddenly and angrily, coming close up to Rogojin. The unexpectedness of this sally on the part of the hitherto silent old man caused some laughter among the intruders.

"Halloa! what's this now?" laughed Rogojin. "You come along with me, old fellow! You shall have as much to drink as you like."

"Oh, it's too horrible!" cried poor Colia, sobbing with shame and annoyance.

"Surely there must be someone among all of you here who will turn this shameless creature out of the room?" cried Varia, suddenly. She was shaking and trembling with rage.

"That's me, I suppose. I'm the shameless creature!" cried Nastasia Philipovna, with amused indifference. "Dear me, and I came–like a fool, as I am–to invite them over to my house for the evening! Look how your sister treats me, Gavrila Ardalionovitch."

For some moments Gania stood as if stunned or struck by lightning, after his sister's speech. But seeing that Nastasia Philipovna was really about to leave the room this time, he sprang at Varia and seized her by the arm like a madman.

"What have you done?" he hissed, glaring at her as though he would like to annihilate her on the spot. He was quite beside himself, and could hardly articulate his words for rage.

"What have I done? Where are you

dragging me to?"

"Do you wish me to beg pardon of this creature because she has come here to insult our mother and disgrace the whole household, you low, base wretch?" cried Varia, looking back at her brother with proud defiance.

A few moments passed as they stood there face to face, Gania still holding her wrist tightly. Varia struggled once–twice–to get free; then could restrain herself no longer, and spat in his face.

"There's a girl for you!" cried Nastasia Philipovna. "Mr. Ptitsin, I congratulate you on your choice."

Gania lost his head. Forgetful of everything he aimed a blow at Varia, which would inevitably have laid her low, but suddenly another hand caught his. Between him and Varia stood the prince.

"Enough–enough!" said the latter, with insistence, but all of a tremble with excitement.

"Are you going to cross my path for ever, damn you!" cried Gania; and, loosening his hold on Varia, he slapped the prince's face with all his force.

Exclamations of horror arose on all sides. The prince grew pale as death; he gazed into Gania's eyes with a strange, wild, reproachful look; his lips trembled and vainly endeavoured to form some words; then his mouth twisted into an incongruous smile.

"Very well–never mind about me; but I shall not allow you to strike her!" he said, at last, quietly. Then, suddenly, he could bear it no longer, and covering his face with his hands, turned to the wall, and murmured in broken accents:

"Oh! how ashamed you will be of this afterwards!"

Gania certainly did look dreadfully abashed. Colia rushed up to comfort the prince, and after him crowded Varia, Rogojin and all, even the general.

"It's nothing, it's nothing!" said the prince,

and again he wore the smile which was so inconsistent with the circumstances.

"Yes, he will be ashamed!" cried Rogojin. "You will be properly ashamed of yourself for having injured such a–such a sheep" (he could not find a better word). "Prince, my dear fellow, leave this and come away with me. I'll show you how Rogojin shows his affection for his friends."

Nastasia Philipovna was also much impressed, both with Gania's action and with the prince's reply.

Her usually thoughtful, pale face, which all this while had been so little in harmony with the jests and laughter which she had seemed to put on for the occasion, was now evidently agitated by new feelings, though she tried to conceal the fact and to look as though she were as ready as ever for jesting and irony.

"I really think I must have seen him somewhere!" she murmured seriously enough.

"Oh, aren't you ashamed of yourself–aren't you ashamed? Are you really the sort of woman you are trying to represent yourself to be? Is it possible?" The prince was now addressing Nastasia, in a tone of reproach, which evidently came from his very heart.

Nastasia Philipovna looked surprised, and smiled, but evidently concealed something beneath her smile and with some confusion and a glance at Gania she left the room.

However, she had not reached the outer hall when she turned round, walked quickly up to Nina Alexandrovna, seized her hand and lifted it to her lips.

"He guessed quite right. I am not that sort of woman," she whispered hurriedly, flushing red all over. Then she turned again and left the room so quickly that no one could imagine what she had come back for. All they saw was that she said something to Nina Alexandrovna in a hurried whisper, and seemed to kiss her hand. Varia, however, both saw and heard all, and watched Nastasia out of the room with an expression of wonder.

Gania recollected himself in time to rush after her in order to show her out, but she had gone. He followed her to the stairs.

"Don't come with me," she cried, "**Au revoir**, till the evening–do you hear? **Au revoir!**"

He returned thoughtful and confused; the riddle lay heavier than ever on his soul. He was troubled about the prince, too, and so bewildered that he did not even observe Rogojin's rowdy band crowd past him and step on his toes, at the door as they went out. They were all talking at once. Rogojin went ahead of the others, talking to Ptitsin, and apparently insisting vehemently upon something very important.

"You've lost the game, Gania" he cried, as he passed the latter.

Gania gazed after him uneasily, but said nothing.

CHAPTER ELEVEN

THE PRINCE NOW LEFT the room and shut himself up in his own chamber. Colia followed him almost at once, anxious to do what he could to console him. The poor boy seemed to be already so attached to him that he could hardly leave him.

"You were quite right to go away!" he said. "The row will rage there worse than ever now; and it's like this every day with us–and all through that Nastasia Philipovna."

"You have so many sources of trouble here,

Colia," said the prince.

"Yes, indeed, and it is all our own fault. But I have a great friend who is much worse off even than we are. Would you like to know him?"

"Yes, very much. Is he one of your school-fellows?"

"Well, not exactly. I will tell you all about him some day.... What do you think of Nastasia Philipovna? She is beautiful, isn't she? I had never seen her before, though I had a great wish to do so. She fascinated me. I could forgive Gania if he were to marry her for love, but for money! Oh dear! that is horrible!"

"Yes, your brother does not attract me much."

"I am not surprised at that. After what you... But I do hate that way of looking at things! Because some fool, or a rogue pretending to be a fool, strikes a man, that man is to be dishonoured for his whole life, unless he wipes out the disgrace with blood, or makes his assailant beg forgiveness on his knees! I think that so very absurd and tyrannical. Lermontoff's Bal Masque is based on that idea–a stupid and unnatural one, in my opinion; but he was hardly more than a child when he wrote it."

"I like your sister very much."

"Did you see how she spat in Gania's face! Varia is afraid of no one. But you did not follow her example, and yet I am sure it was not through cowardice. Here she comes! Speak of a wolf and you see his tail! I felt sure that she would come. She is very generous, though of course she has her faults."

Varia pounced upon her brother.

"This is not the place for you," said she. "Go to father. Is he plaguing you, prince?"

"Not in the least; on the contrary, he interests me."

"Scolding as usual, Varia! It is the worst thing about her. After all, I believe father may have started off with Rogojin. No doubt he is sorry now. Perhaps I had better go and see what he is doing," added Colia, running off.

"Thank God, I have got mother away, and put her to bed without another scene! Gania is worried–and ashamed–not without reason! What a spectacle! I have come to thank you once more, prince, and to ask you if you knew Nastasia Philipovna before?"

"No, I have never known her."

"Then what did you mean, when you said straight out to her that she was not really 'like that'? You guessed right, I fancy. It is quite possible she was not herself at the moment, though I cannot fathom her meaning. Evidently she meant to hurt and insult us. I have heard curious tales about her before now, but if she came to invite us to her house, why did she behave so to my mother? Ptitsin knows her very well; he says he could not understand her today. With Rogojin, too! No one with a spark of self-respect could have talked like that in the house of her... Mother is extremely vexed on your account, too...

"That is nothing!" said the prince, waving his hand.

"But how meek she was when you spoke to her!"

"Meek! What do you mean?"

"You told her it was a shame for her to behave so, and her manner changed at once; she was like another person. You have some influence over her, prince," added Varia, smiling a little.

The door opened at this point, and in came Gania most unexpectedly.

He was not in the least disconcerted to see Varia there, but he stood a moment at the door, and then approached the prince quietly.

"Prince," he said, with feeling, "I was a blackguard. Forgive me!" His face gave evidence of suffering. The prince was considerably amazed, and did not reply at once. "Oh, come, forgive me, forgive me!" Gania insisted, rather impatiently. "If you like, I'll kiss your hand. There!"

The prince was touched; he took Gania's hands, and embraced him heartily, while each kissed the other.

"I never, never thought you were like that," said Muishkin, drawing a deep breath. "I thought you–you weren't capable of–"

"Of what? Apologizing, eh? And where on earth did I get the idea that you were an idiot? You always observe what other people pass by unnoticed; one could talk sense to you, but–"

"Here is another to whom you should apologize," said the prince, pointing to Varia.

"No, no! they are all enemies! I've tried them often enough, believe me," and Gania turned his back on Varia with these words.

"But if I beg you to make it up?" said Varia.

"And you'll go to Nastasia Philipovna's this evening–"

"If you insist: but, judge for yourself, can I go, ought I to go?"

"But she is not that sort of woman, I tell you!" said Gania, angrily. "She was only acting."

"I know that–I know that; but what a part to play! And think what she must take **you** for, Gania! I know she kissed mother's hand, and all that, but she laughed at you, all the same. All this is not good enough for seventy-five thousand roubles, my dear boy. You are capable of honourable feelings still, and that's why I am talking to you so. Oh! **do** take care what you are doing! Don't you know yourself that it will end badly, Gania?"

So saying, and in a state of violent agitation, Varia left the room.

"There, they are all like that," said Gania, laughing, "just as if I do not know all about it much better than they do."

He sat down with these words, evidently intending to prolong his visit.

"If you know it so well," said the prince a little timidly, "why do you choose all this worry for the sake of the seventy-five thousand, which, you confess, does not cover it?"

"I didn't mean that," said Gania; "but while

we are upon the subject, let me hear your opinion. Is all this worry worth seventy-five thousand or not?"

"Certainly not."

"Of course! And it would be a disgrace to marry so, eh?"

"A great disgrace."

"Oh, well, then you may know that I shall certainly do it, now. I shall certainly marry her. I was not quite sure of myself before, but now I am. Don't say a word: I know what you want to tell me–"

"No. I was only going to say that what surprises me most of all is your extraordinary confidence."

"How so? What in?"

"That Nastasia Philipovna will accept you, and that the question is as good as settled; and secondly, that even if she did, you would be able to pocket the money. Of course, I know very little about it, but that's my view. When a man marries for money it often happens that the wife keeps the money in her own hands."

"Of course, you don't know all; but, I assure you, you needn't be afraid, it won't be like that in our case. There are circumstances," said Gania, rather excitedly. "And as to her answer to me, there's no doubt about that. Why should you suppose she will refuse me?"

"Oh, I only judge by what I see. Varvara Ardalionovna said just now–"

"Oh she–they don't know anything about it! Nastasia was only chaffing Rogojin. I was alarmed at first, but I have thought better of it now; she was simply laughing at him. She looks on me as a fool because I show that I meant her money, and doesn't realize that there are other men who would deceive her in far worse fashion. I'm not going to pretend anything, and you'll see she'll marry me, all right. If she likes to live quietly, so she shall; but if she gives me any of her nonsense, I shall leave her at once, but I shall keep the money. I'm not going to look a fool; that's the first thing, not to look a fool."

"But Nastasia Philipovna seems to me to be such a **sensible** woman, and, as such, why should she run blindly into this business? That's what puzzles me so," said the prince.

"You don't know all, you see; I tell you there are things–and besides, I'm sure that she is persuaded that I love her to distraction, and I give you my word I have a strong suspicion that she loves me, too–in her own way, of course. She thinks she will be able to make a sort of slave of me all my life; but I shall prepare a little surprise for her. I don't know whether I ought to be confidential with you, prince; but, I assure you, you are the only decent fellow I have come across. I have not spoken so sincerely as I am doing at this moment for years. There are uncommonly few honest people about, prince; there isn't one honester than Ptitsin, he's the best of the lot. Are you laughing? You don't know, perhaps, that blackguards like honest people, and being one myself I like you. **Why** am I a blackguard? Tell me honestly, now. They all call me a blackguard because of her, and I have got into the way of thinking myself one. That's what is so bad about the business."

"**I** for one shall never think you a blackguard again," said the prince. "I confess I had a poor opinion of you at first, but I have been so joyfully surprised about you just now; it's a good lesson for me. I shall never judge again without a thorough trial. I see now that you are not only not a blackguard, but are not even quite spoiled. I see that you are quite an ordinary man, not original in the least degree, but rather weak."

Gania laughed sarcastically, but said nothing. The prince, seeing that he did not quite like the last remark, blushed, and was silent too.

"Has my father asked you for money?" asked Gania, suddenly.

"No."

"Don't give it to him if he does. Fancy, he was a decent, respectable man once! He was received in the best society; he was not always the liar he is now. Of course, wine is at the bottom of it all; but he is a good deal worse than an innocent liar now. Do you know that he keeps a mistress? I can't understand how mother is so long-suffering. Did he tell you the story of the siege of Kars? Or perhaps the one about his grey horse that talked? He loves to enlarge on these absurd histories." And Gania burst into a fit of laughter. Suddenly he turned to the prince and asked: "Why are you looking at me like that?"

"I am surprised to see you laugh in that way, like a child. You came to make friends with me again just now, and you said, 'I will kiss your hand, if you like,' just as a child would have said it. And then, all at once you are talking of this mad project–of these seventy-five thousand roubles! It all seems so absurd and impossible."

"Well, what conclusion have you reached?"

"That you are rushing madly into the undertaking, and that you would do well to think it over again. It is more than possible that Varvara Ardalionovna is right."

"Ah! now you begin to moralize! I know that I am only a child, very well," replied Gania impatiently. "That is proved by my having this conversation with you. It is not for money only, prince, that I am rushing into this affair," he continued, hardly master of his words, so closely had his vanity been touched. "If I reckoned on that I should certainly be deceived, for I am still too weak in mind and character. I am obeying a passion, an impulse perhaps, because I have but one aim, one that overmasters all else. You imagine that once I am in possession of these seventy-five thousand roubles, I shall rush to buy a carriage... No, I shall go on wearing the old overcoat I have worn for three years, and I shall give up my club. I shall follow the example of men who have made their fortunes. When Ptitsin was seventeen he slept in the street, he sold pen-knives, and began with a copeck; now he has sixty thousand roubles, but to get them, what has he not done? Well, I shall be spared such a hard beginning, and shall start with a little capital. In fifteen years people will say, 'Look, that's Ivolgin, the king of the Jews!' You say that I have no originality. Now mark this, prince–there is nothing so offensive to a man of our time and race than to be told that he is wanting in originality, that he is weak in character, has no particular talent, and is, in short, an ordinary person. You have not even done me the honour of looking upon me as a rogue. Do you know, I could have knocked you down for that just now! You wounded me more cruelly than Epanchin, who thinks me capable of selling him my wife! Observe, it was a perfectly gratuitous idea on his part, seeing there has never been any discussion of it between us! This has exasperated me, and I am determined to make a fortune! I will do it! Once I am rich, I shall be a genius, an extremely original man. One of the vilest and most hateful things connected with money is that it can buy even talent; and will do so as long as the world lasts. You will say that this is childish–or romantic. Well, that will be all the better for me, but the thing shall be done. I will carry it through. He laughs most, who laughs last. Why does Epanchin insult me? Simply because, socially, I am a nobody. However, enough for the present. Colia has put his nose in to tell us dinner is ready, twice. I'm dining out. I shall come and talk to you now and then; you shall be comfortable enough with us. They are sure to make you one of the family. I think you and I will either be great friends or enemies. Look here now, supposing I had kissed your hand just now, as I offered to do in all sincerity, should I have hated you for it afterwards?"

"Certainly, but not always. You would not have been able to keep it up, and would have ended by forgiving me," said the prince, after a pause for reflection, and with a pleasant smile.

"Oho, how careful one has to be with you, prince! Haven't you put a drop of poison in that remark now, eh? By the way–ha, ha, ha!–I forgot to ask, was I right in believing that you were a good deal struck yourself with Nastasia Philipovna."

"Ye-yes."

"Are you in love with her?"

"N-no."

"And yet you flush up as red as a rosebud! Come–it's all right. I'm not going to laugh at you. Do you know she is a very virtuous woman? Believe it or not, as you like. You think she and Totski–not a bit of it, not a bit of it! Not for ever so long! **Au revoir!**"

Gania left the room in great good humour. The prince stayed behind, and meditated alone for a few minutes. At length, Colia popped his head in once more.

"I don't want any dinner, thanks, Colia. I had too good a lunch at General Epanchin's."

Colia came into the room and gave the prince a note; it was from the general and was carefully sealed up. It was clear from Colia's face how painful it was to him to deliver the missive. The prince read it, rose, and took his hat.

"It's only a couple of yards," said Colia, blushing.

"He's sitting there over his bottle–and how they can give him credit, I cannot understand. Don't tell mother I brought you the note, prince; I have sworn not to do it a thousand times, but I'm always so sorry for him. Don't stand on ceremony, give him some trifle, and let that end it."

"Come along, Colia, I want to see your father. I have an idea," said the prince.

CHAPTER TWELVE

COLIA TOOK THE PRINCE to a public-house in the Litaynaya, not far off. In one of the side rooms there sat at a table–looking like one of the regular guests of the establishment–Ardalion Alexandrovitch, with a bottle before him, and a newspaper on his knee. He was waiting for the prince, and no sooner did the latter appear than he began a long harangue about something or other; but so far gone was he that the prince could hardly understand a word.

"I have not got a ten-rouble note," said the prince; "but here is a twenty-five. Change it and give me back the fifteen, or I shall be left without a farthing myself."

"Oh, of course, of course; and you quite understand that I–"

"Yes; and I have another request to make, general. Have you ever been at Nastasia Philipovna's?"

"I? I? Do you mean me? Often, my friend, often! I only pretended I had not in order to avoid a painful subject. You saw today, you were a witness, that I did all that a kind, an indulgent father could do. Now a father of altogether another type shall step into the scene. You shall see; the old soldier shall lay bare this intrigue, or a shameless woman will force her way into a respectable and noble family."

"Yes, quite so. I wished to ask you whether you could show me the way to Nastasia Philipovna's tonight. I must go; I have business with her; I was not invited but I was introduced. Anyhow I am ready to trespass the laws of propriety if only I can get in somehow or other."

"My dear young friend, you have hit on my very idea. It was not for this rubbish I asked you to come over here" (he pocketed the money, however, at this point), "it was to invite your alliance in the campaign against Nastasia Philipovna tonight. How well it sounds, 'General Ivolgin and Prince Muishkin.' That'll fetch her, I think, eh? Capital! We'll go at nine; there's time yet."

"Where does she live?"

"Oh, a long way off, near the Great Theatre, just in the square there–It won't be a large party."

The general sat on and on. He had ordered a fresh bottle when the prince arrived; this took him an hour to drink, and then he had another, and another, during the consumption of which he told pretty nearly the whole story of his life. The prince was in despair. He felt that though he had but applied to this miserable old drunkard because he saw no other way of getting to Nastasia Philipovna's, yet he had been very wrong to put the slightest confidence in such a man.

At last he rose and declared that he would wait no longer. The general rose too, drank the last drops that he could squeeze out of the bottle, and staggered into the street.

Muishkin began to despair. He could not imagine how he had been so foolish as to trust this man. He only wanted one thing, and that was to get to Nastasia Philipovna's, even at the cost of a certain amount of impropriety. But now the scandal threatened to be more than he had bargained for. By this time Ardalion Alexandrovitch was quite intoxicated, and he kept his companion listening while he discoursed eloquently and pathetically on subjects of all kinds, interspersed with torrents of recrimination against the members of his family. He insisted that all his troubles were caused by their bad conduct, and time alone would put an end to them.

At last they reached the Litaynaya. The thaw increased steadily, a warm, unhealthy wind blew through the streets, vehicles splashed through the mud, and the iron shoes of horses and mules rang on the paving stones. Crowds of melancholy people plodded wearily along the footpaths, with here and there a drunken man among them.

"Do you see those brightly-lighted windows?" said the general. "Many of my old comrades-in-arms live about here, and I, who served longer, and suffered more than any of them, am walking on foot to the house of a woman of rather questionable reputation! A man, look you, who has thirteen bullets on his breast!... You don't believe it? Well, I can assure you it was entirely on my account that Pirogoff telegraphed to Paris, and left Sebastopol at the greatest risk during the siege. Nelaton, the Tuileries surgeon, demanded a safe conduct, in the name of science, into the besieged city in order to attend my wounds. The government knows all about it. 'That's the Ivolgin with thirteen bullets in him!' That's how they speak of me.... Do you see that house, prince? One of my old friends lives on the first floor, with his large family. In this and five other houses, three overlooking Nevsky, two in the Morskaya, are all that remain of my personal friends. Nina Alexandrovna gave them up long ago, but I keep in touch with them still... I may say I find refreshment in this little coterie, in thus meeting my old acquaintances and subordinates, who worship me still, in spite of all. General Sokolovitch (by the way, I have not called on him lately, or seen Anna Fedorovna)... You know, my dear prince, when a person does not receive company himself, he gives up going to other people's houses involuntarily. And yet... well... you look as if you didn't believe me.... Well now, why should I not present the son of my old friend and companion to this delightful family–General Ivolgin and

Prince Muishkin? You will see a lovely girl–what am I saying–a lovely girl? No, indeed, two, three! Ornaments of this city and of society: beauty, education, culture–the woman question–poetry–everything! Added to which is the fact that each one will have a dot of at least eighty thousand roubles. No bad thing, eh?... In a word I absolutely must introduce you to them: it is a duty, an obligation. General Ivolgin and Prince Muishkin. Tableau!"

"At once? Now? You must have forgotten..." began the prince.

"No, I have forgotten nothing. Come! This is the house–up this magnificent staircase. I am surprised not to see the porter, but .... it is a holiday... and the man has gone off... Drunken fool! Why have they not got rid of him? Sokolovitch owes all the happiness he has had in the service and in his private life to me, and me alone, but... here we are."

The prince followed quietly, making no further objection for fear of irritating the old man. At the same time he fervently hoped that General Sokolovitch and his family would fade away like a mirage in the desert, so that the visitors could escape, by merely returning downstairs. But to his horror he saw that General Ivolgin was quite familiar with the house, and really seemed to have friends there. At every step he named some topographical or biographical detail that left nothing to be desired on the score of accuracy. When they arrived at last, on the first floor, and the general turned to ring the bell to the right, the prince decided to run away, but a curious incident stopped him momentarily.

"You have made a mistake, general," said he. "The name on the door is Koulakoff, and you were going to see General Sokolovitch."

"Koulakoff... Koulakoff means nothing. This is Sokolovitch's flat, and I am ringing at his door.... What do I care for Koulakoff?... Here comes someone to open."

In fact, the door opened directly, and the

footman informed the visitors that the family were all away.

"What a pity! What a pity! It's just my luck!" repeated Ardalion Alexandrovitch over and over again, in regretful tones. "When your master and mistress return, my man, tell them that General Ivolgin and Prince Muishkin desired to present themselves, and that they were extremely sorry, excessively grieved..."

Just then another person belonging to the household was seen at the back of the hall. It was a woman of some forty years, dressed in sombre colours, probably a housekeeper or a governess. Hearing the names she came forward with a look of suspicion on her face.

"Marie Alexandrovna is not at home," said she, staring hard at the general. "She has gone to her mother's, with Alexandra Michailovna."

"Alexandra Michailovna out, too! How disappointing! Would you believe it, I am always so unfortunate! May I most respectfully ask you to present my compliments to Alexandra Michailovna, and remind her... tell her, that with my whole heart I wish for her what she wished for herself on Thursday evening, while she was listening to Chopin's Ballade. She will remember. I wish it with all sincerity. General Ivolgin and Prince Muishkin!"

The woman's face changed; she lost her suspicious expression.

"I will not fail to deliver your message," she replied, and bowed them out.

As they went downstairs the general regretted repeatedly that he had failed to introduce the prince to his friends.

"You know I am a bit of a poet," said he. "Have you noticed it? The poetic soul, you know." Then he added suddenly– "But after all... after all I believe we made a mistake this time! I remember that the Sokolovitch's live in another house, and what is more, they are just now in Moscow.

Yes, I certainly was at fault. However, it is of no consequence."

"Just tell me," said the prince in reply, "may I count still on your assistance? Or shall I go on alone to see Nastasia Philipovna?"

"Count on my assistance? Go alone? How can you ask me that question, when it is a matter on which the fate of my family so largely depends? You don't know Ivolgin, my friend. To trust Ivolgin is to trust a rock; that's how the first squadron I commanded spoke of me. 'Depend upon Ivolgin,' said they all, 'he is as steady as a rock.' But, excuse me, I must just call at a house on our way, a house where I have found consolation and help in all my trials for years."

"You are going home?"

"No... I wish... to visit Madame Terentieff, the widow of Captain Terentieff, my old subordinate and friend. She helps me to keep up my courage, and to bear the trials of my domestic life, and as I have an extra burden on my mind today..."

"It seems to me," interrupted the prince, "that I was foolish to trouble you just now. However, at present you... Good-bye!"

"Indeed, you must not go away like that, young man, you must not!" cried the general. "My friend here is a widow, the mother of a family; her words come straight from her heart, and find an echo in mine. A visit to her is merely an affair of a few minutes; I am quite at home in her house. I will have a wash, and dress, and then we can drive to the Grand Theatre. Make up your mind to spend the evening with me.... We are just there–that's the house... Why, Colia! you here! Well, is Marfa Borisovna at home or have you only just come?"

"Oh no! I have been here a long while," replied Colia, who was at the front door when the general met him. "I am keeping Hippolyte company. He is worse, and has been in bed all day. I came down to buy some cards. Marfa Borisovna expects you. But what a state you are in, father!" added the boy, noticing his father's unsteady gait. "Well, let us go in."

On meeting Colia the prince determined to accompany the general, though he made up his mind to stay as short a time as possible. He wanted Colia, but firmly resolved to leave the general behind. He could not forgive himself for being so simple as to imagine that Ivolgin would be of any use. The three climbed up the long staircase until they reached the fourth floor where Madame Terentieff lived.

"You intend to introduce the prince?" asked Colia, as they went up.

"Yes, my boy. I wish to present him: General Ivolgin and Prince Muishkin! But what's the matter?... what?... How is Marfa Borisovna?"

"You know, father, you would have done much better not to come at all! She is ready to eat you up! You have not shown yourself since the day before yesterday and she is expecting the money. Why did you promise her any? You are always the same! Well, now you will have to get out of it as best you can."

They stopped before a somewhat low doorway on the fourth floor. Ardalion Alexandrovitch, evidently much out of countenance, pushed Muishkin in front.

"I will wait here," he stammered. "I should like to surprise her. ...."

Colia entered first, and as the door stood open, the mistress of the house peeped out. The surprise of the general's imagination fell very flat, for she at once began to address him in terms of reproach.

Marfa Borisovna was about forty years of age. She wore a dressing-jacket, her feet were in slippers, her face painted, and her hair was in dozens of small plaits. No sooner did she catch sight of Ardalion Alexandrovitch than she screamed:

"There he is, that wicked, mean wretch! I knew it was he! My heart misgave me!"

The old man tried to put a good face on the affair.

"Come, let us go in–it's all right," he whispered in the prince's ear.

But it was more serious than he wished to think. As soon as the visitors had crossed the low dark hall, and entered the narrow reception-room, furnished with half a dozen cane chairs, and two small card-tables, Madame Terentieff, in the shrill tones habitual to her, continued her stream of invectives.

"Are you not ashamed? Are you not ashamed? You barbarian! You tyrant! You have robbed me of all I possessed–you have sucked my bones to the marrow. How long shall I be your victim? Shameless, dishonourable man!"

"Marfa Borisovna! Marfa Borisovna! Here is... the Prince Muishkin! General Ivolgin and Prince Muishkin," stammered the disconcerted old man.

"Would you believe," said the mistress of the house, suddenly addressing the prince, "would you believe that that man has not even spared my orphan children? He has stolen everything I possessed, sold everything, pawned everything; he has left me nothing–nothing! What am I to do with your IOU's, you cunning, unscrupulous rogue? Answer, devourer! answer, heart of stone! How shall I feed my orphans? with what shall I nourish them? And now he has come, he is drunk! He can scarcely stand. How, oh how, have I offended the Almighty, that He should bring this curse upon me! Answer, you worthless villain, answer!"

But this was too much for the general.

"Here are twenty-five roubles, Marfa Borisovna... it is all that I can give... and I owe even these to the prince's generosity–my noble friend. I have been cruelly deceived. Such is... life... Now... Excuse me, I am very weak," he continued, standing in the centre of the room, and bowing to all sides. "I am faint; excuse me! Lenotchka... a cushion... my dear!"

Lenotchka, a little girl of eight, ran to fetch

the cushion at once, and placed it on the rickety old sofa. The general meant to have said much more, but as soon as he had stretched himself out, he turned his face to the wall, and slept the sleep of the just.

With a grave and ceremonious air, Marfa Borisovna motioned the prince to a chair at one of the card-tables. She seated herself opposite, leaned her right cheek on her hand, and sat in silence, her eyes fixed on Muishkin, now and again sighing deeply. The three children, two little girls and a boy, Lenotchka being the eldest, came and leant on the table and also stared steadily at him. Presently Colia appeared from the adjoining room.

"I am very glad indeed to have met you here, Colia," said the prince. "Can you do something for me? I must see Nastasia Philipovna, and I asked Ardalion Alexandrovitch just now to take me to her house, but he has gone to sleep, as you see. Will you show me the way, for I do not know the street? I have the address, though; it is close to the Grand Theatre."

"Nastasia Philipovna? She does not live there, and to tell you the truth my father has never been to her house! It is strange that you should have depended on him! She lives near Wladimir Street, at the Five Corners, and it is quite close by. Will you go directly? It is just half-past nine. I will show you the way with pleasure."

Colia and the prince went off together. Alas! the latter had no money to pay for a cab, so they were obliged to walk.

"I should have liked to have taken you to see Hippolyte," said Colia. "He is the eldest son of the lady you met just now, and was in the next room. He is ill, and has been in bed all day. But he is rather strange, and extremely sensitive, and I thought he might be upset considering the circumstances in which you came... Somehow it touches me less, as it concerns my father, while it is **his**mother. That, of course, makes a great difference. What is a terrible disgrace to a woman, does not disgrace a man, at least not in the same way. Perhaps public opinion is wrong in condemning one sex, and excusing the other. Hippolyte is an extremely clever boy, but so prejudiced. He is really a slave to his opinions."

"Do you say he is consumptive?"

"Yes. It really would be happier for him to die young. If I were in his place I should certainly long for death. He is unhappy about his brother and sisters, the children you saw. If it were possible, if we only had a little money, we should leave our respective families, and live together in a little apartment of our own. It is our dream. But, do you know, when I was talking over your affair with him, he was angry, and said that anyone who did not call out a man who had given him a blow was a coward. He is very irritable to-day, and I left off arguing the matter with him. So Nastasia Philipovna has invited you to go and see her?"

"To tell the truth, she has not."

"Then how do you come to be going there?" cried Colia, so much astonished that he stopped short in the middle of the pavement. "And... and are you going to her 'At Home' in that costume?"

"I don't know, really, whether I shall be allowed in at all. If she will receive me, so much the better. If not, the matter is ended. As to my clothes–what can I do?"

"Are you going there for some particular reason, or only as a way of getting into her society, and that of her friends?"

"No, I have really an object in going... That is, I am going on business it is difficult to explain, but..."

"Well, whether you go on business or not is your affair, I do not want to know. The only important thing, in my eyes, is that you should not be going there simply for the pleasure of spending your evening in such company–cocottes, generals, usurers! If that were the case I should despise and laugh at you. There are terribly few honest people here, and hardly any whom one can respect, although people put on airs–Varia especially! Have you noticed, prince, how many adventurers there are nowadays? Especially here, in our dear Russia. How it has happened I never can understand. There used to be a certain amount of solidity in all things, but now what happens? Everything is exposed to the public gaze, veils are thrown back, every wound is probed by careless fingers. We are for ever present at an orgy of scandalous revelations. Parents blush when they remember their old-fashioned morality. At Moscow lately a father was heard urging his son to stop at nothing–at nothing, mind you!–to get money! The press seized upon the story, of course, and now it is public property. Look at my father, the general! See what he is, and yet, I assure you, he is an honest man! Only... he drinks too much, and his morals are not all we could desire. Yes, that's true! I pity him, to tell the truth, but I dare not say so, because everybody would laugh at me–but I do pity him! And who are the really clever men, after all? Money-grubbers, every one of them, from the first to the last. Hippolyte finds excuses for money-lending, and says it is a necessity. He talks about the economic movement, and the ebb and flow of capital; the devil knows what he means. It makes me angry to hear him talk so, but he is soured by his troubles. Just imagine–the general keeps his mother–but she lends him money! She lends it for a week or ten days at very high interest! Isn't it disgusting? And then, you would hardly believe it, but my mother–Nina Alexandrovna–helps Hippolyte in all sorts of ways, sends him money and clothes. She even goes as far as helping the children, through Hippolyte, because their mother cares nothing about them, and Varia does the same."

"Well, just now you said there were no honest nor good people about, that there were only money-grubbers–and here they are quite close at hand, these honest and good people, your mother and Varia! I think there is a good deal of moral strength in helping people in such circumstances."

"Varia does it from pride, and likes showing off, and giving herself airs. As to my mother, I really do admire her–yes, and honour her. Hippolyte, hardened as he is, feels it. He laughed at first, and thought it vulgar of her–but now, he is sometimes quite touched and overcome by her kindness. H'm! You call that being strong and good? I will remember that! Gania knows nothing about it. He would say that it was encouraging vice."

"Ah, Gania knows nothing about it? It seems there are many things that Gania does not know," exclaimed the prince, as he considered Colia's last words.

"Do you know, I like you very much indeed, prince? I shall never forget about this afternoon."

"I like you too, Colia."

"Listen to me! You are going to live here, are you not?" said Colia. "I mean to get something to do directly, and earn money. Then shall we three live together? You, and I, and Hippolyte? We will hire a flat, and let the general come and visit us. What do you say?"

"It would be very pleasant," returned the prince. "But we must see. I am really rather worried just now. What! are we there already? Is that the house? What a long flight of steps! And there's a porter! Well, Colia I don't know what will come of it all."

The prince seemed quite distracted for the moment.

"You must tell me all about it tomorrow! Don't be afraid. I wish you success; we agree so entirely that I can do so, although I do not understand why you are here. Good-bye!" cried Colia excitedly. "Now I will rush back and tell Hippolyte all about our plans and proposals! But as to your getting in–don't be in the least afraid. You will see her. She is so original about everything. It's the first floor. The porter will show you."

CHAPTER THIRTEEN

THE PRINCE WAS VERY nervous as he reached the outer door; but he did his best to encourage himself with the reflection that the worst thing that could happen to him would be that he would not be received, or, perhaps, received, then laughed at for coming.

But there was another question, which terrified him considerably, and that was: what was he going to do when he **did** get in? And to this question he could fashion no satisfactory reply.

If only he could find an opportunity of coming close up to Nastasia Philipovna and saying to her: “Don’t ruin yourself by marrying this man. He does not love you, he only loves your money. He told me so himself, and so did Aglaya Ivanovna, and I have come on purpose to warn you”–but even that did not seem quite a legitimate or practicable thing to do. Then, again, there was another delicate question, to which he could not find an answer; dared not, in fact, think of it; but at the very idea of which he trembled and blushed. However, in spite of all his fears and heart-quakings he went in, and asked for Nastasia Philipovna.

Nastasia occupied a medium-sized, but distinctly tasteful, flat, beautifully furnished and arranged. At one period of these five years of Petersburg life, Totski had certainly not spared his expenditure upon her. He had calculated upon her eventual love, and tried to tempt her with a lavish outlay upon comforts and luxuries, knowing too well how easily the heart accustoms itself to comforts, and how difficult it is to tear one's self away from luxuries which have become habitual and, little by little, indispensable.

Nastasia did not reject all this, she even loved her comforts and luxuries, but, strangely enough, never became, in the least degree, dependent upon them, and always gave the impression that she could do just as well without them. In fact, she went so far as to inform Totski on several occasions that such was the case, which the latter gentleman considered a very unpleasant communication indeed.

But, of late, Totski had observed many strange and original features and characteristics in Nastasia, which he had neither known nor reckoned upon in former times, and some of these fascinated him, even now, in spite of the fact that all his old calculations with regard to her were long ago cast to the winds.

A maid opened the door for the prince (Nastasia's servants were all females) and, to his surprise, received his request to announce him to her mistress without any astonishment. Neither his dirty boots, nor his wide-brimmed hat, nor his sleeveless cloak, nor his evident confusion of manner, produced the least impression upon her. She helped him off with his cloak, and begged him to wait a moment in the anteroom while she announced him.

The company assembled at Nastasia Philipovna's consisted of none but her most intimate friends, and formed a very small party in comparison with her usual gatherings on this anniversary.

In the first place there were present Totski, and General Epanchin. They were both highly amiable, but both appeared to be labouring under a half-hidden feeling of anxiety as to the result of Nastasia's deliberations with regard to Gania, which result was to be made public this evening.

Then, of course, there was Gania who was by no means so amiable as his elders, but stood apart, gloomy, and miserable, and silent. He had determined not to bring Varia with him; but Nastasia had not even asked after her, though no sooner had he arrived than she had reminded him of the episode between himself and the prince. The general, who had heard nothing of it before, began to listen with some interest, while Gania, drily, but with perfect candour, went through the whole history, including the fact of his apology to the prince. He finished by declaring that the prince was a most extraordinary man, and goodness knows why he had been considered an idiot hitherto, for he was very far from being one.

Nastasia listened to all this with great interest; but the conversation soon turned to Rogojin and his visit, and this theme proved of the greatest attraction to both Totski and the general.

Ptitsin was able to afford some particulars

as to Rogojin's conduct since the afternoon. He declared that he had been busy finding money for the latter ever since, and up to nine o'clock, Rogojin having declared that he must absolutely have a hundred thousand roubles by the evening. He added that Rogojin was drunk, of course; but that he thought the money would be forthcoming, for the excited and intoxicated rapture of the fellow impelled him to give any interest or premium that was asked of him, and there were several others engaged in beating up the money, also.

All this news was received by the company with somewhat gloomy interest. Nastasia was silent, and would not say what she thought about it. Gania was equally uncommunicative. The general seemed the most anxious of all, and decidedly uneasy. The present of pearls which he had prepared with so much joy in the morning had been accepted but coldly, and Nastasia had smiled rather disagreeably as she took it from him. Ferdishenko was the only person present in good spirits.

Totski himself, who had the reputation of being a capital talker, and was usually the life and soul of these entertainments, was as silent as any on this occasion, and sat in a state of, for him, most uncommon perturbation.

The rest of the guests (an old tutor or schoolmaster, goodness knows why invited; a young man, very timid, and shy and silent; a rather loud woman of about forty, apparently an actress; and a very pretty, well-dressed German lady who hardly said a word all the evening) not only had no gift for enlivening the proceedings, but hardly knew what to say for themselves when addressed. Under these circumstances the arrival of the prince came almost as a godsend.

The announcement of his name gave rise to some surprise and to some smiles, especially when it became evident, from Nastasia's astonished look, that she had not thought of inviting him. But her astonishment once over, Nastasia showed such satisfaction that all prepared to greet the prince with cordial smiles of welcome.

"Of course," remarked General Epanchin, "he does this out of pure innocence. It's a little dangerous, perhaps, to encourage this sort of freedom; but it is rather a good thing that he has arrived just at this moment. He may enliven us a little with his originalities."

"Especially as he asked himself," said Ferdishenko.

"What's that got to do with it?" asked the general, who loathed Ferdishenko.

"Why, he must pay toll for his entrance," explained the latter.

"H'm! Prince Muishkin is not Ferdishenko," said the general, impatiently. This worthy gentleman could never quite reconcile himself to the idea of meeting Ferdishenko in society, and on an equal footing.

"Oh general, spare Ferdishenko!" replied the other, smiling. "I have special privileges."

"What do you mean by special privileges?"

"Once before I had the honour of stating them to the company. I will repeat the explanation to-day for your excellency's benefit. You see, excellency, all the world is witty and clever except myself. I am neither. As a kind of compensation I am allowed to tell the truth, for it is a well-known fact that only stupid people tell 'the truth.' Added to this, I am a spiteful man, just because I am not clever. If I am offended or injured I bear it quite patiently until the man injuring me meets with some misfortune. Then I remember, and take my revenge. I return the injury sevenfold, as Ivan Petrovitch Ptitsin says. (Of course he never does so himself.) Excellency, no doubt you recollect Kryloff's fable, 'The Lion and the Ass'? Well now, that's you and I. That fable was written precisely for us."

"You seem to be talking nonsense again, Ferdishenko," growled the general.

"What is the matter, excellency? I know

how to keep my place. When I said just now that we, you and I, were the lion and the ass of Kryloff's fable, of course it is understood that I take the role of the ass. Your excellency is the lion of which the fable remarks:

'A mighty lion, terror of the woods, Was shorn of his great prowess by old age.'

And I, your excellency, am the ass."

"I am of your opinion on that last point," said Ivan Fedorovitch, with ill-concealed irritation.

All this was no doubt extremely coarse, and moreover it was premeditated, but after all Ferdishenko had persuaded everyone to accept him as a buffoon.

"If I am admitted and tolerated here," he had said one day, "it is simply because I talk in this way. How can anyone possibly receive such a man as I am? I quite understand. Now, could I, a Ferdishenko, be allowed to sit shoulder to shoulder with a clever man like Afanasy Ivanovitch? There is one explanation, only one. I am given the position because it is so entirely inconceivable!"

But these vulgarities seemed to please Nastasia Philipovna, although too often they were both rude and offensive. Those who wished to go to her house were forced to put up with Ferdishenko. Possibly the latter was not mistaken in imagining that he was received simply in order to annoy Totski, who disliked him extremely. Gania also was often made the butt of the jester's sarcasms, who used this method of keeping in Nastasia Philipovna's good graces.

"The prince will begin by singing us a fashionable ditty," remarked Ferdishenko, and looked at the mistress of the house, to see what she would say.

"I don't think so, Ferdishenko; please be quiet," answered Nastasia Philipovna dryly.

"A-ah! if he is to be under special patronage, I withdraw my claws."

But Nastasia Philipovna had now risen and advanced to meet the prince.

"I was so sorry to have forgotten to ask you to come, when I saw you," she said, "and I am delighted to be able to thank you personally now, and to express my pleasure at your resolution."

So saying she gazed into his eyes, longing to see whether she could make any guess as to the explanation of his motive in coming to her house. The prince would very likely have made some reply to her kind words, but he was so dazzled by her appearance that he could not speak.

Nastasia noticed this with satisfaction. She was in full dress this evening; and her appearance was certainly calculated to impress all beholders. She took his hand and led him towards her other guests. But just before they reached the drawing-room door, the prince stopped her, and hurriedly and in great agitation whispered to her:

"You are altogether perfection; even your pallor and thinness are perfect; one could not wish you otherwise. I did so wish to come and see you. I–forgive me, please–"

"Don't apologize," said Nastasia, laughing; "you spoil the whole originality of the thing. I think what they say about you must be true, that you are so original.–So you think me perfection, do you?"

"Yes."

"H'm! Well, you may be a good reader of riddles but you are wrong **there**, at all events. I'll remind you of this, tonight."

Nastasia introduced the prince to her guests, to most of whom he was already known.

Totski immediately made some amiable remark. All seemed to brighten up at once, and the conversation became general. Nastasia made the prince sit down next to herself.

"Dear me, there's nothing so very curious about the prince dropping in, after all," remarked Ferdishenko.

"It's quite a clear case," said the hitherto silent Gania. "I have watched the prince almost all day, ever since the moment when he first saw Nastasia Philipovna's portrait, at General Epanchin's. I remember thinking at the time what I am now pretty sure of; and what, I may say in passing, the prince confessed to myself."

Gania said all this perfectly seriously, and without the slightest appearance of joking; indeed, he seemed strangely gloomy.

"I did not confess anything to you," said the prince, blushing. "I only answered your question."

"Bravo! That's frank, at any rate!" shouted Ferdishenko, and there was general laughter.

"Oh prince, prince! I never should have thought it of you;" said General Epanchin. "And I imagined you a philosopher! Oh, you silent fellows!"

"Judging from the fact that the prince blushed at this innocent joke, like a young girl, I should think that he must, as an honourable man, harbour the noblest intentions," said the old toothless schoolmaster, most unexpectedly; he had not so much as opened his mouth before. This remark provoked general mirth, and the old fellow himself laughed loudest of the lot, but ended with a stupendous fit of coughing.

Nastasia Philipovna, who loved originality and drollery of all kinds, was apparently very fond of this old man, and rang the bell for more tea to stop his coughing. It was now half-past ten o'clock.

"Gentlemen, wouldn't you like a little champagne now?" she asked. "I have it all ready; it will cheer us up–do now–no ceremony!"

This invitation to drink, couched, as it was, in such informal terms, came very strangely from Nastasia Philipovna. Her usual entertainments were not quite like this; there was more style about them. However, the wine was not refused; each guest took a glass excepting Gania, who drank nothing.

It was extremely difficult to account for Nastasia's strange condition of mind, which became more evident each moment, and which none could avoid noticing.

She took her glass, and vowed she would empty it three times that evening. She was hysterical, and laughed aloud every other minute with no apparent reason–the next moment relapsing into gloom and thoughtfulness.

Some of her guests suspected that she must be ill; but concluded at last that she was expecting something, for she continued to look at her watch impatiently and unceasingly; she was most absent and strange.

"You seem to be a little feverish tonight," said the actress.

"Yes; I feel quite ill. I have been obliged to put on this shawl–I feel so cold," replied Nastasia. She certainly had grown very pale, and every now and then she tried to suppress a trembling in her limbs.

"Had we not better allow our hostess to

retire?" asked Totski of the general.

"Not at all, gentlemen, not at all! Your presence is absolutely necessary to me tonight," said Nastasia, significantly.

As most of those present were aware that this evening a certain very important decision was to be taken, these words of Nastasia Philipovna's appeared to be fraught with much hidden interest. The general and Totski exchanged looks; Gania fidgeted convulsively in his chair.

"Let's play at some game!" suggested the actress.

"I know a new and most delightful game, added Ferdishenko.

"What is it?" asked the actress.

"Well, when we tried it we were a party of people, like this, for instance; and somebody proposed that each of us, without leaving his place at the table, should relate something about himself. It had to be something that he really and honestly considered the very worst action he had ever committed in his life. But he was to be honest–that was the chief point! He wasn't to be allowed to lie."

"What an extraordinary idea!" said the general.

"That's the beauty of it, general!"

"It's a funny notion," said Totski, "and yet quite natural–it's only a new way of boasting."

"Perhaps that is just what was so fascinating about it."

"Why, it would be a game to cry over–not to laugh at!" said the actress.

"Did it succeed?" asked Nastasia Philipovna. "Come, let's try it, let's try it; we really are not quite so jolly as we might be–let's try it! We may like it; it's original, at all events!"

"Yes," said Ferdishenko; "it's a good idea–come along–the men begin. Of course no one need tell a story if he prefers to be disobliging. We must draw lots! Throw your slips of paper, gentlemen, into this hat, and the prince shall draw for turns. It's a very simple game; all you have to do is to tell the story of the worst action of your life. It's as simple as anything. I'll prompt anyone who forgets the rules!"

No one liked the idea much. Some smiled, some frowned; some objected, but faintly, not wishing to oppose Nastasia's wishes; for this new idea seemed to be rather well received by her. She was still in an excited, hysterical state, laughing convulsively at nothing and everything. Her eyes were blazing, and her cheeks showed two bright red spots against the white. The melancholy appearance of some of her guests seemed to add to her sarcastic humour, and perhaps the very cynicism and cruelty of the game proposed by Ferdishenko pleased her. At all events she was attracted by the idea, and gradually her guests came round to her side; the thing was original, at least, and might turn out to be amusing. "And supposing it's something that one–one can't speak about before ladies?" asked the timid and silent young man.

"Why, then of course, you won't say anything about it. As if there are not plenty of sins to your score without the need of those!" said Ferdishenko.

"But I really don't know which of my actions is the worst," said the lively actress.

"Ladies are exempted if they like."

"And how are you to know that one isn't lying? And if one lies the whole point of the game is lost," said Gania.

"Oh, but think how delightful to hear how one's friends lie! Besides you needn't be afraid, Gania; everybody knows what your worst action is without the need of any lying on your part. Only think, gentlemen,"–and Ferdishenko here grew quite enthusiastic, "only think with what eyes we shall observe one another tomorrow, after our tales have been told!"

"But surely this is a joke, Nastasia Philipovna?" asked Totski. "You don't really mean us to play this game."

"Whoever is afraid of wolves had better not

go into the wood," said Nastasia, smiling.

"But, pardon me, Mr. Ferdishenko, is it possible to make a game out of this kind of thing?" persisted Totski, growing more and more uneasy. "I assure you it can't be a success."

"And why not? Why, the last time I simply told straight off about how I stole three roubles."

"Perhaps so; but it is hardly possible that you told it so that it seemed like truth, or so that you were believed. And, as Gavrila Ardalionovitch has said, the least suggestion of a falsehood takes all point out of the game. It seems to me that sincerity, on the other hand, is only possible if combined with a kind of bad taste that would be utterly out of place here."

"How subtle you are, Afanasy Ivanovitch! You astonish me," cried Ferdishenko. "You will remark, gentlemen, that in saying that I could not recount the story of my theft so as to be believed, Afanasy Ivanovitch has very ingeniously implied that I am not capable of thieving–(it would have been bad taste to say so openly); and all the time he is probably firmly convinced, in his own mind, that I am very well capable of it! But now, gentlemen, to business! Put in your slips, ladies and gentlemen–is yours in, Mr. Totski? So–then we are all ready; now prince, draw, please." The prince silently put his hand into the hat, and drew the names. Ferdishenko was first, then Ptitsin, then the general, Totski next, his own fifth, then Gania, and so on; the ladies did not draw.

"Oh, dear! oh, dear!" cried Ferdishenko. "I did so hope the prince would come out first, and then the general. Well, gentlemen, I suppose I must set a good example! What vexes me much is that I am such an insignificant creature that it matters nothing to anybody whether I have done bad actions or not! Besides, which am I to choose? It's an **embarras de richesse**. Shall I tell how

I became a thief on one occasion only, to convince Afanasy Ivanovitch that it is possible to steal without being a thief?"

"Do go on, Ferdishenko, and don't make unnecessary preface, or you'll never finish," said Nastasia Philipovna. All observed how irritable and cross she had become since her last burst of laughter; but none the less obstinately did she stick to her absurd whim about this new game. Totski sat looking miserable enough. The general lingered over his champagne, and seemed to be thinking of some story for the time when his turn should come.

Part One

CHAPTER FOURTEEN

"I HAVE NO WIT, Nastasia Philipovna," began Ferdishenko, "and therefore I talk too much, perhaps. Were I as witty, now, as Mr. Totski or the general, I should probably have sat silent all the evening, as they have. Now, prince, what do you think?–are there not far more thieves than honest men in this world? Don't you think we may say there does not exist a single person so honest that he has never stolen anything whatever in his life?"

"What a silly idea," said the actress. "Of course it is not the case. I have never stolen anything, for one."

"H'm! very well, Daria Alexeyevna; you have not stolen anything–agreed. But how about the prince, now–look how he is blushing!"

"I think you are partially right, but you exaggerate," said the prince, who had certainly blushed up, of a sudden, for some reason or other.

"Ferdishenko–either tell us your story, or be quiet, and mind your own business. You exhaust all patience," cuttingly and irritably remarked Nastasia Philipovna.

"Immediately, immediately! As for my story, gentlemen, it is too stupid and absurd to tell you.

"I assure you I am not a thief, and yet I have stolen; I cannot explain why. It was at Semeon Ivanovitch Ishenka's country house, one Sunday. He had a dinner party. After dinner the men stayed at the table over their wine. It struck me to ask the daughter of the house to play something on the piano; so I passed through the corner room to join the ladies. In that room, on Maria Ivanovna's writing-table, I observed a three-rouble note. She must have taken it out for some purpose, and left it lying there. There was no one about. I took up the note and put it in my pocket; why, I can't say. I don't know what possessed me to do it, but it was done, and I went quickly back to the dining-room and reseated myself at the dinner-table. I sat and waited there in a great state of excitement. I talked hard, and told lots of stories, and laughed like mad; then I joined the ladies.

"In half an hour or so the loss was discovered, and the servants were being put under examination. Daria, the housemaid was suspected. I exhibited the greatest interest and sympathy, and I remember that poor Daria quite lost her head, and that I began assuring her, before everyone, that I would guarantee her forgiveness on the part of her mistress, if she would confess her guilt. They all stared at the girl, and I remember a wonderful attraction in the reflection that here was I sermonizing away, with the money in my own pocket all the while. I went and spent the three roubles that very evening at a restaurant. I went in and asked for a bottle of Lafite, and drank it up; I wanted to be rid of the money.

"I did not feel much remorse either then or afterwards; but I would not repeat the performance–believe it or not as you please. There–that's all."

"Only, of course that's not nearly your worst action," said the actress, with evident dislike in her face.

"That was a psychological phenomenon, not an action," remarked Totski.

"And what about the maid?" asked Nastasia Philipovna, with undisguised contempt.

"Oh, she was turned out next day, of course. It's a very strict household, there!"

"And you allowed it?"

“I should think so, rather! I was not going to return and confess next day,” laughed Ferdishenko, who seemed a little surprised at the disagreeable impression which his story had made on all parties.

“How mean you were!” said Nastasia.

“Bah! you wish to hear a man tell of his worst actions, and you expect the story to come out goody-goody! One’s worst actions always are mean. We shall see what the general has to say for himself now. All is not gold that glitters, you know; and because a man keeps his carriage he need not be specially virtuous, I assure you, all sorts of people keep carriages. And by what means?”

In a word, Ferdishenko was very angry and rapidly forgetting himself; his whole face was drawn with passion. Strange as it may appear, he had expected much better success for his story. These little errors of taste on Ferdishenko’s part occurred very frequently. Nastasia trembled with rage, and looked fixedly at him, whereupon he relapsed into alarmed silence. He realized that he had gone a little too far.

"Had we not better end this game?" asked Totski.

"It's my turn, but I plead exemption," said Ptitsin.

"You don't care to oblige us?" asked Nastasia.

"I cannot, I assure you. I confess I do not understand how anyone can play this game."

"Then, general, it's your turn," continued Nastasia Philipovna, "and if you refuse, the whole game will fall through, which will disappoint me very much, for I was looking forward to relating a certain 'page of my own life.' I am only waiting for you and Afanasy Ivanovitch to have your turns, for I require the support of your example," she added, smiling.

"Oh, if you put it in that way," cried the general, excitedly, "I'm ready to tell the whole story of my life, but I must confess that I prepared a little story in anticipation of my turn."

Nastasia smiled amiably at him; but evidently her depression and irritability were increasing with every moment. Totski was dreadfully alarmed to hear her promise a revelation out of her own life.

"I, like everyone else," began the general, "have committed certain not altogether graceful actions, so to speak, during the course of my life. But the strangest thing of all in my case is, that I should consider the little anecdote which I am now about to give you as a confession of the worst of my 'bad actions.' It is thirty-five years since it all happened, and yet I cannot to this very day recall the circumstances without, as it were, a sudden pang at the heart.

"It was a silly affair–I was an ensign at the time. You know ensigns–their blood is boiling water, their circumstances generally penurious. Well, I had a servant Nikifor who used to do everything for me in my quarters, economized and managed for me, and even laid hands on anything he could find (belonging to other people), in order to augment our household goods; but a faithful, honest fellow all the same.

"I was strict, but just by nature. At that time we were stationed in a small town. I was quartered at an old widow's house, a lieutenant's widow of eighty years of age. She lived in a wretched little wooden house, and had not even a servant, so poor was she.

"Her relations had all died off–her husband was dead and buried forty years since; and a niece, who had lived with her and bullied her up to three years ago, was dead too; so that she was quite alone.

"Well, I was precious dull with her, especially as she was so childish that there was nothing to be got out of her. Eventually, she stole a fowl of mine; the business is a mystery to this day; but it could have been no one but herself. I requested to be quartered somewhere else, and was shifted to the other end of the town, to the house of a merchant with a large family, and a long beard, as I remember him. Nikifor and I were delighted to go; but the old lady was not pleased at our departure.

"Well, a day or two afterwards, when I returned from drill, Nikifor says to me: 'We oughtn't to have left our tureen with the old lady, I've nothing to serve the soup in.'

"I asked how it came about that the tureen had been left. Nikifor explained that the old lady refused to give it up, because, she said, we had broken her bowl, and she must have our tureen in place of it; she had declared that I had so arranged the matter with herself.

"This baseness on her part of course aroused my young blood to fever heat; I jumped up, and away I flew.

"I arrived at the old woman's house beside myself. She was sitting in a corner all alone, leaning her face on her hand. I fell on her like a clap of thunder. 'You old wretch!' I yelled and all that sort of thing, in real Russian style. Well, when I began cursing at her, a strange thing happened. I looked at her, and she stared back with her eyes starting out of her head, but she did not say a word. She seemed to sway about as she sat, and looked and looked at me in the strangest way. Well, I soon stopped swearing and looked closer at her, asked her questions, but not a word could I get out of her. The flies were buzzing about the room and only this sound broke the silence; the sun was setting outside; I didn't know what to make of it, so I went away.

"Before I reached home I was met and summoned to the major's, so that it was some while before I actually got there. When I came in, Nikifor met me. 'Have you heard, sir, that our old lady is dead?' '**dead**, when?' 'Oh, an hour and a half ago.' That meant nothing more nor less than that she was dying at the moment when I pounced on her and began abusing her.

"This produced a great effect upon me. I used to dream of the poor old woman at nights. I really am not superstitious, but two days after, I went to her funeral, and as time went on I thought more and more about her. I said to myself, 'This woman, this human being, lived to a great age. She had children, a husband and family, friends and relations; her household was busy and cheerful; she was surrounded by smiling faces; and then suddenly they are gone, and she is left alone like a solitary fly... like a fly, cursed with the burden of her age. At last, God calls her to Himself. At sunset, on a lovely summer's evening, my little old woman passes away–a thought, you will notice, which offers much food for reflection–and behold! instead of tears and prayers to start her on her last journey, she has insults and jeers from a young ensign, who stands before her with his hands in his pockets, making a terrible row about a soup tureen!' Of course I was to blame, and even now that I have time to look back at it calmly, I pity the poor old thing no less. I repeat that I wonder at myself, for after all I was not really responsible. Why did she take it into her head to die at that moment? But the more I thought of it, the more I felt the weight of it upon my mind; and I never got quite rid of the impression until I put a couple of old women into an almshouse and kept them there at my own expense. There, that's all. I repeat I dare say I have committed many a grievous sin in my day; but I cannot help always looking back upon this as the worst action I have ever perpetrated."

"H'm! and instead of a bad action, your excellency has detailed one of your noblest deeds," said Ferdishenko. "Ferdishenko is 'done.'"

"Dear me, general," said Nastasia Philipovna, absently, "I really never imagined you had such a good heart."

The general laughed with great satisfaction, and applied himself once more to the champagne.

It was now Totski's turn, and his story was awaited with great curiosity–while all eyes turned on Nastasia Philipovna, as though anticipating that his revelation must be connected somehow with her. Nastasia, during the whole of his story, pulled at the lace trimming of her sleeve, and never once glanced at the speaker. Totski was a handsome man, rather stout, with a very polite and dignified manner. He was always well dressed, and his linen was exquisite. He had plump white hands, and wore a magnificent diamond ring on one finger.

"What simplifies the duty before me considerably, in my opinion," he began, "is that I am bound to recall and relate the very worst action of my life. In such circumstances there can, of course, be no doubt. One's conscience very soon informs one what is the proper narrative to tell. I admit, that among the many silly and thoughtless actions of my life, the memory of one comes prominently forward and reminds me that it lay long like a stone on my heart. Some twenty years since, I paid a visit to Platon Ordintzeff at his country-house. He had just been elected marshal of the nobility, and had come there with his young wife for the winter holidays. Anfisa Alexeyevna's birthday came off just then, too, and there were two balls arranged. At that time Dumas-fils' beautiful work, **La Dame aux Camélias**–a novel which I consider imperishable–had just come into fashion. In the provinces all the ladies were in raptures over it, those who had read it, at least. Camellias were all the fashion. Everyone inquired for them, everybody wanted them; and a grand lot of camellias are to be got in a country town–as you all know–and two balls to provide for!

"Poor Peter Volhofskoi was desperately in love with Anfisa Alexeyevna. I don't know whether there was anything–I mean I don't know whether he could possibly have indulged in any hope. The poor fellow was beside himself to get her a bouquet of camellias. Countess Sotski and Sophia Bespalova, as everyone knew, were coming with white camellia bouquets. Anfisa wished for red ones, for effect. Well, her husband Platon was driven desperate to find some. And the day before the ball, Anfisa's rival snapped up the only red camellias to be had in the place, from under Platon's nose, and Platon–wretched man–was done for. Now if Peter had only been able to step in at this moment with a red bouquet, his little hopes might have made gigantic strides. A woman's gratitude under such circumstances would have been boundless–but it was practically an impossibility.

"The night before the ball I met Peter, looking radiant. 'What is it?' I ask. 'I've found them, Eureka!' 'No! where, where?' 'At Ekshaisk (a little town fifteen miles off) there's a rich old merchant, who keeps a lot of canaries, has no children, and he and his wife are devoted to flowers. He's got some camellias.' 'And what if he won't let you have them?' 'I'll go on my knees and implore till I get them. I won't go away.' 'When shall you start?' 'Tomorrow morning at five o'clock.' 'Go on,' I said, 'and good luck to you.'

"I was glad for the poor fellow, and went home. But an idea got hold of me somehow. I don't know how. It was nearly two in the morning. I rang the bell and ordered the coachman to be waked up and sent to me. He came. I gave him a tip of fifteen roubles, and told him to get the carriage ready at once. In half an hour it was at the door. I got in and off we went.

"By five I drew up at the Ekshaisky inn. I waited there till dawn, and soon after six I was off, and at the old merchant Trepalaf's.

"'Camellias!' I said, 'father, save me, save me, let me have some camellias!' He was a tall, grey old man–a terrible-looking old gentleman. 'Not a bit of it,' he says. 'I won't.' Down I went on my knees. 'Don't say so, don't–think what you're doing!' I cried; 'it's a matter of life and death!' 'If that's the case, take them,' says he. So up I get, and cut such a bouquet of red camellias! He had a whole greenhouse full of them–lovely ones. The old fellow sighs. I pull out a hundred roubles. 'No, no!' says he, 'don't insult me that way.' 'Oh, if that's the case, give it to the village hospital,' I say. 'Ah,' he says, 'that's quite a different matter; that's good of you and generous. I'll pay it in there for you with pleasure.' I liked that old fellow, Russian to the core, **de la vraie souche**. I went home in raptures, but took another road in order to avoid Peter. Immediately on arriving I sent up the bouquet for Anfisa to see when she awoke.

"You may imagine her ecstasy, her gratitude. The wretched Platon, who had almost died since yesterday of the reproaches showered upon him, wept on my shoulder. Of course poor Peter had no chance after this.

"I thought he would cut my throat at first, and went about armed ready to meet him. But he took it differently; he fainted, and had brain fever and convulsions. A month after, when he had hardly recovered, he went off to the Crimea, and there he was shot.

"I assure you this business left me no peace for many a long year. Why did I do it? I was not in love with her myself; I'm afraid it was simply mischief–pure 'cussedness' on my part.

"If I hadn't seized that bouquet from under his nose he might have been alive now, and a happy man. He might have been successful in life, and never have gone to fight the Turks."

Totski ended his tale with the same dignity that had characterized its commencement.

Nastasia Philipovna's eyes were flashing in a most unmistakable way, now; and her lips were all a-quiver by the time Totski finished his story.

All present watched both of them with curiosity.

"You were right, Totski," said Nastasia, "it is a dull game and a stupid one. I'll just tell my story, as I promised, and then we'll play cards."

"Yes, but let's have the story first!" cried the general.

"Prince," said Nastasia Philipovna, unexpectedly turning to Muishkin, "here are my old friends, Totski and General Epanchin, who wish to marry me off. Tell me what you think. Shall I marry or not? As you decide, so shall it be."

Totski grew white as a sheet. The general was struck dumb. All present started and listened intently. Gania sat rooted to his chair.

"Marry whom?" asked the prince, faintly.

"Gavrila Ardalionovitch Ivolgin," said Nastasia, firmly and evenly.

There were a few seconds of dead silence.

The prince tried to speak, but could not form his words; a great weight seemed to lie upon his breast and suffocate him.

"N-no! don't marry him!" he whispered at last, drawing his breath with an effort.

"So be it, then. Gavrila Ardalionovitch," she spoke solemnly and forcibly, "you hear the prince's decision? Take it as my decision; and let that be the end of the matter for good and all."

"Nastasia Philipovna!" cried Totski, in a quaking voice.

"Nastasia Philipovna!" said the general, in persuasive but agitated tones.

Everyone in the room fidgeted in their places, and waited to see what was coming next.

"Well, gentlemen!" she continued, gazing around in apparent astonishment; "what do you all look so alarmed about? Why are you so upset?"

"But–recollect, Nastasia Philipovna," stammered Totski, "you gave a promise, quite a free one, and–and you might have spared us this. I am confused and bewildered, I know; but, in a word, at such a moment, and before company, and all so-so-irregular, finishing off a game with a serious matter like this, a matter of honour, and of heart, and–"

"I don't follow you, Afanasy Ivanovitch; you are losing your head. In the first place, what do you mean by 'before company'? Isn't the company good enough for you? And what's all that about 'a game'? I wished to tell my little story, and I told it! Don't you like it? You heard what I said to the prince? 'As you decide, so it shall be!' If he had said 'yes,' I should have given my consent! But he said 'no,' so I refused. Here was my whole life hanging on his one word! Surely I was serious enough?"

"The prince! What on earth has the prince got to do with it? Who the deuce is the prince?" cried the general, who could conceal his wrath no longer.

"The prince has this to do with it–that I see in him for the first time in all my life, a man endowed with real truthfulness of spirit, and I trust him. He trusted me at first sight, and I trust him!"

"It only remains for me, then, to thank Nastasia Philipovna for the great delicacy with which she has treated me," said Gania, as pale as death, and with quivering lips. "That is my plain duty, of course; but the prince–what has he to do in the matter?"

"I see what you are driving at," said Nastasia Philipovna. "You imply that the prince is after the seventy-five thousand roubles–I quite understand you. Mr. Totski, I forgot to say, 'Take your seventy-five thousand roubles'–I don't want them. I let you go free for nothing–take your freedom! You must need it. Nine years and three months' captivity is enough for anybody. Tomorrow I shall start afresh–today I am a free agent for the first time in my life.

"General, you must take your pearls back, too–give them to your wife–here they are! Tomorrow I shall leave this flat altogether, and then there'll be no more of these pleasant little social gatherings, ladies and gentlemen."

So saying, she scornfully rose from her seat as though to depart.

"Nastasia Philipovna! Nastasia Philipovna!"

The words burst involuntarily from every mouth. All present started up in bewildered excitement; all surrounded her; all had listened uneasily to her wild, disconnected sentences. All felt that something had happened, something had gone very far wrong indeed, but no one could make head or tail of the matter.

At this moment there was a furious ring at the bell, and a great knock at the door–exactly similar to the one which had startled the company at Gania's house in the afternoon.

"Ah, ah! here's the climax at last, at half-past twelve!" cried Nastasia Philipovna. "Sit down, gentlemen, I beg you. Something is about to happen."

So saying, she reseated herself; a strange smile played on her lips. She sat quite still, but watched the door in a fever of impatience.

"Rogojin and his hundred thousand roubles, no doubt of it," muttered Ptitsin to himself.

CHAPTER FIFTEEN

KATIA, THE MAID-SERVANT, made her appearance, terribly frightened.

"Goodness knows what it means, ma'am," she said. "There is a whole collection of men come–all tipsy–and want to see you. They say that 'it's Rogojin, and she knows all about it.'"

"It's all right, Katia, let them all in at once."

"Surely not **all**, ma'am? They seem so disorderly–it's dreadful to see them."

"Yes **all**, Katia, all–every one of them. Let

them in, or they'll come in whether you like or no. Listen! what a noise they are making! Perhaps you are offended, gentlemen, that I should receive such guests in your presence? I am very sorry, and ask your forgiveness, but it cannot be helped–and I should be very grateful if you could all stay and witness this climax. However, just as you please, of course."

The guests exchanged glances; they were annoyed and bewildered by the episode; but it was clear enough that all this had been pre-arranged and expected by Nastasia Philipovna, and that there was no use in trying to stop her now–for she was little short of insane.

Besides, they were naturally inquisitive to see what was to happen. There was nobody who would be likely to feel much alarm. There were but two ladies present; one of whom was the lively actress, who was not easily frightened, and the other the silent German beauty who, it turned out, did not understand a word of Russian, and seemed to be as stupid as she was lovely.

Her acquaintances invited her to their "At Homes" because she was so decorative. She was exhibited to their guests like a valuable picture, or vase, or statue, or firescreen. As for the men, Ptitsin was one of Rogojin's friends; Ferdishenko was as much at home as a fish in the sea, Gania, not yet recovered from his amazement, appeared to be chained to a pillory. The old professor did not in the least understand what was happening; but when he noticed how extremely agitated the mistress of the house, and her friends, seemed, he nearly wept, and trembled with fright: but he would rather have died than leave Nastasia Philipovna at such a crisis, for he loved her as if she were his own granddaughter. Afanasy Ivanovitch greatly disliked having anything to do with the affair, but he was too much interested to leave, in spite of the mad turn things had taken; and a few words that had dropped from the lips of Nastasia puzzled him so much, that he felt he could not go without an explanation. He resolved therefore, to see it out, and to adopt the attitude of silent spectator, as most suited to his dignity. General Epanchin alone determined to depart. He was annoyed at the manner in which his gift had been returned, as though he had condescended, under the influence of passion, to place himself on a level with Ptitsin and Ferdishenko, his self-respect and sense of duty now returned together with a consciousness of what was due to his social rank and official importance. In short, he plainly showed his conviction that a man in his position could have nothing to do with Rogojin and his companions. But Nastasia interrupted him at his first words.

"Ah, general!" she cried, "I was forgetting! If I had only foreseen this unpleasantness! I won't insist on keeping you against your will, although I should have liked you to be beside me now. In any case, I am most grateful to you for your visit, and flattering attention... but if you are afraid..."

"Excuse me, Nastasia Philipovna," interrupted the general, with chivalric generosity. "To whom are you speaking? I have remained until now simply because of my devotion to you, and as for danger, I am only afraid that the carpets may be ruined, and the furniture smashed!... You should shut the door on the lot, in my opinion. But I confess that I am extremely curious to see how it ends."

"Rogojin!" announced Ferdishenko.

"What do you think about it?" said the general in a low voice to Totski. "Is she mad? I mean mad in the medical sense of the word .... eh?"

"I've always said she was predisposed to it," whispered Afanasy Ivanovitch slyly. "Perhaps it is a fever!"

Since their visit to Gania's home, Rogojin's followers had been increased by two new recruits–a dissolute old man, the hero of some ancient scandal, and a retired sub-lieutenant. A laughable story was told of the former. He possessed, it was said, a set of false teeth, and one day when he wanted money for a drinking orgy, he pawned them, and was never able to reclaim them! The officer appeared to be a rival of the gentleman who was so proud of his fists. He was known to none of Rogojin's followers, but as they passed by the Nevsky, where he stood begging, he had joined their ranks. His claim for the charity he desired seemed based on the fact that in the days of his prosperity he had given away as much as fifteen roubles at a time. The rivals seemed more than a little jealous of one another. The athlete appeared injured at the admission of the "beggar" into the company. By nature taciturn, he now merely growled occasionally like a bear, and glared contemptuously upon the "beggar," who, being somewhat of a man of the world, and a diplomatist, tried to insinuate himself into the bear's good graces. He was a much smaller man than the athlete, and doubtless was conscious that he must tread warily. Gently and without argument he alluded to the advantages of the English style in boxing, and showed himself a firm believer in Western institutions. The athlete's lips curled disdainfully, and without honouring his adversary with a formal denial, he exhibited, as if by accident, that peculiarly Russian object–an enormous fist, clenched, muscular, and covered with red hairs! The sight of this pre-eminently national attribute was enough to convince anybody, without words, that it was a serious matter for those who should happen to come into contact with it.

None of the band were very drunk, for the leader had kept his intended visit to Nastasia in view all day, and had done his best to prevent his followers from drinking too much. He was sober himself, but the excitement of this chaotic day–the strangest day of his life–had affected him so that he was in a dazed, wild condition, which almost resembled drunkenness.

He had kept but one idea before him all day, and for that he had worked in an agony of anxiety and a fever of suspense. His lieutenants had worked so hard from five o'clock until eleven, that they actually had collected a hundred thousand roubles for him, but at such terrific expense, that the rate of interest was only mentioned among them in whispers and with bated breath.

As before, Rogojin walked in advance of his troop, who followed him with mingled self-assertion and timidity. They were specially frightened of Nastasia Philipovna herself, for some reason.

Many of them expected to be thrown downstairs at once, without further ceremony, the elegant and irresistible Zaleshoff among them. But the party led by the athlete, without openly showing their hostile intentions, silently nursed contempt and even hatred for Nastasia Philipovna, and marched into her house as they would have marched into an enemy's fortress. Arrived there, the luxury of the rooms seemed to inspire them with a kind of respect, not unmixed with alarm. So many things were entirely new to their experience–the choice furniture, the pictures, the great statue of Venus. They followed their chief into the salon, however, with a kind of impudent curiosity. There, the sight of General Epanchin among the guests, caused many of them to beat a hasty retreat into the adjoining room, the "boxer" and "beggar" being among the first to go. A few only, of whom Lebedeff made one, stood their ground; he had contrived to walk side by side with Rogojin, for he quite understood the importance of a man who had a fortune of a million odd roubles, and who at this moment carried a hundred thousand in his hand. It may be added that the whole company, not excepting

Lebedeff, had the vaguest idea of the extent of their powers, and of how far they could safely go. At some moments Lebedeff was sure that right was on their side; at others he tried uneasily to remember various cheering and reassuring articles of the Civil Code.

Rogojin, when he stepped into the room, and his eyes fell upon Nastasia, stopped short, grew white as a sheet, and stood staring; it was clear that his heart was beating painfully. So he stood, gazing intently, but timidly, for a few seconds. Suddenly, as though bereft of his senses, he moved forward, staggering helplessly, towards the table. On his way he collided against Ptitsin's chair, and put his dirty foot on the lace skirt of the silent lady's dress; but he neither apologized for this, nor even noticed it.

On reaching the table, he placed upon it a strange-looking object, which he had carried with him into the drawing-room.

This was a paper packet, some six or seven inches thick, and eight or nine in length, wrapped in an old newspaper, and tied round three or four times with string.

Having placed this before her, he stood with drooped arms and head, as though awaiting his sentence.

His costume was the same as it had been in the morning, except for a new silk handkerchief round his neck, bright green and red, fastened with a huge diamond pin, and an enormous diamond ring on his dirty forefinger.

Lebedeff stood two or three paces behind his chief; and the rest of the band waited about near the door.

The two maid-servants were both peeping in, frightened and amazed at this unusual and disorderly scene.

"What is that?" asked Nastasia Philipovna, gazing intently at Rogojin, and indicating the paper packet.

"A hundred thousand," replied the latter,

almost in a whisper.

"Oh! so he kept his word–there's a man for you! Well, sit down, please–take that chair. I shall have something to say to you presently. Who are all these with you? The same party? Let them come in and sit down. There's room on that sofa, there are some chairs and there's another sofa! Well, why don't they sit down?"

Sure enough, some of the brave fellows entirely lost their heads at this point, and retreated into the next room. Others, however, took the hint and sat down, as far as they could from the table, however; feeling braver in proportion to their distance from Nastasia.

Rogojin took the chair offered him, but he did not sit long; he soon stood up again, and did not reseat himself. Little by little he began to look around him and discern the other guests. Seeing Gania, he smiled venomously and muttered to himself, "Look at that!"

He gazed at Totski and the general with no apparent confusion, and with very little curiosity. But when he observed that the prince was seated beside Nastasia Philipovna, he could not take his eyes off him for a long while, and was clearly amazed. He could not account for the prince's presence there. It was not in the least surprising that Rogojin should be, at this time, in a more or less delirious condition; for not to speak of the excitements of the day, he had spent the night before in the train, and had not slept more than a wink for forty-eight hours.

"This, gentlemen, is a hundred thousand roubles," said Nastasia Philipovna, addressing the company in general, "here, in this dirty parcel. This afternoon Rogojin yelled, like a madman, that he would bring me a hundred thousand in the evening, and I have been waiting for him all the while. He was bargaining for me, you know; first he offered me eighteen thousand; then he rose to forty, and then to a hundred thousand. And he has kept his word, see! My goodness, how white he is! All this happened this afternoon, at Gania's. I had gone to pay his mother a visit–my future family, you know! And his sister said to my very face, surely somebody will turn this shameless creature out. After which she spat in her brother Gania's face–a girl of character, that!"

"Nastasia Philipovna!" began the general, reproachfully. He was beginning to put his own interpretation on the affair.

"Well, what, general? Not quite good form, eh? Oh, nonsense! Here have I been sitting in my box at the French theatre for the last five years like a statue of inaccessible virtue, and kept out of the way of all admirers, like a silly little idiot! Now, there's this man, who comes and pays down his hundred thousand on the table, before you all, in spite of my five years of innocence and proud virtue, and I dare be sworn he has his sledge outside waiting to carry me off. He values me at a hundred thousand! I see you are still angry with me, Gania! Why, surely you never really wished to take **me** into your family? **me**, Rogojin's mistress! What did the prince say just now?"

"I never said you were Rogojin's mistress–you are **not!**" said the prince, in trembling accents.

"Nastasia Philipovna, dear soul!" cried the actress, impatiently, "do be calm, dear! If it annoys you so–all this–do go away and rest! Of course you would never go with this wretched fellow, in spite of his hundred thousand roubles! Take his money and kick him out of the house; that's the way to treat him and the likes of him! Upon my word, if it were my business, I'd soon clear them all out!"

The actress was a kind-hearted woman, and highly impressionable. She was very angry now.

"Don't be cross, Daria Alexeyevna!" laughed Nastasia. "I was not angry when I spoke; I wasn't reproaching Gania. I don't know how it was that I ever could have indulged the whim of entering an honest family like his. I saw his mother–and kissed her hand, too. I came and stirred up all that fuss, Gania, this afternoon, on purpose to see how much you could swallow–you surprised me, my friend–you did, indeed. Surely you could not marry a woman who accepts pearls like those you knew the general was going to give me, on the very eve of her marriage? And Rogojin! Why, in your own house and before your own brother and sister, he bargained with me! Yet you could come here and expect to be betrothed to me before you left the house! You almost brought your sister, too. Surely what Rogojin said about you is not really true: that you would crawl all the way to the other end of the town, on hands and knees, for three roubles?"

"Yes, he would!" said Rogojin, quietly, but with an air of absolute conviction.

"H'm! and he receives a good salary, I'm told. Well, what should you get but disgrace and misery if you took a wife you hated into your family (for I know very well that you do hate me)? No, no! I believe now that a man like you would murder anyone for money–sharpen a razor and come up behind his best friend and cut his throat like a sheep–I've read of such people. Everyone seems money-mad nowadays. No, no! I may be shameless, but you are far worse. I don't say a word about that other–"

"Nastasia Philipovna, is this really you? You, once so refined and delicate of speech. Oh, what a tongue! What dreadful things you are saying," cried the general, wringing his hands in real grief.

"I am intoxicated, general. I am having a day out, you know–it's my birthday! I have long looked forward to this happy occasion. Daria Alexeyevna, you see that nosegay-man, that Monsieur aux Camelias, sitting there laughing at us?"

"I am not laughing, Nastasia Philipovna; I am only listening with all my attention," said

Totski, with dignity.

"Well, why have I worried him, for five years, and never let him go free? Is he worth it? He is only just what he ought to be–nothing particular. He thinks I am to blame, too. He gave me my education, kept me like a countess. Money–my word! What a lot of money he spent over me! And he tried to find me an honest husband first, and then this Gania, here. And what do you think? All these five years I did not live with him, and yet I took his money, and considered I was quite justified.

"You say, take the hundred thousand and kick that man out. It is true, it is an abominable business, as you say. I might have married long ago, not Gania–Oh, no!–but that would have been abominable too.

"Would you believe it, I had some thoughts of marrying Totski, four years ago! I meant mischief, I confess–but I could have had him, I give you my word; he asked me himself. But I thought, no! it's not worthwhile to take such advantage of him. No! I had better go on to the streets, or accept Rogojin, or become a washerwoman or something–for I have nothing of my own, you know. I shall go away and leave everything behind, to the last rag–he shall have it all back. And who would take me without anything? Ask Gania, there, whether he would. Why, even Ferdishenko wouldn't have me!"

"No, Ferdishenko would not; he is a candid fellow, Nastasia Philipovna," said that worthy. "But the prince would. You sit here making complaints, but just look at the prince. I've been observing him for a long while."

Nastasia Philipovna looked keenly round at the prince.

"Is that true?" she asked.

"Quite true," whispered the prince.

"You'll take me as I am, with nothing?"

"I will, Nastasia Philipovna."

"Here's a pretty business!" cried the general. "However, it might have been expected of him."

The prince continued to regard Nastasia with a sorrowful, but intent and piercing, gaze.

"Here's another alternative for me," said Nastasia, turning once more to the actress; "and he does it out of pure kindness of heart. I know him. I've found a benefactor. Perhaps, though, what they say about him may be true–that he's an–we know what. And what shall you live on, if you are really so madly in love with Rogojin's mistress, that you are ready to marry her–eh?"

"I take you as a good, honest woman, Nastasia Philipovna–not as Rogojin's mistress."

"Who? I?–good and honest?"

"Yes, you."

"Oh, you get those ideas out of novels, you know. Times are changed now, dear prince; the world sees things as they really are. That's all nonsense. Besides, how can you marry? You need a nurse, not a wife."

The prince rose and began to speak in a trembling, timid tone, but with the air of a man absolutely sure of the truth of his words.

"I know nothing, Nastasia Philipovna. I have seen nothing. You are right so far; but I consider that you would be honouring me, and not I you. I am a nobody. You have suffered, you have passed through hell and emerged pure, and that is very much. Why do you shame yourself by desiring to go with Rogojin? You are delirious. You have returned to Mr. Totski his seventy-five thousand roubles, and declared that you will leave this house and all that is in it, which is a line of conduct that not one person here would imitate. Nastasia Philipovna, I love you! I would die for you. I shall never let any man say one word against you, Nastasia Philipovna! and if we are poor, I can work for both."

As the prince spoke these last words a titter was heard from Ferdishenko; Lebedeff laughed too. The general grunted with irritation; Ptitsin and Totski barely restrained their smiles. The rest all sat listening, open-mouthed with wonder.

"But perhaps we shall not be poor; we may be very rich, Nastasia Philipovna," continued the prince, in the same timid, quivering tones. "I don't know for certain, and I'm sorry to say I haven't had an opportunity of finding out all day; but I received a letter from Moscow, while I was in Switzerland, from a Mr. Salaskin, and he acquaints me with the fact that I am entitled to a very large inheritance. This letter–"

The prince pulled a letter out of his pocket.

"Is he raving?" said the general. "Are we really in a mad-house?"

There was silence for a moment. Then Ptitsin spoke.

"I think you said, prince, that your letter was from Salaskin? Salaskin is a very eminent man, indeed, in his own world; he is a wonderfully clever solicitor, and if he really tells you this, I think you may be pretty sure that he is right. It so happens, luckily, that I know his handwriting, for I have lately had business with him. If you would allow me to see it, I should perhaps be able to tell you."

The prince held out the letter silently, but with a shaking hand.

"What, what?" said the general, much agitated.

"What's all this? Is he really heir to anything?"

All present concentrated their attention upon Ptitsin, reading the prince's letter. The general curiosity had received a new fillip. Ferdishenko could not sit still. Rogojin fixed his eyes first on the prince, and then on Ptitsin, and then back again; he was extremely agitated. Lebedeff could not stand it. He crept up and read over Ptitsin's shoulder, with the air of a naughty boy who expects a box on the ear every moment for his indiscretion.

CHAPTER SIXTEEN

"IT'S GOOD BUSINESS," said Ptitsin, at last, folding the letter and handing it back to the prince. "You will receive, without the slightest trouble, by the last will and testament of your aunt, a very large sum of money indeed."

"Impossible!" cried the general, starting up as if he had been shot.

Ptitsin explained, for the benefit of the company, that the prince's aunt had died five months since. He had never known her, but she was his mother's own sister, the daughter of a Moscow merchant, one Paparchin, who had died a bankrupt. But the elder brother of this same Paparchin, had been an eminent and very rich merchant. A year since it had so happened that his only two sons had both died within the same month. This sad event had so affected the old man that he, too, had died very shortly after. He was a widower, and had no relations left, excepting the prince's aunt, a poor woman living on charity, who was herself at the point of death from dropsy; but who had time, before she died, to set Salaskin to work to find her nephew, and to make her will bequeathing her newly-acquired fortune to him.

It appeared that neither the prince, nor the doctor with whom he lived in Switzerland, had thought of waiting for further communications; but the prince had started straight away with Salaskin's letter in his pocket.

"One thing I may tell you, for certain,"

concluded Ptitsin, addressing the prince, "that there is no question about the authenticity of this matter. Anything that Salaskin writes you as regards your unquestionable right to this inheritance, you may look upon as so much money in your pocket. I congratulate you, prince; you may receive a million and a half of roubles, perhaps more; I don't know. All I **do** know is that Paparchin was a very rich merchant indeed."

"Hurrah!" cried Lebedeff, in a drunken voice. "Hurrah for the last of the Muishkins!"

"My goodness me! and I gave him twenty-five roubles this morning as though he were a beggar," blurted out the general, half senseless with amazement. "Well, I congratulate you, I congratulate you!" And the general rose from his seat and solemnly embraced the prince. All came forward with congratulations; even those of Rogojin's party who had retreated into the next room, now crept softly back to look on. For the moment even Nastasia Philipovna was forgotten.

But gradually the consciousness crept back into the minds of each one present that the prince had just made her an offer of marriage. The situation had, therefore, become three times as fantastic as before.

Totski sat and shrugged his shoulders, bewildered. He was the only guest left sitting at this time; the others had thronged round the table in disorder, and were all talking at once.

It was generally agreed, afterwards, in recalling that evening, that from this moment Nastasia Philipovna seemed entirely to lose her senses. She continued to sit still in her place, looking around at her guests with a strange, bewildered expression, as though she were trying to collect her thoughts, and could not. Then she suddenly turned to the prince, and glared at him with frowning brows; but this only lasted one moment. Perhaps it suddenly struck her that all this was a jest, but his face seemed to reassure her. She reflected, and smiled again, vaguely.

"So I am really a princess," she whispered to herself, ironically, and glancing accidentally at Daria Alexeyevna's face, she burst out laughing.

"Ha, ha, ha!" she cried, "this is an unexpected climax, after all. I didn't expect this. What are you all standing up for, gentlemen? Sit down; congratulate me and the prince! Ferdishenko, just step out and order some more champagne, will you? Katia, Pasha," she added suddenly, seeing the servants at the door, "come here! I'm going to be married, did you hear? To the prince. He has a million and a half of roubles; he is Prince Muishkin, and has asked me to marry him. Here, prince, come and sit by me; and here comes the wine. Now then, ladies and gentlemen, where are your congratulations?"

"Hurrah!" cried a number of voices. A rush was made for the wine by Rogojin's followers, though, even among them, there seemed some sort of realization that the situation had changed. Rogojin stood and looked on, with an incredulous smile, screwing up one side of his mouth.

"Prince, my dear fellow, do remember what you are about," said the general, approaching Muishkin, and pulling him by the coat sleeve.

Nastasia Philipovna overheard the remark, and burst out laughing.

"No, no, general!" she cried. "You had better look out! I am the princess now, you know. The prince won't let you insult me. Afanasy Ivanovitch, why don't you congratulate me? I shall be able to sit at table with your new wife, now. Aha! you see what I gain by marrying a prince! A million and a half, and a prince, and an idiot into the bargain, they say. What better could I wish for? Life is only just about to commence for me in earnest. Rogojin, you are a little too late. Away with your paper parcel! I'm going to marry the prince; I'm richer than you are now."

But Rogojin understood how things were

tending, at last. An inexpressibly painful expression came over his face. He wrung his hands; a groan made its way up from the depths of his soul.

"Surrender her, for God's sake!" he said to the prince.

All around burst out laughing.

"What? Surrender her to **you?**" cried Daria Alexeyevna. "To a fellow who comes and bargains for a wife like a moujik! The prince wishes to marry her, and you–"

"So do I, so do I! This moment, if I could! I'd give every farthing I have to do it."

"You drunken moujik," said Daria Alexeyevna, once more. "You ought to be kicked out of the place."

The laughter became louder than ever.

"Do you hear, prince?" said Nastasia Philipovna. "Do you hear how this moujik of a fellow goes on bargaining for your bride?"

"He is drunk," said the prince, quietly, "and he loves you very much."

"Won't you be ashamed, afterwards, to

reflect that your wife very nearly ran away with Rogojin?"

"Oh, you were raving, you were in a fever; you are still half delirious."

"And won't you be ashamed when they tell you, afterwards, that your wife lived at Totski's expense so many years?"

"No; I shall not be ashamed of that. You did not so live by your own will."

"And you'll never reproach me with it?"

"Never."

"Take care, don't commit yourself for a whole lifetime."

"Nastasia Philipovna." said the prince, quietly, and with deep emotion, "I said before that I shall esteem your consent to be my wife as a great honour to myself, and shall consider that it is you who will honour me, not I you, by our marriage. You laughed at these words, and others around us laughed as well; I heard them. Very likely I expressed myself funnily, and I may have looked funny, but, for all that, I believe

I understand where honour lies, and what I said was but the literal truth. You were about to ruin yourself just now, irrevocably; you would never have forgiven yourself for so doing afterwards; and yet, you are absolutely blameless. It is impossible that your life should be altogether ruined at your age. What matter that Rogojin came bargaining here, and that Gavrila Ardalionovitch would have deceived you if he could? Why do you continually remind us of these facts? I assure you once more that very few could find it in them to act as you have acted this day. As for your wish to go with Rogojin, that was simply the idea of a delirious and suffering brain. You are still quite feverish; you ought to be in bed, not here. You know quite well that if you had gone with Rogojin, you would have become a washer-woman next day, rather than stay with him. You are proud, Nastasia Philipovna, and perhaps you have really suffered so much that you imagine yourself to be a desperately guilty woman. You require a great deal of petting and looking after, Nastasia Philipovna, and I will do this. I saw your portrait this morning, and it seemed quite a familiar face to me; it seemed to me that the portrait-face was calling to me for help. I–I shall respect you all my life, Nastasia Philipovna," concluded the prince, as though suddenly recollecting himself, and blushing to think of the sort of company before whom he had said all this.

Ptitsin bowed his head and looked at the ground, overcome by a mixture of feelings. Totski muttered to himself: "He may be an idiot, but he knows that flattery is the best road to success here."

The prince observed Gania's eyes flashing at him, as though they would gladly annihilate him then and there.

"That's a kind-hearted man, if you like," said Daria Alexeyevna, whose wrath was quickly evaporating.

"A refined man, but–lost," murmured the general.

Totski took his hat and rose to go. He and the general exchanged glances, making a private arrangement, thereby, to leave the house together.

"Thank you, prince; no one has ever spoken to me like that before," began Nastasia Philipovna. "Men have always bargained for me, before this; and not a single respectable man has ever proposed to marry me. Do you hear, Afanasy Ivanovitch? What do **you** think of what the prince has just been saying? It was almost immodest, wasn't it? You, Rogojin, wait a moment, don't go yet! I see you don't intend to move however. Perhaps I may go with you yet. Where did you mean to take me to?"

"To Ekaterinhof," replied Lebedeff. Rogojin simply stood staring, with trembling lips, not daring to believe his ears. He was stunned, as though from a blow on the head.

"What are you thinking of, my dear Nastasia?" said Daria Alexeyevna in alarm. "What are you saying?" "You are not going mad, are you?"

Nastasia Philipovna burst out laughing and jumped up from the sofa.

"You thought I should accept this good child's invitation to ruin him, did you?" she cried. "That's Totski's way, not mine. He's fond of children. Come along, Rogojin, get your money ready! We won't talk about marrying just at this moment, but let's see the money at all events. Come! I may not marry you, either. I don't know. I suppose you thought you'd keep the money, if I did! Ha, ha, ha! nonsense! I have no sense of shame left. I tell you I have been Totski's concubine. Prince, you must marry Aglaya Ivanovna, not Nastasia Philipovna, or this fellow Ferdishenko will always be pointing the finger of scorn at you. You aren't afraid, I know; but I should always be afraid that I had ruined you, and that you would reproach me for it. As for what you say about my doing you honour by marrying you–well, Totski can tell you all about that.

You had your eye on Aglaya, Gania, you know you had; and you might have married her if you had not come bargaining. You are all like this. You should choose, once for all, between disreputable women, and respectable ones, or you are sure to get mixed. Look at the general, how he's staring at me!"

"This is too horrible," said the general, starting to his feet. All were standing up now. Nastasia was absolutely beside herself.

"I am very proud, in spite of what I am," she continued. "You called me 'perfection' just now, prince. A nice sort of perfection to throw up a prince and a million and a half of roubles in order to be able to boast of the fact afterwards! What sort of a wife should I make for you, after all I have said? Afanasy Ivanovitch, do you observe I have really and truly thrown away a million of roubles? And you thought that I should consider your wretched seventy-five thousand, with Gania thrown in for a husband, a paradise of bliss!

Take your seventy-five thousand back, sir; you did not reach the hundred thousand. Rogojin cut a better dash than you did. I'll console Gania myself; I have an idea about that. But now I must be off! I've been in prison for ten years. I'm free at last! Well, Rogojin, what are you waiting for? Let's get ready and go."

"Come along!" shouted Rogojin, beside himself with joy. "Hey! all of you fellows! Wine! Round with it! Fill the glasses!"

"Get away!" he shouted frantically, observing that Daria Alexeyevna was approaching to protest against Nastasia's conduct. "Get away, she's mine, everything's mine! She's a queen, get away!"

He was panting with ecstasy. He walked round and round Nastasia Philipovna and told everybody to "keep their distance."

All the Rogojin company were now collected in the drawing-room; some were drinking, some laughed and talked: all were in the highest and wildest spirits. Ferdishenko was doing his best to unite himself to them; the general and Totski again made an attempt to go. Gania, too stood hat in hand ready to go; but seemed to be unable to tear his eyes away from the scene before him.

"Get out, keep your distance!" shouted Rogojin.

"What are you shouting about there!" cried Nastasia "I'm not yours yet. I may kick you out for all you know I haven't taken your money yet; there it all is on the table. Here, give me over that packet! Is there a hundred thousand roubles in that one packet? Pfu! what abominable stuff it looks! Oh! nonsense, Daria Alexeyevna; you surely did not expect me to ruin **him?**" (indicating the prince). "Fancy him nursing me! Why, he needs a nurse himself! The general, there, will be his nurse now, you'll see. Here, prince, look here! Your bride is accepting money. What a disreputable woman she must be! And you wished to marry her! What are you crying about? Is it a bitter dose? Never mind, you shall laugh yet. Trust to time." (In spite of these words there were two large tears rolling down Nastasia's own cheeks.) "It's far better to think twice of it now than afterwards. Oh! you mustn't cry like that! There's Katia crying, too. What is it, Katia, dear? I shall leave you and Pasha a lot of things, I've laid them out for you already; but good-bye, now. I made an honest girl like you serve a low woman like myself. It's better so, prince, it is indeed. You'd begin to despise me afterwards–we should never be happy. Oh! you needn't swear, prince, I shan't believe you, you know. How foolish it would be, too! No, no; we'd better say good-bye and part friends. I am a bit of a dreamer myself, and I used to dream of you once. Very often during those five years down at his estate I used to dream and think, and I always imagined just such a good, honest, foolish fellow as you, one who should come and say to me: 'You are an innocent woman, Nastasia Philipovna, and I adore you.' I dreamt of you often. I used to think so much down there that I nearly went mad; and then this fellow here would come down. He would stay a couple of months out of the twelve, and disgrace and insult and deprave me, and then go; so that I longed to drown myself in the pond a thousand times over; but I did not dare do it. I hadn't the heart, and now–well, are you ready, Rogojin?"

"Ready–keep your distance, all of you!"

"We're all ready," said several of his friends. "The troikas [Sledges drawn by three horses abreast.] are at the door, bells and all."

Nastasia Philipovna seized the packet of bank-notes.

"Gania, I have an idea. I wish to recompense you–why should you lose all? Rogojin, would he crawl for three roubles as far as the Vassiliostrof?"

"Oh, wouldn't he just!"

"Well, look here, Gania. I wish to look into your heart once more, for the last time. You've worried me for the last three months–now it's my turn. Do you see this packet? It contains a hundred thousand roubles. Now, I'm going to throw it into the fire, here–before all these witnesses. As soon as the fire catches hold of it, you put your hands into the fire and pick it out–without gloves, you know. You must have bare hands, and you must turn your sleeves up. Pull it out, I say, and it's all yours. You may burn your fingers a little, of course; but then it's a hundred thousand roubles, remember–it won't take you long to lay hold of it and snatch it out. I shall so much admire you if you put your hands into the fire for my money. All here present may be witnesses that the whole packet of money is yours if you get it out. If you don't get it out, it shall burn. I will let no one else come; away–get away, all of you–it's my money! Rogojin has bought me with it. Is it my money, Rogojin?"

"Yes, my queen; it's your own money, my joy."

"Get away then, all of you. I shall do as I like

with my own–don't meddle! Ferdishenko, make up the fire, quick!"

"Nastasia Philipovna, I can't; my hands won't obey me," said Ferdishenko, astounded and helpless with bewilderment.

"Nonsense," cried Nastasia Philipovna, seizing the poker and raking a couple of logs together. No sooner did a tongue of flame burst out than she threw the packet of notes upon it.

Everyone gasped; some even crossed themselves.

"She's mad–she's mad!" was the cry.

"Oughtn't-oughtn't we to secure her?" asked the general of Ptitsin, in a whisper; "or shall we send for the authorities? Why, she's mad, isn't she–isn't she, eh?"

"N-no, I hardly think she is actually mad," whispered Ptitsin, who was as white as his handkerchief, and trembling like a leaf. He could not take his eyes off the smouldering packet.

"She's mad surely, isn't she?" the general

appealed to Totski.

"I told you she wasn't an ordinary woman," replied the latter, who was as pale as anyone.

"Oh, but, positively, you know–a hundred thousand roubles!"

"Goodness gracious! good heavens!" came from all quarters of the room.

All now crowded round the fire and thronged to see what was going on; everyone lamented and gave vent to exclamations of horror and woe. Some jumped up on chairs in order to get a better view. Daria Alexeyevna ran into the next room and whispered excitedly to Katia and Pasha. The beautiful German disappeared altogether.

"My lady! my sovereign!" lamented Lebedeff, falling on his knees before Nastasia Philipovna, and stretching out his hands towards the fire; "it's a hundred thousand roubles, it is indeed, I packed it up myself, I saw the money! My queen, let me get into the fire after it–say the word–I'll put my whole grey head into the fire for it! I have a poor lame wife and thirteen children. My father died of starvation last week. Nastasia Philipovna, Nastasia Philipovna!" The wretched little man wept, and groaned, and crawled towards the fire.

"Away, out of the way!" cried Nastasia. "Make room, all of you! Gania, what are you standing there for? Don't stand on ceremony. Put in your hand! There's your whole happiness smouldering away, look! Quick!"

But Gania had borne too much that day, and especially this evening, and he was not prepared for this last, quite unexpected trial.

The crowd parted on each side of him and he was left face to face with Nastasia Philipovna, three paces from her. She stood by the fire and waited, with her intent gaze fixed upon him.

Gania stood before her, in his evening clothes, holding his white gloves and hat in his hand, speechless and motionless, with arms folded and eyes fixed on the fire.

A silly, meaningless smile played on his white, death-like lips. He could not take his eyes off the smouldering packet; but it appeared that something new had come to birth in his soul–as though he were vowing to himself that he would bear this trial. He did not move from his place. In a few seconds it became evident to all that he did not intend to rescue the money.

“Hey! look at it, it’ll burn in another minute or two!” cried Nastasia Philipovna. “You’ll hang yourself afterwards, you know, if it does! I’m not joking.”

The fire, choked between a couple of smouldering pieces of wood, had died down for the first few moments after the packet was thrown upon it. But a little tongue of fire now began to lick the paper from below, and soon, gathering courage, mounted the sides of the parcel, and crept around it. In another moment, the whole of it burst into flames, and the exclamations of woe and horror were redoubled.

"Nastasia Philipovna!" lamented Lebedeff again, straining towards the fireplace; but Rogojin dragged him away, and pushed him to the rear once more.

The whole of Rogojin's being was concentrated in one rapturous gaze of ecstasy. He could not take his eyes off Nastasia. He stood drinking her in, as it were. He was in the seventh heaven of delight.

"Oh, what a queen she is!" he ejaculated, every other minute, throwing out the remark for anyone who liked to catch it. "That's the sort of woman for me! Which of you would think of doing a thing like that, you blackguards, eh?" he yelled. He was hopelessly and wildly beside himself with ecstasy.

The prince watched the whole scene, silent and dejected.

"I'll pull it out with my teeth for one thousand," said Ferdishenko.

"So would I," said another, from behind,

"with pleasure. Devil take the thing!" he added, in a tempest of despair, "it will all be burnt up in a minute–It's burning, it's burning!"

"It's burning, it's burning!" cried all, thronging nearer and nearer to the fire in their excitement.

"Gania, don't be a fool! I tell you for the last time."

"Get on, quick!" shrieked Ferdishenko, rushing wildly up to Gania, and trying to drag him to the fire by the sleeve of his coat. "Get it, you dummy, it's burning away fast! Oh–**damn** the thing!"

Gania hurled Ferdishenko from him; then he turned sharp round and made for the door. But he had not gone a couple of steps when he tottered and fell to the ground.

"He's fainted!" the cry went round.

"And the money's burning still," Lebedeff lamented.

"Burning for nothing," shouted others.

"Katia-Pasha! Bring him some water!"

cried Nastasia Philipovna. Then she took the tongs and fished out the packet.

Nearly the whole of the outer covering was burned away, but it was soon evident that the contents were hardly touched. The packet had been wrapped in a threefold covering of newspaper, and the notes were safe. All breathed more freely.

"Some dirty little thousand or so may be touched," said Lebedeff, immensely relieved, "but there's very little harm done, after all."

"It's all his–the whole packet is for him, do you hear–all of you?" cried Nastasia Philipovna, placing the packet by the side of Gania. "He restrained himself, and didn't go after it; so his self-respect is greater than his thirst for money. All right–he'll come to directly–he must have the packet or he'll cut his throat afterwards. There! He's coming to himself. General, Totski, all of you, did you hear me? The money is all Gania's. I give it to him, fully conscious of my action, as recompense for–well, for anything he thinks best. Tell him so. Let it lie here beside him. Off we go, Rogojin! Goodbye, prince. I have seen a man for the first time in my life. Goodbye, Afanasy Ivanovitch–and thanks!"

The Rogojin gang followed their leader and Nastasia Philipovna to the entrance-hall, laughing and shouting and whistling.

In the hall the servants were waiting, and handed her her fur cloak. Martha, the cook, ran in from the kitchen. Nastasia kissed them all round.

"Are you really throwing us all over, little mother? Where, where are you going to? And on your birthday, too!" cried the four girls, crying over her and kissing her hands.

"I am going out into the world, Katia; perhaps I shall be a laundress. I don't know. No more of Afanasy Ivanovitch, anyhow. Give him my respects. Don't think badly of me, girls."

The prince hurried down to the front gate where the party were settling into the troikas, all the bells tinkling a merry accompaniment the while. The general caught him up on the stairs:

"Prince, prince!" he cried, seizing hold of his arm, "recollect yourself! Drop her, prince! You see what sort of a woman she is. I am speaking to you like a father."

The prince glanced at him, but said nothing. He shook himself free, and rushed on downstairs.

The general was just in time to see the prince take the first sledge he could get, and, giving the order to Ekaterinhof, start off in pursuit of the troikas. Then the general's fine grey horse dragged that worthy home, with some new thoughts, and some new hopes and calculations developing in his brain, and with the pearls in his pocket, for he had not forgotten to bring them along with him, being a man of business. Amid his new thoughts and ideas there came, once or twice, the image of Nastasia Philipovna. The general sighed.

"I'm sorry, really sorry," he muttered. "She's

a ruined woman. Mad! mad! However, the prince is not for Nastasia Philipovna now,–perhaps it's as well."

Two more of Nastasia's guests, who walked a short distance together, indulged in high moral sentiments of a similar nature.

"Do you know, Totski, this is all very like what they say goes on among the Japanese?" said Ptitsin. "The offended party there, they say, marches off to his insulter and says to him, 'You insulted me, so I have come to rip myself open before your eyes;' and with these words he does actually rip his stomach open before his enemy, and considers, doubtless, that he is having all possible and necessary satisfaction and revenge. There are strange characters in the world, sir!"

"H'm! and you think there was something of this sort here, do you? Dear me–a very remarkable comparison, you know! But you must have observed, my dear Ptitsin, that I did all I possibly could. I could do no more than I did. And you must admit that there are some rare qualities in this woman. I felt I could not speak in that Bedlam, or I should have been tempted to cry out, when she reproached me, that she herself was my best justification. Such a woman could make anyone forget all reason–everything! Even that moujik, Rogojin, you saw, brought her a hundred thousand roubles! Of course, all that happened tonight was ephemeral, fantastic, unseemly–yet it lacked neither colour nor originality. My God! What might not have been made of such a character combined with such beauty! Yet in spite of all efforts–in spite of all education, even–all those gifts are wasted! She is an uncut diamond.... I have often said so."

And Afanasy Ivanovitch heaved a deep sigh.

Part One

Part Two

Part Two

CHAPTER ONE

TWO DAYS AFTER THE strange conclusion to Nastasia Philipovna's birthday party, with the record of which we concluded the first part of this story, Prince Muishkin hurriedly left St. Petersburg for Moscow, in order to see after some business connected with the receipt of his unexpected fortune.

It was said that there were other reasons for his hurried departure; but as to this, and as to his movements in Moscow, and as to his prolonged absence from St.

Petersburg, we are able to give very little information.

The prince was away for six months, and even those who were most interested in his destiny were able to pick up very little news about him all that while. True, certain rumours did reach his friends, but these were both strange and rare, and each one contradicted the last.

Of course the Epanchin family was much interested in his movements, though he had not had time to bid them farewell before his departure. The general, however, had had an opportunity of seeing him once or twice since the eventful evening, and had spoken very seriously with him; but though he had seen the prince, as I say, he told his family nothing about the circumstance. In fact, for a month or so after his departure it was considered not the thing to mention the prince's name in the Epanchin household. Only Mrs. Epanchin, at the commencement of this period, had announced that she had been "cruelly mistaken in the prince!" and a day or two after, she had added, evidently alluding to him, but not mentioning his name, that it was an unalterable characteristic of hers to be mistaken in people. Then once more, ten days later, after some passage of arms with one of her daughters, she had remarked sententiously. "We have had enough of mistakes. I shall be more careful in future!" However, it was impossible to avoid remarking that there was some sense of oppression in the household–something unspoken, but felt; something strained. All the members of the family wore frowning looks. The general was unusually busy; his family hardly ever saw him.

As to the girls, nothing was said openly, at all events; and probably very little in private. They were proud damsels, and were not always perfectly confidential even among themselves. But they understood each other thoroughly at the first word on all occasions; very often at the first glance, so that there was no need of much talking as a rule.

One fact, at least, would have been perfectly plain to an outsider, had any such person been on the spot; and that was, that the prince had made a very considerable impression upon the family, in spite of the fact that he had but once been inside the house, and then only for a short time. Of course, if analyzed, this impression might have proved to be nothing more than a feeling of curiosity; but be it what it might, there it undoubtedly was.

Little by little, the rumours spread about town became lost in a maze of uncertainty. It was said that some foolish young prince, name unknown, had suddenly come into possession of a gigantic fortune, and had married a French ballet dancer. This was contradicted, and the rumour circulated that it was a young merchant who had come into the enormous fortune and married the great ballet dancer, and that at the wedding the drunken young fool had burned seventy thousand roubles at a candle out of pure bravado.

However, all these rumours soon died down, to which circumstance certain facts largely contributed. For instance, the whole of the Rogojin troop had departed, with him at their head, for Moscow. This was exactly a week after a dreadful orgy at the Ekaterinhof gardens, where Nastasia Philipovna had been present. It became known that after this orgy Nastasia Philipovna had entirely disappeared, and that she had since been traced to Moscow; so that the exodus of the Rogojin band was found consistent with this report.

There were rumours current as to Gania, too; but circumstances soon contradicted these. He had fallen seriously ill, and his illness precluded his appearance in society, and even at business, for over a month. As soon as he had recovered, however, he threw up his situation in the public company under General Epanchin's direction, for some unknown reason, and the post was given to another. He never went near the Epanchins' house at all, and was exceedingly irritable and depressed.

Varvara Ardalionovna married Ptitsin this winter, and it was said that the fact of Gania's retirement from business was the ultimate cause of the marriage, since Gania was now not only unable to support his family, but even required help himself.

We may mention that Gania was no longer mentioned in the Epanchin household any more than the prince was; but that a certain circumstance in connection with the fatal evening at Nastasia's house became known to the general, and, in fact, to all the family the very next day. This fact was that Gania had come home that night, but had refused to go to bed. He had awaited the prince's return from Ekaterinhof with feverish impatience.

On the latter's arrival, at six in the morning, Gania had gone to him in his room, bringing with him the singed packet of money, which he had insisted that the prince should return to Nastasia Philipovna without delay. It was said that when Gania entered the prince's room, he came with anything but friendly feelings, and in a condition of despair and misery; but that after a short conversation, he had stayed on for a couple of hours with him, sobbing continuously and bitterly the whole time. They had parted upon terms of cordial friendship.

The Epanchins heard about this, as well as about the episode at Nastasia Philipovna's. It was strange, perhaps, that the facts should become so quickly, and fairly accurately, known. As far as Gania was concerned, it might have been supposed that the news had come through Varvara Ardalionovna, who had suddenly become a frequent visitor of the Epanchin girls, greatly to their mother's surprise. But though Varvara had seen fit, for some reason, to make friends with them, it was not likely that she would have talked to them about her brother. She had plenty of pride, in spite of the fact that in thus acting she was seeking intimacy with people who had practically shown her brother the door. She and the Epanchin girls had been acquainted in childhood, although of late they had met but rarely. Even now Varvara hardly ever appeared in the drawing-room, but would slip in by a back way. Lizabetha Prokofievna, who disliked Varvara, although she had a great respect for her mother, was much annoyed by this sudden intimacy, and put it down to the general "contrariness" of her daughters, who were "always on the lookout for some new way of opposing her." Nevertheless, Varvara continued her visits.

A month after Muishkin's departure, Mrs. Epanchin received a letter from her old friend Princess Bielokonski (who had lately left for Moscow), which letter put her into the greatest good humour. She did not divulge its contents either to her daughters or the general, but her conduct towards the former became affectionate in the extreme. She even made some sort of confession to them, but they were unable to understand what it was about. She actually relaxed towards the general a little–he had been long disgraced–and though she managed to quarrel with them all the next day, yet she soon came round, and from her general behaviour it was to be concluded that she had had good news of some sort, which she would like, but could not make up her mind, to disclose.

However, a week later she received another letter from the same source, and at last resolved to speak.

She solemnly announced that she had heard from old Princess Bielokonski, who had given her most comforting news about "that queer young prince." Her friend had hunted him up, and found that all was going well with him. He had since called in person upon her, making an extremely favourable impression, for the princess had received him each day since, and had introduced him into several good houses.

The girls could see that their mother concealed a great deal from them, and left out large pieces of the letter in reading it to them.

However, the ice was broken, and it suddenly became possible to mention the prince's name again. And again it became evident how very strong was the impression the young man had made in the household by his one visit there. Mrs. Epanchin was surprised at the effect which the news from Moscow had upon the girls, and they were no less surprised that after solemnly remarking that her most striking characteristic was "being mistaken in people" she should have troubled to obtain for the prince the favour and protection of so powerful an old lady as the Princess Bielokonski. As soon as the ice was thus broken, the general lost no time in showing that he, too, took the greatest interest in the subject. He admitted that he was interested, but said that it was merely in the business side of the question. It appeared that, in the interests of the prince, he had made arrangements in Moscow for a careful watch to be kept upon the prince's business affairs, and especially upon Salaskin. All that had been said as to the prince being an undoubted heir to a fortune turned out to be perfectly true; but the fortune proved to be much smaller than was at first reported. The estate was considerably encumbered with debts; creditors turned up on all sides, and the prince, in spite of all advice and entreaty, insisted upon managing all matters of claim himself–which, of course, meant satisfying everybody all round, although half the claims were absolutely fraudulent.

Mrs. Epanchin confirmed all this. She said the princess had written to much the same effect, and added that there was no curing a fool. But it was plain, from her expression of face, how strongly she approved of this particular young fool's doings. In conclusion, the general observed that his wife took as great an interest in the prince as though he were her own son; and that she had commenced to be especially affectionate towards Aglaya was a self-evident fact.

All this caused the general to look grave and important. But, alas! this agreeable state of affairs very soon changed once more.

A couple of weeks went by, and suddenly the general and his wife were once more gloomy and silent, and the ice was as firm as ever. The fact was, the general, who had heard first, how Nastasia Philipovna had fled to Moscow and had been discovered there by Rogojin; that she had then disappeared once more, and been found again by Rogojin, and how after that she had almost promised to marry him, now received news that she had once more disappeared, almost on the very day fixed for her wedding, flying somewhere into the interior of Russia this time, and that Prince Muishkin had left all his affairs in the hands of Salaskin and disappeared also–but whether he was with Nastasia, or had only set off in search of her, was unknown.

Lizabetha Prokofievna received confirmatory news from the princess–and alas, two months after the prince's first departure from St. Petersburg, darkness and mystery once more enveloped his whereabouts and actions, and in the Epanchin family the ice of silence once more formed over the subject. Varia, however, informed the girls of what had happened, she having received the news from Ptitsin, who generally knew more than most people.

To make an end, we may say that there were many changes in the Epanchin household in the spring, so that it was not difficult to forget the prince, who sent no news of himself.

The Epanchin family had at last made up

their minds to spend the summer abroad, all except the general, who could not waste time in "travelling for enjoyment," of course. This arrangement was brought about by the persistence of the girls, who insisted that they were never allowed to go abroad because their parents were too anxious to marry them off. Perhaps their parents had at last come to the conclusion that husbands might be found abroad, and that a summer's travel might bear fruit. The marriage between Alexandra and Totski had been broken off. Since the prince's departure from St. Petersburg no more had been said about it; the subject had been dropped without ceremony, much to the joy of Mrs. General, who, announced that she was "ready to cross herself with both hands" in gratitude for the escape. The general, however, regretted Totski for a long while. "Such a fortune!" he sighed, "and such a good, easy-going fellow!"

After a time it became known that Totski

had married a French marquise, and was to be carried off by her to Paris, and then to Brittany.

"Oh, well," thought the general, "he's lost to us for good, now."

So the Epanchins prepared to depart for the summer.

But now another circumstance occurred, which changed all the plans once more, and again the intended journey was put off, much to the delight of the general and his spouse.

A certain Prince S— arrived in St. Petersburg from Moscow, an eminent and honourable young man. He was one of those active persons who always find some good work with which to employ themselves. Without forcing himself upon the public notice, modest and unobtrusive, this young prince was concerned with much that happened in the world in general.

He had served, at first, in one of the civil departments, had then attended to matters connected with the local government of provincial towns, and had of late been a corresponding member of several important scientific societies. He was a man of excellent family and solid means, about thirty-five years of age.

Prince S— made the acquaintance of the general's family, and Adelaida, the second girl, made a great impression upon him. Towards the spring he proposed to her, and she accepted him. The general and his wife were delighted. The journey abroad was put off, and the wedding was fixed for a day not very distant.

The trip abroad might have been enjoyed later on by Mrs. Epanchin and her two remaining daughters, but for another circumstance.

It so happened that Prince S— introduced a distant relation of his own into the Epanchin family–one Evgenie Pavlovitch, a young officer of about twenty-eight years of age, whose conquests among the ladies in Moscow had been proverbial. This young gentleman no sooner set eyes on Aglaya than he became a frequent visitor at the house. He was witty, well-educated, and extremely wealthy, as the general very soon discovered. His past reputation was the only thing against him.

Nothing was said; there were not even any hints dropped; but still, it seemed better to the parents to say nothing more about going abroad this season, at all events. Aglaya herself perhaps was of a different opinion.

All this happened just before the second appearance of our hero upon the scene.

By this time, to judge from appearances, poor Prince Muishkin had been quite forgotten in St. Petersburg. If he had appeared suddenly among his acquaintances, he would have been received as one from the skies; but we must just glance at one more fact before we conclude this preface.

Colia Ivolgin, for some time after the prince's departure, continued his old life. That is, he went to school, looked after his father, helped Varia in the house, and ran her errands, and went frequently to see his friend, Hippolyte.

The lodgers had disappeared very quickly–Ferdishenko soon after the events at Nastasia Philipovna's, while the prince went to Moscow, as we know. Gania and his mother went to live with Varia and Ptitsin immediately after the latter's wedding, while the general was housed in a debtor's prison by reason of certain IOU's given to the captain's widow under the impression that they would never be formally used against him. This unkind action much surprised poor Ardalion Alexandrovitch, the victim, as he called himself, of an "unbounded trust in the nobility of the human heart."

When he signed those notes of hand he never dreamt that they would be a source of future trouble. The event showed that he was mistaken. "Trust in anyone after this! Have the least confidence in man or woman!" he cried in bitter tones, as he sat with his new friends in prison, and recounted to them his favourite stories of the siege of Kars, and the resuscitated soldier. On the whole, he accommodated himself very well to his new position. Ptitsin and Varia declared that he was in the right place, and Gania was of the same opinion. The only person who deplored his fate was poor Nina Alexandrovna, who wept bitter tears over him, to the great surprise of her household, and, though always in feeble health, made a point of going to see him as often as possible.

Since the general's "mishap," as Colia called it, and the marriage of his sister, the boy had quietly possessed himself of far more freedom. His relations saw little of him, for he rarely slept at home. He made many new friends; and was moreover, a frequent visitor at the debtor's prison, to which he invariably accompanied his mother. Varia, who used to be always correcting him, never spoke to him now on the subject of his frequent absences, and the whole household was surprised to see Gania, in spite of his depression, on quite friendly terms with his brother. This was something new, for Gania had been wont to look upon Colia as a kind of errand-boy, treating him with contempt, threatening to "pull his ears," and in general driving him almost wild with irritation. It seemed now that Gania really needed his brother, and the latter, for his part, felt as if he could forgive Gania much since he had returned the hundred thousand roubles offered to him by Nastasia Philipovna. Three months after the departure of the prince, the Ivolgin family discovered that Colia had made acquaintance with the Epanchins, and was on very friendly terms with the daughters. Varia heard of it first, though Colia had not asked her to introduce him. Little by little the family grew quite fond of him. Madame Epanchin at first looked on him with disdain, and received him coldly, but in a short time he grew to please her, because, as she said, he "was candid and no flatterer"–a very true description. From the first he put himself on an equality with his new friends, and though he sometimes read newspapers and books to the mistress of the house, it was simply because he liked to be useful.

One day, however, he and Lizabetha Prokofievna quarrelled seriously about the "woman question," in the course of a lively discussion on that burning subject. He told her that she was a tyrant, and that he would never set foot in her house again. It may seem incredible, but a day or two after, Madame Epanchin sent a servant with a note begging him to return, and Colia, without standing on his dignity, did so at once.

Aglaya was the only one of the family whose good graces he could not gain, and who always spoke to him haughtily, but it so happened that the boy one day succeeded in giving the proud maiden a surprise.

It was about Easter, when, taking advantage of a momentary tête-à-tête Colia handed Aglaya a letter, remarking that he "had orders to deliver it to her privately." She stared at him in amazement, but he did not wait to hear what she had to say, and went out. Aglaya broke the seal, and read as follows:

"Once you did me the honour of giving me your confidence. Perhaps you have quite forgotten me now! How is it that I am writing to you? I do not know; but I am conscious of an irresistible desire to remind you of my existence, especially you. How many times I have needed all three of you; but only you have dwelt always in my mind's eye. I need you–I need you very much. I will not write about myself. I have nothing to tell you. But I long for you to be happy. Are you happy? That is all I wished to say to you– Your brother,

"Pr. L. Muishkin."

On reading this short and disconnected note, Aglaya suddenly blushed all over, and became very thoughtful.

It would be difficult to describe her thoughts at that moment. One of them was, "Shall I show it to anyone?" But she was ashamed to show it. So she ended by hiding it in her table drawer, with a very strange, ironical smile upon her lips.

Next day, she took it out, and put it into a large book, as she usually did with papers which she wanted to be able to find easily. She laughed when, about a week later, she happened to notice the name of the book, and saw that it was Don Quixote, but it would be difficult to say exactly why.

I cannot say, either, whether she showed the letter to her sisters.

But when she had read it herself once more, it suddenly struck her that surely that conceited boy, Colia, had not been the one chosen correspondent of the prince all this while. She determined to ask him, and did so with an exaggerated show of carelessness. He informed her haughtily that though he had given the prince his permanent address when the latter left town, and had offered his services, the prince had never before given him any commission to perform, nor had he written until the following lines arrived, with Aglaya's letter. Aglaya took the note, and read it.

"Dear Colia,–Please be so kind as to give the enclosed sealed letter to Aglaya Ivanovna. Keep well–Ever your loving,

"Pr. L. Muishkin."

"It seems absurd to trust a little pepper-box like you," said Aglaya, as she returned the note, and walked past the "pepper-box" with an expression of great contempt.

This was more than Colia could bear. He had actually borrowed Gania's new green tie for the occasion, without saying why he wanted it, in order to impress her. He was very deeply mortified.

CHAPTER TWO

IT WAS THE BEGINNING of June, and for a whole week the weather in St. Petersburg had been magnificent. The Epanchins had a luxurious country-house at Pavlofsk, [One of the fashionable summer resorts near St. Petersburg.] and to this spot Mrs. Epanchin determined to proceed without further delay. In a couple of days all was ready, and the family had left town. A day or two after this removal to Pavlofsk, Prince Muishkin arrived in St. Petersburg by the morning train from Moscow. No one met him; but, as he stepped out of the carriage, he suddenly became aware of two strangely glowing eyes fixed upon him from among the crowd that met the train. On endeavouring to re-discover the eyes, and see to whom they belonged, he could find nothing to guide him. It must have been a hallucination. But the disagreeable impression remained, and without this, the prince was sad and thoughtful already, and seemed to be much preoccupied.

His cab took him to a small and bad hotel near the Litaynaya. Here he engaged a couple of rooms, dark and badly furnished. He washed and changed, and hurriedly left the hotel again, as though anxious to waste no time. Anyone who now saw him for the first time since he left Petersburg would judge that he had improved vastly so far as his exterior was concerned. His clothes certainly were very different; they were more fashionable, perhaps even too much so, and anyone inclined to mockery might have found something to smile at in his appearance. But what is there that people will not smile at?

The prince took a cab and drove to a street near the Nativity, where he soon discovered the house he was seeking. It was a small wooden villa, and he was struck by its attractive and clean appearance; it stood in a pleasant little garden, full of flowers. The windows looking on the street were open, and the sound of a voice, reading aloud or making a speech, came through them. It rose at times to a shout, and was interrupted occasionally by bursts of laughter.

Prince Muishkin entered the court-yard, and ascended the steps. A cook with her sleeves turned up to the elbows opened the door. The visitor asked if Mr. Lebedeff were at home.

"He is in there," said she, pointing to the salon.

The room had a blue wall-paper, and was well, almost pretentiously, furnished, with its round table, its divan, and its bronze clock under a glass shade. There was a narrow pier-glass against the wall, and a chandelier adorned with lustres hung by a bronze chain from the ceiling.

When the prince entered, Lebedeff was standing in the middle of the room, his back to the door. He was in his shirt-sleeves, on account of the extreme heat, and he seemed to have just reached the peroration of his speech, and was impressively beating his breast.

His audience consisted of a youth of about fifteen years of age with a clever face, who had a book in his hand, though he was not reading; a young lady of twenty, in deep mourning, stood near him with an infant in her arms; another girl of thirteen, also in black, was laughing loudly, her mouth wide open; and on the sofa lay a handsome young man, with black hair and eyes, and a suspicion of beard and whiskers. He frequently interrupted the speaker and argued with him, to the great delight of the others.

"Lukian Timofeyovitch! Lukian Timofeyovitch! Here's someone to see you! Look here!... a gentleman to speak to you!... Well, it's not my fault!" and the cook turned and went away red with anger.

Lebedeff started, and at sight of the prince stood like a statue for a moment. Then he moved up to him with an ingratiating smile, but stopped short again.

"Prince! ex-ex-excellency!" he stammered. Then suddenly he ran towards the girl with the infant, a movement so unexpected by her that she staggered and fell back, but next moment he was threatening the other child, who was standing, still laughing, in the doorway. She screamed, and ran towards the kitchen. Lebedeff stamped his foot angrily; then, seeing the prince regarding him with amazement, he murmured apologetically– "Pardon to show respect!... he-he!"

"You are quite wrong..." began the prince.

"At once... at once... in one moment!"

He rushed like a whirlwind from the room, and Muishkin looked inquiringly at the others.

They were all laughing, and the guest joined in the chorus.

"He has gone to get his coat," said the boy.

"How annoying!" exclaimed the prince. "I thought... Tell me, is he..."

"You think he is drunk?" cried the young man on the sofa. "Not in the least. He's only had three or four small glasses, perhaps five; but what is that? The usual thing!"

As the prince opened his mouth to answer, he was interrupted by the girl, whose sweet face wore an expression of absolute frankness.

"He never drinks much in the morning; if you have come to talk business with him, do it now. It is the best time. He sometimes comes back drunk in the evening; but just now he passes the greater part of the evening in tears, and reads passages of

Holy Scripture aloud, because our mother died five weeks ago."

"No doubt he ran off because he did not know what to say to you," said the youth on the divan. "I bet he is trying to cheat you, and is thinking how best to do it."

Just then Lebedeff returned, having put on his coat.

"Five weeks!" said he, wiping his eyes. "Only five weeks! Poor orphans!"

"But why wear a coat in holes," asked the girl, "when your new one is hanging behind the door? Did you not see it?"

"Hold your tongue, dragon-fly!" he scolded. "What a plague you are!" He stamped his foot irritably, but she only laughed, and answered:

"Are you trying to frighten me? I am not Tania, you know, and I don't intend to run away. Look, you are waking Lubotchka, and she will have convulsions again. Why do you shout like that?"

"Well, well! I won't again," said the master

of the house, his anxiety getting the better of his temper. He went up to his daughter, and looked at the child in her arms, anxiously making the sign of the cross over her three times. "God bless her! God bless her!" he cried with emotion. "This little creature is my daughter Luboff," addressing the prince. "My wife, Helena, died–at her birth; and this is my big daughter Vera, in mourning, as you see; and this, this, oh, this," pointing to the young man on the divan...

"Well, go on! never mind me!" mocked the other. "Don't be afraid!"

"Excellency! Have you read that account of the murder of the Zemarin family, in the newspaper?" cried Lebedeff, all of a sudden.

"Yes," said Muishkin, with some surprise.

"Well, that is the murderer! It is he–in fact–"

"What do you mean?" asked the visitor.

"I am speaking allegorically, of course; but he will be the murderer of a Zemarin family in the future. He is getting ready. ..."

They all laughed, and the thought crossed

the prince's mind that perhaps Lebedeff was really trifling in this way because he foresaw inconvenient questions, and wanted to gain time.

"He is a traitor! a conspirator!" shouted Lebedeff, who seemed to have lost all control over himself. "A monster! a slanderer! Ought I to treat him as a nephew, the son of my sister Anisia?"

"Oh! do be quiet! You must be drunk! He has taken it into his head to play the lawyer, prince, and he practices speechifying, and is always repeating his eloquent pleadings to his children. And who do you think was his last client? An old woman who had been robbed of five hundred roubles, her all, by some rogue of a usurer, besought him to take up her case, instead of which he defended the usurer himself, a Jew named Zeidler, because this Jew promised to give him fifty roubles...."

"It was to be fifty if I won the case, only five if I lost," interrupted Lebedeff, speaking in a low tone, a great contrast to his earlier manner.

"Well! naturally he came to grief: the law is not administered as it used to be, and he only got laughed at for his pains. But he was much pleased with himself in spite of that. 'Most learned judge!' said he, 'picture this unhappy man, crippled by age and infirmities, who gains his living by honourable toil–picture him, I repeat, robbed of his all, of his last mouthful; remember, I entreat you, the words of that learned legislator, "Let mercy and justice alike rule the courts of law."' Now, would you believe it, excellency, every morning he recites this speech to us from beginning to end, exactly as he spoke it before the magistrate. To-day we have heard it for the fifth time. He was just starting again when you arrived, so much does he admire it. He is now preparing to undertake another case. I think, by the way, that you are Prince Muishkin? Colia tells me you are the cleverest man he has ever known...."

"The cleverest in the world," interrupted his uncle hastily.

"I do not pay much attention to that opinion," continued the young man calmly. "Colia is very fond of you, but he," pointing to Lebedeff, "is flattering you. I can assure you I have no intention of flattering you, or anyone else, but at least you have some common-sense. Well, will you judge between us? Shall we ask the prince to act as arbitrator?" he went on, addressing his uncle.

"I am so glad you chanced to come here, prince."

"I agree," said Lebedeff, firmly, looking round involuntarily at his daughter, who had come nearer, and was listening attentively to the conversation.

"What is it all about?" asked the prince, frowning. His head ached, and he felt sure that Lebedeff was trying to cheat him in some way, and only talking to put off the explanation that he had come for.

"I will tell you all the story. I am his nephew; he did speak the truth there, although he is generally telling lies. I am at the University, and have not yet finished my course. I mean to do so, and I shall, for I have a determined character. I must, however, find something to do for the present, and therefore I have got employment on the railway at twenty-four roubles a month. I admit that my uncle has helped me once or twice before. Well, I had twenty roubles in my pocket, and I gambled them away. Can you believe that I should be so low, so base, as to lose money in that way?"

"And the man who won it is a rogue, a rogue whom you ought not to have paid!" cried Lebedeff.

"Yes, he is a rogue, but I was obliged to pay him," said the young man. "As to his being a rogue, he is assuredly that, and I am not saying it because he beat you. He is an ex-lieutenant, prince, dismissed from the service, a teacher of boxing, and one of Rogojin's followers. They are all lounging about the pavements now that Rogojin has turned them off. Of course, the worst of it is that, knowing he was a rascal, and a card-sharper, I none the less played palki with him, and risked my last rouble. To tell the truth, I thought to myself, 'If I lose, I will go to my uncle, and I am sure he will not refuse to help me.' Now that was base–cowardly and base!"

"That is so," observed Lebedeff quietly; "cowardly and base."

"Well, wait a bit, before you begin to triumph," said the nephew viciously; for the words seemed to irritate him. "He is delighted! I came to him here and told him everything: I acted honourably, for I did not excuse myself. I spoke most severely of my conduct, as everyone here can witness. But I must smarten myself up before I take up my new post, for I am really like a tramp. Just look at my boots! I cannot possibly appear like this, and if I am not at the bureau at the time appointed, the job will be given to someone else; and I shall have to try for another. Now I only beg for fifteen roubles, and I give my word that I will never ask him for anything again. I am also ready to promise to repay my debt in three months' time, and I will keep my word, even if I have to live on bread and water. My salary will amount to seventy-five roubles in three months. The sum I now ask, added to what I have borrowed already, will make a total of about thirty-five roubles, so you see I shall have enough to pay him and confound him! if he wants interest, he shall have that, too! Haven't I always paid back the money he lent me before? Why should he be so mean now? He grudges my having paid that lieutenant; there can be no other reason! That's the kind he is–a dog in the manger!"

"And he won't go away!" cried Lebedeff. "He has installed himself here, and here he remains!"

"I have told you already, that I will not go away until I have got what I ask. Why are you smiling, prince? You look as if you disapproved of me."

"I am not smiling, but I really think you are in the wrong, somewhat," replied Muishkin, reluctantly.

"Don't shuffle! Say plainly that you think that I am quite wrong, without any 'somewhat'! Why 'somewhat'?"

"I will say you are quite wrong, if you wish."

"If I wish! That's good, I must say! Do you think I am deceived as to the flagrant impropriety of my conduct? I am quite aware that his money is his own, and that my action–is much like an attempt at extortion. But you-you don't know what life is! If people don't learn by experience, they never understand. They must be taught. My intentions are perfectly honest; on my conscience he will lose nothing, and I will pay back the money with interest. Added to which he has had the moral satisfaction of seeing me disgraced. What does he want more? and what is he good for if he never helps anyone? Look what he does himself! just ask him about his dealings with others, how he deceives people! How did he manage to buy this house? You may cut off my head if he has not let you in for something–and if he is not trying to cheat you again. You are smiling. You don't believe me?"

"It seems to me that all this has nothing to do with your affairs," remarked the prince.

"I have lain here now for three days," cried the young man without noticing, "and I have seen a lot! Fancy! he suspects his daughter, that angel, that orphan, my cousin–he suspects her, and every evening he searches her room, to see if she has a lover hidden in it! He comes here too on tiptoe, creeping softly–oh, so softly–and looks under the sofa–my bed, you know. He is mad with suspicion, and sees a thief in every corner. He runs about all night long;

he was up at least seven times last night, to satisfy himself that the windows and doors were barred, and to peep into the oven. That man who appears in court for scoundrels, rushes in here in the night and prays, lying prostrate, banging his head on the ground by the half-hour–and for whom do you think he prays? Who are the sinners figuring in his drunken petitions? I have heard him with my own ears praying for the repose of the soul of the Countess du Barry! Colia heard it too. He is as mad as a March hare!"

"You hear how he slanders me, prince," said Lebedeff, almost beside himself with rage. "I may be a drunkard, an evil-doer, a thief, but at least I can say one thing for myself. He does not know–how should he, mocker that he is?–that when he came into the world it was I who washed him, and dressed him in his swathing-bands, for my sister Anisia had lost her husband, and was in great poverty. I was very little better off than she, but I sat up night after night with her, and nursed both mother and child; I used to go downstairs and steal wood for them from the house-porter. How often did I sing him to sleep when I was half dead with hunger! In short, I was more than a father to him, and now–now he jeers at me! Even if I did cross myself, and pray for the repose of the soul of the Comtesse du Barry, what does it matter? Three days ago, for the first time in my life, I read her biography in an historical dictionary. Do you know who she was? You there!" addressing his nephew. "Speak! do you know?"

"Of course no one knows anything about her but you," muttered the young man in a would-be jeering tone.

"She was a Countess who rose from shame to reign like a Queen. An Empress wrote to her, with her own hand, as '**Ma chère cousine**.' At a **lever-du-roi** one morning (do you know what a **lever-du-roi** was?)–a Cardinal, a Papal legate, offered to put on her stockings; a high and holy person like that looked on it as an honour! Did you know this? I see by your expression that you did not! Well, how did she die? Answer!"

"Oh! do stop–you are too absurd!"

"This is how she died. After all this honour and glory, after having been almost a Queen, she was guillotined by that butcher, Samson. She was quite innocent, but it had to be done, for the satisfaction of the fishwives of Paris. She was so terrified, that she did not understand what was happening. But when Samson seized her head, and pushed her under the knife with his foot, she cried out: 'Wait a moment! wait a moment, monsieur!' Well, because of that moment of bitter suffering, perhaps the Saviour will pardon her other faults, for one cannot imagine a greater agony. As I read the story my heart bled for her. And what does it matter to you, little worm, if I implored the Divine mercy for her, great sinner as she was, as I said my evening prayer? I might have done it because

I doubted if anyone had ever crossed himself for her sake before. It may be that in the other world she will rejoice to think that a sinner like herself has cried to heaven for the salvation of her soul. Why are you laughing? You believe nothing, atheist! And your story was not even correct! If you had listened to what I was saying, you would have heard that I did not only pray for the Comtesse du Barry. I said, 'Oh Lord! give rest to the soul of that great sinner, the Comtesse du Barry, and to all unhappy ones like her.' You see that is quite a different thing, for how many sinners there are, how many women, who have passed through the trials of this life, are now suffering and groaning in purgatory! I prayed for you, too, in spite of your insolence and impudence, also for your fellows, as it seems that you claim to know how I pray..."

"Oh! that's enough in all conscience! Pray for whom you choose, and the devil take them and you! We have a scholar here; you did not know that, prince?" he continued, with a sneer. "He reads all sorts of books and memoirs now."

"At any rate, your uncle has a kind heart," remarked the prince, who really had to force himself to speak to the nephew, so much did he dislike him.

"Oh, now you are going to praise him! He will be set up! He puts his hand on his heart, and he is delighted! I never said he was a man without heart, but he is a rascal–that's the pity of it. And then, he is addicted to drink, and his mind is unhinged, like that of most people who have taken more than is good for them for years. He loves his children–oh, I know that well enough! He respected my aunt, his late wife... and he even has a sort of affection for me. He has remembered me in his will."

"I shall leave you nothing!" exclaimed his uncle angrily.

"Listen to me, Lebedeff," said the prince in a decided voice, turning his back on the young man. "I know by experience that when you choose, you can be business-like... I have very little time to spare, and if you... By the way–excuse me–what is your Christian name? I have forgotten it."

"Ti-Ti-Timofey."

"And?"

"Lukianovitch."

Everyone in the room began to laugh.

"He is telling lies!" cried the nephew. "Even now he cannot speak the truth. He is not called Timofey Lukianovitch, prince, but Lukian Timofeyovitch. Now do tell us why you must needs lie about it? Lukian or Timofey, it is all the same to you, and what difference can it make to the prince? He tells lies without the least necessity, simply by force of habit, I assure you."

"Is that true?" said the prince impatiently.

"My name really is Lukian Timofeyovitch," acknowledged Lebedeff, lowering his eyes, and putting his hand on his heart.

"Well, for God's sake, what made you say the other?"

"To humble myself," murmured Lebedeff.

"What on earth do you mean? Oh I if only I knew where Colia was at this moment!" cried the prince, standing up, as if to go.

"I can tell you all about Colia," said the young man

"Oh! no, no!" said Lebedeff, hurriedly.

"Colia spent the night here, and this morning went after his father, whom you let out of prison by paying his debts–Heaven only knows why! Yesterday the general promised to come and lodge here, but he did not appear. Most probably he slept at the hotel close by. No doubt Colia is there, unless he has gone to Pavlofsk to see the Epanchins. He had a little money, and was intending to go there yesterday. He must be either at the hotel or at Pavlofsk."

"AtPavlofsk!HeisatPavlofsk,undoubtedly!" interrupted Lebedeff.... "But come–let us go into the garden–we will have coffee there...." And Lebedeff seized the prince's arm, and led him from the room. They went across the yard, and found themselves in a delightful little garden with the trees already in their summer dress of green, thanks to the unusually fine weather. Lebedeff invited his guest to sit down on a green seat before a table of the same colour fixed in the earth, and took a seat facing him. In a few minutes the coffee appeared, and the prince did not refuse it. The host kept his eyes fixed on Muishkin, with an expression of passionate servility.

"I knew nothing about your home before," said the prince absently, as if he were thinking of something else.

"Poor orphans," began Lebedeff, his face assuming a mournful air, but he stopped short, for the other looked at him inattentively, as if he had already forgotten his own remark. They waited a few minutes in silence, while Lebedeff sat with his eyes fixed mournfully on the young man's face.

"Well!" said the latter, at last rousing himself. "Ah! yes! You know why I came, Lebedeff.

Your letter brought me. Speak! Tell me all about it."

The clerk, rather confused, tried to say something, hesitated, began to speak, and again stopped. The prince looked at him gravely.

"I think I understand, Lukian Timofeyovitch: you were not sure that I should come. You did not think I should start at the first word from you, and you merely wrote to relieve your conscience. However, you see now that I have come, and I have had enough of trickery. Give up serving, or trying to serve, two masters. Rogojin has been here these three weeks. Have you managed to sell her to him as you did before? Tell me the truth."

"He discovered everything, the monster... himself......"

"Don't abuse him; though I dare say you have something to complain of...."

"He beat me, he thrashed me unmercifully!" replied Lebedeff vehemently. "He set a dog on me in Moscow, a bloodhound, a terrible beast that chased me all down the street."

"You seem to take me for a child, Lebedeff. Tell me, is it a fact that she left him while they were in Moscow?"

"Yes, it is a fact, and this time, let me tell you, on the very eve of their marriage! It was a question of minutes when she slipped off to Petersburg. She came to me directly she arrived–'Save me, Lukian! find me some refuge, and say nothing to the prince!' She is afraid of you, even more than she is of him, and in that she shows her wisdom!" And Lebedeff slily put his finger to his brow as he said the last words.

"And now it is you who have brought them together again?"

"Excellency, how could I, how could I prevent it?"

"That will do. I can find out for myself. Only tell me, where is she now? At his house? With him?"

"Oh no! Certainly not! 'I am free,' she says;

you know how she insists on that point. 'I am entirely free.' She repeats it over and over again. She is living in Petersburgskaia, with my sister-in-law, as I told you in my letter."

"She is there at this moment?"

"Yes, unless she has gone to Pavlofsk: the fine weather may have tempted her, perhaps, into the country, with Daria Alexeyevna. 'I am quite free,' she says. Only yesterday she boasted of her freedom to Nicolai Ardalionovitch–a bad sign," added Lebedeff, smiling.

"Colia goes to see her often, does he not?"

"He is a strange boy, thoughtless, and inclined to be indiscreet."

"Is it long since you saw her?"

"I go to see her every day, every day."

"Then you were there yesterday?"

"N-no: I have not been these three last days."

"It is a pity you have taken too much wine, Lebedeff I want to ask you something...

but..."

"All right! all right! I am not drunk," replied the clerk, preparing to listen.

"Tell me, how was she when you left her?"

"She is a woman who is seeking..."

"Seeking?"

"She seems always to be searching about, as if she had lost something. The mere idea of her coming marriage disgusts her; she looks on it as an insult. She cares as much for **him** as for a piece of orange-peel–not more. Yet I am much mistaken if she does not look on him with fear and trembling. She forbids his name to be mentioned before her, and they only meet when unavoidable. He understands, well enough! But it must be gone through. She is restless, mocking, deceitful, violent...."

"Deceitful and violent?"

"Yes, violent. I can give you a proof of it. A few days ago she tried to pull my hair because I said something that annoyed her. I tried to soothe her by reading the

Apocalypse aloud."

"What?" exclaimed the prince, thinking he had not heard aright.

"By reading the Apocalypse. The lady has a restless imagination, he-he! She has a liking for conversation on serious subjects, of any kind; in fact they please her so much, that it flatters her to discuss them. Now for fifteen years at least I have studied the Apocalypse, and she agrees with me in thinking that the present is the epoch represented by the third horse, the black one whose rider holds a measure in his hand. It seems to me that everything is ruled by measure in our century; all men are clamouring for their rights; 'a measure of wheat for a penny, and three measures of barley for a penny.' But, added to this, men desire freedom of mind and body, a pure heart, a healthy life, and all God's good gifts. Now by pleading their rights alone, they will never attain all this, so the white horse, with his rider Death, comes next, and is followed by Hell. We talked about this matter when we met, and it impressed her very much."

"Do you believe all this?" asked Muishkin, looking curiously at his companion.

"I both believe it and explain it. I am but a poor creature, a beggar, an atom in the scale of humanity. Who has the least respect for Lebedeff? He is a target for all the world, the butt of any fool who chooses to kick him. But in interpreting revelation I am the equal of anyone, great as he may be! Such is the power of the mind and the spirit. I have made a lordly personage tremble, as he sat in his armchair... only by talking to him of things concerning the spirit. Two years ago, on Easter Eve, His Excellency Nil Alexeyovitch, whose subordinate I was then, wished to hear what I had to say, and sent a message by Peter Zakkaritch to ask me to go to his private room. 'They tell me you expound the prophecies relating to Antichrist,' said he, when we were alone. 'Is that so?' 'Yes,' I answered unhesitatingly, and I began to give some comments on the Apostle's allegorical vision. At first he smiled, but when we reached the numerical computations and correspondences, he trembled, and turned pale. Then he begged me to close the book, and sent me away, promising to put my name on the reward list. That took place as I said on the eve of Easter, and eight days later his soul returned to God."

"What?"

"It is the truth. One evening after dinner he stumbled as he stepped out of his carriage. He fell, and struck his head on the curb, and died immediately. He was seventy-three years of age, and had a red face, and white hair; he deluged himself with scent, and was always smiling like a child. Peter Zakkaritch recalled my interview with him, and said, '**you foretold his death.**'"

The prince rose from his seat, and Lebedeff, surprised to see his guest preparing to go so soon, remarked: "You are not interested?" in a respectful tone.

"I am not very well, and my head aches. Doubtless the effect of the journey," replied the prince, frowning.

"You should go into the country," said Lebedeff timidly.

The prince seemed to be considering the suggestion.

"You see, I am going into the country myself in three days, with my children and belongings. The little one is delicate; she needs change of air; and during our absence this house will be done up. I am going to Pavlofsk."

"You are going to Pavlofsk too?" asked the prince sharply. "Everybody seems to be going there. Have you a house in that neighbourhood?"

"I don't know of many people going to Pavlofsk, and as for the house, Ivan Ptitsin has let me one of his villas rather cheaply. It is a pleasant place, lying on a hill surrounded by trees, and one can live there for a mere song. There is good music to be heard, so no wonder it is popular. I shall stay in the lodge. As to the villa itself..."

"Have you let it?"

"N-no–not exactly."

"Let it to me," said the prince.

Now this was precisely what Lebedeff had made up his mind to do in the last three minutes. Not that he had any difficulty in finding a tenant; in fact the house was occupied at present by a chance visitor, who had told Lebedeff that he would perhaps take it for the summer months. The clerk knew very well that this "**perhaps**" meant "**certainly**," but as he thought he could make more out of a tenant like the prince, he felt justified in speaking vaguely about the present inhabitant's intentions. "This is quite a coincidence," thought he, and when the subject of price was mentioned, he made a gesture with his hand, as if to waive away a question of so little importance.

"Oh well, as you like!" said Muishkin. "I will think it over. You shall lose nothing!"

They were walking slowly across the garden.

"But if you... I could..." stammered Lebedeff, "if... if you please, prince, tell you something on the subject which would interest you, I am sure." He spoke in wheedling tones, and wriggled as he walked along.

Muishkin stopped short.

"Daria Alexeyevna also has a villa at Pavlofsk."

"Well?"

"A certain person is very friendly with her, and intends to visit her pretty often."

"Well?"

"Aglaya Ivanovna..."

"Oh stop, Lebedeff!" interposed Muishkin, feeling as if he had been touched on an open wound. "That... that has nothing to do with me. I should like to know when you are going to start. The sooner the better as far as I am concerned, for I am at an hotel."

They had left the garden now, and were crossing the yard on their way to the gate.

"Well, leave your hotel at once and come here; then we can all go together to Pavlofsk the day after tomorrow."

"I will think about it," said the prince dreamily, and went off.

The clerk stood looking after his guest, struck by his sudden absent-mindedness. He had not even remembered to say goodbye, and Lebedeff was the more surprised at the omission, as he knew by experience how courteous the prince usually was.

CHAPTER THREE

IT WAS NOW CLOSE on twelve o'clock.

The prince knew that if he called at the Epanchins' now he would only find the general, and that the latter might probably carry him straight off to Pavlofsk with him; whereas there was one visit he was most anxious to make without delay.

So at the risk of missing General Epanchin altogether, and thus postponing his visit to Pavlofsk for a day, at least, the prince decided to go and look for the house he desired to find.

The visit he was about to pay was, in some respects, a risky one. He was in two minds about it, but knowing that the house was in the Gorohovaya, not far from the Sadovaya, he determined to go in that direction, and to try to make up his mind on the way.

Arrived at the point where the Gorohovaya crosses the Sadovaya, he was surprised to find how excessively agitated he was. He had no idea that his heart could beat so painfully.

One house in the Gorohovaya began to attract his attention long before he reached it, and the prince remembered afterwards that he had said to himself: “That is the house, I’m sure of it.” He came up to it quite curious to discover whether he had guessed right, and felt that he would be disagreeably impressed to find that he had actually done so. The house was a large gloomy-looking structure, without the slightest claim to architectural beauty, in colour a dirty green.

There are a few of these old houses, built towards the end of the last century, still standing in that part of St. Petersburg, and showing little change from their original form and colour. They are solidly built, and are remarkable for the thickness of their walls, and for the fewness of their windows, many of which are covered by gratings. On the ground-floor there is usually a money-changer's shop, and the owner lives over it. Without as well as within, the houses seem inhospitable and mysterious–an impression which is difficult to explain, unless it has something to do with the actual architectural style. These houses are almost exclusively inhabited by the merchant class.

Arrived at the gate, the prince looked up at the legend over it, which ran:

"House of Rogojin, hereditary and honourable citizen."

He hesitated no longer; but opened the glazed door at the bottom of the outer stairs and made his way up to the second storey.

The place was dark and gloomy-looking; the walls of the stone staircase were painted a dull red. Rogojin and his mother and brother occupied the whole of the second floor. The servant who opened the door to Muishkin led him, without taking his name, through several rooms and up and down many steps until they arrived at a door, where he knocked.

Parfen Rogojin opened the door himself.

On seeing the prince he became deadly white, and apparently fixed to the ground, so that he was more like a marble statue than a human being. The prince had expected some surprise, but Rogojin evidently considered his visit an impossible and miraculous event. He stared with an expression almost of terror, and his lips twisted into a bewildered smile.

"Parfen! perhaps my visit is ill-timed. I–I can go away again if you like," said Muishkin at last, rather embarrassed.

"No, no; it's all right, come in," said Parfen, recollecting himself.

They were evidently on quite familiar terms.

In Moscow they had had many occasions of meeting; indeed, some few of those meetings were but too vividly impressed upon their memories. They had not met now, however, for three months.

The deathlike pallor, and a sort of slight convulsion about the lips, had not left Rogojin's face. Though he welcomed his guest, he was still obviously much disturbed. As he invited the prince to sit down near the table, the latter happened to turn towards him, and was startled by the strange expression on his face. A painful recollection flashed into his mind. He stood for a time, looking straight at Rogojin, whose eyes seemed to blaze like fire. At last Rogojin smiled, though he still looked agitated and shaken.

"What are you staring at me like that for?" he muttered. "Sit down."

The prince took a chair.

"Parfen," he said, "tell me honestly, did you know that I was coming to Petersburg or no?"

"Oh, I supposed you were coming," the other replied, smiling sarcastically, "and I was right in my supposition, you see; but how was I to know that you would come **today?**"

A certain strangeness and impatience in his manner impressed the prince very forcibly.

"And if you had known that I was coming today, why be so irritated about it?" he asked, in quiet surprise.

"Why did you ask me?"

"Because when I jumped out of the train this morning, two eyes glared at me just as yours did a moment since."

"Ha! and whose eyes may they have been?" said Rogojin, suspiciously. It seemed to the prince that he was trembling.

"I don't know; I thought it was a hallucination. I often have hallucinations nowadays. I feel just as I did five years ago when my fits were about to come on."

"Well, perhaps it was a hallucination, I don't know," said Parfen.

He tried to give the prince an affectionate smile, and it seemed to the latter as though in this smile of his something had broken, and that he could not mend it, try as he would.

"Shall you go abroad again then?" he asked, and suddenly added, "Do you remember how we came up in the train from Pskoff together? You and your cloak and leggings, eh?"

And Rogojin burst out laughing, this time with unconcealed malice, as though he were glad that he had been able to find an opportunity for giving vent to it.

"Have you quite taken up your quarters here?" asked the prince

"Yes, I'm at home. Where else should I go to?"

"We haven't met for some time. Meanwhile I have heard things about you which I should not have believed to be possible."

"What of that? People will say anything," said Rogojin drily.

"At all events, you've disbanded your troop–and you are living in your own house instead of being fast and loose about the place; that's all very good. Is this house all yours, or joint property?"

"It is my mother's. You get to her apartments by that passage."

"Where's your brother?"

"In the other wing."

"Is he married?"

"Widower. Why do you want to know all this?"

The prince looked at him, but said nothing. He had suddenly relapsed into musing, and had probably not heard the question at all. Rogojin did not insist upon an answer, and there was silence for a few moments.

"I guessed which was your house from a hundred yards off," said the prince at last.

"Why so?"

"I don't quite know. Your house has the

aspect of yourself and all your family; it bears the stamp of the Rogojin life; but ask me why I think so, and I can tell you nothing. It is nonsense, of course. I am nervous about this kind of thing troubling me so much. I had never before imagined what sort of a house you would live in, and yet no sooner did I set eyes on this one than I said to myself that it must be yours."

"Really!" said Rogojin vaguely, not taking in what the prince meant by his rather obscure remarks.

The room they were now sitting in was a large one, lofty but dark, well furnished, principally with writing-tables and desks covered with papers and books. A wide sofa covered with red morocco evidently served Rogojin for a bed. On the table beside which the prince had been invited to seat himself lay some books; one containing a marker where the reader had left off, was a volume of Solovieff's History. Some oil-paintings in worn gilded frames hung on the walls, but it was impossible to make out what subjects they represented, so blackened were they by smoke and age. One, a life-sized portrait, attracted the prince's attention. It showed a man of about fifty, wearing a long riding-coat of German cut. He had two medals on his breast; his beard was white, short and thin; his face yellow and wrinkled, with a sly, suspicious expression in the eyes.

"That is your father, is it not?" asked the prince.

"Yes, it is," replied Rogojin with an unpleasant smile, as if he had expected his guest to ask the question, and then to make some disagreeable remark.

"Was he one of the Old Believers?"

"No, he went to church, but to tell the truth he really preferred the old religion. This was his study and is now mine. Why did you ask if he were an Old Believer?"

"Are you going to be married here?"

"Ye-yes!" replied Rogojin, starting at the unexpected question.

"Soon?"

"You know yourself it does not depend on me."

"Parfen, I am not your enemy, and I do not intend to oppose your intentions in any way. I repeat this to you now just as I said it to you once before on a very similar occasion. When you were arranging for your projected marriage in Moscow, I did not interfere with you–you know I did not. That first time she fled to me from you, from the very altar almost, and begged me to 'save her from you.' Afterwards she ran away from me again, and you found her and arranged your marriage with her once more; and now, I hear, she has run away from you and come to Petersburg. Is it true? Lebedeff wrote me to this effect, and that's why I came here. That you had once more arranged matters with Nastasia Philipovna I only learned last night in the train from a friend of yours, Zaleshoff–if you wish to know.

"I confess I came here with an object. I

wished to persuade Nastasia to go abroad for her health; she requires it. Both mind and body need a change badly. I did not intend to take her abroad myself. I was going to arrange for her to go without me. Now I tell you honestly, Parfen, if it is true that all is made up between you, I will not so much as set eyes upon her, and I will never even come to see you again.

"You know quite well that I am telling the truth, because I have always been frank with you. I have never concealed my own opinion from you. I have always told you that I consider a marriage between you and her would be ruin to her. You would also be ruined, and perhaps even more hopelessly. If this marriage were to be broken off again, I admit I should be greatly pleased; but at the same time I have not the slightest intention of trying to part you. You may be quite easy in your mind, and you need not suspect me. You know yourself whether I was ever really your rival or not, even when she ran away and came to me.

"There, you are laughing at me–I know why you laugh. It is perfectly true that we lived apart from one another all the time, in different towns. I told you before that I did not love her with love, but with pity! You said then that you understood me; did you really understand me or not? What hatred there is in your eyes at this moment! I came to relieve your mind, because you are dear to me also. I love you very much, Parfen; and now I shall go away and never come back again. Goodbye."

The prince rose.

"Stay a little," said Parfen, not leaving his chair and resting his head on his right hand. "I haven't seen you for a long time."

The prince sat down again. Both were silent for a few moments.

"When you are not with me I hate you, Lef Nicolaievitch. I have loathed you every day of these three months since I last saw you. By heaven I have!" said Rogojin. "I could have poisoned you at any minute. Now, you have been with me but a quarter of an hour, and all my malice seems to have melted away, and you are as dear to me as ever. Stay here a little longer."

"When I am with you you trust me; but as soon as my back is turned you suspect me," said the prince, smiling, and trying to hide his emotion.

"I trust your voice, when I hear you speak. I quite understand that you and I cannot be put on a level, of course."

"Why did you add that?–There! Now you are cross again," said the prince, wondering.

"We were not asked, you see. We were made different, with different tastes and feelings, without being consulted. You say you love her with pity. I have no pity for her. She hates me–that's the plain truth of the matter. I dream of her every night, and always that she is laughing at me with another man. And so she does laugh at me. She thinks no more of marrying me than if she were changing her shoe. Would you believe it, I haven't seen her for five days, and I daren't go near her. She asks me what I come for, as if she were not content with having disgraced me–"

"Disgraced you! How?"

"Just as though you didn't know! Why, she ran away from me, and went to you. You admitted it yourself, just now."

"But surely you do not believe that she..."

"That she did not disgrace me at Moscow with that officer, Zemtuznikoff? I know for certain she did, after having fixed our marriage-day herself!"

"Impossible!" cried the prince.

"I know it for a fact," replied Rogojin, with conviction.

"It is not like her, you say? My friend, that's absurd. Perhaps such an act would horrify her, if she were with you, but it is quite different where I am concerned. She looks on me as vermin. Her affair with Keller was simply to make a laughing-stock of me. You don't know what a fool she made of me in Moscow; and the money I spent over her! The money! the money!"

"And you can marry her now, Parfen! What will come of it all?" said the prince, with dread in his voice.

Rogojin gazed back gloomily, and with a terrible expression in his eyes, but said nothing.

"I haven't been to see her for five days," he repeated, after a slight pause. "I'm afraid of being turned out. She says she's still her own mistress, and may turn me off altogether, and go abroad. She told me this herself," he said, with a peculiar glance at Muishkin. "I think she often does it merely to frighten me. She is always laughing at me, for some reason or other; but at other times she's angry, and won't say a word, and that's what I'm afraid of. I took her a shawl one day, the like of which she might never have seen, although she did live in luxury and she gave it away to her maid,

Katia. Sometimes when I can keep away no longer, I steal past the house on the sly, and once I watched at the gate till dawn–I thought something was going on–and she saw me from the window. She asked me what I should do if I found she had deceived me. I said, 'You know well enough.'"

"What did she know?" cried the prince.

"How was I to tell?" replied Rogojin, with an angry laugh. "I did my best to catch her tripping in Moscow, but did not succeed. However, I caught hold of her one day, and said: 'You are engaged to be married into a respectable family, and do you know what sort of a woman you are? **That's** the sort of woman you are,' I said."

"You told her that?"

"Yes."

"Well, go on."

"She said, 'I wouldn't even have you for a footman now, much less for a husband.' 'I shan't leave the house,' I said, 'so it doesn't matter.' 'Then I shall call somebody and have you kicked out,' she cried. So then I rushed at her, and beat her till she was bruised all over."

"Impossible!" cried the prince, aghast.

"I tell you it's true," said Rogojin quietly, but with eyes ablaze with passion.

"Then for a day and a half I neither slept, nor ate, nor drank, and would not leave her. I knelt at her feet: 'I shall die here,' I said, 'if you don't forgive me; and if you have me turned out, I shall drown myself; because, what should I be without you now?' She was like a madwoman all that day; now she would cry; now she would threaten me with a knife; now she would abuse me. She called in Zaleshoff and Keller, and showed me to them, shamed me in their presence. 'Let's all go to the theatre,' she says, 'and leave him here if he won't go–it's not my business. They'll give you some tea, Parfen Semeonovitch, while I am away, for you must be hungry.' She came back from the theatre alone. 'Those cowards wouldn't come,' she said. 'They are afraid of you, and tried to frighten me, too. "He won't go away as he came," they said, "he'll cut your throat–see if he doesn't." Now, I shall go to my bedroom, and I shall not even lock my door, just to show you how much I am afraid of you. You must be shown that once for all. Did you have tea?' 'No,' I said, 'and I don't intend to.' 'Ha, ha! you are playing off your pride against your stomach! That sort of heroism doesn't sit well on you,' she said.

"With that she did as she had said she would; she went to bed, and did not lock her door. In the morning she came out. 'Are you quite mad?' she said, sharply. 'Why, you'll die of hunger like this.' 'Forgive me,' I said. 'No, I won't, and I won't marry you. I've said it. Surely you haven't sat in this chair all night without sleeping?' 'I didn't sleep,' I said. 'H'm! how sensible of you. And are you going to have no breakfast or dinner today?' 'I told you I wouldn't. Forgive me!' 'You've no idea how unbecoming this sort of thing is to you,' she said, 'it's like putting a saddle on a cow's back. Do you think you are frightening me? My word, what a dreadful thing that you should sit here and eat no food! How terribly frightened I am!' She wasn't angry long, and didn't seem to remember my offence at all. I was surprised, for she is a vindictive, resentful woman–but then I thought that perhaps she despised me too much to feel any resentment against me. And that's the truth.

"She came up to me and said, 'Do you know who the Pope of Rome is?' 'I've heard of him,' I said. 'I suppose you've read the Universal History, Parfen Semeonovitch, haven't you?' she asked. 'I've learned nothing at all,' I said. 'Then I'll lend it to you to read. You must know there was a Roman Pope once, and he was very angry with a certain Emperor; so the Emperor came and neither ate nor drank, but knelt before the Pope's palace till he should be forgiven. And what sort of vows do you think that Emperor was making during all those days on his knees? Stop, I'll read it to you!' Then she read me a lot of verses, where it said that the Emperor spent all the time vowing vengeance against the Pope. 'You don't mean to say you don't approve of the poem, Parfen Semeonovitch,' she says. 'All you have read out is perfectly true,' say I. 'Aha!' says she, 'you admit it's true, do you? And you are making vows to yourself that if I marry you, you will remind me of all this, and take it out of me.' 'I don't know,' I say, 'perhaps I was thinking like that, and perhaps I was not. I'm not thinking of anything just now.' 'What are your thoughts, then?' 'I'm thinking that when you rise from your chair and go past me, I watch you, and follow you with my eyes; if your dress does but rustle, my heart sinks; if you leave the room, I remember every little word and action, and what your voice sounded like, and what you said. I thought of nothing all last night, but sat here listening to your sleeping breath, and heard you move a little, twice.' 'And as for your attack upon me,' she says, 'I suppose you never once thought of **that?**' 'Perhaps I did think of it, and perhaps not,' I say. 'And what if I don't either forgive you or marry, you?' 'I tell you I shall go and drown myself.' 'H'm!' she said, and then relapsed into silence. Then she got angry, and went out. 'I suppose you'd murder me before you drowned yourself, though!' she cried as she left the room.

"An hour later, she came to me again, looking melancholy. 'I will marry you, Parfen Semeonovitch,' she says, not because I'm frightened of you, but because it's all the same to me how I ruin myself. And how can I do it better? Sit down; they'll bring you some dinner directly. And if I do marry you, I'll be a faithful wife to you–you need not doubt that.' Then she thought a bit, and said, 'At all events, you are not a flunkey; at first, I thought you were no better than a flunkey.' And she arranged the wedding and fixed the day straight away on the spot.

"Then, in another week, she had run away again, and came here to Lebedeff's; and when I found her here, she said to me, 'I'm not going to renounce you altogether, but I wish to put off the wedding a bit longer yet–just as long as I like–for I am still my own mistress; so you may wait, if you like.' That's how the matter stands between us now. What do you think of all this, Lef Nicolaievitch?"

"'What do you think of it yourself?" replied the prince, looking sadly at Rogojin.

"As if I can think anything about it! I–" He was about to say more, but stopped in despair.

The prince rose again, as if he would leave.

"At all events, I shall not interfere with you!" he murmured, as though making answer to some secret thought of his own.

"I'll tell you what!" cried Rogojin, and his eyes flashed fire. "I can't understand your yielding her to me like this; I don't understand it. Have you given up loving her altogether?

At first you suffered badly–I know it–I saw it. Besides, why did you come post-haste after us? Out of pity, eh? He, he, he!" His mouth curved in a mocking smile.

"Do you think I am deceiving you?" asked the prince.

"No! I trust you–but I can't understand. It seems to me that your pity is greater than my love." A hungry longing to speak his mind out seemed to flash in the man's eyes, combined with an intense anger.

"Your love is mingled with hatred, and therefore, when your love passes, there will be the greater misery," said the prince. "I tell you this, Parfen–"

"What! that I'll cut her throat, you mean?"

The prince shuddered.

"You'll hate her afterwards for all your present love, and for all the torment you are suffering on her account now. What seems to me the most extraordinary thing is, that she can again consent to marry you, after all that has passed between you. When I heard the news yesterday, I could hardly bring myself to believe it. Why, she has run twice from you, from the very altar rails, as it were. She must have some presentiment of evil. What can she want with you now? Your money? Nonsense! Besides, I should think you must have made a fairly large hole in your fortune already. Surely it is not because she is so very anxious to find a husband? She could find many a one besides yourself. Anyone would be better than you, because you will murder her, and I feel sure she must know that but too well by now. Is it because you love her so passionately? Indeed, that may be it. I have heard that there are women who want just that kind of love... but still..." The prince paused, reflectively.

"What are you grinning at my father's portrait again for?" asked Rogojin, suddenly. He was carefully observing every change in the expression of the prince's face.

"I smiled because the idea came into my

head that if it were not for this unhappy passion of yours you might have, and would have, become just such a man as your father, and that very quickly, too. You'd have settled down in this house of yours with some silent and obedient wife. You would have spoken rarely, trusted no one, heeded no one, and thought of nothing but making money."

"Laugh away! She said exactly the same, almost word for word, when she saw my father's portrait. It's remarkable how entirely you and she are at one now-a-days."

"What, has she been here?" asked the prince with curiosity.

"Yes! She looked long at the portrait and asked all about my father. 'You'd be just such another,' she said at last, and laughed. 'You have such strong passions, Parfen,' she said, 'that they'd have taken you to Siberia in no time if you had not, luckily, intelligence as well. For you have a good deal of intelligence.' (She said this–believe it or not. The first time I ever heard anything of that sort from her.) 'You'd soon have thrown up all this rowdyism that you indulge in now, and you'd have settled down to quiet, steady money-making, because you have little education; and here you'd have stayed just like your father before you. And you'd have loved your money so that you'd amass not two million, like him, but ten million; and you'd have died of hunger on your money bags to finish up with, for you carry everything to extremes.' There, that's exactly word for word as she said it to me. She never talked to me like that before. She always talks nonsense and laughs when she's with me. We went all over this old house together. 'I shall change all this,' I said, 'or else I'll buy a new house for the wedding.' 'No, no!' she said, 'don't touch anything; leave it all as it is; I shall live with your mother when I marry you.'

"I took her to see my mother, and she was as respectful and kind as though she were her own daughter. Mother has been almost demented ever since father died–she's an old woman. She sits and bows from her chair to everyone she sees. If you left her alone and didn't feed her for three days, I don't believe she would notice it. Well, I took her hand, and I said, 'Give your blessing to this lady, mother, she's going to be my wife.' So Nastasia kissed mother's hand with great feeling. 'She must have suffered terribly, hasn't she?' she said. She saw this book here lying before me. 'What! have you begun to read Russian history?' she asked. She told me once in Moscow, you know, that I had better get Solovieff's Russian History and read it, because I knew nothing. 'That's good,' she said, 'you go on like that, reading books. I'll make you a list myself of the books you ought to read first–shall I?' She had never once spoken to me like this before; it was the first time I felt I could breathe before her like a living creature."

"I'm very, very glad to hear of this, Parfen," said the prince, with real feeling. "Who knows? Maybe God will yet bring you near to one another."

"Never, never!" cried Rogojin, excitedly.

"Look here, Parfen; if you love her so much, surely you must be anxious to earn her respect? And if you do so wish, surely you may hope to? I said just now that I considered it extraordinary that she could still be ready to marry you. Well, though I cannot yet understand it, I feel sure she must have some good reason, or she wouldn't do it. She is sure of your love; but besides that, she must attribute **something** else to you–some good qualities, otherwise the thing would not be. What you have just said confirms my words. You say yourself that she found it possible to speak to you quite differently from her usual manner. You are suspicious, you know, and jealous, therefore when anything annoying happens to you, you exaggerate its significance. Of course, of course, she does not think so ill of you as you say. Why, if she did, she would simply be walking to death by drowning or by the knife, with her eyes wide open, when she married you. It is impossible! As if anybody would go to their death deliberately!"

Rogojin listened to the prince's excited words with a bitter smile. His conviction was, apparently, unalterable.

"How dreadfully you look at me, Parfen!" said the prince, with a feeling of dread.

"Water or the knife?" said the latter, at last. "Ha, ha–that's exactly why she is going to marry me, because she knows for certain that the knife awaits her. Prince, can it be that you don't even yet see what's at the root of it all?"

"I don't understand you."

"Perhaps he really doesn't understand me! They do say that you are a–you know what! She loves another–there, you can understand that much! Just as I love her, exactly so she loves another man. And that other man is–do you know who? It's you. There–you didn't know that, eh?"

"I?"

"You, you! She has loved you ever since that day, her birthday! Only she thinks she cannot marry you, because it would be the ruin of you. 'Everybody knows what sort of a woman I am,' she says. She told me all this herself, to my very face! She's afraid of disgracing and ruining you, she says, but it doesn't matter about me. She can marry me all right! Notice how much consideration she shows for me!"

"But why did she run away to me, and then again from me to–"

"From you to me? Ha, ha! that's nothing! Why, she always acts as though she were in a delirium now-a-days! Either she says, 'Come on, I'll marry you! Let's have the wedding quickly!' and fixes the day, and seems in a hurry for it, and when it begins to come near she feels frightened; or else some other idea gets into her head–goodness knows! you've seen her–you know how she goes on–laughing and crying and raving! There's nothing extraordinary about her having run away from you! She ran away because she found out how dearly she loved you. She could not bear to be near you. You said just now that I had found her at Moscow, when she ran away from you. I didn't do anything of the sort; she came to me herself, straight from you. 'Name the day–I'm ready!' she said. 'Let's have some champagne, and go and hear the gipsies sing!' I tell you she'd have thrown herself into the water long ago if it were not for me! She doesn't do it because I am, perhaps, even more dreadful to her than the water! She's marrying me out of spite; if she marries me, I tell you, it will be for spite!"

"But how do you, how can you–" began the prince, gazing with dread and horror at Rogojin.

"Why don't you finish your sentence? Shall I tell you what you were thinking to yourself just then? You were thinking, 'How can she marry him after this? How can it possibly be permitted?' Oh, I know what you were thinking about!"

"I didn't come here for that purpose, Parfen. That was not in my mind–"

"That may be! Perhaps you didn't **come** with the idea, but the idea is certainly there **now!** Ha, ha! well, that's enough! What are you upset about? Didn't you really know it all before? You astonish me!"

"All this is mere jealousy–it is some malady of yours, Parfen! You exaggerate everything," said the prince, excessively agitated. "What are you doing?"

"Let go of it!" said Parfen, seizing from the prince's hand a knife which the latter had at that moment taken up from the table, where it lay beside the history. Parfen replaced it where it had been.

"I seemed to know it–I felt it, when I was coming back to Petersburg," continued the prince, "I did not want to come, I wished to forget all this, to uproot it from my memory altogether! Well, good-bye–what is the matter?"

He had absently taken up the knife a second time, and again Rogojin snatched it from his hand, and threw it down on the table. It was a plain looking knife, with a bone handle, a blade about eight inches long, and broad in proportion, it did not clasp.

Seeing that the prince was considerably struck by the fact that he had twice seized this knife out of his hand, Rogojin caught it up with some irritation, put it inside the book, and threw the latter across to another table.

"Do you cut your pages with it, or what?" asked Muishkin, still rather absently, as though unable to throw off a deep preoccupation into which the conversation had thrown him.

"Yes."

"It's a garden knife, isn't it?"

"Yes. Can't one cut pages with a garden

knife?"

"It's quite new."

"Well, what of that? Can't I buy a new knife if I like?" shouted Rogojin furiously, his irritation growing with every word.

The prince shuddered, and gazed fixedly at Parfen. Suddenly he burst out laughing.

"Why, what an idea!" he said. "I didn't mean to ask you any of these questions; I was thinking of something quite different! But my head is heavy, and I seem so absent-minded nowadays! Well, good-bye–I can't remember what I wanted to say–good-bye!"

"Not that way," said Rogojin.

"There, I've forgotten that too!"

"This way–come along–I'll show you."

CHAPTER FOUR

THEY PASSED THROUGH THE same rooms which the prince had traversed on his arrival. In the largest there were pictures on the walls, portraits and landscapes of little interest. Over the door, however, there was one of strange and rather striking shape; it was six or seven feet in length, and not more than a foot in height. It represented the Saviour just taken from the cross.

The prince glanced at it, but took no further notice. He moved on hastily, as though anxious to get out of the house. But Rogojin suddenly stopped underneath the picture.

"My father picked up all these pictures very cheap at auctions, and so on," he said; "they are all rubbish, except the one over the door, and that is valuable. A man offered five hundred roubles for it last week."

"Yes–that's a copy of a Holbein," said the prince, looking at it again, "and a good copy, too, so far as I am able to judge. I saw the picture abroad, and could not forget it–what's the matter?"

Rogojin had dropped the subject of the picture and walked on. Of course his strange frame of mind was sufficient to account for his conduct; but, still, it seemed queer to the prince that he should so abruptly drop a conversation commenced by himself. Rogojin did not take any notice of his question.

"Lef Nicolaievitch," said Rogojin, after a pause, during which the two walked along a little further, "I have long wished to ask you, do you believe in God?"

"How strangely you speak, and how odd you look!" said the other, involuntarily.

"I like looking at that picture," muttered Rogojin, not noticing, apparently, that the prince had not answered his question.

"That picture! That picture!" cried Muishkin, struck by a sudden idea. "Why, a man's faith might be ruined by looking at that picture!"

"So it is!" said Rogojin, unexpectedly. They had now reached the front door.

The prince stopped.

"How?" he said. "What do you mean? I was half joking, and you took me up quite seriously! Why do you ask me whether I believe in God?"

"Oh, no particular reason. I meant to ask you before–many people are unbelievers nowadays, especially Russians, I have been told. You ought to know–you've lived abroad."

Rogojin laughed bitterly as he said these words, and opening the door, held it for the prince to pass out. Muishkin looked surprised, but went out. The other followed him as far as the landing of the outer stairs, and shut the door behind him. They both now stood facing one another, as though oblivious of where they were, or what they had to do next.

"Well, good-bye!" said the prince, holding out his hand.

"Good-bye," said Rogojin, pressing it hard, but quite mechanically.

The prince made one step forward, and then turned round.

"As to faith," he said, smiling, and evidently unwilling to leave Rogojin in this state–"as to faith, I had four curious conversations in two days, a week or so ago. One morning I met a man in the train, and made acquaintance with him at once. I had often heard of him as a very learned man, but an atheist; and I was very glad of the opportunity of conversing with so eminent and clever a person. He doesn't believe in God, and he talked a good deal about it, but all the while it appeared to me that he was speaking **outside the subject**. And it has always struck me, both in speaking to such men and in reading their books, that they do not seem really to be touching on that at all, though on the surface they may appear to do so. I told him this, but I dare say I did not clearly express what I meant, for he could not understand me.

"That same evening I stopped at a small provincial hotel, and it so happened that a dreadful murder had been committed there the night before, and everybody was talking about it. Two peasants–elderly men and old friends–had had tea together there the night before, and were to occupy the same bedroom. They were not drunk but one of them had noticed for the first time that his friend possessed a silver watch which he was wearing on a chain. He was by no means a thief, and was, as peasants go, a rich man; but this watch so fascinated him that he could not restrain himself. He took a knife, and when his friend turned his back, he came up softly behind, raised his eyes to heaven, crossed himself, and saying earnestly–'God forgive me, for Christ's sake!' he cut his friend's throat like a sheep, and took the watch."

Rogojin roared with laughter. He laughed as though he were in a sort of fit. It was strange to see him laughing so after the sombre mood he had been in just before.

"Oh, I like that! That beats anything!" he cried convulsively, panting for breath. "One is an absolute unbeliever; the other is such a thorough-going believer that he murders his friend to the tune of a prayer! Oh, prince, prince, that's too good for anything! You can't have invented it. It's the best thing I've heard!"

"Next morning I went out for a stroll through the town," continued the prince, so soon as Rogojin was a little quieter, though his laughter still burst out at intervals, "and soon observed a drunken-looking soldier staggering about the pavement. He came up to me and said, 'Buy my silver cross, sir! You shall have it for fourpence–it's real silver.' I looked, and there he held a cross, just taken off his own neck, evidently, a large tin one, made after the Byzantine pattern. I fished out fourpence, and put his cross on my own neck, and I could see by his face that he was as pleased as he could be at the thought that he had succeeded in cheating a foolish gentleman, and away he went to drink the value of his cross. At that time everything that I saw made a tremendous impression upon me. I had understood nothing about Russia before, and had only vague and fantastic memories of it. So I thought, 'I will wait awhile before I condemn this Judas. Only God knows what may be hidden in the hearts of drunkards.'

"Well, I went homewards, and near the hotel I came across a poor woman, carrying a child–a baby of some six weeks old. The mother was quite a girl herself. The baby was smiling up at her, for the first time in its life, just at that moment; and while I watched the woman she suddenly crossed herself, oh, so devoutly! 'What is it, my good woman?' I asked her. (I was never but asking questions then!) 'Exactly as is a mother's joy when her baby smiles for the first time into her eyes, so is God's joy when one of His children turns and prays to Him for the first time, with all his heart!' This is what that poor woman said to me, almost word for word; and such a deep, refined, truly religious thought it was–a thought in which the whole essence of Christianity was expressed in one flash–that is, the recognition of God as our Father, and of God's joy in men as His own children, which is the chief idea of Christ. She was a simple country-woman–a mother, it's true–and perhaps, who knows, she may have been the wife of the drunken soldier!

"Listen, Parfen; you put a question to me

just now. This is my reply. The essence of religious feeling has nothing to do with reason, or atheism, or crime, or acts of any kind–it has nothing to do with these things–and never had. There is something besides all this, something which the arguments of the atheists can never touch. But the principal thing, and the conclusion of my argument, is that this is most clearly seen in the heart of a Russian. This is a conviction which I have gained while I have been in this Russia of ours. Yes, Parfen! there is work to be done; there is work to be done in this Russian world! Remember what talks we used to have in Moscow! And I never wished to come here at all; and I never thought to meet you like this, Parfen! Well, well–good-bye–good-bye! God be with you!"

He turned and went downstairs.

"Lef Nicolaievitch!" cried Parfen, before he had reached the next landing. "Have you got that cross you bought from the soldier with you?"

"Yes, I have," and the prince stopped again.

"Show it me, will you?"

A new fancy! The prince reflected, and then mounted the stairs once more. He pulled out the cross without taking it off his neck.

"Give it to me," said Parfen.

"Why? do you–"

The prince would rather have kept this particular cross.

"I'll wear it; and you shall have mine. I'll take it off at once."

"You wish to exchange crosses? Very well, Parfen, if that's the case, I'm glad enough– that makes us brothers, you know."

The prince took off his tin cross, Parfen his gold one, and the exchange was made.

Parfen was silent. With sad surprise the prince observed that the look of distrust, the bitter, ironical smile, had still not altogether left his newly-adopted brother's face. At moments, at all events, it showed itself but too plainly,

At last Rogojin took the prince's hand, and stood so for some moments, as though he could not make up his mind. Then he drew him along, murmuring almost inaudibly,

"Come!"

They stopped on the landing, and rang the bell at a door opposite to Parfen's own lodging.

An old woman opened to them and bowed low to Parfen, who asked her some questions hurriedly, but did not wait to hear her answer. He led the prince on through several dark, cold-looking rooms, spotlessly clean, with white covers over all the furniture.

Without the ceremony of knocking, Parfen entered a small apartment, furnished like a drawing-room, but with a polished mahogany partition dividing one half of it from what was probably a bedroom. In one corner of this room sat an old woman in an arm-chair, close to the stove. She did not look very old, and her face was a pleasant, round one; but she was white-haired and, as one could detect at the first glance, quite in her second childhood. She wore a black woollen dress, with a black handkerchief round her neck and shoulders, and a white cap with black ribbons. Her feet were raised on a footstool. Beside her sat another old woman, also dressed in mourning, and silently knitting a stocking; this was evidently a companion. They both looked as though they never broke the silence. The first old woman, so soon as she saw Rogojin and the prince, smiled and bowed courteously several times, in token of her gratification at their visit.

"Mother," said Rogojin, kissing her hand, "here is my great friend, Prince Muishkin; we have exchanged crosses; he was like a real brother to me at Moscow at one time, and did a great deal for me. Bless him, mother, as you would bless your own son. Wait a moment, let me arrange your hands for you."

But the old lady, before Parfen had time to touch her, raised her right hand, and, with three fingers held up, devoutly made the sign of the cross three times over the prince. She then nodded her head kindly at him once more.

"There, come along, Lef Nicolaievitch; that's all I brought you here for," said Rogojin.

When they reached the stairs again he added:

"She understood nothing of what I said to her, and did not know what I wanted her to do, and yet she blessed you; that shows she wished to do so herself. Well, goodbye; it's time you went, and I must go too."

He opened his own door.

"Well, let me at least embrace you and say goodbye, you strange fellow!" cried the prince, looking with gentle reproach at Rogojin, and advancing towards him. But the latter had hardly raised his arms when he dropped them again. He could not make up his mind to it; he turned away from the prince in order to avoid looking at him. He could not embrace him.

"Don't be afraid," he muttered, indistinctly, "though I have taken your cross, I shall not murder you for your watch." So saying, he laughed suddenly, and strangely. Then in a moment his face became transfigured; he grew deadly white, his lips trembled, his eyes burned like fire. He stretched out his arms and held the prince tightly to him, and said in a strangled voice:

"Well, take her! It's Fate! She's yours. I surrender her.... Remember Rogojin!" And pushing the prince from him, without looking back at him, he hurriedly entered his own flat, and banged the door.

CHAPTER FIVE

IT WAS LATE NOW, nearly half-past two, and the prince did not find General Epanchin at home. He left a card, and determined to look up Colia, who had a room at a small hotel near. Colia was not in, but he was informed that he might be back shortly, and had left word that if he were not in by half-past three it was to be understood that he had gone to Pavlofsk to General Epanchin's, and would dine there. The prince decided to wait till half-past three, and ordered some dinner. At half-past three there was no sign of Colia. The prince waited until four o'clock, and then strolled off mechanically wherever his feet should carry him.

In early summer there are often magnificent days in St. Petersburg–bright, hot and still. This happened to be such a day.

For some time the prince wandered about without aim or object. He did not know the town well. He stopped to look about him on bridges, at street corners. He entered a confectioner's shop to rest, once. He was in a state of nervous excitement and perturbation; he noticed nothing and no one; and he felt a craving for solitude, to be alone with his thoughts and his emotions, and to give himself up to them passively. He loathed the idea of trying to answer the questions that would rise up in his heart and mind. "I am not to blame for all this," he thought to himself, half unconsciously.

Towards six o'clock he found himself at the station of the Tsarsko-Selski railway.

He was tired of solitude now; a new rush of feeling took hold of him, and a flood of light chased away the gloom, for a moment, from his soul. He took a ticket to Pavlofsk, and determined to get there as fast as he could, but something stopped him; a reality, and not a fantasy, as he was inclined to think it. He was about to take his place in a carriage, when he suddenly threw away his ticket and came out again, disturbed and thoughtful. A few moments later, in the street, he recalled something that had bothered him all the afternoon. He caught himself engaged in a strange occupation which he now recollected he had taken up at odd moments for the last few hours–it was looking about all around him for something, he did not know what. He had forgotten it for a while, half an hour or so, and now, suddenly, the uneasy search had recommenced.

But he had hardly become conscious of this curious phenomenon, when another recollection suddenly swam through his brain, interesting him for the moment, exceedingly. He remembered that the last time he had been engaged in looking around him for the unknown something, he was standing before a cutler's shop, in the window of which were exposed certain goods for sale. He was extremely anxious now to discover whether this shop and these goods really existed, or whether the whole thing had been a hallucination.

He felt in a very curious condition today, a condition similar to that which had preceded his fits in bygone years.

He remembered that at such times he had been particularly absentminded, and could not discriminate between objects and persons unless he concentrated special attention upon them.

He remembered seeing something in the window marked at sixty copecks. Therefore, if the shop existed and if this object were really in the window, it would prove that he had been able to concentrate his attention on this article at a moment when, as a general rule, his absence of mind would have been too great to admit of any such concentration; in fact, very shortly after he had left the railway station in such a state of agitation.

So he walked back looking about him for the shop, and his heart beat with intolerable impatience. Ah! here was the very shop, and there was the article marked “60 cop.” Of course, it’s sixty copecks, he thought, and certainly worth no more. This idea amused him and he laughed.

But it was a hysterical laugh; he was feeling terribly oppressed. He remembered clearly that just here, standing before this window, he had suddenly turned round, just as earlier in the day he had turned and found the dreadful eyes of Rogojin fixed upon him. Convinced, therefore, that in this respect at all events he had been under no delusion, he left the shop and went on.

This must be thought out; it was clear that there had been no hallucination at the station then, either; something had actually happened to him, on both occasions; there was no doubt of it. But again a loathing for all mental exertion overmastered him; he would not think it out now, he would put it off and think of something else. He remembered that during his epileptic fits, or rather immediately preceding them, he had always experienced a moment or two when his whole heart, and mind, and body seemed to wake up to vigour and light; when he became filled with joy and hope, and all his anxieties seemed to be swept away for ever; these moments were but presentiments, as it were, of the one final second (it was never more than a second) in which the fit came upon him. That second, of course, was inexpressible. When his attack was over, and the prince reflected on his symptoms, he used to say to himself: “These moments, short as they are, when I feel such extreme consciousness of myself, and consequently more of life than at other times, are due only to the disease–to the sudden rupture of normal conditions. Therefore they are not really a higher kind of life, but a lower." This reasoning, however, seemed to end in a paradox, and lead to the further consideration:–"What matter though it be only disease, an abnormal tension of the brain, if when I recall and analyze the moment, it seems to have been one of harmony and beauty in the highest degree–an instant of deepest sensation, overflowing with unbounded joy and rapture, ecstatic devotion, and completest life?" Vague though this sounds, it was perfectly comprehensible to Muishkin, though he knew that it was but a feeble expression of his sensations.

That there was, indeed, beauty and harmony in those abnormal moments, that they really contained the highest synthesis of life, he could not doubt, nor even admit the possibility of doubt. He felt that they were not analogous to the fantastic and unreal dreams due to intoxication by hashish, opium or wine. Of that he could judge, when the attack was over. These instants were characterized–to define it in a word–by an intense quickening of the sense of personality. Since, in the last conscious moment preceding the attack, he could say to himself, with full understanding of his words: "I would give my whole life for this one instant," then doubtless to him it really was worth a lifetime. For the rest, he thought the dialectical part of his argument of little worth; he saw only too clearly that the result of these ecstatic moments was stupefaction, mental darkness, idiocy. No argument was possible on that point. His conclusion, his estimate of the "moment," doubtless contained some error, yet the reality of the sensation troubled him. What's more unanswerable than a fact? And this fact had occurred. The prince had confessed unreservedly to himself that the feeling of intense beatitude in that crowded moment made the moment worth a lifetime. "I feel then," he said one day to Rogojin in Moscow, "I feel then as if I understood those amazing words–'There shall be no more time.'" And he added with a smile: "No doubt the epileptic Mahomet refers to that same moment when he says that he visited all the dwellings of Allah, in less time than was needed to empty his pitcher of water." Yes, he had often met Rogojin in Moscow, and many were the subjects they discussed. "He told me I had been a brother to him," thought the prince. "He said so today, for the first time."

He was sitting in the Summer Garden on a seat under a tree, and his mind dwelt on the matter. It was about seven o'clock, and the place was empty. The stifling atmosphere foretold a storm, and the prince felt a certain charm in the contemplative mood which possessed him. He found pleasure, too, in gazing at the exterior objects around him. All the time he was trying to forget some thing, to escape from some idea that haunted him; but melancholy thoughts came back, though he would so willingly have escaped from them. He remembered suddenly how he had been talking to the waiter, while he dined, about a recently committed murder which the whole town was discussing, and as he thought of it something strange came over him. He was seized all at once by a violent desire, almost a temptation, against which he strove in vain.

He jumped up and walked off as fast as he could towards the "Petersburg Side." [One of the quarters of St. Petersburg.] He had asked someone, a little while before, to show him which was the Petersburg Side, on the banks of the Neva. He had not gone there, however; and he knew very well that it was of no use to go now, for he would certainly not find Lebedeff's relation at home. He had the address, but she must certainly have gone to Pavlofsk, or Colia would have let him know. If he were to go now, it would merely be out of curiosity, but a sudden, new idea had come into his head.

However, it was something to move on and know where he was going. A minute later he was still moving on, but without knowing anything. He could no longer think out his new idea. He tried to take an interest in all he saw; in the sky, in the Neva. He spoke to some children he met. He felt his epileptic condition becoming more and more developed. The evening was very close; thunder was heard some way off.

The prince was haunted all that day by the face of Lebedeff's nephew whom he had seen for the first time that morning, just as one is haunted at times by some persistent musical refrain. By a curious association of ideas, the young man always appeared as the murderer of whom Lebedeff had spoken when introducing him to Muishkin. Yes, he had read something about the murder, and that quite recently. Since he came to Russia, he had heard many stories of this kind, and was interested in them. His conversation with the waiter, an hour ago, chanced to be on the subject of this murder of the Zemarins, and the latter had agreed with him about it. He thought of the waiter again, and decided that he was no fool, but a steady, intelligent man: though, said he to himself, "God knows what he may really be; in a country with which one is unfamiliar it is difficult to understand the people one meets." He was beginning to have a passionate faith in the Russian soul, however, and what discoveries he had made in the last six months, what unexpected discoveries! But every soul is a mystery, and depths of mystery lie in the soul of a Russian. He had been intimate with Rogojin, for example, and a brotherly friendship had sprung up between them–yet did he really know him? What chaos and ugliness fills the world at times! What a self-satisfied rascal is that nephew of Lebedeff's! "But what am I thinking," continued the prince to himself. “Can he really have committed that crime? Did he kill those six persons? I seem to be confusing things... how strange it all is.... My head goes round... And Lebedeff’s daughter–how sympathetic and charming her face was as she held the child in her arms! What an innocent look and child-like laugh she had! It is curious that I had forgotten her until now. I expect Lebedeff adores her–and I really believe, when I think of it, that as sure as two and two make four, he is fond of that nephew, too!”

Well, why should he judge them so hastily! Could he really say what they were, after one short visit? Even Lebedeff seemed an enigma today. Did he expect to find him so? He had never seen him like that before. Lebedeff and the Comtesse du Barry! Good Heavens! If Rogojin should really kill someone, it would not, at any rate, be such a senseless, chaotic affair. A knife made to a special pattern, and six people killed in a kind of delirium. But Rogojin also had a knife made to a special pattern. Can it be that Rogojin wishes to murder anyone? The prince began to tremble violently. “It is a crime on my part to imagine anything so base, with such cynical frankness.” His face reddened with shame at the thought; and then there came across him as in a flash the memory of the incidents at the Pavlofsk station, and at the other station in the morning; and the question asked him by Rogojin about **the eyes** and Rogojin’s cross, that he was even now wearing; and the benediction of Rogojin’s mother; and his embrace on the darkened staircase–that last supreme renunciation–and now, to find himself full of this new “idea,” staring into shop-windows, and looking round for things–how base he was!

Despair overmastered his soul; he would not go on, he would go back to his hotel; he even turned and went the other way; but a moment after he changed his mind again and went on in the old direction.

Why, here he was on the Petersburg Side already, quite close to the house! Where was his "idea"? He was marching along without it now. Yes, his malady was coming back, it was clear enough; all this gloom and heaviness, all these "ideas," were nothing more nor less than a fit coming on; perhaps he would have a fit this very day.

But just now all the gloom and darkness had fled, his heart felt full of joy and hope, there was no such thing as doubt. And yes, he hadn't seen her for so long; he really must see her. He wished he could meet Rogojin; he would take his hand, and they would go to her together. His heart was pure, he was no rival of Parfen's. Tomorrow, he would go and tell him that he had seen her. Why, he had only come for the sole purpose of seeing her, all the way from Moscow! Perhaps she might be here still, who knows? She might not have gone away to Pavlofsk yet.

Yes, all this must be put straight and above-board, there must be no more passionate renouncements, such as Rogojin's. It must all be clear as day. Cannot Rogojin's soul bear the light? He said he did not love her with sympathy and pity; true, he added that "your pity is greater than my love," but he was not quite fair on himself there. Kin! Rogojin reading a book–wasn't that sympathy beginning? Did it not show that he comprehended his relations with her? And his story of waiting day and night for her forgiveness? That didn't look quite like passion alone.

And as to her face, could it inspire nothing but passion? Could her face inspire passion at all now? Oh, it inspired suffering, grief, overwhelming grief of the soul! A poignant, agonizing memory swept over the prince's heart.

Yes, agonizing. He remembered how he had suffered that first day when he thought he observed in her the symptoms of madness. He had almost fallen into despair. How could he have lost his hold upon her when she ran away from him to Rogojin? He ought to have run after her himself, rather than wait for news as he had done. Can Rogojin have failed to observe, up to now, that she is mad? Rogojin attributes her strangeness to other causes, to passion! What insane jealousy! What was it he had hinted at in that suggestion of his? The prince suddenly blushed, and shuddered to his very heart.

But why recall all this? There was insanity on both sides. For him, the prince, to love this woman with passion, was unthinkable. It would be cruel and inhuman. Yes. Rogojin is not fair to himself; he has a large heart; he has aptitude for sympathy. When he learns the truth, and finds what a pitiable being is this injured, broken, half-insane creature, he will forgive her all the torment she has caused him. He will become her slave, her brother, her friend. Compassion will teach even Rogojin, it will show him how to reason. Compassion is the chief law of human existence. Oh, how guilty he felt towards Rogojin! And, for a few warm, hasty words spoken in Moscow, Parfen had called him "brother," while he–but no, this was delirium! It would all come right! That gloomy Parfen had implied that his faith was waning; he must suffer dreadfully. He said he liked to look at that picture; it was not that he liked it, but he felt the need of looking at it. Rogojin was not merely a passionate soul; he was a fighter. He was fighting for the restoration of his dying faith. He must have something to hold on to and believe, and someone to believe in. What a strange picture that of Holbein's is! Why, this is the street, and here's the house, No. 16.

The prince rang the bell, and asked for Nastasia Philipovna. The lady of the house came out, and stated that Nastasia had gone to stay with Daria Alexeyevna at Pavlofsk, and might be there some days.

Madame Filisoff was a little woman of forty, with a cunning face, and crafty, piercing eyes. When, with an air of mystery, she asked her visitor's name, he refused at first to answer, but in a moment he changed his mind, and left strict instructions that it should be given to Nastasia Philipovna. The urgency of his request seemed to impress Madame Filisoff, and she put on a knowing expression, as if to say, "You need not be afraid, I quite understand." The prince's name evidently was a great surprise to her. He stood and looked absently at her for a moment, then turned, and took the road back to his hotel. But he went away not as he came. A great change had suddenly come over him. He went blindly forward; his knees shook under him; he was tormented by "ideas"; his lips were blue, and trembled with a feeble, meaningless smile. His demon was upon him once more.

What had happened to him? Why was his brow clammy with drops of moisture, his knees shaking beneath him, and his soul oppressed with a cold gloom? Was it because he had just seen these dreadful eyes again? Why, he had left the Summer Garden on purpose to see them; that had been his "idea." He had wished to assure himself that he would see them once more at that house. Then why was he so overwhelmed now, having seen them as he expected? just as though he had not expected to see them! Yes, they were the very same eyes; and no doubt about it. The same that he had seen in the crowd that morning at the station, the same that he had surprised in Rogojin's rooms some hours later, when the latter had replied to his inquiry with a sneering laugh, "Well, whose eyes were they?" Then for the third time they had appeared just as he was getting into the train on his way to see Aglaya. He had had a strong impulse to rush up to Rogojin, and repeat his words of the morning "Whose eyes are they?" Instead he had fled from the station, and knew nothing more, until he found himself gazing into the window of a cutler's shop, and wondering if a knife with a staghorn handle would cost more than sixty copecks. And as the prince sat dreaming in the Summer Garden under a lime-tree, a wicked demon had come and whispered in his car: "Rogojin has been spying upon you and watching you all the morning in a frenzy of desperation. When he finds you have not gone to Pavlofsk–a terrible discovery for him–he will surely go at once to that house in Petersburg Side, and watch for you there, although only this morning you gave your word of honour not to see **her**, and swore that you had not come to Petersburg for that purpose." And thereupon the prince had hastened off to that house, and what was there in the fact that he had met Rogojin there? He had only seen a wretched, suffering creature, whose state of mind was gloomy and miserable, but most comprehensible. In the morning Rogojin had seemed to be trying to keep out of the way; but at the station this afternoon he had stood out, he had concealed himself, indeed, less than the prince himself; at the house, now, he had stood fifty yards off on the other side of the road, with folded hands, watching, plainly in view and apparently desirous of being seen. He had stood there like an accuser, like a judge, not like a–a what?

And why had not the prince approached him and spoken to him, instead of turning away and pretending he had seen nothing, although their eyes met? (Yes, their eyes had met, and they had looked at each other.) Why, he had himself wished to take Rogojin by the hand and go in together, he had himself determined to go to him on the morrow and tell him that he had seen her, he had repudiated the demon as he walked to the house, and his heart had been full of joy.

Was there something in the whole aspect of the man, today, sufficient to justify the prince's terror, and the awful suspicions of his demon? Something seen, but indescribable, which filled him with dreadful presentiments? Yes, he was convinced of it–convinced of what? (Oh, how mean and hideous of him to feel this conviction, this presentiment! How he blamed himself for it!) "Speak if you dare, and tell me, what is the presentiment?" he repeated to himself, over and over again. "Put it into words, speak out clearly and distinctly. Oh, miserable coward that I am!" The prince flushed with shame for his own baseness. "How shall I ever look this man in the face again? My God, what a day! And what a nightmare, what a nightmare!"

There was a moment, during this long, wretched walk back from the Petersburg Side, when the prince felt an irresistible desire to go straight to Rogojin's, wait for him, embrace him with tears of shame and contrition, and tell him of his distrust, and finish with it–once for all.

But here he was back at his hotel.

How often during the day he had thought of this hotel with loathing–its corridor, its rooms, its stairs. How he had dreaded coming back to it, for some reason.

"What a regular old woman I am today," he had said to himself each time, with annoyance. "I believe in every foolish presentiment that comes into my head."

He stopped for a moment at the door; a great flush of shame came over him. "I am a coward, a wretched coward," he said, and moved forward again; but once more he paused.

Among all the incidents of the day, one recurred to his mind to the exclusion of the rest; although now that his self-control was regained, and he was no longer under the influence of a nightmare, he was able to think of it calmly. It concerned the knife on Rogojin's table. "Why should not Rogojin have as many knives on his table as he chooses?" thought the prince, wondering at his suspicions, as he had done when he found himself looking into the cutler's window. "What could it have to do with me?"

he said to himself again, and stopped as if rooted to the ground by a kind of paralysis of limb such as attacks people under the stress of some humiliating recollection.

The doorway was dark and gloomy at any time; but just at this moment it was rendered doubly so by the fact that the thunder-storm had just broken, and the rain was coming down in torrents.

And in the semi-darkness the prince distinguished a man standing close to the stairs, apparently waiting.

There was nothing particularly significant in the fact that a man was standing back in the doorway, waiting to come out or go upstairs; but the prince felt an irresistible conviction that he knew this man, and that it was Rogojin. The man moved on up the stairs; a moment later the prince passed up them, too. His heart froze within him. "In a minute or two I shall know all," he thought.

The staircase led to the first and second corridors of the hotel, along which lay the guests' bedrooms. As is often the case in Petersburg houses, it was narrow and very dark, and turned around a massive stone column.

On the first landing, which was as small as the necessary turn of the stairs allowed, there was a niche in the column, about half a yard wide, and in this niche the prince felt convinced that a man stood concealed. He thought he could distinguish a figure standing there. He would pass by quickly and not look. He took a step forward, but could bear the uncertainty no longer and turned his head.

The eyes–the same two eyes–met his! The man concealed in the niche had also taken a step forward. For one second they stood face to face.

Suddenly the prince caught the man by the shoulder and twisted him round towards the light, so that he might see his face more clearly.

Rogojin's eyes flashed, and a smile of

insanity distorted his countenance. His right hand was raised, and something glittered in it. The prince did not think of trying to stop it. All he could remember afterwards was that he seemed to have called out:

"Parfen! I won't believe it."

Next moment something appeared to burst open before him: a wonderful inner light illuminated his soul. This lasted perhaps half a second, yet he distinctly remembered hearing the beginning of the wail, the strange, dreadful wail, which burst from his lips of its own accord, and which no effort of will on his part could suppress.

Next moment he was absolutely unconscious; black darkness blotted out everything.

He had fallen in an epileptic fit.

As is well known, these fits occur instantaneously. The face, especially the eyes, become terribly disfigured, convulsions seize the limbs, a terrible cry breaks from the sufferer, a wail from which everything human seems to be blotted out, so that it is impossible to believe that the man who has just fallen is the same who emitted the dreadful cry. It seems more as though some other being, inside the stricken one, had cried. Many people have borne witness to this impression; and many cannot behold an epileptic fit without a feeling of mysterious terror and dread.

Such a feeling, we must suppose, overtook Rogojin at this moment, and saved the prince's life. Not knowing that it was a fit, and seeing his victim disappear head foremost into the darkness, hearing his head strike the stone steps below with a crash, Rogojin rushed downstairs, skirting the body, and flung himself headlong out of the hotel, like a raving madman.

The prince's body slipped convulsively down the steps till it rested at the bottom. Very soon, in five minutes or so, he was discovered, and a crowd collected around him.

A pool of blood on the steps near his head gave rise to grave fears. Was it a case of accident, or had there been a crime? It was, however, soon recognized as a case of epilepsy, and identification and proper measures for restoration followed one another, owing to a fortunate circumstance. Colia Ivolgin had come back to his hotel about seven o'clock, owing to a sudden impulse which made him refuse to dine at the Epanchins', and, finding a note from the prince awaiting him, had sped away to the latter's address. Arrived there, he ordered a cup of tea and sat sipping it in the coffee-room. While there he heard excited whispers of someone just found at the bottom of the stairs in a fit; upon which he had hurried to the spot, with a presentiment of evil, and at once recognized the prince.

The sufferer was immediately taken to his room, and though he partially regained consciousness, he lay long in a semi-dazed condition.

The doctor stated that there was no danger to be apprehended from the wound on the head, and as soon as the prince could understand what was going on around him, Colia hired a carriage and took him away to Lebedeff's. There he was received with much cordiality, and the departure to the country was hastened on his account. Three days later they were all at Pavlofsk.

CHAPTER SIX

LEBEDEFF'S COUNTRY-HOUSE WAS not large, but it was pretty and convenient, especially the part which was let to the prince.

A row of orange and lemon trees and jasmines, planted in green tubs, stood on the fairly wide terrace. According to Lebedeff, these trees gave the house a most delightful aspect. Some were there when he bought it, and he was so charmed with the effect that he promptly added to their number. When the tubs containing these plants arrived at the villa and were set in their places, Lebedeff kept running into the street to enjoy the view of the house, and every time he did so the rent to be demanded from the future tenant went up with a bound.

This country villa pleased the prince very much in his state of physical and mental exhaustion. On the day that they left for Pavlofsk, that is the day after his attack, he appeared almost well, though in reality he felt very far from it. The faces of those around him for the last three days had made a pleasant impression. He was pleased to see, not only Colia, who had become his inseparable companion, but Lebedeff himself and all the family, except the nephew, who had left the house. He was also glad to receive a visit from General Ivolgin, before leaving St. Petersburg.

It was getting late when the party arrived at Pavlofsk, but several people called to see the prince, and assembled in the verandah. Gania was the first to arrive. He had grown so pale and thin that the prince could hardly recognize him. Then came Varia and Ptitsin, who were rusticating in the neighbourhood. As to General Ivolgin, he scarcely budged from Lebedeff's house, and seemed to have moved to Pavlofsk with him. Lebedeff did his best to keep Ardalion Alexandrovitch by him, and to prevent him from invading the prince's quarters. He chatted with him confidentially, so that they might have been taken for old friends. During those three days the prince had noticed that they frequently held long conversations; he often heard their voices raised in argument on deep and learned subjects, which evidently pleased Lebedeff. He seemed as if he could not do without the general. But it was not only Ardalion Alexandrovitch whom Lebedeff kept out of the prince's way. Since they had come to the villa, he treated his own family the same. Upon the pretext that his tenant needed quiet, he kept him almost in isolation, and Muishkin protested in vain against this excess of zeal. Lebedeff stamped his feet at his daughters and drove them away if they attempted to join the prince on the terrace; not even Vera was excepted.

"They will lose all respect if they are allowed to be so free and easy; besides it is not proper for them," he declared at last, in answer to a direct question from the prince.

"Why on earth not?" asked the latter. "Really, you know, you are making yourself a nuisance, by keeping guard over me like this. I get bored all by myself; I have told you so over and over again, and you get on my nerves more than ever by waving your hands and creeping in and out in the mysterious way you do."

It was a fact that Lebedeff, though he was so anxious to keep everyone else from disturbing the patient, was continually in and out of the prince's room himself. He invariably began by opening the door a crack and peering in to see if the prince was there, or if he had escaped; then he would creep softly up to the arm-chair, sometimes making Muishkin jump by his sudden appearance. He always asked if the patient wanted anything, and when the latter replied that he only wanted to be left in peace, he would turn away obediently and make for the door on tip-toe, with deprecatory gestures to imply that he had only just looked in, that he would not speak a word, and would go away and not intrude again; which did not prevent him from reappearing in ten minutes or a quarter of an hour. Colia had free access to the prince, at which Lebedeff was quite disgusted and indignant. He would listen at the door for half an hour at a time while the two were talking. Colia found this out, and naturally told the prince of his discovery.

"Do you think yourself my master, that you try to keep me under lock and key like this?" said the prince to Lebedeff. "In the country, at least, I intend to be free, and you may make up your mind that I mean to see whom I like, and go where I please."

"Why, of course," replied the clerk, gesticulating with his hands.

The prince looked him sternly up and down.

"Well, Lukian Timofeyovitch, have you brought the little cupboard that you had at the head of your bed with you here?"

"No, I left it where it was."

"Impossible!"

"It cannot be moved; you would have to pull the wall down, it is so firmly fixed."

"Perhaps you have one like it here?"

"I have one that is even better, much better; that is really why I bought this house."

"Ah! What visitor did you turn away from my door, about an hour ago?"

"The-the general. I would not let him in; there is no need for him to visit you, prince... I have the deepest esteem for him, he is a–a great man. You don't believe it? Well, you will see, and yet, most excellent prince, you had much better not receive him."

"May I ask why? and also why you walk about on tiptoe and always seem as if you were going to whisper a secret in my ear whenever you come near me?"

"I am vile, vile; I know it!" cried Lebedeff, beating his breast with a contrite air. "But will not the general be too hospitable for you?"

"Too hospitable?"

"Yes. First, he proposes to come and live in my house. Well and good; but he sticks at nothing; he immediately makes himself one of the family. We have talked over our respective relations several times, and discovered that we are connected by marriage. It seems also that you are a sort of nephew on his mother's side; he was explaining it to me again only yesterday. If you are his nephew, it follows that I must also be a relation of yours, most excellent prince. Never mind about that, it is only a foible; but just now he assured me that all his life, from the day he was made an ensign to the 11th of last June, he has entertained at least two hundred guests at his table every day. Finally, he went so far as to say that they never rose from the table; they dined, supped, and had tea, for fifteen hours at a stretch. This went on for thirty years without a break; there was barely time to change the table-cloth; directly one person left, another took his place. On feast-days he entertained as many as three hundred guests, and they numbered seven hundred on the thousandth anniversary of the foundation of the Russian Empire. It amounts to a passion with him; it makes one uneasy to hear of it. It is terrible to have to entertain people who do things on such a scale. That is why I wonder whether such a man is not too hospitable for you and me."

"But you seem to be on the best of terms with him?"

"Quite fraternal–I look upon it as a joke. Let

us be brothers-in-law, it is all the same to me,–rather an honour than not. But in spite of the two hundred guests and the thousandth anniversary of the Russian Empire, I can see that he is a very remarkable man. I am quite sincere. You said just now that I always looked as if I was going to tell you a secret; you are right. I have a secret to tell you: a certain person has just let me know that she is very anxious for a secret interview with you."

"Why should it be secret? Not at all; I will call on her myself tomorrow."

"No, oh no!" cried Lebedeff, waving his arms; "if she is afraid, it is not for the reason you think. By the way, do you know that the monster comes every day to inquire after your health?"

"You call him a monster so often that it makes me suspicious."

"You must have no suspicions, none whatever," said Lebedeff quickly. "I only want you to know that the person in question is not afraid of him, but of something quite, quite different."

"What on earth is she afraid of, then? Tell me plainly, without any more beating about the bush," said the prince, exasperated by the other's mysterious grimaces.

"Ah that is the secret," said Lebedeff, with a smile.

"Whose secret?"

"Yours. You forbade me yourself to mention it before you, most excellent prince," murmured Lebedeff. Then, satisfied that he had worked up Muishkin's curiosity to the highest pitch, he added abruptly: "She is afraid of Aglaya Ivanovna."

The prince frowned for a moment in silence, and then said suddenly:

"Really, Lebedeff, I must leave your house. Where are Gavrila Ardalionovitch and the Ptitsins? Are they here? Have you chased them away, too?"

"They are coming, they are coming; and the general as well. I will open all the doors;

I will call all my daughters, all of them, this very minute," said Lebedeff in a low voice, thoroughly frightened, and waving his hands as he ran from door to door.

At that moment Colia appeared on the terrace; he announced that Lizabetha Prokofievna and her three daughters were close behind him.

Moved by this news, Lebedeff hurried up to the prince.

"Shall I call the Ptitsins, and Gavrila Ardalionovitch? Shall I let the general in?" he asked.

"Why not? Let in anyone who wants to see me. I assure you, Lebedeff, you have misunderstood my position from the very first; you have been wrong all along. I have not the slightest reason to hide myself from anyone," replied the prince gaily.

Seeing him laugh, Lebedeff thought fit to laugh also, and though much agitated his satisfaction was quite visible.

Colia was right; the Epanchin ladies

were only a few steps behind him. As they approached the terrace other visitors appeared from Lebedeff's side of the house–the Ptitsins, Gania, and Ardalion Alexandrovitch.

The Epanchins had only just heard of the prince's illness and of his presence in Pavlofsk, from Colia; and up to this time had been in a state of considerable bewilderment about him. The general brought the prince's card down from town, and Mrs. Epanchin had felt convinced that he himself would follow his card at once; she was much excited.

In vain the girls assured her that a man who had not written for six months would not be in such a dreadful hurry, and that probably he had enough to do in town without needing to bustle down to Pavlofsk to see them. Their mother was quite angry at the very idea of such a thing, and announced her absolute conviction that he would turn up the next day at latest.

So next day the prince was expected all

the morning, and at dinner, tea, and supper; and when he did not appear in the evening, Mrs. Epanchin quarrelled with everyone in the house, finding plenty of pretexts without so much as mentioning the prince's name.

On the third day there was no talk of him at all, until Aglaya remarked at dinner: "Mamma is cross because the prince hasn't turned up," to which the general replied that it was not his fault.

Mrs. Epanchin misunderstood the observation, and rising from her place she left the room in majestic wrath. In the evening, however, Colia came with the story of the prince's adventures, so far as he knew them. Mrs. Epanchin was triumphant; although Colia had to listen to a long lecture. "He idles about here the whole day long, one can't get rid of him; and then when he is wanted he does not come. He might have sent a line if he did not wish to inconvenience himself."

At the words "one can't get rid of him," Colia was very angry, and nearly flew into a rage;

but he resolved to be quiet for the time and show his resentment later. If the words had been less offensive he might have forgiven them, so pleased was he to see Lizabetha Prokofievna worried and anxious about the prince's illness.

She would have insisted on sending to Petersburg at once, for a certain great medical celebrity; but her daughters dissuaded her, though they were not willing to stay behind when she at once prepared to go and visit the invalid. Aglaya, however, suggested that it was a little unceremonious to go **en masse** to see him.

"Very well then, stay at home," said Mrs. Epanchin, "and a good thing too, for Evgenie Pavlovitch is coming down and there will be no one at home to receive him."

Of course, after this, Aglaya went with the rest. In fact, she had never had the slightest intention of doing otherwise.

Prince S., who was in the house, was requested to escort the ladies. He had been much interested when he first heard of the prince from the Epanchins. It appeared that they had known one another before, and had spent some time together in a little provincial town three months ago. Prince S. had greatly taken to him, and was delighted with the opportunity of meeting him again.

The general had not come down from town as yet, nor had Evgenie Pavlovitch arrived.

It was not more than two or three hundred yards from the Epanchins' house to Lebedeff's. The first disagreeable impression experienced by Mrs. Epanchin was to find the prince surrounded by a whole assembly of other guests–not to mention the fact that some of those present were particularly detestable in her eyes. The next annoying circumstance was when an apparently strong and healthy young fellow, well dressed, and smiling, came forward to meet her on the terrace, instead of the half-dying unfortunate whom she had expected to see.

She was astonished and vexed, and her

disappointment pleased Colia immensely. Of course he could have undeceived her before she started, but the mischievous boy had been careful not to do that, foreseeing the probably laughable disgust that she would experience when she found her dear friend, the prince, in good health. Colia was indelicate enough to voice the delight he felt at his success in managing to annoy Lizabetha Prokofievna, with whom, in spite of their really amicable relations, he was constantly sparring.

"Just wait a while, my boy!" said she; "don't be too certain of your triumph." And she sat down heavily, in the arm-chair pushed forward by the prince.

Lebedeff, Ptitsin, and General Ivolgin hastened to find chairs for the young ladies. Varia greeted them joyfully, and they exchanged confidences in ecstatic whispers.

"I must admit, prince, I was a little put out to see you up and about like this–I expected to find you in bed; but I give you my word, I was only annoyed for an instant, before I collected my thoughts properly. I am always wiser on second thoughts, and I dare say you are the same. I assure you I am as glad to see you well as though you were my own son,–yes, and more; and if you don't believe me the more shame to you, and it's not my fault. But that spiteful boy delights in playing all sorts of tricks. You are his patron, it seems. Well, I warn you that one fine morning I shall deprive myself of the pleasure of his further acquaintance."

"What have I done wrong now?" cried Colia. "What was the good of telling you that the prince was nearly well again? You would not have believed me; it was so much more interesting to picture him on his death-bed."

"How long do you remain here, prince?" asked Madame Epanchin.

"All the summer, and perhaps longer."

"You are alone, aren't you,–not married?"

"No, I'm not married!" replied the prince, smiling at the ingenuousness of this little feeler.

"Oh, you needn't laugh! These things do happen, you know! Now then–why didn't you come to us? We have a wing quite empty. But just as you like, of course. Do you lease it from **him?**–this fellow, I mean," she added, nodding towards Lebedeff. "And why does he always wriggle so?"

At that moment Vera, carrying the baby in her arms as usual, came out of the house, on to the terrace. Lebedeff kept fidgeting among the chairs, and did not seem to know what to do with himself, though he had no intention of going away. He no sooner caught sight of his daughter, than he rushed in her direction, waving his arms to keep her away; he even forgot himself so far as to stamp his foot.

"Is he mad?" asked Madame Epanchin suddenly.

"No, he..."

"Perhaps he is drunk? Your company is

rather peculiar," she added, with a glance at the other guests....

"But what a pretty girl! Who is she?"

"That is Lebedeff's daughter–Vera Lukianovna."

"Indeed? She looks very sweet. I should like to make her acquaintance."

The words were hardly out of her mouth, when Lebedeff dragged Vera forward, in order to present her.

"Orphans, poor orphans!" he began in a pathetic voice.

"The child she carries is an orphan, too. She is Vera's sister, my daughter Luboff. The day this babe was born, six weeks ago, my wife died, by the will of God Almighty.... Yes... Vera takes her mother's place, though she is but her sister... nothing more... nothing more..."

"And you! You are nothing more than a fool, if you'll excuse me! Well! well! you know that yourself, I expect," said the lady indignantly.

Lebedeff bowed low. "It is the truth," he

replied, with extreme respect.

"Oh, Mr. Lebedeff, I am told you lecture on the Apocalypse. Is it true?" asked Aglaya.

"Yes, that is so... for the last fifteen years."

"I have heard of you, and I think read of you in the newspapers."

"No, that was another commentator, whom the papers named. He is dead, however, and I have taken his place," said the other, much delighted.

"We are neighbours, so will you be so kind as to come over one day and explain the Apocalypse to me?" said Aglaya. "I do not understand it in the least."

"Allow me to warn you," interposed General Ivolgin, "that he is the greatest charlatan on earth." He had taken the chair next to the girl, and was impatient to begin talking. "No doubt there are pleasures and amusements peculiar to the country," he continued, "and to listen to a pretended student holding forth on the book of the Revelations may be as good as any other. It may even be original.

But... you seem to be looking at me with some surprise–may I introduce myself–General Ivolgin–I carried you in my arms as a baby–"

"Delighted, I'm sure," said Aglaya; "I am acquainted with Varvara Ardalionovna and Nina Alexandrovna." She was trying hard to restrain herself from laughing.

Mrs. Epanchin flushed up; some accumulation of spleen in her suddenly needed an outlet. She could not bear this General Ivolgin whom she had once known, long ago–in society.

"You are deviating from the truth, sir, as usual!" she remarked, boiling over with indignation; "you never carried her in your life!"

"You have forgotten, mother," said Aglaya, suddenly. "He really did carry me about,–in Tver, you know. I was six years old, I remember. He made me a bow and arrow, and I shot a pigeon. Don't you remember shooting a pigeon, you and I, one day?"

"Yes, and he made me a cardboard helmet, and a little wooden sword–I remember!" said Adelaida.

"Yes, I remember too!" said Alexandra. "You quarrelled about the wounded pigeon, and Adelaida was put in the corner, and stood there with her helmet and sword and all."

The poor general had merely made the remark about having carried Aglaya in his arms because he always did so begin a conversation with young people. But it happened that this time he had really hit upon the truth, though he had himself entirely forgotten the fact. But when Adelaida and Aglaya recalled the episode of the pigeon, his mind became filled with memories, and it is impossible to describe how this poor old man, usually half drunk, was moved by the recollection.

"I remember–I remember it all!" he cried. "I was captain then. You were such a lovely little thing–Nina Alexandrovna!–Gania, listen! I was received then by General Epanchin."

"Yes, and look what you have come to now!" interrupted Mrs. Epanchin. "However, I see you have not quite drunk your better feelings away. But you've broken your wife's heart, sir–and instead of looking after your children, you have spent your time in public-houses and debtors' prisons! Go away, my friend, stand in some corner and weep, and bemoan your fallen dignity, and perhaps God will forgive you yet! Go, go! I'm serious! There's nothing so favourable for repentance as to think of the past with feelings of remorse!"

There was no need to repeat that she was serious. The general, like all drunkards, was extremely emotional and easily touched by recollections of his better days. He rose and walked quietly to the door, so meekly that Mrs. Epanchin was instantly sorry for him.

"Ardalion Alexandrovitch," she cried after him, "wait a moment, we are all sinners!

When you feel that your conscience reproaches you a little less, come over to me and we'll have a talk about the past! I dare say I am fifty times more of a sinner than you are! And now go, go, good-bye, you had better not stay here!" she added, in alarm, as he turned as though to come back.

"Don't go after him just now, Colia, or he'll be vexed, and the benefit of this moment will be lost!" said the prince, as the boy was hurrying out of the room.

"Quite true! Much better to go in half an hour or so," said Mrs. Epanchin.

"That's what comes of telling the truth for once in one's life!" said Lebedeff. "It reduced him to tears."

"Come, come! the less **you** say about it the better–to judge from all I have heard about you!" replied Mrs. Epanchin.

The prince took the first opportunity of informing the Epanchin ladies that he had intended to pay them a visit that day, if they had not themselves come this afternoon, and Lizabetha Prokofievna replied that she hoped he would still do so.

By this time some of the visitors had disappeared.

Ptitsin had tactfully retreated to Lebedeff's wing; and Gania soon followed him.

The latter had behaved modestly, but with dignity, on this occasion of his first meeting with the Epanchins since the rupture. Twice Mrs. Epanchin had deliberately examined him from head to foot; but he had stood fire without flinching. He was certainly much changed, as anyone could see who had not met him for some time; and this fact seemed to afford Aglaya a good deal of satisfaction.

"That was Gavrila Ardalionovitch, who just went out, wasn't it?" she asked suddenly, interrupting somebody else's conversation to make the remark.

"Yes, it was," said the prince.

"I hardly knew him; he is much changed, and for the better!"

"I am very glad," said the prince.

"He has been very ill," added Varia.

"How has he changed for the better?" asked Mrs. Epanchin. "I don't see any change for the better! What's better in him? Where did you get **that** idea from? **what**'s better?"

"There's nothing better than the 'poor knight'!" said Colia, who was standing near the last speaker's chair.

"I quite agree with you there!" said Prince S., laughing.

"So do I," said Adelaida, solemnly.

"**What** poor knight?" asked Mrs. Epanchin, looking round at the face of each of the speakers in turn. Seeing, however, that Aglaya was blushing, she added, angrily:

"What nonsense you are all talking! What do you mean by poor knight?"

"It's not the first time this urchin, your favourite, has shown his impudence by twisting other people's words," said Aglaya, haughtily.

Every time that Aglaya showed temper

(and this was very often), there was so much childish pouting, such "school-girlishness," as it were, in her apparent wrath, that it was impossible to avoid smiling at her, to her own unutterable indignation. On these occasions she would say, "How can they, how **dare** they laugh at me?"

This time everyone laughed at her, her sisters, Prince S., Prince Muishkin (though he himself had flushed for some reason), and Colia. Aglaya was dreadfully indignant, and looked twice as pretty in her wrath.

"He's always twisting round what one says," she cried.

"I am only repeating your own exclamation!" said Colia. "A month ago you were turning over the pages of your Don Quixote, and suddenly called out 'there is nothing better than the poor knight.' I don't know whom you were referring to, of course, whether to Don Quixote, or Evgenie Pavlovitch, or someone else, but you certainly said these words, and afterwards there was a long conversation..."

"You are inclined to go a little too far, my good boy, with your guesses," said Mrs. Epanchin, with some show of annoyance.

"But it's not I alone," cried Colia. "They all talked about it, and they do still. Why, just now Prince S. and Adelaida Ivanovna declared that they upheld 'the poor knight'; so evidently there does exist a 'poor knight'; and if it were not for Adelaida Ivanovna, we should have known long ago who the 'poor knight' was."

"Why, how am I to blame?" asked Adelaida, smiling.

"You wouldn't draw his portrait for us, that's why you are to blame! Aglaya Ivanovna asked you to draw his portrait, and gave you the whole subject of the picture. She invented it herself; and you wouldn't."

"What was I to draw? According to the lines she quoted:

"'From his face he never lifted. That eternal mask of steel.'"

"What sort of a face was I to draw? I couldn't draw a mask."

"I don't know what you are driving at; what mask do you mean?" said Mrs. Epanchin, irritably. She began to see pretty clearly though what it meant, and whom they referred to by the generally accepted title of "poor knight." But what specially annoyed her was that the prince was looking so uncomfortable, and blushing like a ten-year-old child.

"Well, have you finished your silly joke?" she added, "and am I to be told what this 'poor knight' means, or is it a solemn secret which cannot be approached lightly?"

But they all laughed on.

"It's simply that there is a Russian poem," began Prince S., evidently anxious to change the conversation, "a strange thing, without beginning or end, and all about a 'poor knight.' A month or so ago, we were all talking and laughing, and looking up a subject for one of Adelaida's pictures–you know it is the principal business of this family to find subjects for Adelaida's pictures. Well, we happened upon this 'poor knight.' I don't remember who thought of it first–"

"Oh! Aglaya Ivanovna did," said Colia.

"Very likely–I don't recollect," continued Prince S.

"Some of us laughed at the subject; some liked it; but she declared that, in order to make a picture of the gentleman, she must first see his face. We then began to think over all our friends' faces to see if any of them would do, and none suited us, and so the matter stood; that's all. I don't know why Nicolai Ardalionovitch has brought up the joke now. What was appropriate and funny then, has quite lost all interest by this time."

"Probably there's some new silliness about it," said Mrs. Epanchin, sarcastically.

"There is no silliness about it at all–only the profoundest respect," said Aglaya, very seriously. She had quite recovered her temper; in fact, from certain signs, it was fair to conclude that she was delighted to see this joke going so far; and a careful observer might have remarked that her satisfaction dated from the moment when the fact of the prince's confusion became apparent to all.

"'Profoundest respect!' What nonsense! First, insane giggling, and then, all of a sudden, a display of 'profoundest respect.' Why respect? Tell me at once, why have you suddenly developed this 'profound respect,' eh?"

"Because," replied Aglaya gravely, "in the poem the knight is described as a man capable of living up to an ideal all his life. That sort of thing is not to be found every day among the men of our times. In the poem it is not stated exactly what the ideal was, but it was evidently some vision, some revelation of pure Beauty, and the knight wore round his neck, instead of a scarf, a rosary. A device–A. N. B.–the meaning of which is not explained, was inscribed on his shield–"

"No, A. N. D.," corrected Colia.

"I say A. N. B., and so it shall be!" cried Aglaya, irritably. "Anyway, the 'poor knight' did not care what his lady was, or what she did. He had chosen his ideal, and he was bound to serve her, and break lances for her, and acknowledge her as the ideal of pure Beauty, whatever she might say or do afterwards. If she had taken to stealing, he would have championed her just the same. I think the poet desired to embody in this one picture the whole spirit of medieval chivalry and the platonic love of a pure and high-souled knight. Of course it's all an ideal, and in the 'poor knight' that spirit reached the utmost limit of asceticism. He is a Don Quixote, only serious and not comical. I used not to understand him, and laughed at him, but now I love the 'poor knight,' and respect his actions."

So ended Aglaya; and, to look at her, it was difficult, indeed, to judge whether she was joking or in earnest.

"Pooh! he was a fool, and his actions were the actions of a fool," said Mrs. Epanchin; "and as for you, young woman, you ought to know better. At all events, you are not to talk like that again. What poem is it? Recite it! I want to hear this poem! I have hated poetry all my life. Prince, you must excuse this nonsense. We neither of us like this sort of thing! Be patient!"

They certainly were put out, both of them.

The prince tried to say something, but he was too confused, and could not get his words out. Aglaya, who had taken such liberties in her little speech, was the only person present, perhaps, who was not in the least embarrassed. She seemed, in fact, quite pleased.

She now rose solemnly from her seat, walked to the centre of the terrace, and stood in front of the prince's chair. All looked on with some surprise, and Prince S. and her sisters with feelings of decided alarm, to see what new frolic she was up to; it had gone quite far enough already, they thought. But Aglaya evidently thoroughly enjoyed the affectation and ceremony with which she was introducing her recitation of the poem.

Mrs. Epanchin was just wondering whether she would not forbid the performance after all, when, at the very moment that Aglaya commenced her declamation, two new guests, both talking loudly, entered from the street. The new arrivals were General Epanchin and a young man.

Their entrance caused some slight commotion.

CHAPTER SEVEN

THE YOUNG FELLOW ACCOMPANYING the general was about twenty-eight, tall, and well built, with a handsome and clever face, and bright black eyes, full of fun and intelligence.

Aglaya did not so much as glance at the new arrivals, but went on with her recitation, gazing at the prince the while in an affected manner, and at him alone. It was clear to him that she was doing all this with some special object.

But the new guests at least somewhat eased his strained and uncomfortable position. Seeing them approaching, he rose from his chair, and nodding amicably to the general, signed to him not to interrupt the recitation. He then got behind his chair, and stood there with his left hand resting on the back of it. Thanks to this change of position, he was able to listen to the ballad with far less embarrassment than before. Mrs. Epanchin had also twice motioned to the new arrivals to be quiet, and stay where they were.

The prince was much interested in the young man who had just entered. He easily concluded that this was Evgenie Pavlovitch Radomski, of whom he had already heard mention several times. He was puzzled, however, by the young man's plain clothes, for he had always heard of Evgenie Pavlovitch as a military man. An ironical smile played on Evgenie's lips all the while the recitation was proceeding, which showed that he, too, was probably in the secret of the 'poor knight' joke. But it had become quite a different matter with Aglaya. All the affectation of manner which she had displayed at the beginning disappeared as the ballad proceeded. She spoke the lines in so serious and exalted a manner, and with so much taste, that she even seemed to justify the exaggerated solemnity with which she had stepped forward. It was impossible to discern in her now anything but a deep feeling for the spirit of the poem which she had undertaken to interpret.

Her eyes were aglow with inspiration, and a slight tremor of rapture passed over her lovely features once or twice. She continued to recite:

"Once there came a vision glorious, Mystic, dreadful, wondrous fair; Burned itself into his spirit, And abode for ever there! "Never more–from that sweet moment–Gazéd he on womankind; He was dumb to love and wooing. And to all their graces blind. "Full of love for that sweet vision, Brave and pure he took the field; With his blood he stained the letters N. P. B. upon his shield. "'Lumen caeli, sancta Rosa!' Shouting on the foe he fell, And like thunder rang his war-cry O'er the cowering infidel. "Then within his distant castle, Home returned, he dreamed his days–Silent, sad,–and when death took him. He was mad, the legend says."

When recalling all this afterwards the prince could not for the life of him understand how to reconcile the beautiful, sincere, pure nature of the girl with the irony of this jest. That it was a jest there was no doubt whatever; he knew that well enough, and had good reason, too, for his conviction; for during her recitation of the ballad Aglaya had deliberately changed the letters A. N. B. into N. P. B. He was quite sure she had not done this by accident, and that his ears had not deceived him. At all events her performance–which was a joke, of course, if rather a crude one,–was premeditated. They had evidently talked (and laughed) over the 'poor knight' for more than a month.

Yet Aglaya had brought out these letters N. P. B. not only without the slightest appearance of irony, or even any particular accentuation, but with so even and unbroken an appearance of seriousness that assuredly anyone might have supposed that these initials were the original ones written in the ballad. The thing made an uncomfortable impression upon the prince. Of course Mrs. Epanchin saw nothing either in the change of initials or in the insinuation embodied therein. General Epanchin only knew that there was a recitation of verses going on, and took no further interest in the matter. Of the rest of the audience, many had understood the allusion and wondered both at the daring of the lady and at the motive underlying it, but tried to show no sign of their feelings. But Evgenie Pavlovitch (as the prince was ready to wager) both comprehended and tried his best to show that he comprehended; his smile was too mocking to leave any doubt on that point.

"How beautiful that is!" cried Mrs. Epanchin, with sincere admiration. "Whose is it?"

"Pushkin's, mama, of course! Don't disgrace us all by showing your ignorance," said Adelaida.

"As soon as we reach home give it to me to read."

"I don't think we have a copy of Pushkin in the house."

"There are a couple of torn volumes somewhere; they have been lying about from time immemorial," added Alexandra.

"Send Feodor or Alexey up by the very first train to buy a copy, then.–Aglaya, come here–kiss me, dear, you recited beautifully! but," she added in a whisper, "if you were sincere I am sorry for you. If it was a joke, I do not approve of the feelings which prompted you to do it, and in any case you would have done far better not to recite it at all. Do you understand?–Now come along, young woman; we've sat here too long. I'll speak to you about this another time."

Meanwhile the prince took the opportunity of greeting General Epanchin, and the general introduced Evgenie Pavlovitch to him.

"I caught him up on the way to your house," explained the general. "He had heard that we were all here."

"Yes, and I heard that you were here, too," added Evgenie Pavlovitch; "and since I had long promised myself the pleasure of seeking not only your acquaintance but your friendship, I did not wish to waste time, but came straight on. I am sorry to hear that you are unwell."

"Oh, but I'm quite well now, thank you, and very glad to make your acquaintance. Prince S. has often spoken to me about you," said Muishkin, and for an instant the two men looked intently into one another's eyes.

The prince remarked that Evgenie Pavlovitch's plain clothes had evidently made a great impression upon the company present, so much so that all other interests seemed to be effaced before this surprising fact.

His change of dress was evidently a matter of some importance. Adelaida and Alexandra poured out a stream of questions; Prince S., a relative of the young man, appeared annoyed; and Ivan Fedorovitch quite excited. Aglaya alone was not interested. She merely looked closely at Evgenie for a minute, curious perhaps as to whether civil or military clothes became him best, then turned away and paid no more attention to him or his costume. Lizabetha Prokofievna asked no questions, but it was clear that she was uneasy, and the prince fancied that Evgenie was not in her good graces.

"He has astonished me," said Ivan Fedorovitch. "I nearly fell down with surprise. I could hardly believe my eyes when I met him in Petersburg just now. Why this haste? That's what I want to know. He has always said himself that there is no need to break windows."

Evgenie Pavlovitch remarked here that he had spoken of his intention of leaving the service long ago. He had, however, always made more or less of a joke about it, so no one had taken him seriously. For that matter he joked about everything, and his friends never knew what to believe, especially if he did not wish them to understand him.

"I have only retired for a time," said he, laughing. "For a few months; at most for a year."

"But there is no necessity for you to retire at all," complained the general, "as far as I know."

"I want to go and look after my country estates. You advised me to do that yourself," was the reply. "And then I wish to go abroad."

After a few more expostulations, the conversation drifted into other channels, but the prince, who had been an attentive listener, thought all this excitement about so small a matter very curious. "There must be more in it than appears," he said to himself.

"I see the 'poor knight' has come on the scene again," said Evgenie Pavlovitch, stepping to Aglaya's side.

To the amazement of the prince, who overheard the remark, Aglaya looked haughtily and inquiringly at the questioner, as though she would give him to know, once for all, that there could be no talk between them about the 'poor knight,' and that she did not understand his question.

"But not now! It is too late to send to town for a Pushkin now. It is much too late, I say!" Colia was exclaiming in a loud voice. "I have told you so at least a hundred times."

"Yes, it is really much too late to send to town now," said Evgenie Pavlovitch, who had escaped from Aglaya as rapidly as possible. "I am sure the shops are shut in Petersburg; it is past eight o'clock," he added, looking at his watch.

"We have done without him so far," interrupted Adelaida in her turn. "Surely we can wait until to-morrow."

"Besides," said Colia, "it is quite unusual, almost improper, for people in our position to take any interest in literature. Ask Evgenie Pavlovitch if I am not right. It is much more fashionable to drive a waggonette with red wheels."

"You got that from some magazine, Colia," remarked Adelaida.

"He gets most of his conversation in that way," laughed Evgenie Pavlovitch. "He borrows whole phrases from the reviews. I have long had the pleasure of knowing both Nicholai Ardalionovitch and his conversational methods, but this time he was not repeating something he had read; he was alluding, no doubt, to my yellow waggonette, which has, or had, red wheels. But I have exchanged it, so you are rather behind the times, Colia."

The prince had been listening attentively to Radomski's words, and thought his manner very pleasant. When Colia chaffed him about his waggonette he had replied with perfect equality and in a friendly fashion. This pleased Muishkin.

At this moment Vera came up to Lizabetha Prokofievna, carrying several large and beautifully bound books, apparently quite new.

"What is it?" demanded the lady.

"This is Pushkin," replied the girl. "Papa told me to offer it to you."

"What? Impossible!" exclaimed Mrs. Epanchin.

"Not as a present, not as a present! I should not have taken the liberty," said Lebedeff, appearing suddenly from behind his daughter. "It is our own Pushkin, our family copy, Annenkoff's edition; it could not be bought now. I beg to suggest, with great respect, that your excellency should buy it, and thus quench the noble literary thirst which is consuming you at this moment," he concluded grandiloquently.

"Oh! if you will sell it, very good–and

thank you. You shall not be a loser! But for goodness' sake, don't twist about like that, sir! I have heard of you; they tell me you are a very learned person. We must have a talk one of these days. You will bring me the books yourself?"

"With the greatest respect... and... and veneration," replied Lebedeff, making extraordinary grimaces.

"Well, bring them, with or without respect, provided always you do not drop them on the way; but on the condition," went on the lady, looking full at him, "that you do not cross my threshold. I do not intend to receive you today. You may send your daughter Vera at once, if you like. I am much pleased with her."

"Why don't you tell him about them?" said Vera impatiently to her father. "They will come in, whether you announce them or not, and they are beginning to make a row. Lef Nicolaievitch,"–she addressed herself to the prince–"four men are here asking for you. They have waited some time, and are beginning to make a fuss, and papa will not bring them in."

"Who are these people?" said the prince.

"They say that they have come on business, and they are the kind of men, who, if you do not see them here, will follow you about the street. It would be better to receive them, and then you will get rid of them. Gavrila Ardalionovitch and Ptitsin are both there, trying to make them hear reason."

"Pavlicheff's son! It is not worth while!" cried Lebedeff. "There is no necessity to see them, and it would be most unpleasant for your excellency. They do not deserve..."

"What? Pavlicheff's son!" cried the prince, much perturbed. "I know... I know–but I entrusted this matter to Gavrila Ardalionovitch. He told me..."

At that moment Gania, accompanied by Ptitsin, came out to the terrace. From an adjoining room came a noise of angry voices, and General Ivolgin, in loud tones, seemed to be trying to shout them down. Colia rushed off at once to investigate the cause of the uproar.

"This is most interesting!" observed Evgenie Pavlovitch.

"I expect he knows all about it!" thought the prince.

"What, the son of Pavlicheff? And who may this son of Pavlicheff be?" asked General Epanchin with surprise; and looking curiously around him, he discovered that he alone had no clue to the mystery. Expectation and suspense were on every face, with the exception of that of the prince, who stood gravely wondering how an affair so entirely personal could have awakened such lively and widespread interest in so short a time.

Aglaya went up to him with a peculiarly serious look.

"It will be well," she said, "if you put an end to this affair yourself **at once**: but you must allow us to be your witnesses. They want to throw mud at you, prince, and you must be triumphantly vindicated. I give you joy beforehand!"

"And I also wish for justice to be done, once for all," cried Madame Epanchin, "about this impudent claim. Deal with them promptly, prince, and don't spare them! I am sick of hearing about the affair, and many a quarrel I have had in your cause. But I confess I am anxious to see what happens, so do make them come out here, and we will remain. You have heard people talking about it, no doubt?" she added, turning to Prince S.

"Of course," said he. "I have heard it spoken about at your house, and I am anxious to see these young men!"

"They are Nihilists, are they not?"

"No, they are not Nihilists," explained Lebedeff, who seemed much excited. "This is another lot–a special group. According to my nephew they are more advanced even than the Nihilists. You are quite wrong, excellency, if you think that your presence will intimidate them; nothing intimidates them. Educated men, learned men even, are to be found among Nihilists; these go further, in that they are men of action. The movement is, properly speaking, a derivative from Nihilism–though they are only known indirectly, and by hearsay, for they never advertise their doings in the papers. They go straight to the point. For them, it is not a question of showing that Pushkin is stupid, or that Russia must be torn in pieces. No; but if they have a great desire for anything, they believe they have a right to get it even at the cost of the lives, say, of eight persons. They are checked by no obstacles. In fact, prince, I should not advise you..."

But Muishkin had risen, and was on his way to open the door for his visitors.

"You are slandering them, Lebedeff," said he, smiling.

"You are always thinking about your

nephew's conduct. Don't believe him, Lizabetha Prokofievna. I can assure you Gorsky and Daniloff are exceptions–and that these are only... mistaken. However, I do not care about receiving them here, in public. Excuse me, Lizabetha Prokofievna. They are coming, and you can see them, and then I will take them away. Please come in, gentlemen!"

Another thought tormented him: He wondered was this an arranged business–arranged to happen when he had guests in his house, and in anticipation of his humiliation rather than of his triumph? But he reproached himself bitterly for such a thought, and felt as if he should die of shame if it were discovered. When his new visitors appeared, he was quite ready to believe himself infinitely less to be respected than any of them.

Four persons entered, led by General Ivolgin, in a state of great excitement, and talking eloquently.

"He is for me, undoubtedly!" thought the prince, with a smile. Colia also had joined the party, and was talking with animation to Hippolyte, who listened with a jeering smile on his lips.

The prince begged the visitors to sit down. They were all so young that it made the proceedings seem even more extraordinary. Ivan Fedorovitch, who really understood nothing of what was going on, felt indignant at the sight of these youths, and would have interfered in some way had it not been for the extreme interest shown by his wife in the affair. He therefore remained, partly through curiosity, partly through good-nature, hoping that his presence might be of some use. But the bow with which General Ivolgin greeted him irritated him anew; he frowned, and decided to be absolutely silent.

As to the rest, one was a man of thirty, the retired officer, now a boxer, who had been with Rogojin, and in his happier days had given fifteen roubles at a time to beggars.

Evidently he had joined the others as a comrade to give them moral, and if necessary material, support. The man who had been spoken of as "Pavlicheff's son," although he gave the name of Antip Burdovsky, was about twenty-two years of age, fair, thin and rather tall. He was remarkable for the poverty, not to say uncleanliness, of his personal appearance: the sleeves of his overcoat were greasy; his dirty waistcoat, buttoned up to his neck, showed not a trace of linen; a filthy black silk scarf, twisted till it resembled a cord, was round his neck, and his hands were unwashed. He looked round with an air of insolent effrontery. His face, covered with pimples, was neither thoughtful nor even contemptuous; it wore an expression of complacent satisfaction in demanding his rights and in being an aggrieved party. His voice trembled, and he spoke so fast, and with such stammerings, that he might have been taken for a foreigner, though the purest Russian blood ran in his veins. Lebedeff's nephew, whom the reader has seen already, accompanied him, and also the youth named Hippolyte Terentieff. The latter was only seventeen or eighteen. He had an intelligent face, though it was usually irritated and fretful in expression. His skeleton-like figure, his ghastly complexion, the brightness of his eyes, and the red spots of colour on his cheeks, betrayed the victim of consumption to the most casual glance. He coughed persistently, and panted for breath; it looked as though he had but a few weeks more to live. He was nearly dead with fatigue, and fell, rather than sat, into a chair. The rest bowed as they came in; and being more or less abashed, put on an air of extreme self-assurance. In short, their attitude was not that which one would have expected in men who professed to despise all trivialities, all foolish mundane conventions, and indeed everything, except their own personal interests.

"Antip Burdovsky," stuttered the son of

Pavlicheff.

"Vladimir Doktorenko," said Lebedeff's nephew briskly, and with a certain pride, as if he boasted of his name.

"Keller," murmured the retired officer.

"Hippolyte Terentieff," cried the last-named, in a shrill voice.

They sat now in a row facing the prince, and frowned, and played with their caps. All appeared ready to speak, and yet all were silent; the defiant expression on their faces seemed to say, "No, sir, you don't take us in!" It could be felt that the first word spoken by anyone present would bring a torrent of speech from the whole deputation.

CHAPTER EIGHT

"I DID NOT EXPECT YOU, GENTLEMEN," began the prince. "I have been ill until to-day. A month ago," he continued, addressing himself to Antip Burdovsky, "I put your business into Gavrila Ardalionovitch Ivolgin's hands, as I told you then. I do not in the least object to having a personal interview... but you will agree with me that this is hardly the time... I propose that we go into another room, if you will not keep me long... As you see, I have friends here, and believe me..."

"Friends as many as you please, but allow me," interrupted the harsh voice of Lebedeff's nephew–"allow me to tell you that you might have treated us rather more politely, and not have kept us waiting at least two hours...

"No doubt... and I... is that acting like a prince? And you... you may be a general! But I... I am not your valet! And I... I..." stammered Antip Burdovsky.

He was extremely excited; his lips trembled, and the resentment of an embittered soul was in his voice. But he spoke so indistinctly that hardly a dozen words could be gathered.

"It was a princely action!" sneered Hippolyte.

"If anyone had treated me so," grumbled the boxer.

"I mean to say that if I had been in Burdovsky's place...I..."

"Gentlemen, I did not know you were there; I have only just been informed, I assure you," repeated Muishkin.

"We are not afraid of your friends, prince," remarked Lebedeff's nephew, "for we are within our rights."

The shrill tones of Hippolyte interrupted him. "What right have you... by what right do you demand us to submit this matter, about Burdovsky... to the judgment of your friends? We know only too well what the judgment of your friends will be!..."

This beginning gave promise of a stormy discussion. The prince was much discouraged, but at last he managed to make himself heard amid the vociferations of his excited visitors.

"If you," he said, addressing Burdovsky–"if you prefer not to speak here, I offer again to go into another room with you... and as to your waiting to see me, I repeat that I only this instant heard..."

"Well, you have no right, you have no right, no right at all!... Your friends indeed!"... gabbled Burdovsky, defiantly examining the faces round him, and becoming more and more excited. "You have no right!..." As he ended thus abruptly, he leant forward, staring at the prince with his short-sighted, bloodshot eyes. The latter was so astonished, that he did not reply, but looked steadily at him in return.

"Lef Nicolaievitch!" interposed Madame Epanchin, suddenly, "read this at once, this very moment! It is about this business."

She held out a weekly comic paper, pointing to an article on one of its pages. Just as the visitors were coming in, Lebedeff, wishing to ingratiate himself with the great lady, had pulled this paper from his pocket, and presented it to her, indicating a few columns marked in pencil. Lizabetha Prokofievna had had time to read some of it, and was greatly upset.

"Would it not be better to peruse it alone... later," asked the prince, nervously.

"No, no, read it–read it at once directly, and aloud, aloud!" cried she, calling Colia to her and giving him the journal.–"Read it aloud, so that everyone may hear it!"

An impetuous woman, Lizabetha Prokofievna sometimes weighed her anchors and put out to sea quite regardless of the possible storms she might encounter. Ivan Fedorovitch felt a sudden pang of alarm, but the others were merely curious, and somewhat surprised. Colia unfolded the paper, and began to read, in his clear, high-pitched voice, the following article:

"Proletarians and scions of nobility! An episode of the brigandage of today and every day! Progress! Reform! Justice!"

"Strange things are going on in our so-called Holy Russia in this age of reform and great enterprises; this age of patriotism in which hundreds of millions are yearly sent abroad; in which industry is encouraged, and the hands of Labour paralyzed, etc.; there is no end to this, gentlemen, so let us come to the point. A strange thing has happened

to a scion of our defunct aristocracy. (De profundis!) The grandfathers of these scions ruined themselves at the gaming-tables; their fathers were forced to serve as officers or subalterns; some have died just as they were about to be tried for innocent thoughtlessness in the handling of public funds. Their children are sometimes congenital idiots, like the hero of our story; sometimes they are found in the dock at the Assizes, where they are generally acquitted by the jury for edifying motives; sometimes they distinguish themselves by one of those burning scandals that amaze the public and add another blot to the stained record of our age. Six months ago–that is, last winter–this particular scion returned to Russia, wearing gaiters like a foreigner, and shivering with cold in an old scantily-lined cloak. He had come from Switzerland, where he had just undergone a successful course

of treatment for idiocy (sic!). Certainly Fortune favoured him, for, apart from the interesting malady of which he was cured in Switzerland (can there be a cure for idiocy?) his story proves the truth of the Russian proverb that 'happiness is the right of certain classes!' Judge for yourselves. Our subject was an infant in arms when he lost his father, an officer who died just as he was about to be court-martialled for gambling away the funds of his company, and perhaps also for flogging a subordinate to excess (remember the good old days, gentlemen). The orphan was brought up by the charity of a very rich Russian landowner. In the good old days, this man, whom we will call P—, owned four thousand souls as serfs (souls as serfs!–can you understand such an expression, gentlemen? I cannot; it must be looked up in a dictionary before one can understand it; these things of a bygone day are already unintelligible to us). He appears to have been one of those Russian parasites who lead an idle existence abroad, spending the summer at some spa, and the winter in Paris, to the greater profit of the organizers of public balls. It may safely be said that the manager of the Chateau des Fleurs (lucky man!) pocketed at least a third of the money paid by Russian peasants to their lords in the days of serfdom. However this may be, the gay P— brought up the orphan like a prince, provided him with tutors and governesses (pretty, of course!) whom he chose himself in Paris. But the little aristocrat, the last of his noble race, was an idiot. The governesses, recruited at the Chateau des Fleurs, laboured in vain; at twenty years of age their pupil could not speak in any language, not even Russian. But ignorance of the latter was still excusable. At last P— was seized with a strange notion; he imagined that in Switzerland they could change an idiot into a man of sense. After all, the idea was quite logical; a parasite and landowner naturally supposed that intelligence was a marketable commodity like everything else, and that in Switzerland especially it could be bought for money. The case was entrusted to a celebrated Swiss professor, and cost thousands of roubles; the treatment lasted five years. Needless to say, the idiot did not become intelligent, but it is alleged that he grew into something more or less resembling a man. At this stage P— died suddenly, and, as usual, he had made no will and left his affairs in disorder. A crowd of eager claimants arose, who cared nothing about any last scion of a noble race undergoing treatment in Switzerland, at the expense of the deceased, as a congenital idiot. Idiot though he was, the noble scion tried to cheat his professor,

and they say he succeeded in getting him to continue the treatment gratis for two years, by concealing the death of his benefactor. But the professor himself was a charlatan. Getting anxious at last when no money was forthcoming, and alarmed above all by his patient's appetite, he presented him with a pair of old gaiters and a shabby cloak and packed him off to Russia, third class. It would seem that Fortune had turned her back upon our hero. Not at all; Fortune, who lets whole populations die of hunger, showered all her gifts at once upon the little aristocrat, like Kryloff's Cloud which passes over an arid plain and empties itself into the sea. He had scarcely arrived in St. Petersburg, when a relation of his mother's (who was of bourgeois origin, of course), died at Moscow. He was a merchant, an Old Believer, and he had no children. He left a fortune of several millions in good current coin, and everything came

to our noble scion, our gaitered baron, formerly treated for idiocy in a Swiss lunatic asylum. Instantly the scene changed, crowds of friends gathered round our baron, who meanwhile had lost his head over a celebrated demi-mondaine; he even discovered some relations; moreover a number of young girls of high birth burned to be united to him in lawful matrimony. Could anyone possibly imagine a better match? Aristocrat, millionaire, and idiot, he has every advantage! One might hunt in vain for his equal, even with the lantern of Diogenes; his like is not to be had even by getting it made to order!"

"Oh, I don't know what this means" cried Ivan Fedorovitch, transported with indignation.

"Leave off, Colia," begged the prince. Exclamations arose on all sides.

"Let him go on reading at all costs!" ordered Lizabetha Prokofievna, evidently preserving her composure by a desperate effort. “Prince, if the reading is stopped, you and I will quarrel.”

Colia had no choice but to obey. With crimson cheeks he read on unsteadily:

“But while our young millionaire dwelt as it were in the Empyrean, something new occurred. One fine morning a man called upon him, calm and severe of aspect, distinguished, but plainly dressed. Politely, but in dignified terms, as befitted his errand, he briefly explained the motive for his visit. He was a lawyer of enlightened views; his client was a young man who had consulted him in confidence. This young man was no other than the son of P—, though he bears another name. In his youth P—, the sensualist, had seduced a young girl, poor but respectable. She was a serf, but had received a European education. Finding that a child was expected, he hastened her marriage with a man of

noble character who had loved her for a long time. He helped the young couple for a time, but he was soon obliged to give up, for the high-minded husband refused to accept anything from him. Soon the careless nobleman forgot all about his former mistress and the child she had borne him; then, as we know, he died intestate. P—'s son, born after his mother's marriage, found a true father in the generous man whose name he bore. But when he also died, the orphan was left to provide for himself, his mother now being an invalid who had lost the use of her limbs. Leaving her in a distant province, he came to the capital in search of pupils. By dint of daily toil he earned enough to enable him to follow the college courses, and at last to enter the university. But what can one earn by teaching the children of Russian merchants at ten copecks a lesson, especially with an invalid mother to keep? Even her death did not much diminish the hardships of the young man's struggle for existence. Now this is the question: how, in the name of justice, should our scion have argued the case? Our readers will think, no doubt, that he would say to himself: 'P— showered benefits upon me all my life; he spent tens of thousands of roubles to educate me, to provide me with governesses, and to keep me under treatment in Switzerland. Now I am a millionaire, and P—'s son, a noble young man who is not responsible for the faults of his careless and forgetful father, is wearing himself out giving ill-paid lessons. According to justice, all that was done for me ought to have been done for him. The enormous sums spent upon me were not really mine; they came to me by an error of blind Fortune, when they ought to have gone to P—'s son. They should have gone to benefit him, not me, in whom P— interested himself by a mere caprice, instead of doing his duty as a father. If I wished to behave nobly, justly, and with delicacy, I ought to bestow half my fortune upon the son of my benefactor; but as economy is my favourite virtue, and I know this is not a case in which the law can intervene, I will not give up half my millions. But it would be too openly vile, too flagrantly infamous, if I did not at least restore to P—'s son the tens of thousands of roubles spent in curing my idiocy. This is simply a case of conscience and of strict justice. Whatever would have become of me if P— had not looked after my education, and had taken care of his own son instead of me?'

"No, gentlemen, our scions of the nobility do not reason thus. The lawyer, who had taken up the matter purely out of friendship to the young man, and almost against his will, invoked every consideration of justice, delicacy, honour, and even plain figures; in vain, the ex-patient of the Swiss lunatic asylum was inflexible. All this might pass, but the sequel is absolutely unpardonable, and not to be excused by any interesting malady. This millionaire, having but just discarded the old gaiters of his professor, could not even understand that the noble young man slaving away at his lessons was not asking for charitable help, but for his rightful due, though the debt was not a legal one; that, correctly speaking, he was not asking for anything, but it was merely his friends who had thought fit to bestir themselves on his behalf. With the cool insolence of a bloated capitalist, secure in his millions, he majestically drew a banknote for fifty roubles from his pocket-book and sent it to the noble young man as a humiliating piece of charity. You can hardly believe it, gentlemen! You are scandalized and disgusted; you cry out in indignation!

But that is what he did! Needless to say, the money was returned, or rather flung back in his face. The case is not within the province of the law, it must be referred to the tribunal of public opinion; this is what we now do, guaranteeing the truth of all the details which we have related."

When Colia had finished reading, he handed the paper to the prince, and retired silently to a corner of the room, hiding his face in his hands. He was overcome by a feeling of inexpressible shame; his boyish sensitiveness was wounded beyond endurance. It seemed to him that something extraordinary, some sudden catastrophe had occurred, and that he was almost the cause of it, because he had read the article aloud.

Yet all the others were similarly affected. The girls were uncomfortable and ashamed. Lizabetha Prokofievna restrained her violent anger by a great effort; perhaps she bitterly regretted her interference in the matter; for the present she kept silence. The prince felt as very shy people often do in such a case; he was so ashamed of the conduct of other people, so humiliated for his guests, that he dared not look them in the face. Ptitsin, Varia, Gania, and Lebedeff himself, all looked rather confused. Stranger still, Hippolyte and the "son of Pavlicheff" also seemed slightly surprised, and Lebedeff's nephew was obviously far from pleased. The boxer alone was perfectly calm; he twisted his moustaches with affected dignity, and if his eyes were cast down it was certainly not in confusion, but rather in noble modesty, as if he did not wish to be insolent in his triumph. It was evident that he was delighted with the article.

"The devil knows what it means," growled Ivan Fedorovitch, under his breath; "it must have taken the united wits of fifty footmen to write it."

"May I ask your reason for such an insulting supposition, sir?" said Hippolyte, trembling with rage.

"You will admit yourself, general, that for an honourable man, if the author is an honourable man, that is an–an insult," growled the boxer suddenly, with convulsive jerkings of his shoulders.

"In the first place, it is not for you to address me as 'sir,' and, in the second place, I refuse to give you any explanation," said Ivan Fedorovitch vehemently; and he rose without another word, and went and stood on the first step of the flight that led from the verandah to the street, turning his back on the company. He was indignant with Lizabetha Prokofievna, who did not think of moving even now.

"Gentlemen, gentlemen, let me speak at last," cried the prince, anxious and agitated. "Please let us understand one another. I say nothing about the article, gentlemen, except that every word is false; I say this because you know it as well as I do. It is shameful. I should be surprised if any one of you could have written it."

"I did not know of its existence till this moment," declared Hippolyte. "I do not approve of it."

"I knew it had been written, but I would not have advised its publication," said Lebedeff's nephew, "because it is premature."

"I knew it, but I have a right. I... I..." stammered the "son of Pavlicheff."

"What! Did you write all that yourself? Is it possible?" asked the prince, regarding Burdovsky with curiosity.

"One might dispute your right to ask such questions," observed Lebedeff's nephew.

"I was only surprised that Mr. Burdovsky should have–however, this is what I have to say. Since you had already given the matter publicity, why did you object just now, when I began to speak of it to my friends?"

"At last!" murmured Lizabetha Prokofievna indignantly.

Lebedeff could restrain himself no longer;

he made his way through the row of chairs.

"Prince," he cried, "you are forgetting that if you consented to receive and hear them, it was only because of your kind heart which has no equal, for they had not the least right to demand it, especially as you had placed the matter in the hands of Gavrila Ardalionovitch, which was also extremely kind of you. You are also forgetting, most excellent prince, that you are with friends, a select company; you cannot sacrifice them to these gentlemen, and it is only for you to have them turned out this instant. As the master of the house I shall have great pleasure ...."

"Quite right!" agreed General Ivolgin in a loud voice.

"That will do, Lebedeff, that will do–" began the prince, when an indignant outcry drowned his words.

"Excuse me, prince, excuse me, but now that will not do," shouted Lebedeff's nephew, his voice dominating all the others. "The matter must be clearly stated, for it is obviously not properly understood. They are calling in some legal chicanery, and upon that ground they are threatening to turn us out of the house! Really, prince, do you think we are such fools as not to be aware that this matter does not come within the law, and that legally we cannot claim a rouble from you? But we are also aware that if actual law is not on our side, human law is for us, natural law, the law of common-sense and conscience, which is no less binding upon every noble and honest man–that is, every man of sane judgment–because it is not to be found in miserable legal codes. If we come here without fear of being turned out (as was threatened just now) because of the imperative tone of our demand, and the unseemliness of such a visit at this late hour (though it was not late when we arrived, we were kept waiting in your anteroom), if, I say, we came in without fear, it is just because we expected to find you a man of sense; I mean, a man of honour and conscience. It is quite true that we did not present ourselves humbly, like your flatterers and parasites, but holding up our heads as befits independent men. We present no petition, but a proud and free demand (note it well, we do not beseech, we demand!). We ask you fairly and squarely in a dignified manner. Do you believe that in this affair of Burdovsky you have right on your side? Do you admit that Pavlicheff overwhelmed you with benefits, and perhaps saved your life? If you admit it (which we take for granted), do you intend, now that you are a millionaire, and do you not think it in conformity with justice, to indemnify Burdovsky? Yes or no? If it is yes, or, in other words, if you possess what you call honour and conscience, and we more justly call common-sense, then accede to our demand, and the matter is at an end. Give us satisfaction, without entreaties or thanks from us; do not expect thanks from us, for what you do will be done not for our sake, but for the sake of justice. If you refuse to satisfy us, that is, if your answer is no, we will go away at once, and there will be an end of the matter. But we will tell you to your face before the present company that you are a man of vulgar and undeveloped mind; we will openly deny you the right to speak in future of your honour and conscience, for you have not paid the fair price of such a right. I have no more to say–I have put the question before you. Now turn us out if you dare. You can do it; force is on your side. But remember that we do not beseech, we demand! We do not beseech, we demand!"

With these last excited words, Lebedeff's nephew was silent.

"We demand, we demand, we demand, we do not beseech," spluttered Burdovsky, red as a lobster.

The speech of Lebedeff's nephew caused a certain stir among the company; murmurs arose, though with the exception of Lebedeff, who was still very much excited, everyone was careful not to interfere in the matter. Strangely enough, Lebedeff, although on the prince's side, seemed quite proud of his nephew's eloquence. Gratified vanity was visible in the glances he cast upon the assembled company.

"In my opinion, Mr. Doktorenko," said the prince, in rather a low voice, "you are quite right in at least half of what you say. I would go further and say that you are altogether right, and that I quite agree with you, if there were not something lacking in your speech. I cannot undertake to say precisely what it is, but you have certainly omitted something, and you cannot be quite just while there is something lacking. But let us put that aside and return to the point. Tell me what induced you to publish this article. Every word of it is a calumny, and I think, gentlemen, that you have been guilty of a mean action."

"Allow me–"

"Sir–"

“What? What? What?” cried all the visitors at once, in violent agitation.

“As to the article,” said Hippolyte in his croaking voice, “I have told you already that we none of us approve of it! There is the writer,” he added, pointing to the boxer, who sat beside him. “I quite admit that he has written it in his old regimental manner, with an equal disregard for style and decency. I know he is a cross between a fool and an adventurer; I make no bones about telling him so to his face every day. But after all he is half justified; publicity is the lawful right of every man; consequently, Burdovsky is not excepted. Let him answer for his own blunders. As to the objection which I made just now in the name of all, to the presence of your friends, I think I ought to explain, gentlemen, that I only did so to assert our rights, though we really wished to have witnesses; we had agreed unanimously upon the point before we came in. We do not care who your witnesses may be, or whether they are your friends or not. As they cannot fail to recognize Burdovsky's right (seeing that it is mathematically demonstrable), it is just as well that the witnesses should be your friends. The truth will only be more plainly evident."

"It is quite true; we had agreed upon that point," said Lebedeff's nephew, in confirmation.

"If that is the case, why did you begin by making such a fuss about it?" asked the astonished prince.

The boxer was dying to get in a few words; owing, no doubt, to the presence of the ladies, he was becoming quite jovial.

"As to the article, prince," he said, "I admit that I wrote it, in spite of the severe criticism of my poor friend, in whom I always overlook many things because of his unfortunate state of health. But I wrote and published it in the form of a letter, in the paper of a friend. I showed it to no one but Burdovsky, and I did not read it all through, even to him. He immediately gave me permission to publish it, but you will admit that I might have done so without his consent. Publicity is a noble, beneficent, and universal right. I hope, prince, that you are too progressive to deny this?"

"I deny nothing, but you must confess that your article–"

"Is a bit thick, you mean? Well, in a way that is in the public interest; you will admit that yourself, and after all one cannot overlook a blatant fact. So much the worse for the guilty parties, but the public welfare must come before everything. As to certain inaccuracies and figures of speech, so to speak, you will also admit that the motive, aim, and intention, are the chief thing. It is a question, above all, of making a wholesome example; the individual case can be examined afterwards; and as to the style–well, the thing was meant to be humorous, so to speak, and, after all, everybody writes like that; you must admit it yourself! Ha, ha!"

"But, gentlemen, I assure you that you are quite astray," exclaimed the prince. "You have published this article upon the supposition that I would never consent to satisfy Mr. Burdovsky. Acting on that conviction, you have tried to intimidate me by this publication and to be revenged for my supposed refusal. But what did you know of my intentions? It may be that I have resolved to satisfy Mr. Burdovsky's claim. I now declare openly, in the presence of these witnesses, that I will do so."

"The noble and intelligent word of an intelligent and most noble man, at last!" exclaimed the boxer.

"Good God!" exclaimed Lizabetha Prokofievna involuntarily.

"This is intolerable," growled the general.

"Allow me, gentlemen, allow me," urged the prince.

"I will explain matters to you. Five weeks

ago I received a visit from Tchebaroff, your agent, Mr. Burdovsky. You have given a very flattering description of him in your article, Mr. Keller," he continued, turning to the boxer with a smile, "but he did not please me at all. I saw at once that Tchebaroff was the moving spirit in the matter, and, to speak frankly, I thought he might have induced you, Mr. Burdovsky, to make this claim, by taking advantage of your simplicity."

"You have no right.... I am not simple," stammered Burdovsky, much agitated.

"You have no sort of right to suppose such things," said Lebedeff's nephew in a tone of authority.

"It is most offensive!" shrieked Hippolyte; "it is an insulting suggestion, false, and most ill-timed."

"I beg your pardon, gentlemen; please excuse me," said the prince. "I thought absolute frankness on both sides would be best, but have it your own way. I told Tchebaroff that, as I was not in Petersburg,

I would commission a friend to look into the matter without delay, and that I would let you know, Mr. Burdovsky. Gentlemen, I have no hesitation in telling you that it was the fact of Tchebaroff's intervention that made me suspect a fraud. Oh! do not take offence at my words, gentlemen, for Heaven's sake do not be so touchy!" cried the prince, seeing that Burdovsky was getting excited again, and that the rest were preparing to protest. "If I say I suspected a fraud, there is nothing personal in that. I had never seen any of you then; I did not even know your names; I only judged by Tchebaroff; I am speaking quite generally–if you only knew how I have been 'done' since I came into my fortune!"

"You are shockingly naive, prince," said Lebedeff's nephew in mocking tones.

"Besides, though you are a prince and a millionaire, and even though you may really be simple and good-hearted, you can hardly be outside the general law," Hippolyte declared loudly.

"Perhaps not; it is very possible," the prince agreed hastily, "though I do not know what general law you allude to. I will go on–only please do not take offence without good cause. I assure you I do not mean to offend you in the least. Really, it is impossible to speak three words sincerely without your flying into a rage! At first I was amazed when Tchebaroff told me that Pavlicheff had a son, and that he was in such a miserable position. Pavlicheff was my benefactor, and my father's friend. Oh, Mr. Keller, why does your article impute things to my father without the slightest foundation? He never squandered the funds of his company nor ill-treated his subordinates, I am absolutely certain of it; I cannot imagine how you could bring yourself to write such a calumny! But your assertions concerning Pavlicheff are absolutely intolerable! You do not scruple to make a libertine of that noble man; you call him a sensualist as coolly as if you were speaking the truth, and yet it would not be possible to find a chaster man. He was even a scholar of note, and in correspondence with several celebrated scientists, and spent large sums in the interests of science. As to his kind heart and his good actions, you were right indeed when you said that I was almost an idiot at that time, and could hardly understand anything–(I could speak and understand Russian, though),–but now I can appreciate what I remember–"

"Excuse me," interrupted Hippolyte, "is not this rather sentimental? You said you wished to come to the point; please remember that it is after nine o'clock."

"Very well, gentlemen–very well," replied the prince. "At first I received the news with mistrust, then I said to myself that I might be mistaken, and that Pavlicheff might possibly have had a son. But I was absolutely amazed at the readiness with which the son had revealed the secret of his birth at the expense of his mother's honour. For Tchebaroff had already menaced me with publicity in our interview....”

“What nonsense!” Lebedeff’s nephew interrupted violently.

“You have no right–you have no right!” cried Burdovsky.

“The son is not responsible for the misdeeds of his father; and the mother is not to blame,” added Hippolyte, with warmth.

“That seems to me all the more reason for sparing her,” said the prince timidly.

“Prince, you are not only simple, but your simplicity is almost past the limit,” said Lebedeff’s nephew, with a sarcastic smile.

“But what right had you?” said Hippolyte in a very strange tone.

“None–none whatever,” agreed the prince hastily. “I admit you are right there, but it was involuntary, and I immediately said to myself that my personal feelings had nothing to do with it,–that if I thought it right to satisfy the demands of Mr. Burdovsky, out of respect for the memory of Pavlicheff, I ought to do so in any case, whether I esteemed Mr. Burdovsky or not. I only mentioned this, gentlemen, because it seemed so unnatural to me for a son to betray his mother's secret in such a way. In short, that is what convinced me that Tchebaroff must be a rogue, and that he had induced Mr. Burdovsky to attempt this fraud."

"But this is intolerable!" cried the visitors, some of them starting to their feet.

"Gentlemen, I supposed from this that poor Mr. Burdovsky must be a simple-minded man, quite defenceless, and an easy tool in the hands of rogues. That is why I thought it my duty to try and help him as 'Pavlicheff's son'; in the first place by rescuing him from the influence of Tchebaroff, and secondly by making myself his friend. I have resolved to give him ten thousand roubles; that is about the sum which I calculate that Pavlicheff must have spent on me."

"What, only ten thousand!" cried Hippolyte.

"Well, prince, your arithmetic is not up to much, or else you are mighty clever at it, though you affect the air of a simpleton," said Lebedeff's nephew.

"I will not accept ten thousand roubles," said Burdovsky.

"Accept, Antip," whispered the boxer eagerly, leaning past the back of Hippolyte's chair to give his friend this piece of advice. "Take it for the present; we can see about more later on."

"Look here, Mr. Muishkin," shouted Hippolyte, "please understand that we are not fools, nor idiots, as your guests seem to imagine; these ladies who look upon us with such scorn, and especially this fine gentleman" (pointing to Evgenie Pavlovitch) "whom I have not the honour of knowing, though I think I have heard some talk about him–"

"Really, really, gentlemen," cried the prince in great agitation, "you are misunderstanding me again. In the first place, Mr. Keller, you have greatly overestimated my fortune in your article. I am far from being a millionaire. I have barely a tenth of what you suppose. Secondly, my treatment in Switzerland was very far from costing tens of thousands of roubles. Schneider received six hundred roubles a year, and he was only paid for the first three years. As to the pretty governesses whom Pavlicheff is supposed to have brought from Paris, they only exist in Mr. Keller's imagination; it is another calumny. According to my calculations, the sum spent on me was very considerably under ten thousand roubles, but I decided on that sum, and you must admit that in paying a debt I could not offer Mr. Burdovsky more, however kindly disposed I might be towards him; delicacy forbids it; I should seem to be offering him charity instead of rightful payment. I don't know how you cannot see that, gentlemen! Besides, I had no intention of leaving the matter there. I meant to intervene amicably later on and help to improve poor Mr. Burdovsky's position. It is clear that he has been deceived, or he would never have agreed to anything so vile as the scandalous revelations about his mother in Mr. Keller's article. But, gentlemen, why are you getting angry again? Are we never to come to an understanding? Well, the event has proved me right! I have just seen with my own eyes the proof that my conjecture was correct!" he added, with increasing eagerness.

He meant to calm his hearers, and did not perceive that his words had only increased their irritation.

"What do you mean? What are you convinced of?" they demanded angrily.

"In the first place, I have had the opportunity of getting a correct idea of Mr. Burdovsky. I see what he is for myself. He is an innocent man, deceived by everyone! A defenceless victim, who deserves indulgence! Secondly, Gavrila Ardalionovitch, in whose hands I had placed the matter, had his first interview with me barely an hour ago. I had not heard from him for some time, as I was away, and have been ill for three days since my return to St. Petersburg. He tells me that he has exposed the designs of Tchebaroff and has proof that justifies my opinion of him. I know, gentlemen, that many people think me an idiot. Counting upon my reputation as a man whose purse-strings are easily loosened, Tchebaroff thought it would be a simple matter to fleece me, especially by trading on my gratitude to Pavlicheff. But the main point is–listen, gentlemen, let me finish!–the main point is that Mr. Burdovsky is not Pavlicheff's son at all. Gavrila Ardalionovitch has just told me of his discovery, and assures me that he has positive proofs. Well, what do you think of that? It is scarcely credible, even after all the tricks that have been played upon me. Please note that we have positive proofs! I can hardly believe it myself, I assure you; I do not yet believe it; I am still doubtful, because Gavrila Ardalionovitch has not had time to go into details; but there can be no further doubt that Tchebaroff is a rogue! He has deceived poor Mr. Burdovsky, and all of you, gentlemen, who have come forward so nobly to support your friend–(he evidently needs support, I quite see that!). He has abused your credulity and involved you all in an attempted fraud, for when all is said and done this claim is nothing else!"

"What! a fraud? What, he is not Pavlicheff's son? Impossible!"

These exclamations but feebly expressed the profound bewilderment into which the prince's words had plunged Burdovsky's companions.

"Certainly it is a fraud! Since Mr. Burdovsky is not Pavlicheff's son, his claim is neither more nor less than attempted fraud (supposing, of course, that he had known the truth), but the fact is that he has been deceived. I insist on this point in order to justify him; I repeat that his simple-mindedness makes him worthy of pity, and that he cannot stand alone; otherwise he would have behaved like a scoundrel in this matter. But I feel certain that he does not understand it! I was just the same myself before I went to Switzerland; I stammered incoherently; one tries to express oneself and cannot. I understand that. I am all the better able to pity Mr. Burdovsky, because I know from experience what it is to be like that, and so I have a right to speak. Well, though there is no such person as 'Pavlicheff's son,' and it is all nothing but a humbug, yet I will keep to my decision, and I am prepared to give up ten thousand roubles in memory of Pavlicheff. Before Mr. Burdovsky made this claim, I proposed to found a school with this money, in memory of my benefactor, but I shall honour his memory quite as well by giving the ten thousand roubles to Mr. Burdovsky, because, though he was not Pavlicheff's son, he was treated almost as though he were. That is what gave a rogue the opportunity of deceiving him; he really did think himself Pavlicheff's son. Listen, gentlemen; this matter must be settled; keep calm; do not get angry; and sit down! Gavrila Ardalionovitch will explain everything to you at once, and I confess that I am very anxious to hear all the details myself. He says that he has even been to Pskoff to see your mother, Mr. Burdovsky; she is not dead, as the article which was just read to us makes out. Sit down, gentlemen, sit down!"

The prince sat down, and at length prevailed upon Burdovsky's company to do likewise. During the last ten or twenty minutes, exasperated by continual interruptions, he had raised his voice, and spoken with great vehemence. Now, no doubt, he bitterly regretted several words and expressions which had escaped him in his excitement. If he had not been driven beyond the limits of endurance, he would not have ventured to express certain conjectures so openly. He had no sooner sat down than his heart was torn by sharp remorse. Besides insulting Burdovsky with the supposition, made in the presence of witnesses, that he was suffering from the complaint for which he had himself been treated in Switzerland, he reproached himself with the grossest indelicacy in having offered him the ten thousand roubles before everyone. "I ought to have waited till to-morrow and offered him the money when we were alone," thought Muishkin. "Now it is too late, the mischief is done! Yes, I am an idiot, an absolute idiot!" he said to himself, overcome with shame and regret.

Till then Gavrila Ardalionovitch had sat apart in silence. When the prince called upon him, he came and stood by his side, and in a calm, clear voice began to render an account of the mission confided to him. All conversation ceased instantly. Everyone, especially the Burdovsky party, listened with the utmost curiosity.

CHAPTER NINE

"YOU WILL NOT DENY, I am sure," said Gavrila Ardalionovitch, turning to Burdovsky, who sat looking at him with wide-open eyes, perplexed and astonished. "You will not deny, seriously, that you were born just two years after your mother's legal marriage to Mr. Burdovsky, your father. Nothing would be easier than to prove the date of your birth from well-known facts; we can only look on Mr. Keller's version as a work of imagination, and one, moreover, extremely offensive both to you and your mother. Of course he distorted the truth in order to strengthen your claim, and to serve your interests. Mr. Keller said that he previously consulted you about his article in the paper, but did not read it to you as a whole. Certainly he could not have read that passage..."

"As a matter of fact, I did not read it," interrupted the boxer, "but its contents had been given me on unimpeachable authority, and I..."

"Excuse me, Mr. Keller," interposed Gavrila Ardalionovitch. "Allow me to speak. I assure you your article shall be mentioned in its proper place, and you can then explain everything, but for the moment I would rather not anticipate. Quite accidentally, with the help of my sister, Varvara Ardalionovna Ptitsin, I obtained from one of her intimate friends, Madame Zoubkoff, a letter written to her twenty-five years ago, by Nicolai Andreevitch Pavlicheff, then abroad. After getting into communication with this lady, I went by her advice to Timofei Fedorovitch Viazovkin, a retired colonel, and one of Pavlicheff's oldest friends. He gave me two more letters written by the latter when he was still in foreign parts. These three documents, their dates, and the facts mentioned in them, prove in the most undeniable manner, that eighteen months before your birth, Nicolai Andreevitch went abroad, where he remained for three consecutive years. Your mother, as you are well aware, has never been out of Russia.... It is too late to read the letters now; I am content to state the fact. But if you desire it, come to me tomorrow morning, bring witnesses and writing experts with you, and I will prove the absolute truth of my story. From that moment the question will be decided."

These words caused a sensation among the listeners, and there was a general movement of relief. Burdovsky got up abruptly.

"If that is true," said he, "I have been

deceived, grossly deceived, but not by Tchebaroff: and for a long time past, a long time. I do not wish for experts, not I, nor to go to see you. I believe you. I give it up.... But I refuse the ten thousand roubles. Good-bye."

"Wait five minutes more, Mr. Burdovsky," said Gavrila Ardalionovitch pleasantly. "I have more to say. Some rather curious and important facts have come to light, and it is absolutely necessary, in my opinion, that you should hear them. You will not regret, I fancy, to have the whole matter thoroughly cleared up."

Burdovsky silently resumed his seat, and bent his head as though in profound thought. His friend, Lebedeff's nephew, who had risen to accompany him, also sat down again. He seemed much disappointed, though as self-confident as ever. Hippolyte looked dejected and sulky, as well as surprised. He had just been attacked by a violent fit of coughing, so that his handkerchief was stained with blood. The boxer looked thoroughly frightened.

"Oh, Antip!" cried he in a miserable voice, "I did say to you the other day–the day before yesterday–that perhaps you were not really Pavlicheff's son!"

There were sounds of half-smothered laughter at this.

"Now, that is a valuable piece of information, Mr. Keller," replied Gania. "However that may be, I have private information which convinces me that Mr. Burdovsky, though doubtless aware of the date of his birth, knew nothing at all about Pavlicheff's sojourn abroad. Indeed, he passed the greater part of his life out of Russia, returning at intervals for short visits. The journey in question is in itself too unimportant for his friends to recollect it after more than twenty years; and of course Mr. Burdovsky could have known nothing about it, for he was not born. As the event has proved, it was not impossible to find evidence of his absence, though I must confess that chance has helped me in a quest which might very well have come to nothing. It was really almost impossible for Burdovsky or Tchebaroff to discover these facts, even if it had entered their heads to try. Naturally they never dreamt..."

Here the voice of Hippolyte suddenly intervened.

"Allow me, Mr. Ivolgin," he said irritably. "What is the good of all this rigmarole? Pardon me. All is now clear, and we acknowledge the truth of your main point. Why go into these tedious details? You wish perhaps to boast of the cleverness of your investigation, to cry up your talents as detective? Or perhaps your intention is to excuse Burdovsky, by proving that he took up the matter in ignorance? Well, I consider that extremely impudent on your part! You ought to know that Burdovsky has no need of being excused or justified by you or anyone else! It is an insult! The affair is quite painful enough for him without that.

Will nothing make you understand?"

"Enough! enough! Mr. Terentieff," interrupted Gania.

"Don't excite yourself; you seem very ill, and I am sorry for that. I am almost done, but there are a few facts to which I must briefly refer, as I am convinced that they ought to be clearly explained once for all...." A movement of impatience was noticed in his audience as he resumed: "I merely wish to state, for the information of all concerned, that the reason for Mr. Pavlicheff's interest in your mother, Mr. Burdovsky, was simply that she was the sister of a serf-girl with whom he was deeply in love in his youth, and whom most certainly he would have married but for her sudden death. I have proofs that this circumstance is almost, if not quite, forgotten. I may add that when your mother was about ten years old, Pavlicheff took her under his care, gave her a good education, and later, a considerable dowry. His relations were alarmed, and feared he might go so far as to marry her, but she gave her hand to a young land-surveyor named Burdovsky when she reached the age of twenty. I can even say definitely that it was a marriage of affection. After his wedding your father gave up his occupation as land-surveyor, and with his wife's dowry of fifteen thousand roubles went in for commercial speculations. As he had had no experience, he was cheated on all sides, and took to drink in order to forget his troubles. He shortened his life by his excesses, and eight years after his marriage he died. Your mother says herself that she was left in the direst poverty, and would have died of starvation had it not been for Pavlicheff, who generously allowed her a yearly pension of six hundred roubles. Many people recall his extreme fondness for you as a little boy. Your mother confirms this, and agrees with others in thinking that he loved you the more because you were a sickly child, stammering in your speech, and almost deformed–for it is known that all his life Nicolai Andreevitch had a partiality for unfortunates of every kind, especially children. In my opinion this is most important. I may add that I discovered yet another fact, the last on which I employed my detective powers. Seeing how fond Pavlicheff was of you,–it was thanks to him you went to school, and also had the advantage of special teachers–his relations and servants grew to believe that you were his son, and that your father had been betrayed by his wife. I may point out that this idea was only accredited generally during the last years of Pavlicheff's life, when his next-of-kin were trembling about the succession, when the earlier story was quite forgotten, and when all opportunity for discovering the truth had seemingly passed away. No doubt you, Mr. Burdovsky, heard this conjecture, and did not hesitate to accept it as true. I have had the honour of making your mother's acquaintance, and I find that she knows all about these reports. What she does not know is that you, her son, should have listened to them so complaisantly. I found your respected mother at Pskoff, ill and in deep poverty, as she has been ever since the death of your benefactor. She told me with tears of gratitude how you had supported her; she expects much of you, and believes fervently in your future success..."

"Oh, this is unbearable!" said Lebedeff's nephew impatiently. "What is the good of all this romancing?"

"It is revolting and unseemly!" cried Hippolyte, jumping up in a fury.

Burdovsky alone sat silent and motionless.

"What is the good of it?" repeated Gavrila Ardalionovitch, with pretended surprise. "Well, firstly, because now perhaps Mr. Burdovsky is quite convinced that Mr. Pavlicheff's love for him came simply from generosity of soul, and not from paternal duty. It was most necessary to impress this fact upon his mind, considering that he approved of the article written by Mr.

Keller. I speak thus because I look on you, Mr. Burdovsky, as an honourable man. Secondly, it appears that there was no intention of cheating in this case, even on the part of Tchebaroff. I wish to say this quite plainly, because the prince hinted a while ago that I too thought it an attempt at robbery and extortion. On the contrary, everyone has been quite sincere in the matter, and although Tchebaroff may be somewhat of a rogue, in this business he has acted simply as any sharp lawyer would do under the circumstances. He looked at it as a case that might bring him in a lot of money, and he did not calculate badly; because on the one hand he speculated on the generosity of the prince, and his gratitude to the late Mr. Pavlicheff, and on the other to his chivalrous ideas as to the obligations of honour and conscience. As to Mr. Burdovsky, allowing for his principles, we may acknowledge that he engaged in the business with very little personal aim in view. At the instigation of Tchebaroff and his other friends, he decided to make the attempt in the service of truth, progress, and humanity. In short, the conclusion may be drawn that, in spite of all appearances, Mr. Burdovsky is a man of irreproachable character, and thus the prince can all the more readily offer him his friendship, and the assistance of which he spoke just now..."

"Hush! hush! Gavrila Ardalionovitch!" cried Muishkin in dismay, but it was too late.

"I said, and I have repeated it over and over again," shouted Burdovsky furiously, "that I did not want the money. I will not take it... why...I will not... I am going away!"

He was rushing hurriedly from the terrace, when Lebedeff's nephew seized his arms, and said something to him in a low voice. Burdovsky turned quickly, and drawing an addressed but unsealed envelope from his pocket, he threw it down on a little table beside the prince.

"There's the money!... How dare you?... The money!"

"Those are the two hundred and fifty roubles you dared to send him as a charity, by the hands of Tchebaroff," explained Doktorenko.

"The article in the newspaper put it at fifty!" cried Colia.

"I beg your pardon," said the prince, going up to Burdovsky. "I have done you a great wrong, but I did not send you that money as a charity, believe me. And now I am again to blame. I offended you just now." (The prince was much distressed; he seemed worn out with fatigue, and spoke almost incoherently.) "I spoke of swindling... but I did not apply that to you. I was deceived .... I said you were... afflicted... like me... But you are not like me... you give lessons... you support your mother. I said you had dishonoured your mother, but you love her. She says so herself... I did not know... Gavrila Ardalionovitch did not tell me that... Forgive me! I dared to offer you ten thousand roubles, but I was wrong. I ought to have done it differently, and now... there is no way of doing it, for you despise me..."

"I declare, this is a lunatic asylum!" cried Lizabetha Prokofievna.

"Of course it is a lunatic asylum!" repeated Aglaya sharply, but her words were overpowered by other voices. Everybody was talking loudly, making remarks and comments; some discussed the affair gravely, others laughed. Ivan Fedorovitch Epanchin was extremely indignant. He stood waiting for his wife with an air of offended dignity. Lebedeff's nephew took up the word again.

"Well, prince, to do you justice, you certainly know how to make the most of your–let us call it infirmity, for the sake of politeness; you have set about offering your money and friendship in such a way that no self-respecting man could possibly accept them. This is an excess of ingenuousness or of malice–you ought to know better than anyone which word best fits the case."

"Allow me, gentlemen," said Gavrila Ardalionovitch, who had just examined the contents of the envelope, "there are only a hundred roubles here, not two hundred and fifty. I point this out, prince, to prevent misunderstanding."

"Never mind, never mind," said the prince, signing to him to keep quiet.

"But we do mind," said Lebedeff's nephew vehemently. "Prince, your 'never mind' is an insult to us. We have nothing to hide; our actions can bear daylight. It is true that there are only a hundred roubles instead of two hundred and fifty, but it is all the same."

"Why, no, it is hardly the same," remarked Gavrila Ardalionovitch, with an air of ingenuous surprise.

"Don't interrupt, we are not such fools as you think, Mr. Lawyer," cried Lebedeff's nephew angrily. "Of course there is a difference between a hundred roubles and two hundred and fifty, but in this case the principle is the main point, and that a hundred and fifty roubles are missing is only a side issue. The point to be emphasized is that Burdovsky will not accept your highness's charity; he flings it back in your face, and it scarcely matters if there are a hundred roubles or two hundred and fifty. Burdovsky has refused ten thousand roubles; you heard him. He would not have returned even a hundred roubles if he was dishonest! The hundred and fifty roubles were paid to Tchebaroff for his travelling expenses. You may jeer at our stupidity and at our inexperience in business matters; you have done all you could already to make us look ridiculous; but do not dare to call us dishonest. The four of us will club together every day to repay the hundred and fifty roubles to the prince, if we have to pay it in instalments of a rouble at a time, but we will repay it, with interest. Burdovsky is poor, he has no millions. After his journey to see the prince Tchebaroff sent in his bill. We counted on winning... Who would not have done the same in such a case?”

“Who indeed?” exclaimed Prince S.

“I shall certainly go mad, if I stay here!” cried Lizabetha Prokofievna.

“It reminds me,” said Evgenie Pavlovitch, laughing, “of the famous plea of a certain lawyer who lately defended a man for murdering six people in order to rob them. He excused his client on the score of poverty. ‘It is quite natural,’ he said in conclusion, ‘considering the state of misery he was in, that he should have thought of murdering these six people; which of you, gentlemen, would not have done the same in his place?’”

“Enough,” cried Lizabetha Prokofievna abruptly, trembling with anger, “we have had enough of this balderdash!”

In a state of terrible excitement she threw back her head, with flaming eyes, casting looks of contempt and defiance upon the whole company, in which she could no longer distinguish friend from foe. She had restrained herself so long that she felt forced to vent her rage on somebody. Those who knew Lizabetha Prokofievna saw at once how it was with her. “She flies into these rages sometimes,” said Ivan Fedorovitch to Prince S. the next day, “but she is not often so violent as she was yesterday; it does not happen more than once in three years.”

“Be quiet, Ivan Fedorovitch! Leave me alone!” cried Mrs. Epanchin. “Why do you offer me your arm now? You had not sense enough to take me away before. You are my husband, you are a father, it was your duty to drag me away by force, if in my folly I refused to obey you and go quietly. You might at least have thought of your daughters. We can find our way out now without your help. Here is shame enough for a year! Wait a moment ‘till I thank the prince! Thank you, prince, for the entertainment you have given us! It was most amusing to hear these young men... It is vile, vile! A chaos, a scandal, worse than a nightmare!

Is it possible that there can be many such people on earth? Be quiet, Aglaya! Be quiet, Alexandra! It is none of your business! Don't fuss round me like that, Evgenie Pavlovitch; you exasperate me! So, my dear," she cried, addressing the prince, "you go so far as to beg their pardon! He says, 'Forgive me for offering you a fortune.' And you, you mountebank, what are you laughing at?" she cried, turning suddenly on Lebedeff's nephew. "'We refuse ten thousand roubles; we do not beseech, we demand!' As if he did not know that this idiot will call on them tomorrow to renew his offers of money and friendship. You will, won't you? You will? Come, will you, or won't you?"

"I shall," said the prince, with gentle humility.

"You hear him! You count upon it, too," she continued, turning upon Doktorenko. "You are as sure of him now as if you had the money in your pocket. And there you are playing the swaggerer to throw dust in our eyes! No, my dear sir, you may take other people in! I can see through all your airs and graces, I see your game!"

"Lizabetha Prokofievna!" exclaimed the prince.

"Come, Lizabetha Prokofievna, it is quite time for us to be going, we will take the prince with us," said Prince S. with a smile, in the coolest possible way.

The girls stood apart, almost frightened; their father was positively horrified. Mrs. Epanchin's language astonished everybody. Some who stood a little way off smiled furtively, and talked in whispers. Lebedeff wore an expression of utmost ecstasy.

"Chaos and scandal are to be found everywhere, madame," remarked Doktorenko, who was considerably put out of countenance.

"Not like this! Nothing like the spectacle you have just given us, sir," answered Lizabetha Prokofievna, with a sort of hysterical rage. "Leave me alone, will you?"

she cried violently to those around her, who were trying to keep her quiet. “No, Evgenie Pavlovitch, if, as you said yourself just now, a lawyer said in open court that he found it quite natural that a man should murder six people because he was in misery, the world must be coming to an end. I had not heard of it before. Now I understand everything. And this stutterer, won’t he turn out a murderer?” she cried, pointing to Burdovsky, who was staring at her with stupefaction. “I bet he will! He will have none of your money, possibly, he will refuse it because his conscience will not allow him to accept it, but he will go murdering you by night and walking off with your cashbox, with a clear conscience! He does not call it a dishonest action but ‘the impulse of a noble despair’; ‘a negation’; or the devil knows what! Bah! everything is upside down, everyone walks head downwards. A young girl, brought up at home, suddenly jumps into a cab in the middle of the street, saying: ‘Good-bye, mother, I married Karlitch, or Ivanitch, the other day!' And you think it quite right? You call such conduct estimable and natural? The 'woman question'? Look here," she continued, pointing to Colia, "the other day that whippersnapper told me that this was the whole meaning of the 'woman question.' But even supposing that your mother is a fool, you are none the less, bound to treat her with humanity. Why did you come here tonight so insolently? 'Give us our rights, but don't dare to speak in our presence. Show us every mark of deepest respect, while we treat you like the scum of the earth.' The miscreants have written a tissue of calumny in their article, and these are the men who seek for truth, and do battle for the right! 'We do not beseech, we demand, you will get no thanks from us, because you will be acting to satisfy your own conscience!' What morality! But, good heavens! if you declare that the prince's generosity will, excite no gratitude in you, he might answer that he is not, bound to be grateful to Pavlicheff, who also was only satisfying his own conscience. But you counted on the prince's, gratitude towards Pavlicheff; you never lent him any money; he owes you nothing; then what were you counting upon if not on his gratitude? And if you appeal to that sentiment in others, why should you expect to be exempted from it? They are mad! They say society is savage and inhuman because it despises a young girl who has been seduced. But if you call society inhuman you imply that the young girl is made to suffer by its censure. How then, can you hold her up to the scorn of society in the newspapers without realizing that you are making her suffering, still greater? Madmen! Vain fools! They don't believe in God, they don't believe in Christ! But you are so eaten up by pride and vanity, that you will end by devouring each other–that is my prophecy! Is not this absurd? Is it not monstrous chaos? And after all this, that shameless creature will go and beg their pardon! Are there many people like you? What are you smiling at? Because I am not ashamed to disgrace myself before you?– Yes, I am disgraced–it can't be helped now! But don't you jeer at me, you scum!" (this was aimed at Hippolyte). "He is almost at his last gasp, yet he corrupts others. You, have got hold of this lad–" (she pointed to Colia); "you, have turned his head, you have taught him to be an atheist, you don't believe in God, and you are not too old to be whipped, sir! A plague upon you! And so, Prince Lef Nicolaievitch, you will call on them tomorrow, will you?" she asked the prince breathlessly, for the second time.

"Yes."

"Then I will never speak to you again." She made a sudden movement to go, and then turned quickly back. "And you will call on that atheist?" she continued, pointing to Hippolyte. "How dare you grin at me like that?" she shouted furiously, rushing at the invalid, whose mocking smile drove her to distraction.

Exclamations arose on all sides.

"Lizabetha Prokofievna! Lizabetha Prokofievna! Lizabetha Prokofievna!"

"Mother, this is disgraceful!" cried Aglaya.

Mrs. Epanchin had approached Hippolyte and seized him firmly by the arm, while her eyes, blazing with fury, were fixed upon his face.

"Do not distress yourself, Aglaya Ivanovitch," he answered calmly; "your mother knows that one cannot strike a dying man. I am ready to explain why I was laughing. I shall be delighted if you will let me–"

A violent fit of coughing, which lasted a full minute, prevented him from finishing his sentence.

"He is dying, yet he will not stop holding forth!" cried Lizabetha Prokofievna. She loosed her hold on his arm, almost terrified, as she saw him wiping the blood from his lips. "Why do you talk? You ought to go home to bed."

"So I will," he whispered hoarsely. "As soon as I get home I will go to bed at once; and I know I shall be dead in a fortnight; Botkine told me so himself last week. That is why I should like to say a few farewell words, if you will let me."

"But you must be mad! It is ridiculous! You should take care of yourself; what is the use of holding a conversation now? Go home to bed, do!" cried Mrs. Epanchin in horror.

"When I do go to bed I shall never get up again," said Hippolyte, with a smile. "I meant to take to my bed yesterday and stay there till I died, but as my legs can still carry me, I put it off for two days, so as to come here with them to-day–but I am very tired."

"Oh, sit down, sit down, why are you standing?"

Lizabetha Prokofievna placed a chair for him with her own hands.

"Thank you," he said gently. "Sit opposite to me, and let us talk. We must have a talk now, Lizabetha Prokofievna; I am very anxious for it." He smiled at her once more. "Remember that today, for the last time, I am out in the air, and in the company of my fellow-men, and that in a fortnight I shall certainly be no longer in this world. So, in a way, this is my farewell to nature and to men. I am not very sentimental, but do you know, I am quite glad that all this has happened at Pavlofsk, where at least one can see a green tree."

"But why talk now?" replied Lizabetha Prokofievna, more and more alarmed; "You are quite feverish. Just now you would not stop shouting, and now you can hardly breathe. You are gasping."

"I shall have time to rest. Why will you not grant my last wish? Do you know, Lizabetha Prokofievna, that I have dreamed of meeting you for a long while? I had often heard of you from Colia; he is almost the only person who still comes to see me. You are an original and eccentric woman; I have seen that for myself–Do you know, I have even been rather fond of you?"

"Good heavens! And I very nearly struck him!"

"You were prevented by Aglaya Ivanovna. I think I am not mistaken? That is your daughter, Aglaya Ivanovna? She is so beautiful that I recognized her directly, although I had never seen her before. Let me, at least, look on beauty for the last time in my life," he said with a wry smile. "You are here with the prince, and your husband, and a large company. Why should you refuse to gratify my last wish?"

"Give me a chair!" cried Lizabetha Prokofievna, but she seized one for herself and sat down opposite to Hippolyte. "Colia, you must go home with him," she commanded, "and tomorrow I will come my self."

"Will you let me ask the prince for a cup of tea?... I am exhausted. Do you know what you might do, Lizabetha Prokofievna? I think you wanted to take the prince home with you for tea. Stay here, and let us spend the evening together. I am sure the prince will give us all some tea. Forgive me for being so free and easy–but I know you are kind, and the prince is kind, too. In fact, we are all good-natured people–it is really quite comical."

The prince bestirred himself to give orders. Lebedeff hurried out, followed by Vera.

"It is quite true," said Mrs. Epanchin decisively. "Talk, but not too loud, and don't excite yourself. You have made me sorry for you. Prince, you don't deserve that I should stay and have tea with you, yet I will, all the same, but I won't apologize. I apologize to nobody! Nobody! It is absurd! However, forgive me, prince, if I blew you up–that is, if you like, of course. But please don't let me keep anyone," she added suddenly to her husband and daughters, in a tone of resentment, as though they had grievously offended her. "I can come home alone quite well."

But they did not let her finish, and gathered round her eagerly. The prince immediately invited everyone to stay for tea, and apologized for not having thought of it before. The general murmured a few polite words, and asked Lizabetha Prokofievna if she did not feel cold on the terrace. He very nearly asked Hippolyte how long he had been at the University, but stopped himself in time. Evgenie Pavlovitch and Prince S. suddenly grew extremely gay and amiable. Adelaida and Alexandra had not recovered from their surprise, but it was now mingled with satisfaction; in short, everyone seemed very much relieved that Lizabetha Prokofievna had got over her paroxysm. Aglaya alone still frowned, and sat apart in silence. All the other guests stayed on as well; no one wanted to go, not even General Ivolgin, but Lebedeff said something to him in passing which did not seem to please him, for he immediately went and sulked in a corner. The prince took care to offer tea to Burdovsky and his friends as well as the rest. The invitation made them rather uncomfortable. They muttered that they would wait for Hippolyte, and went and sat by themselves in a distant corner of the verandah. Tea was served at once; Lebedeff had no doubt ordered it for himself and his family before the others arrived. It was striking eleven.

CHAPTER TEN

AFTER MOISTENING HIS LIPS with the tea which Vera Lebedeff brought him, Hippolyte set the cup down on the table, and glanced round. He seemed confused and almost at a loss.

"Just look, Lizabetha Prokofievna," he began, with a kind of feverish haste; "these china cups are supposed to be extremely valuable. Lebedeff always keeps them locked up in his china-cupboard; they were part of his wife's dowry. Yet he has brought them out tonight–in your honour, of course! He is so pleased–" He was about to add something else, but could not find the words.

"There, he is feeling embarrassed; I expected as much," whispered Evgenie Pavlovitch suddenly in the prince's ear. "It is a bad sign; what do you think? Now, out of spite, he will come out with something so outrageous that even Lizabetha Prokofievna will not be able to stand it."

Muishkin looked at him inquiringly.

"You do not care if he does?" added Evgenie Pavlovitch. "Neither do I; in fact, I should be glad, merely as a proper punishment for our dear Lizabetha Prokofievna. I am very anxious that she should get it, without delay, and I shall stay till she does. You seem feverish."

"Never mind; by-and-by; yes, I am not feeling well," said the prince impatiently, hardly listening. He had just heard Hippolyte mention his own name.

"You don't believe it?" said the invalid, with

a nervous laugh. "I don't wonder, but the prince will have no difficulty in believing it; he will not be at all surprised."

"Do you hear, prince–do you hear that?" said Lizabetha Prokofievna, turning towards him.

There was laughter in the group around her, and Lebedeff stood before her gesticulating wildly.

"He declares that your humbug of a landlord revised this gentleman's article–the article that was read aloud just now–in which you got such a charming dressing-down."

The prince regarded Lebedeff with astonishment.

"Why don't you say something?" cried Lizabetha Prokofievna, stamping her foot.

"Well," murmured the prince, with his eyes still fixed on Lebedeff, "I can see now that he did."

"Is it true?" she asked eagerly.

"Absolutely, your excellency," said Lebedeff, without the least hesitation.

Mrs. Epanchin almost sprang up in amazement at his answer, and at the assurance of his tone.

“He actually seems to boast of it!” she cried.

“I am base–base!” muttered Lebedeff, beating his breast, and hanging his head.

“What do I care if you are base or not? He thinks he has only to say, ‘I am base,’ and there is an end of it. As to you, prince, are you not ashamed?–I repeat, are you not ashamed, to mix with such riff-raff? I will never forgive you!”

“The prince will forgive me!” said Lebedeff with emotional conviction.

Keller suddenly left his seat, and approached Lizabetha Prokofievna.

“It was only out of generosity, madame,” he said in a resonant voice, “and because I would not betray a friend in an awkward position, that I did not mention this revision before; though you heard him yourself threatening to kick us down the steps. To clear the matter up, I declare now that I did have recourse to his assistance, and that I paid him six roubles for it. But I did not ask him to correct my style; I simply went to him for information concerning the facts, of which I was ignorant to a great extent, and which he was competent to give. The story of the gaiters, the appetite in the Swiss professor's house, the substitution of fifty roubles for two hundred and fifty–all such details, in fact, were got from him. I paid him six roubles for them; but he did not correct the style."

"I must state that I only revised the first part of the article," interposed Lebedeff with feverish impatience, while laughter rose from all around him; "but we fell out in the middle over one idea, so I never corrected the second part. Therefore I cannot be held responsible for the numerous grammatical blunders in it."

"That is all he thinks of!" cried Lizabetha Prokofievna.

"May I ask when this article was revised?" said Evgenie Pavlovitch to Keller.

"Yesterday morning," he replied, "we had an interview which we all gave our word of honour to keep secret."

"The very time when he was cringing before you and making protestations of devotion! Oh, the mean wretches! I will have nothing to do with your Pushkin, and your daughter shall not set foot in my house!"

Lizabetha Prokofievna was about to rise, when she saw Hippolyte laughing, and turned upon him with irritation.

"Well, sir, I suppose you wanted to make me look ridiculous?"

"Heaven forbid!" he answered, with a forced smile. "But I am more than ever struck by your eccentricity, Lizabetha Prokofievna. I admit that I told you of Lebedeff's duplicity, on purpose. I knew the effect it would have on you,–on you alone, for the prince will forgive him. He has probably forgiven him already, and is racking his brains to find some excuse for him–is not that the truth, prince?"

He gasped as he spoke, and his strange agitation seemed to increase.

"Well?" said Mrs. Epanchin angrily, surprised at his tone; "well, what more?"

"I have heard many things of the kind about you...they delighted me... I have learned to hold you in the highest esteem," continued Hippolyte.

His words seemed tinged with a kind of sarcastic mockery, yet he was extremely agitated, casting suspicious glances around him, growing confused, and constantly losing the thread of his ideas. All this, together with his consumptive appearance, and the frenzied expression of his blazing eyes, naturally attracted the attention of everyone present.

"I might have been surprised (though I admit I know nothing of the world), not only that you should have stayed on just now in the company of such people as myself and my friends, who are not of your class, but that you should let these... young ladies listen to such a scandalous affair, though no doubt novel-reading has taught them all there is to know. I may be mistaken; I hardly know what I am saying; but surely no one but you would have stayed to please a whippersnapper (yes, a whippersnapper; I admit it) to spend the evening and take part in everything–only to be ashamed of it tomorrow. (I know I express myself badly.) I admire and appreciate it all extremely, though the expression on the face of his excellency, your husband, shows that he thinks it very improper. He-he!" He burst out laughing, and was seized with a fit of coughing which lasted for two minutes and prevented him from speaking.

"He has lost his breath now!" said Lizabetha Prokofievna coldly, looking at him with more curiosity than pity: "Come, my dear boy, that is quite enough–let us make an end of this."

Ivan Fedorovitch, now quite out of patience, interrupted suddenly. "Let me remark in my turn, sir," he said in tones of deep annoyance, "that my wife is here as the guest of Prince Lef Nicolaievitch, our friend and neighbour, and that in any case, young man, it is not for you to pass judgment on the conduct of Lizabetha Prokofievna, or to make remarks aloud in my presence concerning what feelings you think may be read in my face. Yes, my wife stayed here," continued the general, with increasing irritation, "more out of amazement than anything else. Everyone can understand that a collection of such strange young men would attract the attention of a person interested in contemporary life. I stayed myself, just as I sometimes stop to look on in the street when I see something that may be regarded as-as-as-"

"As a curiosity," suggested Evgenie Pavlovitch, seeing his excellency involved in a comparison which he could not complete.

"That is exactly the word I wanted," said the general with satisfaction–"a curiosity.

However, the most astonishing and, if I may so express myself, the most painful, thing in this matter, is that you cannot even understand, young man, that Lizabetha Prokofievna, only stayed with you because you are ill,–if you really are dying–moved by the pity awakened by your plaintive appeal, and that her name, character, and social position place her above all risk of contamination. Lizabetha Prokofievna!" he continued, now crimson with rage, "if you are coming, we will say goodnight to the prince, and–"

"Thank you for the lesson, general," said Hippolyte, with unexpected gravity, regarding him thoughtfully.

"Two minutes more, if you please, dear Ivan Fedorovitch," said Lizabetha Prokofievna to her husband; "it seems to me that he is in a fever and delirious; you can see by his eyes what a state he is in; it is impossible to let him go back to Petersburg tonight. Can you put him up, Lef Nicolaievitch? I hope you are not bored, dear prince," she added suddenly to Prince S. "Alexandra, my dear, come here! Your hair is coming down."

She arranged her daughter's hair, which was not in the least disordered, and gave her a kiss. This was all that she had called her for.

"I thought you were capable of development," said Hippolyte, coming out of his fit of abstraction. "Yes, that is what I meant to say," he added, with the satisfaction of one who suddenly remembers something he had forgotten. "Here is Burdovsky, sincerely anxious to protect his mother; is not that so? And he himself is the cause of her disgrace. The prince is anxious to help Burdovsky and offers him friendship and a large sum of money, in the sincerity of his heart. And here they stand like two sworn enemies–ha, ha, ha! You all hate Burdovsky because his behaviour with regard to his mother is shocking and repugnant to you; do you not? Is not that true? Is it not true? You all have a passion for beauty and distinction in outward forms; that is all you care for, isn't it? I have suspected for a long time that you cared for nothing else! Well, let me tell you that perhaps there is not one of you who loved your mother as Burdovsky loved his. As to you, prince, I know that you have sent money secretly to Burdovsky's mother through Gania. Well, I bet now," he continued with an hysterical laugh, "that Burdovsky will accuse you of indelicacy, and reproach you with a want of respect for his mother! Yes, that is quite certain! Ha, ha, ha!"

He caught his breath, and began to cough once more.

"Come, that is enough! That is all now; you have no more to say? Now go to bed; you are burning with fever," said Lizabetha Prokofievna impatiently. Her anxious eyes had never left the invalid. "Good heavens, he is going to begin again!"

"You are laughing, I think? Why do you keep laughing at me?" said Hippolyte irritably to Evgenie Pavlovitch, who certainly was laughing.

"I only want to know, Mr. Hippolyte–excuse me, I forget your surname."

"Mr. Terentieff," said the prince.

"Oh yes, Mr. Terentieff. Thank you prince. I heard it just now, but had forgotten it. I want to know, Mr. Terentieff, if what I have heard about you is true. It seems you are convinced that if you could speak to the people from a window for a quarter of an hour, you could make them all adopt your views and follow you?"

"I may have said so," answered Hippolyte, as if trying to remember. "Yes, I certainly said so," he continued with sudden animation, fixing an unflinching glance on his questioner. "What of it?"

"Nothing. I was only seeking further information, to put the finishing touch."

Evgenie Pavlovitch was silent, but Hippolyte kept his eyes fixed upon him, waiting impatiently for more.

"Well, have you finished?" said Lizabetha Prokofievna to Evgenie. "Make haste, sir; it is time he went to bed. Have you more to say?" She was very angry.

"Yes, I have a little more," said Evgenie Pavlovitch, with a smile. "It seems to me that all you and your friends have said, Mr. Terentieff, and all you have just put forward with such undeniable talent, may be summed up in the triumph of right above all, independent of everything else, to the exclusion of everything else; perhaps even before having discovered what constitutes the right. I may be mistaken?"

"You are certainly mistaken; I do not even understand you. What else?"

Murmurs arose in the neighbourhood of Burdovsky and his companions; Lebedeff's nephew protested under his breath.

"I have nearly finished," replied Evgenie

Pavlovitch.

"I will only remark that from these premises one could conclude that might is right–I mean the right of the clenched fist, and of personal inclination. Indeed, the world has often come to that conclusion. Prudhon upheld that might is right. In the American War some of the most advanced Liberals took sides with the planters on the score that the blacks were an inferior race to the whites, and that might was the right of the white race."

"Well?"

"You mean, no doubt, that you do not deny that might is right?"

"What then?"

"You are at least logical. I would only point out that from the right of might, to the right of tigers and crocodiles, or even Daniloff and Gorsky, is but a step."

"I know nothing about that; what else?"

Hippolyte was scarcely listening. He kept saying "well?" and "what else?"

mechanically, without the least curiosity, and by mere force of habit.

"Why, nothing else; that is all."

"However, I bear you no grudge," said Hippolyte suddenly, and, hardly conscious of what he was doing, he held out his hand with a smile. The gesture took Evgenie Pavlovitch by surprise, but with the utmost gravity he touched the hand that was offered him in token of forgiveness.

"I can but thank you," he said, in a tone too respectful to be sincere, "for your kindness in letting me speak, for I have often noticed that our Liberals never allow other people to have an opinion of their own, and immediately answer their opponents with abuse, if they do not have recourse to arguments of a still more unpleasant nature."

"What you say is quite true," observed General Epanchin; then, clasping his hands behind his back, he returned to his place on the terrace steps, where he yawned with an air of boredom.

"Come, sir, that will do; you weary me," said Lizabetha Prokofievna suddenly to Evgenie Pavlovitch.

Hippolyte rose all at once, looking troubled and almost frightened.

"It is time for me to go," he said, glancing round in perplexity. "I have detained you... I wanted to tell you everything... I thought you all... for the last time... it was a whim..."

He evidently had sudden fits of returning animation, when he awoke from his semi-delirium; then, recovering full self-possession for a few moments, he would speak, in disconnected phrases which had perhaps haunted him for a long while on his bed of suffering, during weary, sleepless nights.

"Well, good-bye," he said abruptly. "You think it is easy for me to say good-bye to you? Ha, ha!"

Feeling that his question was somewhat gauche, he smiled angrily. Then as if vexed that he could not ever express what he really meant, he said irritably, in a loud voice:

"Excellency, I have the honour of inviting you to my funeral; that is, if you will deign to honour it with your presence. I invite you all, gentlemen, as well as the general."

He burst out laughing again, but it was the laughter of a madman. Lizabetha Prokofievna approached him anxiously and seized his arm. He stared at her for a moment, still laughing, but soon his face grew serious.

"Do you know that I came here to see those trees?" pointing to the trees in the park. "It is not ridiculous, is it? Say that it is not ridiculous!" he demanded urgently of Lizabetha Prokofievna. Then he seemed to be plunged in thought. A moment later he raised his head, and his eyes sought for someone. He was looking for Evgenie Pavlovitch, who was close by on his right as before, but he had forgotten this, and his eyes ranged over the assembled company. "Ah! you have not gone!" he said, when he caught sight of him at last. “You kept on laughing just now, because I thought of speaking to the people from the window for a quarter of an hour. But I am not eighteen, you know; lying on that bed, and looking out of that window, I have thought of all sorts of things for such a long time that... a dead man has no age, you know. I was saying that to myself only last week, when I was awake in the night. Do you know what you fear most? You fear our sincerity more than anything, although you despise us! The idea crossed my mind that night... You thought I was making fun of you just now, Lizabetha Prokofievna? No, the idea of mockery was far from me; I only meant to praise you. Colia told me the prince called you a child–very well–but let me see, I had something else to say...” He covered his face with his hands and tried to collect his thoughts.

“Ah, yes–you were going away just now, and I thought to myself: ‘I shall never see these people again–never again! This is the last time I shall see the trees, too. I shall see nothing after this but the red brick wall of Meyer's house opposite my window. Tell them about it–try to tell them,' I thought. 'Here is a beautiful young girl–you are a dead man; make them understand that. Tell them that a dead man may say anything–and Mrs. Grundy will not be angry–ha-ha! You are not laughing?" He looked anxiously around. "But you know I get so many queer ideas, lying there in bed. I have grown convinced that nature is full of mockery–you called me an atheist just now, but you know this nature... why are you laughing again? You are very cruel!" he added suddenly, regarding them all with mournful reproach. "I have not corrupted Colia," he concluded in a different and very serious tone, as if remembering something again.

"Nobody here is laughing at you. Calm yourself," said Lizabetha Prokofievna, much moved. "You shall see a new doctor tomorrow; the other was mistaken; but sit down, do not stand like that! You are delirious–" Oh, what shall we do with him she cried in anguish, as she made him sit down again in the arm-chair.

A tear glistened on her cheek. At the sight of it Hippolyte seemed amazed. He lifted his hand timidly and, touched the tear with his finger, smiling like a child.

"I... you," he began joyfully. "You cannot tell how I... he always spoke so enthusiastically of you, Colia here; I liked his enthusiasm. I was not corrupting him! But I must leave him, too–I wanted to leave them all–there was not one of them–not one! I wanted to be a man of action–I had a right to be. Oh! what a lot of things I wanted! Now I want nothing; I renounce all my wants; I swore to myself that I would want nothing; let them seek the truth without me! Yes, nature is full of mockery! Why"–he continued with sudden warmth–"does she create the choicest beings only to mock at them? The only human being who is recognized as perfect, when nature showed him to mankind, was given the mission to say things which have caused the shedding of so much blood that it would have drowned mankind if it had all been shed at once! Oh! it is better for me to die! I should tell some dreadful lie too; nature would so contrive it! I have corrupted nobody. I wanted to live for the happiness of all men, to find and spread the truth. I used to look out of my window at the wall of Meyer's house, and say to myself that if I could speak for a quarter of an hour I would convince the whole world, and now for once in my life I have come into contact with... you–if not with the others! And what is the result? Nothing! The sole result is that you despise me! Therefore I must be a fool, I am useless, it is time I disappeared! And I shall leave not even a memory! Not a sound, not a trace, not a single deed! I have not spread a single truth!... Do not laugh at the fool! Forget him! Forget him forever! I beseech you, do not be so cruel as to remember! Do you know that if I were not consumptive, I would kill myself?"

Though he seemed to wish to say much more, he became silent. He fell back into his chair, and, covering his face with his hands, began to sob like a little child.

"Oh! what on earth are we to do with him?" cried Lizabetha Prokofievna. She hastened to him and pressed his head against her bosom, while he sobbed convulsively.

"Come, come, come! There, you must not cry, that will do. You are a good child! God will forgive you, because you knew no better. Come now, be a man! You know presently you will be ashamed."

Hippolyte raised his head with an effort, saying:

"I have little brothers and sisters, over there, poor avid innocent. She will corrupt them! You are a saint! You are a child yourself–save them! Snatch them from that... she is... it is shameful! Oh! help them! God will repay you a hundredfold. For the love of God, for the love of Christ!"

"Speak, Ivan Fedorovitch! What are we to do?" cried Lizabetha Prokofievna, irritably. "Please break your majestic silence! I tell you, if you cannot come to some decision, I will stay here all night myself. You have tyrannized over me enough, you autocrat!"

She spoke angrily, and in great excitement, and expected an immediate reply. But in such a case, no matter how many are present, all prefer to keep silence: no one will take the initiative, but all reserve their comments till afterwards. There were some present–Varvara Ardalionovna, for instance–who would have willingly sat there till morning without saying a word. Varvara had sat apart all the evening without opening her lips, but she listened to everything with the closest attention; perhaps she had her reasons for so doing.

"My dear," said the general, "it seems to me that a sick-nurse would be of more use here than an excitable person like you. Perhaps it would be as well to get some sober, reliable man for the night. In any case we must consult the prince, and leave the patient to rest at once. Tomorrow we can see what can be done for him."

"It is nearly midnight; we are going. Will he come with us, or is he to stay here?" Doktorenko asked crossly of the prince.

"You can stay with him if you like," said Muishkin.

"There is plenty of room here."

Suddenly, to the astonishment of all, Keller went quickly up to the general.

"Excellency," he said, impulsively, "if you want a reliable man for the night, I am ready to sacrifice myself for my friend–such a soul as he has! I have long thought him a great man, excellency! My article showed my lack of education, but when he criticizes he scatters pearls!"

Ivan Fedorovitch turned from the boxer with a gesture of despair.

"I shall be delighted if he will stay; it would certainly be difficult for him to get back to Petersburg," said the prince, in answer to the eager questions of Lizabetha Prokofievna.

"But you are half asleep, are you not? If you don't want him, I will take him back to my house! Why, good gracious! He can hardly stand up himself! What is it? Are you ill?"

Not finding the prince on his death-bed, Lizabetha Prokofievna had been misled by his appearance to think him much better than he was. But his recent illness, the painful memories attached to it, the fatigue of this evening, the incident with "Pavlicheff's son," and now this scene with Hippolyte, had all so worked on his oversensitive nature that he was now almost in a fever. Moreover, a new trouble, almost a fear, showed itself in his eyes; he watched Hippolyte anxiously as if expecting something further.

Suddenly Hippolyte arose. His face, shockingly pale, was that of a man overwhelmed with shame and despair. This was shown chiefly in the look of fear and hatred which he cast upon the assembled company, and in the wild smile upon his trembling lips. Then he cast down his eyes, and with the same smile, staggered towards Burdovsky and Doktorenko, who stood at the entrance to the verandah. He had decided to go with them.

"There! that is what I feared!" cried the prince. "It was inevitable!"

Hippolyte turned upon him, a prey to maniacal rage, which set all the muscles of his face quivering.

"Ah! that is what you feared! It was inevitable, you say! Well, let me tell you that if I hate anyone here–I hate you all," he cried, in a hoarse, strained voice–"but you, you, with your jesuitical soul, your soul of sickly sweetness, idiot, beneficent millionaire–I hate you worse than anything or anyone on earth! I saw through you and hated you long ago; from the day I first heard of you. I hated you with my whole heart. You have contrived all this! You have driven me into this state! You have made a dying man disgrace himself. You, you, you are the cause of my abject cowardice! I would kill you if I remained alive! I do not want your benefits; I will accept none from anyone; do you hear? Not from any one! I want nothing! I was delirious, do not dare to triumph! I curse every one of you, once for all!"

Breath failed him here, and he was obliged to stop.

"He is ashamed of his tears!" whispered Lebedeff to Lizabetha Prokofievna. "It was inevitable. Ah! what a wonderful man the prince is! He read his very soul."

But Mrs. Epanchin would not deign to look at Lebedeff. Drawn up haughtily, with her head held high, she gazed at the "riff-raff," with scornful curiosity. When Hippolyte had finished, Ivan Fedorovitch shrugged his shoulders, and his wife looked him angrily up and down, as if to demand the meaning of his movement. Then she turned to the prince.

"Thanks, prince, many thanks, eccentric friend of the family, for the pleasant evening you have provided for us. I am sure you are quite pleased that you have managed to mix us up with your extraordinary affairs. It is quite enough, dear family friend; thank you for giving us an opportunity of getting to know you so well."

She arranged her cloak with hands that trembled with anger as she waited for the "riff-raff" to go. The cab which Lebedeff's son had gone to fetch a quarter of an hour ago, by Doktorenko's order, arrived at that moment. The general thought fit to put in a word after his wife.

"Really, prince, I hardly expected after–after all our friendly intercourse–and you see, Lizabetha Prokofievna–"

"Papa, how can you?" cried Adelaida, walking quickly up to the prince and holding out her hand.

He smiled absently at her; then suddenly he felt a burning sensation in his ear as an angry voice whispered:

"If you do not turn those dreadful people out of the house this very instant, I shall hate you all my life–all my life!" It was Aglaya. She seemed almost in a frenzy, but she turned away before the prince could look at her. However, there was no one left to turn out of the house, for they had managed meanwhile to get Hippolyte into the cab, and it had driven off.

"Well, how much longer is this going to last, Ivan Fedorovitch? What do you think? Shall I soon be delivered from these odious youths?"

"My dear, I am quite ready; naturally... the prince."

Ivan Fedorovitch held out his hand to Muishkin, but ran after his wife, who was leaving with every sign of violent indignation, before he had time to shake it. Adelaida, her fiance, and Alexandra, said good-bye to their host with sincere friendliness. Evgenie Pavlovitch did the same, and he alone seemed in good spirits.

"What I expected has happened! But I am sorry, you poor fellow, that you should have had to suffer for it," he murmured, with a most charming smile.

Aglaya left without saying good-bye. But the evening was not to end without a last adventure. An unexpected meeting was yet in store for Lizabetha Prokofievna.

She had scarcely descended the terrace steps leading to the high road that skirts the park at Pavlofsk, when suddenly there dashed by a smart open carriage, drawn by a pair of beautiful white horses. Having passed some ten yards beyond the house, the carriage suddenly drew up, and one of the two ladies seated in it turned sharp round as though she had just caught sight of some acquaintance whom she particularly wished to see.

"Evgenie Pavlovitch! Is that you?" cried a clear, sweet voice, which caused the prince, and perhaps someone else, to tremble. "Well, I **am** glad I've found you at last! I've sent to town for you twice today myself! My messengers have been searching for you everywhere!"

Evgenie Pavlovitch stood on the steps like one struck by lightning. Mrs. Epanchin stood still too, but not with the petrified expression of Evgenie. She gazed haughtily at the audacious person who had addressed her companion, and then turned a look of astonishment upon Evgenie himself.

"There's news!" continued the clear voice. "You need not be anxious about Kupferof's IOU's–Rogojin has bought them up. I persuaded him to!–I dare say we shall settle Biscup too, so it's all right, you see! **Au revoir**, tomorrow! And don't worry!" The carriage moved on, and disappeared.

"The woman's mad!" cried Evgenie, at last, crimson with anger, and looking confusedly around. “I don’t know what she’s talking about! What IOU’s? Who is she?” Mrs. Epanchin continued to watch his face for a couple of seconds; then she marched briskly and haughtily away towards her own house, the rest following her.

A minute afterwards, Evgenie Pavlovitch reappeared on the terrace, in great agitation.

“Prince,” he said, “tell me the truth; do you know what all this means?”

“I know nothing whatever about it!” replied the latter, who was, himself, in a state of nervous excitement.

“No?”

“No!”

“Well, nor do I!” said Evgenie Pavlovitch, laughing suddenly. “I haven’t the slightest knowledge of any such IOU’s as she mentioned, I swear I haven’t–What’s the matter, are you fainting?”

“Oh, no–no–I’m all right, I assure you!”

Part Two

CHAPTER ELEVEN

THE ANGER OF THE Epanchin family was unappeased for three days. As usual the prince reproached himself, and had expected punishment, but he was inwardly convinced that Lizabetha Prokofievna could not be seriously angry with him, and that she probably was more angry with herself. He was painfully surprised, therefore, when three days passed with no word from her. Other things also troubled and perplexed him, and one of these grew more important in his eyes as the days went by. He had begun to blame himself for two opposite tendencies–on the one hand to extreme, almost "senseless," confidence in his fellows, on the other to a "vile, gloomy suspiciousness."

By the end of the third day the incident of the eccentric lady and Evgenie Pavlovitch had attained enormous and mysterious proportions in his mind. He sorrowfully asked himself whether he had been the cause of this new "monstrosity," or was it... but he refrained from saying who else might be in fault. As for the letters N.P.B., he looked on that as a harmless joke, a mere childish piece of mischief–so childish that he felt it would be shameful, almost dishonourable, to attach any importance to it.

The day after these scandalous events, however, the prince had the honour of receiving a visit from Adelaida and her fiance, Prince S. They came, ostensibly, to inquire after his health. They had wandered out for a walk, and called in "by accident," and talked for almost the whole of the time they were with him about a certain most lovely tree in the park, which Adelaida had set her heart upon for a picture. This, and a little amiable conversation on Prince S.'s part, occupied the time, and not a word was said about last evening's episodes. At length Adelaida burst out laughing, apologized, and explained that they had come incognito; from which, and from the circumstance that they said nothing about the prince's either walking back with them or coming to see them later on, the latter inferred that he was in Mrs. Epanchin's black books. Adelaida mentioned a watercolour that she would much like to show him, and explained that she would either send it by Colia, or bring it herself the next day–which to the prince seemed very suggestive.

At length, however, just as the visitors were on the point of departing, Prince S. seemed suddenly to recollect himself. "Oh yes, by-the-by," he said, "do you happen to know, my dear Lef Nicolaievitch, who that lady was who called out to Evgenie Pavlovitch last night, from the carriage?"

"It was Nastasia Philipovna," said the prince; "didn't you know that? I cannot tell you who her companion was."

"But what on earth did she mean? I assure you it is a real riddle to me–to me, and to others, too!" Prince S. seemed to be under the influence of sincere astonishment.

"She spoke of some bills of Evgenie Pavlovitch's," said the prince, simply, "which Rogojin had bought up from someone; and implied that Rogojin would not press him."

"Oh, I heard that much, my dear fellow! But the thing is so impossibly absurd! A man of property like Evgenie to give IOU's to a money-lender, and to be worried about them! It is ridiculous. Besides, he cannot possibly be on such intimate terms with Nastasia Philipovna as she gave us to understand; that's the principal part of the mystery! He has given me his word that he knows nothing whatever about the matter, and of course I believe him. Well, the question is, my dear prince, do you know anything about it? Has any sort of suspicion of the meaning of it come across you?"

"No, I know nothing whatever about it. I assure you I had nothing at all to do with it."

"Oh, prince, how strange you have become! I assure you, I hardly know you for your old self. How can you suppose that I ever suggested you could have had a finger in such a business? But you are not quite yourself today, I can see." He embraced the prince, and kissed him.

"What do you mean, though," asked Muishkin, "'by such a business'? I don't see any particular 'business' about it at all!"

"Oh, undoubtedly, this person wished somehow, and for some reason, to do Evgenie Pavlovitch a bad turn, by attributing to him–before witnesses–qualities which he neither has nor can have," replied Prince S.

drily enough.

Muiskhin looked disturbed, but continued to gaze intently and questioningly into Prince S.'s face. The latter, however, remained silent.

"Then it was not simply a matter of bills?" Muishkin said at last, with some impatience. "It was not as she said?"

"But I ask you, my dear sir, how can there be anything in common between Evgenie Pavlovitch, and–her, and again Rogojin? I tell you he is a man of immense wealth–as I know for a fact; and he has further expectations from his uncle. Simply Nastasia Philipovna–"

Prince S. paused, as though unwilling to continue talking about Nastasia Philipovna.

"Then at all events he knows her!" remarked the prince, after a moment's silence.

"Oh, that may be. He may have known her some time ago–two or three years, at least. He used to know Totski. But it is impossible that there should be any intimacy between them. She has not even been in the place–many people don't even know that she has returned from Moscow! I have only observed her carriage about for the last three days or so."

"It's a lovely carriage," said Adelaida.

"Yes, it was a beautiful turn-out, certainly!"

The visitors left the house, however, on no less friendly terms than before. But the visit was of the greatest importance to the prince, from his own point of view. Admitting that he had his suspicions, from the moment of the occurrence of last night, perhaps even before, that Nastasia had some mysterious end in view, yet this visit confirmed his suspicions and justified his fears. It was all clear to him; Prince S. was wrong, perhaps, in his view of the matter, but he was somewhere near the truth, and was right in so far as that he understood there to be an intrigue of some sort going on. Perhaps Prince S. saw it all more clearly than he had allowed his hearers to understand. At all events, nothing could be plainer than that he and Adelaida had come for the express purpose of obtaining explanations, and that they suspected him of being concerned in the affair. And if all this were so, then **she** must have some terrible object in view! What was it? There was no stopping **her**, as Muishkin knew from experience, in the performance of anything she had set her mind on! "Oh, she is mad, mad!" thought the poor prince.

But there were many other puzzling occurrences that day, which required immediate explanation, and the prince felt very sad. A visit from Vera Lebedeff distracted him a little. She brought the infant Lubotchka with her as usual, and talked cheerfully for some time. Then came her younger sister, and later the brother, who attended a school close by. He informed Muishkin that his father had lately found a new interpretation of the star called "wormwood," which fell upon the water-springs, as described in the

Apocalypse. He had decided that it meant the network of railroads spread over the face of Europe at the present time. The prince refused to believe that Lebedeff could have given such an interpretation, and they decided to ask him about it at the earliest opportunity. Vera related how Keller had taken up his abode with them on the previous evening. She thought he would remain for some time, as he was greatly pleased with the society of General Ivolgin and of the whole family. But he declared that he had only come to them in order to complete his education! The prince always enjoyed the company of Lebedeff's children, and today it was especially welcome, for Colia did not appear all day. Early that morning he had started for Petersburg. Lebedeff also was away on business. But Gavrila Ardalionovitch had promised to visit Muishkin, who eagerly awaited his coming.

About seven in the evening, soon after dinner, he arrived. At the first glance it struck the prince that he, at any rate, must know all the details of last night's affair. Indeed, it would have been impossible for him to remain in ignorance considering the intimate relationship between him, Varvara Ardalionovna, and Ptitsin. But although he and the prince were intimate, in a sense, and although the latter had placed the Burdovsky affair in his hands–and this was not the only mark of confidence he had received–it seemed curious how many matters there were that were tacitly avoided in their conversations. Muishkin thought that Gania at times appeared to desire more cordiality and frankness. It was apparent now, when he entered, that he was convinced that the moment for breaking the ice between them had come at last.

But all the same Gania was in haste, for his sister was waiting at Lebedeff's to consult him on an urgent matter of business. If he had anticipated impatient questions, or impulsive confidences, he was soon undeceived. The prince was thoughtful, reserved, even a little absent-minded, and asked none of the questions–one in particular–that Gania had expected. So he imitated the prince's demeanour, and talked fast and brilliantly upon all subjects but the one on which their thoughts were engaged. Among other things Gania told his host that Nastasia Philipovna had been only four days in Pavlofsk, and that everyone was talking about her already. She was staying with Daria Alexeyevna, in an ugly little house in Mattrossky Street, but drove about in the smartest carriage in the place. A crowd of followers had pursued her from the first, young and old. Some escorted her on horse-back when she took the air in her carriage.

She was as capricious as ever in the choice of her acquaintances, and admitted few into her narrow circle. Yet she already had a numerous following and many champions on whom she could depend in time of need. One gentleman on his holiday had broken off his engagement on her account, and an old general had quarrelled with his only son for the same reason.

She was accompanied sometimes in her carriage by a girl of sixteen, a distant relative of her hostess. This young lady sang very well; in fact, her music had given a kind of notoriety to their little house. Nastasia, however, was behaving with great discretion on the whole. She dressed quietly, though with such taste as to drive all the ladies in Pavlofsk mad with envy, of that, as well as of her beauty and her carriage and horses.

"As for yesterday's episode," continued Gania, "of course it was pre-arranged." Here he paused, as though expecting to be asked how he knew that. But the prince did not inquire. Concerning Evgenie Pavlovitch, Gania stated, without being asked, that he believed the former had not known Nastasia

Philipovna in past years, but that he had probably been introduced to her by somebody in the park during these four days. As to the question of the IOU's she had spoken of, there might easily be something in that; for though Evgenie was undoubtedly a man of wealth, yet certain of his affairs were equally undoubtedly in disorder. Arrived at this interesting point, Gania suddenly broke off, and said no more about Nastasia's prank of the previous evening.

At last Varvara Ardalionovna came in search of her brother, and remained for a few minutes. Without Muishkin's asking her, she informed him that Evgenie Pavlovitch was spending the day in Petersburg, and perhaps would remain there over tomorrow; and that her husband had also gone to town, probably in connection with Evgenie Pavlovitch's affairs.

"Lizabetha Prokofievna is in a really fiendish temper today," she added, as she went out, "but the most curious thing is that

Aglaya has quarrelled with her whole family; not only with her father and mother, but with her sisters also. It is not a good sign." She said all this quite casually, though it was extremely important in the eyes of the prince, and went off with her brother. Regarding the episode of "Pavlicheff's son," Gania had been absolutely silent, partly from a kind of false modesty, partly, perhaps, to "spare the prince's feelings." The latter, however, thanked him again for the trouble he had taken in the affair.

Muishkin was glad enough to be left alone. He went out of the garden, crossed the road, and entered the park. He wished to reflect, and to make up his mind as to a certain "step." This step was one of those things, however, which are not thought out, as a rule, but decided for or against hastily, and without much reflection. The fact is, he felt a longing to leave all this and go away–go anywhere, if only it were far enough, and at once, without bidding farewell to anyone. He felt a presentiment that if he remained but a few days more in this place, and among these people, he would be fixed there irrevocably and permanently. However, in a very few minutes he decided that to run away was impossible; that it would be cowardly; that great problems lay before him, and that he had no right to leave them unsolved, or at least to refuse to give all his energy and strength to the attempt to solve them. Having come to this determination, he turned and went home, his walk having lasted less than a quarter of an hour. At that moment he was thoroughly unhappy.

Lebedeff had not returned, so towards evening Keller managed to penetrate into the prince's apartments. He was not drunk, but in a confidential and talkative mood. He announced that he had come to tell the story of his life to Muishkin, and had only remained at Pavlofsk for that purpose. There was no means of turning him out; nothing short of an earthquake would have removed him.

In the manner of one with long hours before him, he began his history; but after a few incoherent words he jumped to the conclusion, which was that "having ceased to believe in God Almighty, he had lost every vestige of morality, and had gone so far as to commit a theft." "Could you imagine such a thing?" said he.

"Listen to me, Keller," returned the prince. "If I were in your place, I should not acknowledge that unless it were absolutely necessary for some reason. But perhaps you are making yourself out to be worse than you are, purposely?"

"I should tell it to no one but yourself, prince, and I only name it now as a help to my soul's evolution. When I die, that secret will die with me! But, excellency, if you knew, if you only had the least idea, how difficult it is to get money nowadays! Where to find it is the question. Ask for a loan, the answer is always the same: 'Give us gold, jewels, or diamonds, and it will be quite easy.' Exactly what one has not got! Can you picture that to yourself? I got angry at last, and said, 'I suppose you would accept emeralds?' 'Certainly, we accept emeralds with pleasure. Yes!' 'Well, that's all right,' said I. 'Go to the devil, you den of thieves!' And with that I seized my hat, and walked out."

"Had you any emeralds?" asked the prince.

"What? I have emeralds? Oh, prince! with what simplicity, with what almost pastoral simplicity, you look upon life!"

Could not something be made of this man under good influences? asked the prince of himself, for he began to feel a kind of pity for his visitor. He thought little of the value of his own personal influence, not from a sense of humility, but from his peculiar way of looking at things in general. Imperceptibly the conversation grew more animated and more interesting, so that neither of the two felt anxious to bring it to a close. Keller confessed, with apparent sincerity, to having been guilty of many acts of such a nature that it astonished the prince that he could mention them, even to him. At every fresh avowal he professed the deepest repentance, and described himself as being "bathed in tears"; but this did not prevent him from putting on a boastful air at times, and some of his stories were so absurdly comical that both he and the prince laughed like madmen.

"One point in your favour is that you seem to have a child-like mind, and extreme truthfulness," said the prince at last. "Do you know that that atones for much?"

"I am assuredly noble-minded, and chivalrous to a degree!" said Keller, much softened. "But, do you know, this nobility of mind exists in a dream, if one may put it so? It never appears in practice or deed. Now, why is that? I can never understand."

"Do not despair. I think we may say without fear of deceiving ourselves, that you have now given a fairly exact account of your life. I, at least, think it would be impossible to add much to what you have just told me."

"Impossible?" cried Keller, almost pityingly. "Oh prince, how little you really seem to understand human nature!"

"Is there really much more to be added?" asked the prince, with mild surprise. "Well, what is it you really want of me? Speak out; tell me why you came to make your confession to me?"

"What did I want? Well, to begin with, it is good to meet a man like you. It is a pleasure to talk over my faults with you. I know you for one of the best of men... and then... then..."

He hesitated, and appeared so much embarrassed that the prince helped him out.

"Then you wanted me to lend you money?"

The words were spoken in a grave tone, and even somewhat shyly.

Keller started, gave an astonished look at the speaker, and thumped the table with his fist.

"Well, prince, that's enough to knock me

down! It astounds me! Here you are, as simple and innocent as a knight of the golden age, and yet... yet... you read a man's soul like a psychologist! Now, do explain it to me, prince, because I... I really do not understand!... Of course, my aim was to borrow money all along, and you... you asked the question as if there was nothing blameable in it–as if you thought it quite natural."

"Yes... from you it is quite natural."

"And you are not offended?"

"Why should I be offended?"

"Well, just listen, prince. I remained here last evening, partly because I have a great admiration for the French archbishop Bourdaloue. I enjoyed a discussion over him till three o'clock in the morning, with Lebedeff; and then... then–I swear by all I hold sacred that I am telling you the truth–then I wished to develop my soul in this frank and heartfelt confession to you. This was my thought as I was sobbing myself to sleep at dawn. Just as I was losing consciousness, tears in my soul, tears on my face (I remember how I lay there sobbing), an idea from hell struck me. 'Why not, after confessing, borrow money from him?' You see, this confession was a kind of masterstroke; I intended to use it as a means to your good grace and favour–and then–then I meant to walk off with a hundred and fifty roubles. Now, do you not call that base?"

"It is hardly an exact statement of the case," said the prince in reply. "You have confused your motives and ideas, as I need scarcely say too often happens to myself. I can assure you, Keller, I reproach myself bitterly for it sometimes. When you were talking just now I seemed to be listening to something about myself. At times I have imagined that all men were the same," he continued earnestly, for he appeared to be much interested in the conversation, "and that consoled me in a certain degree, for a **double** motive is a thing most difficult to fight against. I have tried, and I know. God knows whence they arise, these ideas that you speak of as base. I fear these double motives more than ever just now, but I am not your judge, and in my opinion it is going too far to give the name of baseness to it–what do you think? You were going to employ your tears as a ruse in order to borrow money, but you also say–in fact, you have sworn to the fact–that independently of this your confession was made with an honourable motive. As for the money, you want it for drink, do you not? After your confession, that is weakness, of course; but, after all, how can anyone give up a bad habit at a moment's notice? It is impossible. What can we do? It is best, I think, to leave the matter to your own conscience. How does it seem to you?" As he concluded the prince looked curiously at Keller; evidently this problem of double motives had often been considered by him before.

"Well, how anybody can call you an idiot after that, is more than I can understand!"

cried the boxer.

The prince reddened slightly.

"Bourdaloue, the archbishop, would not have spared a man like me," Keller continued, "but you, you have judged me with humanity. To show how grateful I am, and as a punishment, I will not accept a hundred and fifty roubles. Give me twenty-five–that will be enough; it is all I really need, for a fortnight at least. I will not ask you for more for a fortnight. I should like to have given Agatha a present, but she does not really deserve it. Oh, my dear prince, God bless you!"

At this moment Lebedeff appeared, having just arrived from Petersburg. He frowned when he saw the twenty-five rouble note in Keller's hand, but the latter, having got the money, went away at once. Lebedeff began to abuse him.

"You are unjust; I found him sincerely repentant," observed the prince, after listening for a time.

"What is the good of repentance like that?

It is the same exactly as mine yesterday, when I said, 'I am base, I am base,'–words, and nothing more!"

"Then they were only words on your part? I thought, on the contrary..."

"Well, I don't mind telling you the truth–you only! Because you see through a man somehow. Words and actions, truth and falsehood, are all jumbled up together in me, and yet I am perfectly sincere. I feel the deepest repentance, believe it or not, as you choose; but words and lies come out in the infernal craving to get the better of other people. It is always there–the notion of cheating people, and of using my repentant tears to my own advantage! I assure you this is the truth, prince! I would not tell any other man for the world! He would laugh and jeer at me–but you, you judge a man humanely."

"Why, Keller said the same thing to me nearly word for word a few minutes ago!" cried Muishkin. "And you both seem inclined to boast about it! You astonish me, but I think he is more sincere than you, for you make a regular trade of it. Oh, don't put on that pathetic expression, and don't put your hand on your heart! Have you anything to say to me? You have not come for nothing..."

Lebedeff grinned and wriggled.

"I have been waiting all day for you, because I want to ask you a question; and, for once in your life, please tell me the truth at once. Had you anything to do with that affair of the carriage yesterday?"

Lebedeff began to grin again, rubbed his hands, sneezed, but spoke not a word in reply.

"I see you had something to do with it."

"Indirectly, quite indirectly! I am speaking the truth–I am indeed! I merely told a certain person that I had people in my house, and that such and such personages might be found among them."

"I am aware that you sent your son to that house–he told me so himself just now, but what is this intrigue?" said the prince, impatiently.

"It is not my intrigue!" cried Lebedeff, waving his hand.

"It was engineered by other people, and is, properly speaking, rather a fantasy than an intrigue!"

"But what is it all about? Tell me, for Heaven's sake! Cannot you understand how nearly it touches me? Why are they blackening Evgenie Pavlovitch's reputation?"

Lebedeff grimaced and wriggled again.

"Prince!" said he. "Excellency! You won't let me tell you the whole truth; I have tried to explain; more than once I have begun, but you have not allowed me to go on..."

The prince gave no answer, and sat deep in thought. Evidently he was struggling to decide.

"Very well! Tell me the truth," he said, dejectedly.

"Aglaya Ivanovna..." began Lebedeff, promptly.

"Be silent! At once!" interrupted the prince, red with indignation, and perhaps with shame, too. "It is impossible and absurd! All that has been invented by you, or fools like you! Let me never hear you say a word again on that subject!"

Late in the evening Colia came in with a whole budget of Petersburg and Pavlofsk news. He did not dwell much on the Petersburg part of it, which consisted chiefly of intelligence about his friend Hippolyte, but passed quickly to the Pavlofsk tidings. He had gone straight to the Epanchins' from the station.

"There's the deuce and all going on there!" he said. "First of all about the row last night, and I think there must be something new as well, though I didn't like to ask. Not a word about **you**, prince, the whole time! The most interesting fact was that Aglaya had been quarrelling with her people about Gania. Colia did not know any details, except that it had been a terrible quarrel! Also Evgenie

Pavlovitch had called, and met with an excellent reception all round. And another curious thing: Mrs. Epanchin was so angry that she called Varia to her–Varia was talking to the girls–and turned her out of the house 'once for all' she said. I heard it from Varia herself–Mrs. Epanchin was quite polite, but firm; and when Varia said good-bye to the girls, she told them nothing about it, and they didn't know they were saying goodbye for the last time. I'm sorry for Varia, and for Gania too; he isn't half a bad fellow, in spite of his faults, and I shall never forgive myself for not liking him before! I don't know whether I ought to continue to go to the Epanchins' now," concluded Colia–"I like to be quite independent of others, and of other people's quarrels if I can; but I must think over it."

"I don't think you need break your heart over Gania," said the prince; "for if what you say is true, he must be considered dangerous in the Epanchin household, and if so, certain hopes of his must have been encouraged."

"What? What hopes?" cried Colia; "you surely don't mean Aglaya?–oh, no!–"

"You're a dreadful sceptic, prince," he continued, after a moment's silence. "I have observed of late that you have grown sceptical about everything. You don't seem to believe in people as you did, and are always attributing motives and so on–am I using the word 'sceptic' in its proper sense?"

"I believe so; but I'm not sure."

"Well, I'll change it, right or wrong; I'll say that you are not sceptical, but **jealous**. There! you are deadly jealous of Gania, over a certain proud damsel! Come!" Colia jumped up, with these words, and burst out laughing. He laughed as he had perhaps never laughed before, and still more when he saw the prince flushing up to his temples. He was delighted that the prince should be jealous about Aglaya. However, he stopped immediately on seeing that the other was really hurt, and the conversation continued, very earnestly, for an hour or more.

Next day the prince had to go to town, on business. Returning in the afternoon, he happened upon General Epanchin at the station. The latter seized his hand, glancing around nervously, as if he were afraid of being caught in wrong-doing, and dragged him into a first-class compartment. He was burning to speak about something of importance.

"In the first place, my dear prince, don't be angry with me. I would have come to see you yesterday, but I didn't know how Lizabetha Prokofievna would take it. My dear fellow, my house is simply a hell just now, a sort of sphinx has taken up its abode there. We live in an atmosphere of riddles; I can't make head or tail of anything. As for you, I feel sure you are the least to blame of any of us, though you certainly have been the cause of a good deal of trouble. You see, it's all very pleasant to be a philanthropist; but it can be carried too far. Of course I admire kind-heartedness, and I esteem my wife, but–"

The general wandered on in this disconnected way for a long time; it was clear that he was much disturbed by some circumstance which he could make nothing of.

"It is plain to me, that **you** are not in it at all," he continued, at last, a little less vaguely, "but perhaps you had better not come to our house for a little while. I ask you in the friendliest manner, mind; just till the wind changes again. As for Evgenie Pavlovitch," he continued with some excitement, "the whole thing is a calumny, a dirty calumny. It is simply a plot, an intrigue, to upset our plans and to stir up a quarrel. You see, prince, I'll tell you privately, Evgenie and ourselves have not said a word yet, we have no formal understanding, we are in no way bound on either side, but the word may be said very soon, don't you see, **very** soon, and all this is most injurious, and is meant to be so. Why? I'm sure I can't tell you. She's an extraordinary woman, you see, an eccentric woman; I tell you I am so frightened of that woman that I can't sleep. What a carriage that was, and where did it come from, eh? I declare, I was base enough to suspect Evgenie at first; but it seems certain that that cannot be the case, and if so, why is she interfering here? That's the riddle, what does she want? Is it to keep Evgenie to herself? But, my dear fellow, I swear to you, I swear he doesn't even **know** her, and as for those bills, why, the whole thing is an invention! And the familiarity of the woman! It's quite clear we must treat the impudent creature's attempt with disdain, and redouble our courtesy towards Evgenie. I told my wife so.

"Now I'll tell you my secret conviction. I'm certain that she's doing this to revenge herself on me, on account of the past, though I assure you that all the time I was blameless. I blush at the very idea. And now she turns up again like this, when I thought she had finally disappeared! Where's Rogojin all this time? I thought she was Mrs. Rogojin, long ago."

The old man was in a state of great mental perturbation. The whole of the journey, which occupied nearly an hour, he continued in this strain, putting questions and answering them himself, shrugging his shoulders, pressing the prince's hand, and assuring the latter that, at all events, he had no suspicion whatever of **him**. This last assurance was satisfactory, at all events. The general finished by informing him that Evgenie's uncle was head of one of the civil service departments, and rich, very rich, and a gourmand. "And, well, Heaven preserve him, of course–but Evgenie gets his money, don't you see? But, for all this, I'm uncomfortable, I don't know why. There's something in the air, I feel there's something nasty in the air, like a bat, and I'm by no means comfortable."

And it was not until the third day that the formal reconciliation between the prince and the Epanchins took place, as said before.

Part Two

CHAPTER TWELVE

IT WAS SEVEN IN the evening, and the prince was just preparing to go out for a walk in the park, when suddenly Mrs. Epanchin appeared on the terrace.

"In the first place, don't dare to suppose," she began, "that I am going to apologize. Nonsense! You were entirely to blame."

The prince remained silent.

"Were you to blame, or not?"

"No, certainly not, no more than yourself, though at first I thought I was."

"Oh, very well, let's sit down, at all events, for I don't intend to stand up all day. And remember, if you say, one word about 'mischievous urchins,' I shall go away and break with you altogether. Now then, did you, or did you not, send a letter to Aglaya, a couple of months or so ago, about Eastertide?"

"Yes!"

"What for? What was your object? Show me the letter." Mrs. Epanchin's eyes flashed; she was almost trembling with impatience.

"I have not got the letter," said the prince, timidly, extremely surprised at the turn the conversation had taken. "If anyone has it, if it still exists, Aglaya Ivanovna must have it."

"No finessing, please. What did you write about?"

"I am not finessing, and I am not in the least afraid of telling you; but I don't see the slightest reason why I should not have written."

"Be quiet, you can talk afterwards! What

was the letter about? Why are you blushing?"

The prince was silent. At last he spoke.

"I don't understand your thoughts, Lizabetha Prokofievna; but I can see that the fact of my having written is for some reason repugnant to you. You must admit that I have a perfect right to refuse to answer your questions; but, in order to show you that I am neither ashamed of the letter, nor sorry that I wrote it, and that I am not in the least inclined to blush about it" (here the prince's blushes redoubled), "I will repeat the substance of my letter, for I think I know it almost by heart."

So saying, the prince repeated the letter almost word for word, as he had written it.

"My goodness, what utter twaddle, and what may all this nonsense have signified, pray? If it had any meaning at all!" said Mrs. Epanchin, cuttingly, after having listened with great attention.

"I really don't absolutely know myself; I know my feeling was very sincere. I had moments at that time full of life and hope."

"What sort of hope?"

"It is difficult to explain, but certainly not the hopes you have in your mind. Hopes–well, in a word, hopes for the future, and a feeling of joy that **there**, at all events, I was not entirely a stranger and a foreigner. I felt an ecstasy in being in my native land once more; and one sunny morning I took up a pen and wrote her that letter, but why to **her**, I don't quite know. Sometimes one longs to have a friend near, and I evidently felt the need of one then," added the prince, and paused.

"Are you in love with her?"

"N-no! I wrote to her as to a sister; I signed myself her brother."

"Oh yes, of course, on purpose! I quite understand."

"It is very painful to me to answer these questions, Lizabetha Prokofievna."

"I dare say it is; but that's no affair of mine. Now then, assure me truly as before Heaven, are you lying to me or not?"

"No, I am not lying."

"Are you telling the truth when you say you are not in love?"

"I believe it is the absolute truth."

"'I believe,' indeed! Did that mischievous urchin give it to her?"

"I asked Nicolai Ardalionovitch..."

"The urchin! the urchin!" interrupted Lizabetha Prokofievna in an angry voice. "I do not want to know if it were Nicolai Ardalionovitch! The urchin!"

"Nicolai Ardalionovitch..."

"The urchin, I tell you!"

"No, it was not the urchin: it was Nicolai Ardalionovitch," said the prince very firmly, but without raising his voice.

"Well, all right! All right, my dear! I shall put that down to your account."

She was silent a moment to get breath, and to recover her composure.

"Well!–and what's the meaning of the 'poor knight,' eh?"

"I don't know in the least; I wasn't present

when the joke was made. It **is** a joke. I suppose, and that's all."

"Well, that's a comfort, at all events. You don't suppose she could take any interest in you, do you? Why, she called you an 'idiot' herself."

"I think you might have spared me that," murmured the prince reproachfully, almost in a whisper.

"Don't be angry; she is a wilful, mad, spoilt girl. If she likes a person she will pitch into him, and chaff him. I used to be just such another. But for all that you needn't flatter yourself, my boy; she is not for you. I don't believe it, and it is not to be. I tell you so at once, so that you may take proper precautions. Now, I want to hear you swear that you are not married to that woman?"

"Lizabetha Prokofievna, what are you thinking of?" cried the prince, almost leaping to his feet in amazement.

"Why? You very nearly were, anyhow."

"Yes–I nearly was," whispered the prince,

hanging his head.

"Well then, have you come here for **her?** Are you in love with **her?** With **that** creature?"

"I did not come to marry at all," replied the prince.

"Is there anything you hold sacred?"

"There is."

"Then swear by it that you did not come here to marry **her!**"

"I'll swear it by whatever you please."

"I believe you. You may kiss me; I breathe freely at last. But you must know, my dear friend, Aglaya does not love you, and she shall never be your wife while I am out of my grave. So be warned in time. Do you hear me?"

"Yes, I hear."

The prince flushed up so much that he could not look her in the face.

"I have waited for you with the greatest impatience (not that you were worth it). Every night I have drenched my pillow with tears, not for you, my friend, not for you, don't flatter yourself! I have my own grief, always the same, always the same. But I'll tell you why I have been awaiting you so impatiently, because I believe that Providence itself sent you to be a friend and a brother to me. I haven't a friend in the world except Princess Bielokonski, and she is growing as stupid as a sheep from old age. Now then, tell me, yes or no? Do you know why she called out from her carriage the other night?"

"I give you my word of honour that I had nothing to do with the matter and know nothing about it."

"Very well, I believe you. I have my own ideas about it. Up to yesterday morning I thought it was really Evgenie Pavlovitch who was to blame; now I cannot help agreeing with the others. But why he was made such a fool of I cannot understand. However, he is not going to marry Aglaya, I can tell you that. He may be a very excellent fellow, but–so it shall be. I was not at all sure of accepting him before, but now I have quite made up my mind that I won't have him. 'Put me in my coffin first and then into my grave, and then you may marry my daughter to whomsoever you please,' so I said to the general this very morning. You see how I trust you, my boy."

"Yes, I see and understand."

Mrs. Epanchin gazed keenly into the prince's eyes. She was anxious to see what impression the news as to Evgenie Pavlovitch had made upon him.

"Do you know anything about Gavrila Ardalionovitch?" she asked at last.

"Oh yes, I know a good deal."

"Did you know he had communications with Aglaya?"

"No, I didn't," said the prince, trembling a little, and in great agitation. "You say Gavrila Ardalionovitch has private communications with Aglaya?–Impossible!"

"Only quite lately. His sister has been

working like a rat to clear the way for him all the winter."

"I don't believe it!" said the prince abruptly, after a short pause. "Had it been so I should have known long ago."

"Oh, of course, yes; he would have come and wept out his secret on your bosom. Oh, you simpleton–you simpleton! Anyone can deceive you and take you in like a–like a,–aren't you ashamed to trust him? Can't you see that he humbugs you just as much as ever he pleases?"

"I know very well that he does deceive me occasionally, and he knows that I know it, but–" The prince did not finish his sentence.

"And that's why you trust him, eh? So I should have supposed. Good Lord, was there ever such a man as you? Tfu! and are you aware, sir, that this Gania, or his sister Varia, have brought her into correspondence with Nastasia Philipovna?"

"Brought whom?" cried Muishkin.

"Aglaya."

"I don't believe it! It's impossible! What object could they have?" He jumped up from his chair in his excitement.

"Nor do I believe it, in spite of the proofs. The girl is self-willed and fantastic, and insane! She's wicked, wicked! I'll repeat it for a thousand years that she's wicked; they **all** are, just now, all my daughters, even that 'wet hen' Alexandra. And yet I don't believe it. Because I don't choose to believe it, perhaps; but I don't. Why haven't you been?" she turned on the prince suddenly. "Why didn't you come near us all these three days, eh?"

The prince began to give his reasons, but she interrupted him again.

"Everybody takes you in and deceives you; you went to town yesterday. I dare swear you went down on your knees to that rogue, and begged him to accept your ten thousand roubles!"

"I never thought of doing any such thing. I have not seen him, and he is not a rogue, in my opinion. I have had a letter from him."

"Show it me!"

The prince took a paper from his pocket-book, and handed it to Lizabetha Prokofievna. It ran as follows:

"Sir,

"In the eyes of the world I am sure that I have no cause for pride or self-esteem. I am much too insignificant for that. But what may be so to other men's eyes is not so to yours. I am convinced that you are better than other people. Doktorenko disagrees with me, but I am content to differ from him on this point. I will never accept one single copeck from you, but you have helped my mother, and I am bound to be grateful to you for that, however weak it may seem. At any rate, I have changed my opinion about you, and I think right to inform you of the fact; but I also suppose that there can be no further intercourse between us.

"Antip Burdovsky.

"P.S.–The two hundred roubles I owe you shall certainly be repaid in time."

"How extremely stupid!" cried Mrs. Epanchin, giving back the letter abruptly. "It was not worth the trouble of reading. Why are you smiling?"

"Confess that you are pleased to have read it."

"What! Pleased with all that nonsense! Why, cannot you see that they are all infatuated with pride and vanity?"

"He has acknowledged himself to be in the wrong. Don't you see that the greater his vanity, the more difficult this admission must have been on his part? Oh, what a little child you are, Lizabetha Prokofievna!"

"Are you tempting me to box your ears for you, or what?"

"Not at all. I am only proving that you are glad about the letter. Why conceal your real feelings? You always like to do it."

"Never come near my house again!" cried Mrs. Epanchin, pale with rage. "Don't let me see as much as a **shadow** of you about the place! Do you hear?"

"Oh yes, and in three days you'll come and invite me yourself. Aren't you ashamed now? These are your best feelings; you are only tormenting yourself."

"I'll die before I invite you! I shall forget your very name! I've forgotten it already!"

She marched towards the door.

"But I'm forbidden your house as it is, without your added threats!" cried the prince after her.

"What? Who forbade you?"

She turned round so suddenly that one might have supposed a needle had been stuck into her.

The prince hesitated. He perceived that he had said too much now.

"**Who** forbade you?" cried Mrs. Epanchin once more.

"Aglaya Ivanovna told me–"

"When? Speak–quick!"

"She sent to say, yesterday morning, that

I was never to dare to come near the house again."

Lizabetha Prokofievna stood like a stone.

"What did she send? Whom? Was it that boy? Was it a message?–quick!"

"I had a note," said the prince.

"Where is it? Give it here, at once."

The prince thought a moment. Then he pulled out of his waistcoat pocket an untidy slip of paper, on which was scrawled:

"Prince Lef Nicolaievitch,–If you think fit, after all that has passed, to honour our house with a visit, I can assure you you will not find me among the number of those who are in any way delighted to see you.

"Aglaya Epanchin."

Mrs. Epanchin reflected a moment. The next minute she flew at the prince, seized his hand, and dragged him after her to the door.

"Quick–come along!" she cried, breathless with agitation and impatience. "Come along with me this moment!"

"But you declared I wasn't–"

"Don't be a simpleton. You behave just as though you weren't a man at all. Come on! I shall see, now, with my own eyes. I shall see all."

"Well, let me get my hat, at least."

"Here's your miserable hat. He couldn't even choose a respectable shape for his hat! Come on! She did that because I took your part and said you ought to have come–little vixen!–else she would never have sent you that silly note. It's a most improper note, I call it; most improper for such an intelligent, well-brought-up girl to write. H'm! I dare say she was annoyed that you didn't come; but she ought to have known that one can't write like that to an idiot like you, for you'd be sure to take it literally." Mrs. Epanchin was dragging the prince along with her all the time, and never let go of his hand for an instant. "What are you listening for?" she added, seeing that she had committed herself a little. "She wants a clown like you–she hasn't seen one for some time–to play with. That's why she is anxious for you to come to the house. And right glad I am that she'll make a thorough good fool of you. You deserve it; and she can do it–oh! she can, indeed!–as well as most people."

CONTINUES IN VOLUME TWO

www.ingramcontent.com/pod-product-compliance
Lightning Source LLC
Chambersburg PA
CBHW020919310726
48980CB00011B/964/J

* 9 7 8 1 8 3 4 1 2 3 9 7 4 *